Tall, Skinny Cappuccino

Tall, Skinny Cappuccino

KIMBERLY HUFF

Mapletree Publishing Company
Denver, Colorado

Printed in the United States of America
13 12 11 10 09 08   1 2 3 4 5 6 7

Cover design by TLC Graphics   www.tlcgraphics.com

Library of Congress Cataloging-in-Publication Data
Huff, Kimberly, 1981-
Tall, skinny cappuccino / by Kimberly Huff.
        p. cm.
ISBN 978-1-60065-104-5 (alk. paper)
1. Women journalists—Fiction. 2. Periodicals—Publishing—Fiction. 3.
Boston (Mass.)—Fiction. 4. Chick lit. I. Title.
        PS3608.U3497T35 2008
        813'.6—dc22
                                        2007015097

Printed on acid-free paper

Mapletree Publishing Company
Denver, Colorado 80130
800-537-0414
www.mapletreepublishing.com
The Mapletree logo is a trademark of
Mapletree Publishing Company

*To my daddy, my kindred dreamer.
Thank you for believing in me, for funding my dreams,
and for telling me I can do anything. And to God—
for giving me something to write about.*

1

"Do you see that red-headed vixen waiting for her drink by the bar?" I whisper to Mandy from our usual table at Starbucks.

"You mean Miss Indecent Exposure over there reading *The Times*!" Mandy says with a laugh. Of course she reads *The Times*. All classy people read *The Times*, though I bet she only scans the horoscope section.

"Yeah. Well, say hello to the new senior editor of *The Beantown Scene*," I say bitterly, leaning back in my chair.

"You're joking," Mandy says. She turns her attention toward the window, where my new boss stands like a goddess in a display case.

"I mean, why can't she just go to the Starbucks down the street?" I muse. "Or how about Dunkin Donuts? I mean, the girl could definitely use a donut. Look at that waistline! I bet she hasn't eaten in years."

"You're not joking!" Mandy exclaims, giving me her full attention. "Oh my gosh, Emma. You're being serious! Long Legs is your new boss." She eyes the beautiful, leggy super model who is now my official boss. I haven't told Mandy this, but this isn't the first time I've seen Natasha. We've actually crossed paths three times in the last two weeks. I thought it was mere coincidence, but how naïve can I be? She was *so* scoping out

1

the competition. And what a vixen! I swear if she unbuttons her shirts any further she'll be arrested for indecent exposure. Allow me to misquote Humphrey Bogart by saying that of all the coffee shops in all the world, she happens to flit into in mine, commanding the attention of everyone in the establishment.

And she's *so* the kind of woman everybody loves to hate, sort of a Gwyneth Paltrow meets Jessica Simpson. You know, the kind of woman who walks into a room and has all the men forgetting about their wives and girlfriends. She's about 5'11" with a long, wavy mane you'd only see on Julia Roberts. Her tanned legs go on for miles, and what better way to flaunt them than with a skirt that could double as a headband? Sporting the latest Louis Vuitton handbag and three-inch Manola Blahniks, I assure you this goddess is nothing short of perfection.

"Sorry, I was just having an epiphany over Natasha's little ensemble," I say to Mandy, leaning in. "I mean, look at those shoes. Who does she think she is, Sarah Jessica Parker? We live in Boston for crying out loud! Hello, cobblestones!"

"Natasha?" Mandy snorts. "Well that figures. Of course that's her name. Girls like that always have exotic names."

"Like Monique," I say, flipping my hair dramatically over my shoulder.

"Or Mischa." We both laugh.

"But what happened?" Mandy asks, dropping her smile. "I thought they practically printed your new business cards." I thought so too. Silly, Emma!

"Well, it turns out they received Natasha's resume last week, and she's way more qualified than I am," I say bitterly. Mandy slaps her hand on the table.

"But you've been there for three years!"

"My very reaction, but whatever. It happens." I take a

2

quick sip of my latte and look out the window. Mandy raises her eyebrows. I sigh and stare into my cup. "Okay. Initially, yes, I was pretty upset. But why should I be surprised? You and I both know that things like that don't happen to me." It's true. I'm not one of those people who gets promoted, proposed to, or even asked out on hot dates. I'm lucky to even have a job, a job that at times just seems like a stepping stone for greater things, but at least it's a job. "And it was considerate of Richard to give me a heads up before Natasha moved into her nice corner office yesterday afternoon." I give Mandy a reassuring smile.

"Yeah, you tell yourself that," Mandy says as she rolls her eyes. I set down my cup in defeat.

"Okay, so I'm still a little upset."

"A little?" she asks quietly. Gosh, Mandy reads me like a book.

"Yes, a little," I say defensively, "and only because I have to report to Miss Long Legs every morning."

"That's ridiculous, and you know it. Why are you putting up a front for me? That job was yours, and everybody knows it, including what's-her-name over there. If you ask me, her lack of clothing got her the job."

Mandy has always been one to speak her mind. That's probably why she's an up-and-coming broadcast journalist. Any day now she'll have her own talk show. I've known her since we were forced to work together on a history project in the fourth grade. I did all the work, and she in turn allowed me to raid her closet. You could say she's the reason I don't wear white until Easter Sunday and always have my toenails painted. I swear, the two of us are like night and day, but strangely, we're soul mates. She's my Ethel, and I'm her Lucy.

"Well, I could've borrowed one of your little skirts," I say with a straight face. "Though I can't say I have the same svelte figure as our Amazon friend." Not that I'm fat. My body is what you'd call a pear, probably because I hate to exercise. Not that I'm ashamed of it or anything. All the construction workers seem to like it.

Want to know the truth? I'm devastated that I didn't get the job. I've been writing for *Bean Town Scene* for three years, and I've had about all I can take. I wouldn't complain if I could write about something that actually mattered, but I've been writing about gossip and entertainment since I began working for the magazine. Call me a dreamer, but I thought for sure they would recognize my talent and move me to a column that actually took a brain to write. Not that I'm entirely void of gratitude. I love writing about the glitz and glamour of one our nation's greatest cities, but that's not all there is to life. I want to write about what America is doing to help AIDS in Africa, not about what celebrity is going to Africa on vacation.

And because *Bean Town Scene* is a weekly publication, I never have time to do anything extra, much less look for another job. I'm lucky to squeeze in a night class once a week, and that's for mere pleasure. (Loser, I know.) On the surface it sounds like a dream job, and I guess it is. I mean, who doesn't love fashion and dining at hip, new bistros? But I didn't bust my tail at Harvard for six years just to write about the newest hangouts in Cambridge. My classmates are writing for publications like *The Globe* and *Time Magazine* for crying out loud! How can anybody take me seriously when the only voice I have is on whether velour jumpsuits are in or out this season? (FYI: they are so over!)

I must admit, however, the job does have its perks. I've met a handful of celebrities, including Tom Brady and Ben Affleck. I even scored season tickets to the Red Sox last year, though I regifted them as fast as you can say "baseball." Instead, Mom and Dad enjoyed a beautiful season at Fenway Park.

And this Friday I've even been invited to a black tie

benefit at the Ritz-Carlton. Carmichael Advertising is sponsoring a lobster dinner to raise money for cancer research. Apparently this big-wig Carmichael firm is making a dent in the business world. Its headquarters are in New York City, but the firm just recently opened an office in Boston. I've never met the CEO, but my sister Zoë says he's a rich, haughty playboy. How typical.

Actually my job has nothing to do with my invite to the benefit. I'm going with Zoë.

"So have you bought shoes yet?" Mandy asks between gulps of her frappuccino. This is why I love this girl. It's snowing bullets outside and she's drinking a milkshake as if it were a hot summer's day.

"Uh ... well, the thing is ..." I trail off.

"Emma, the benefit's tomorrow night!" she says. "And you know how you are about shoes."

She's right. If there's one thing I hate to shop for more than a bathing suit, it's shoes. Probably because I hate feet. I've always wanted to wear stilettos, but they just draw attention to my big, awkward appendages. And I don't even think they make my size.

"I know. I'll go after work."

"No, go during lunch. That is, if Miss Lollipop lets you go to lunch. I bet she hasn't eaten in years," Mandy says. Since high school, we've referred to girls as lollipops when their heads are bigger than their bodies due to starvation. (For example: Lindsay Lohan and Nicole Richie.) No offense to them or anything, they just make me very hungry.

"Yeah," I laugh, "Natasha is so ..."

"Natasha is so what?" I hear from behind me. Shoot a monkey. I whip my blonde hair around and see Natasha standing behind me. Did she hear me?

"Hi-ya, Natasha," I say, forcing a smile. "I was just telling Mandy about your new job. Congratulations by the way!" I'm getting a crick in my neck from looking up at her.

"Well, I know you really wanted the job," she says as she gives me the glance-over, "but I do have more experience. After all, I did come from *Vogue*."

I see Mandy's jaw drop out of the corner of my eye.

"Excuse me, but ..." she begins, but I grab her arm. It would totally bite to lose my job today.

"Gee, it's getting late," I say as I look down at my watchless wrist.

"Yes, well, I'm headed to the office," Natasha says, flicking her hair over her shoulder. "I want to put in an early start. You may want to do the same." I open my mouth to speak, but she beats me to it. "Ciao," she says as she pivots on her stilettos and trots off, turning heads as she exits.

"What a terrible human being," Mandy says hotly as we get up to leave.

"I know."

"But enough about her." She smiles, grabs my shoulders, and looks me squarely in the eye. "Go find yourself some stunning, big shoes and call me later. I want you looking like a princess tomorrow night."

As I watch Mandy's short brown bob disappear into the crowd, I can't help but stare up at the sky and ask, "Why can't something good happen to me for once?"

"Good morning, Emma," chirps a sweet, twangy voice from the cubicle to my right.

"Good morning, Gwyneth," I call back jokingly. Gwen never should have told me she hates being called by her real name. I think it has something to do with Gwyneth Paltrow naming her kid after produce.

Gwen pops her head over her cubicle wall. "Did you see what *she's* wearing today?" she says in a whisper.

Gwen is so cute. She's trying so hard to hate Natasha on my behalf, but she's really no good at it. Gwen loves everyone, and everyone loves Gwen.

"Actually, I bumped into her this morning."

"What?" she asks. She slides around to my cubicle to hear more.

I begin giving Gwen a recap of this morning but am interrupted mid-story by her phone. I don't even have to guess who it is. Matthew calls Gwen every morning at nine o'clock sharp. They've been married for over a year but still act as if they're on their honeymoon. Gwen says Matthew is super romantic, but I think he's really cheesy.

Gwen and I started working for *Bean Town Scene* around the same time. She's a petite southern belle from

Nashville who went away to school and never made it home. I know she misses her family terribly, but she did manage to land herself a publicity job and a rather dishy husband. And who do you figure set them up?

I met Gwen's husband, Matthew, at the opening of Casablanca, a French eatery located in the South End. We had a few laughs over spinach crepes, but I knew after five minutes that it wasn't going anywhere. At the time he was a law student, and between you and me, I can't stand lawyers. Plus, he's Jewish, and wouldn't I have to like convert or something? It's a shame, really, because Matthew is now a wealthy attorney with a lot of clout. I guess it wasn't my turn. Besides, he had a huge piece of spinach lodged between his front teeth. God does these things for a reason, you know.

"Do you want to hit ABP for lunch today?" Gwen asks as she hangs up the phone and makes her way back to my cube. I pause from typing on the computer.

"I can't. I have to buy a pair of shoes for the stupid benefit tomorrow night." I roll my eyes as Gwen takes a seat on my desk.

"Stupid benefit. I thought you were excited." But before we can finish talking, Natasha walks by and we're forced back in our chairs.

After three hours of intense working: you know, shopping on eBay and surfing people.com (I know, I feel guilty already), my phone rings.

"Emma Mosley," I say in my professional voice. I feel so cool when I do that.

"You will never guess what I just heard!" a spunky voice squeals on the other end. I lean back in my chair, happy for the break.

"Zoë? Hey sis, you sound winded. Are you just now making it to the gym?"

"What do you think?" she asks. That's a no. If I know Zoë, she's already run her daily eight miles. But that's her idea of fun. She's a personal trainer. I think I was born into the wrong family because I only run when I'm being chased. "Listen," she breaks into my thoughts. "I just talked to Samantha, and you will never guess what she told me about Natasha."

"She knows Natasha?" I ask, though I shouldn't be surprised.

Samantha is Zoë's best friend. She's a pharmaceutical sales rep, but I secretly call her "The Drug Bunny." You should see the things she wears to work. I'm sorry, but short skirts are so *Melrose Place* and didn't they cancel that show? But I can't say anything to Zoë. Samantha's her close friend, if you could call that friendship. I'd say it's more a shopping buddy, but that's just me.

The truth is Zoë has never had a best friend. She's one of those girls who always has to have a boyfriend. Not that I'm a feminist or anything, but it's ridiculous to think that another human being can complete you. We're human. We're flawed. And my gosh, women need girlfriends!

Zoë once again interrupts my thoughts.

"Natasha is divorced!" she blurts out.

"No!" I gasp.

"That's why she's so rich. She was married to some ancient stockbroker. I'm talking like 30 years her senior, but it only lasted a few months." Ew! I'm getting a mental picture of his saggy butt. "And he's loaded. Or should I say, he was loaded? Last year she hired a private investigator and busted him for having an affair with his secretary."

"That is so Lifetime!"

"I know! And it gets juicier. The prenup had some infidelity clause, so she sued him for everything. Now she's a millionaire and owns her own townhouse in the Back Bay and all that jazz." I almost want to say that she earned it by marrying Mr. Geriatrics, but I refrain. I shake my head.

"Whatever happened to the sanctity of marriage?" I mutter.

"Right. Look, I gotta run. Don't forget to buy shoes." And with this she hangs up. I glance up at the clock and realize it's shoe shopping time.

As I collect my stuff and head toward the elevator, I can't help but feel sorry for Natasha. She may have the money, the looks, even the career, but she can't be happy. I bet she feels so ugly and alone. That poor thing. She could really use a friend.

"Hold the elevator!" I yell. As the elevator door re-opens, I walk straight into Natasha.

"Oh!" I say. Why can't I just have good intentions without having to act on them? Gritting my teeth, I open my mouth to speak a word of encouragement but am interrupted by her ringing cell phone. Darn.

"Hey baby," she says in what I imagine is a finishing school voice. "I got a loud display of roses sitting on my new desk."

You know what, I think as I get off the elevator. I don't think I feel sorry for Miss Perfection anymore.

3

As I enter the double doors of Saks Fifth Avenue, a feeling of nostalgia washes over me. The thing is, I used to have a bit of a shopping problem. Okay, it was more like a shopping addiction. I didn't think it was that serious, but my family and friends seemed to think otherwise.

About two years ago I came home from another glorious day frolicking about Newbury Street, with packages galore under my arms, and opened the door to an intervention. Mandy and Zoë were worried that my shopping was getting "excessive" and they took the liberty of calling my mother, who in turn called my grandmother, my aunt, and even my third cousin. Heck, the entire Mosley family tree was in my living room. I was so mad I could have killed them. As if they didn't both benefit from my shopping sprees. I distinctly remember Mandy telling me about all the attention she received from my leather pants. But after hearing their speeches and cries of concern, I was humbled. Like watching *Oprah*, there were tears, hugs, and a few gallons of ice cream. Four hours later, I agreed to Shopaholics Anonymous, which lasted for about a month.

The people in that meeting were whacked beyond belief! They made me so crazy I actually started smoking, and I hate smokers. Yet there I was, lighting up like a Christmas tree. I was so embarrassed by my new habit that I'd wake up at odd hours in the night so Mandy wouldn't catch me. I even lied and told her I smelled like cigarettes because Gwen started smoking. But just like shopping, I couldn't conceal my newfound habit for long.

One afternoon she asked me point-blank, and I couldn't lie. All it took was one I'm-so-disappointed-in-you look and a trip to the American Cancer Society's Web site, and it was adios Marlboro Lights.

And hello chocolate. What is it with having a vice, anyway? I always believed that too many made you a weak person, but everybody deserves one, right? So maybe I'm rationalizing my addictive personality, but it's only because I'm passionate. For five weeks I hit every chocolate store this side of Boylston Street. I even filled out an application at Lindt. Naturally, my newfound addiction triggered a sudden growth spurt in my backside, but I convinced myself that it was better than smoking. Besides, gluttony only applies to 500-pound people who have to be lifted by a crane. But like all bad habits, this one also caught up with me. When I could no longer fit into my favorite pair of Sevens, I nixed all vices and decided to live a life in moderation. I must admit that it's been rather pleasant, but I'm always on the lookout for another vice. Maybe the next one will be exercise.

So here I am, back at Saks, facing all my ghosts. I feel like a recovering alchy in a liquor store, but since I'm pressed for time, this shouldn't be too difficult. As I browse the shoe department, I'm filled with dread. Why am I going to this stupid benefit, anyway? According to the papers, this Jonathan Carmichael is the next JFK, Jr. He started Carmichael Advertising in New York about six years ago and already has offices in two other cities. Zoë says his picture has graced every magazine cover in New York City, and he was most recently named *People* magazine's "Sexiest Man in Advertising." Boy, am I glad I canceled my subscription. There's nothing more unattractive than a man too big for his Calvin Kleins.

I browse endless pairs of shoes in a state of total frustration until my eyes fall on a pair of Manola Blahniks quite similar to the ones Natasha is sporting today. I set down my Gucci knockoff and glance down at the price.

"Five hundred dollars!" I gasp in horror. I cower as other shoppers stare at me. Surely I didn't see that right. I look again. Yep! Five hundred dollars. Oh my gosh! Even when I was a shopaholic, I had more sense than to spend five hundred bucks on a pair of shoes. You put your stinky feet in them for Pete's sake! But even though I know how shallow it is to spend that much money on clothes, especially when there are so many starving children in the world, I've always wondered what it would feel like to be designer-clad from head to toe. On second thought, maybe I'll try it. It's better to try the stuff on and *then* donate money to the Red Cross, isn't it?

As usual, all the sales women are busy with their high-end customers, so I'm left to fend for myself. Unfortunately, the stilettos on display are a size seven, and I wear a size ten. You know what, they'll do. I dash to find myself a matching designer dress. After all, I'm only trying them on.

Five minutes later, I'm zipping up a $5,000 cashmere and silk strapless dress, feeling like Grace Kelly. It's as if my backside has disappeared somewhere in this God-sent creation. Elegant and simple. Calvin Klein really knows what a woman wants.

It takes a good four minutes to shove the Manolo Blahniks on my big feet, but with a little lotion they slide on without too much pain. Now I know how Cinderella's wicked stepsisters felt when they tried to shove their big feet into her glass slipper. (Except in this case, the glass slipper is a pair of $500 Manolo Blahniks, but that's beside the point.)

As I stand up to take a look at my Oscar-worthy ensemble, I feel a sharp pain shoot up my legs.

"Owwwww," I howl. My knees buckle, and I go crashing to the dressing room floor. What is going on? I reach for my throbbing foot. Or should I say feet? I've never felt this kind of pain before. Oh my gosh, claustrophobia. I can't move!

"Get off me!" I yell at the shoes as if they had ears. Oh gosh, they're stuck. They're stuck! I have $500 shoes stuck on my feet! What do I do? I can't breathe. Oh, man. I think I'm having a heart attack. Doesn't a sharp pain shoot up your body just before your heart stops? Or is it up your arm? I think it's the arm.

Confession: I'm not the coolest person when it comes to intense circumstances such as these. A bit high-maintenance, really. I once got my hand stuck in a vending machine at the mall because my Diet Coke was jammed. The maintenance guy had to come in and take the machine apart. All in the name of 65 cents! But that pales in comparison to this. This is worse, way worse. I could lose my feet! They may be ugly and all, but at least they get me to the kitchen.

Okay Emma, think. What would MacGyver do? Well, that's easy. He'd build a shopping mall out of the shoebox. Okay, first things first. I need to get out of this dress. If I know myself at all, then this is a disaster waiting to happen.

Trying my best to think happy thoughts, I throw on my black gauchos. Thank goodness I wasn't wearing tight pants today! After hanging Calvin Klein on his rightful hanger and blowing him a little kiss, I open the door and peek out of the dressing room. I really can't walk another step. Oh, but I have to. I'll be just like the little engine that could. Say it out loud.

"I think I can. I think I can," I mumble as I creep out the door. "Hello! Is anyone there?" The one time you want one of those annoying sales people pestering to get you another size, there's no one in sight. How typical.

"Help," I plead in sheer desperation. This is bad. This is really bad. I could lose my feet. Oh, what a story that would be. I can just see it now: "Young Journalist Loses Her Feet in Tragic Shopping Incident." At least I'd make *The Boston Globe.*

"Hello, people. Is anyone there?" What is this? The Twilight Zone? "Oh my gosh, I give up," I whimper as I slide down the wall, bend my knees into my chest and lower my head. My eyes begin to tear.

"Are you okay?" I hear in the distance. Must be my imagination. I continue sulking and talking to myself.

"Why am I such a dope?" I softly beat my head on my knees. "Seriously, who does this?"

"Are you okay?" The voice is louder and sounds amused.

"Huh?" I ask, and slowly raise my head. Oh my gosh! Standing before me is the most gorgeous human being I've ever laid eyes on. Suddenly I feel very dizzy, and I don't think it's the shoes. He has to be at least 6'3", and his eyes ... be still my beating heart, I've never seen eyes so dark and intense. I mean, it's just not normal to look like that. Let me rephrase that. It's not normal for someone who looks like that to talk to me.

"Are you okay?" he asks for the third time, crouching down to my level. Well shoot, boy! I am now!

"Uh ... yeah. Of course I am," I say cheerfully, trying to mask the pain as I attempt to stand. My legs give way, but luckily my big butt softens the fall.

Without hesitation, Mr. Mystery Man grabs my arm and helps me up, but his very touch makes me stumble again. When I finally get to my feet, I smile softly, praying that I don't have lipstick on my teeth. He looks down and returns a smile that makes me want to melt. His dad has to be a dentist.

"Should I even ask?" he says, raising his eyebrows.

"You don't want to know," I say as I tighten my grip on his arms. And what wonderful arms they are. Even under his tie-less suit, I can tell the man works out.

"Well, now I'm kinda curious," he says with a gleam in his eye. I stare into his slate eyes as I attempt to articulate some sort of a response.

"I have big feet," I blurt, trying to pull my gaze away from his face. So much for sophistication.

"Can you walk?" he asks. He glances at my wobbly legs. I'm way too distracted by his dark, wavy hair and beautiful dimples to even respond.

"Um, huh? What?" I ask, snapping out of my daze.

"Can you walk?" he asks again.

"Of course I can." No I can't.

"Are you sure, or is this one of those things you girls do when you say something but mean something else?" Did I get pegged or what?

"No," I say decidedly.

"No it isn't that girl thing or no you can't walk?" he asks with a smile. I put weight on my foot and a sharp pain shoots up my thigh.

"I'm completely crippled," I finally confess. He eyes me for a moment.

"Hop on, Big Foot," he says as he squats next to me. I let out a nervous laugh.

"You must be joking," I say.

"Surely you're not too prideful to be helped." Forget my pride. I lost that when I opened my big mouth. The real dilemma is whether or not he can lift me? Why did I have to eat all that pizza last night?

"Of course I'm not," I say as I bend down and put my hands around his neck. Gosh, he smells good. As I take another inhalation, Mr. Wonderful stands up and carries me away. I don't care where I'm going, just as long as he's going too.

4

This has got to be the most embarrassing moment of my adult life, and I've had some doozies. I once went on a date with a Kennedy. He was a cousin to a second cousin of a nephew of Robert Kennedy but still as blue-blooded as the rest of the clan. I met him in my political science class. I can't say he was all that attractive, but the words "Kennedy Compound" and "Martha's Vineyard" kept ringing in my ear so I agreed to go out with him. We went to some charity ball at The Four Seasons, and it must've been the clam chowder or something because I totally blanked on his name. I tried to glide my way through the evening, using phrases like "Hey you," but as fate would have it, I ran into an old English professor. When introducing him, I accidentally called my date John. After that he completely ignored me for the rest of the semester.

And there was the time I fell asleep on the New York subway. I'm not sure what I was dreaming about, but I awoke to the sound of my own voice yelling, "You like that, Big Daddy!"

Mr. Hottie carries me into a dressing room and sets me down on a bench. Together we tug and pull until the shoes come off. I sit and stretch my toes for a minute.

Dark Eyes stands and puts his hands on his hips.

"So tell me how you got your shoes stuck?" he asks with a laugh. I can't believe I'm in a dressing room with a complete stranger. My mom would die.

"If I tell you, then I'll have to kill you," I say. Shut up, Emma. That was so cheesy. You know better!

"Let me guess. Hot date?" he teases. Oh my gosh, he is so flirting with me. Isn't he? It's been so long since a man has flirted with me that I think I've forgotten how to flirt back.

"Ha," I say as I stall for thought time. Come on, Emma. It's like riding a bike. "I don't think I've had a hot date in oh ... ever." What kind of answer was that? That's almost as lame as Baby telling Johnny, "I carried a watermelon" in *Dirty Dancing*. I take a seat and reach for my black boots. I need to relax. But seriously, how can I relax when the most beautiful man I've ever seen in my life is helping me into my shoes. They may be Steve Maddens and they may zip up to my knee, but this really is Cinderella.

"Now I find that quite surprising," he says as he helps me to my feet. Did you hear that? He so wants me to have his children.

"Actually, I was trying on shoes for some benefit I have to go to," I say as I roll my eyes. "It's my first one." Gosh my feet hurt.

"Really?" he asks as we make our way out the dressing room and toward the registers. I'm a bit curious as to why he's buying a handbag in the middle of the day, but I can't ask him that. I barely know the guy, but what if he's a cross dresser or something?

"Yeah, but I already know that benefits are for old people with lots of money."

"And no sense of where to invest it?" he adds, getting into line at the cash register.

"Exactly." He shakes his head.

"Urban legend."

"Really?" I ask inquisitively. He laughs.

"Yeah, it'll be fine. Just smile and act like you know what you're talking about." Do I ever?

"I'm Emma Mosley, by the way." I reach out my hand to shake his. He pauses for a moment, but comes to and reaches for mine.

"Jack," he says. Skin on skin. I'm melting.

"So tell me something, Jack?" I say as I shift my weight between feet. Gosh, they're sore. "What's a guy like you doing buying a purse in the middle of a work day?" I'm sorry, but I can't help myself. The guy could be gay. Or worse, married. That would totally bite.

He hands the cashier his credit card and smiles. "It's my secretary's birthday. She has a thing for purses." I eye the label on the purse and let out a low whistle.

"Coach, huh? I'm impressed," I say as I look straight into his eyes.

"Well, she's been good to me," he says, as if dropping almost $300 on a birthday gift were nothing. He slides his wallet into his back pocket and turns to me. "So tell me something, Emma. And I want you to be completely honest." My heart is pounding in my chest. Is he proposing to me already?

"Emerald cut," I blurt without thinking. Crap! Did I just say that?

"What?" he asks with a confused look on his precious face. The cashier's eyes dart at me as she hands him his package. I shoot her a look that implies "I know." I turn my attention back to Jack.

"Uh ... nothing. You were saying?"

"Well, I was just wondering," he says as he leans in closer. I hope he can't hear my heart pounding.

"Yes," I interrupt excitedly. Shut up, Emma!

"If I could take you to lunch." Oh. Well, it's definitely not a proposal, but it's a start. A start to something bigger. Oh gosh! What does this mean? Okay, stop over-thinking. I, Emma Mosley, vow not to analyze or over-think today. At least not for the next hour. But I wonder what's going to happen? Okay, starting now.

"Well Jack, it just so happens that the way to my heart is through my stomach." Okay, maybe I could have thought more before saying that.

As we make our way to the street, I excuse myself to phone Natasha with some lame excuse about checking out a new restaurant on Newbury Street, which isn't exactly a lie. I'm sure there's a new restaurant *somewhere* on Newbury Street, I just don't know where it is.

"What do you mean you're reviewing a new restaurant?" Natasha says. "Your article's due today. And what little café are you talking about? I don't know of any. What's it called?" Oh, please. Like she's heard of every restaurant on Newbury Street. The woman doesn't even eat!

"Uh, it's new," I say as I slump to the steps of Saks. "Oh, look at that. The waiter's here. I'll have the story on your desk at the end of the day. Bye," I say and hang up the phone before she has time to respond. I'm so going to get fired.

"Is everything all right?" Jack says as he joins me on the steps.

"Fine, except that my boss is a total..." Crap, I'm supposed to be a lady. He slides his hands casually into his coat pockets and waits for me to finish.

"A total what?" he prods.

"Tell me the truth," I ask as I turn toward him. "On a scale from one to ten, how bad is it to hang up on your boss?"

"You hung up on your boss!" he says loud enough for passersby to hear us. I bite my thumbnail and cringe.

"It's that bad, huh?"

"Well, it's not going to get you a promotion," he says.

"But I think I can keep you from getting fired," he says as he stands and helps me to my feet. "Well, at least for today."

"This should be interesting," I say as I follow him to the main street.

"Did I hear you say something about reviewing a restaurant on Newbury Street?"

"Were you eavesdropping on me, Jack?" I say teasingly.

"You were talking pretty loudly, Emma."

"True. Okay, lay it on me."

"Well, as your luck would have it, I know of a bistro that just opened up on the corner of Newbury and Berkeley. So technically you're not a liar."

"Well, shoot. That's what I was going for," I joke.

"What do you say, Disney Eyes? Can I buy you lunch?" he says as he turns to face me. Disney Eyes? Oh my gosh. That's what my daddy called me when I was little. Maybe that's a sign.

"Sounds perfect," I say, trying to conceal the gleam in my tone. We walk in silence as we make our way to Boylston Street, where Jack hails a taxi.

"Jack," I say nervously as the cab pulls up. He turns to look at me. "I feel kinda bad that you keep helping me out of trouble. I don't know how to thank you." Please say by having your children.

"Thank me by eating more than a salad," he says with a straight face. "I hate it when girls do that." Okay, who is this guy, and what is his flaw?

"That'll never be a problem," I say as Jack opens the door. He puts his hand on the small of my back as he helps me into the car. I wonder if men have a clue how special this gesture makes a woman feel. Maybe my luck is about to change.

5

As I step off the elevator onto the fifteenth floor of my office building, I suddenly remember our mandatory staff meeting. Oh my gosh! I look down at my watch. Crap! I'm twenty minutes late! I take off in a sprint to the board room.

"Look who finally decided to grace us with her presence," Natasha announces as I enter the room.

"I'm sorry I'm late," I mutter as I scramble to find an empty seat. "That bistro was really crowded."

"We're not in high school, Miss Mosley. We don't need to hear your whereabouts," she snaps.

"Yes, ma'am," I remark sarcastically. Everyone laughs. So sue me. I'm not Gandhi.

"Very funny, Emma. Now did you get the review?" Simmer down, I want to snap back. It was only a joke, though I guess I deserve the harsh treatment; I did hang up on her.

"I got it," I say with a toss of my head. And I promise to stop lying, I think as I look down at my unpolished fingernails.

"Fine then," she says. "Moving on."

As she continues droning to the entire group, I gaze

out the window and recap the last two hours. The last two hours, I might add, that have left me completely dumbfounded.

"So what were you like as a child?" Jack asks as he takes a bite of a croissant. I still can't believe I'm at Atlantis. It opened a few weeks ago, and I had to call three times for a reservation next month. But not Jack. He walked right up to the maitre d' and shook his hand as if they were brothers.

"Oh trust me. You don't want to know," I say embarrassingly as I take the final bite of raspberry chicken crepes. I look down at my empty plate. Gee, those went fast. I know *Glamour* says not to eat an entire meal on your first date, but come on, I had to. Who doesn't finish a free meal?

"Tell me some Little Emma stories," he says as he leans back in his chair. "I bet you were always in trouble."

"What makes you say that?" I laugh. How did he know?

"Just a hunch," he says with a charming grin. My gosh, his smile makes my heart pound. Literally, the entire hour I've known him, my heart has been racing. I wonder if that means I'm burning calories.

"First tell me how you got that," I say, pointing to the scar above his left eyebrow. It's very faint, but I noticed it when he was helping me out of my shoes.

"This," he says as he rubs his finger across it. "I'm surprised you noticed it." Great, now he knows I've been staring at him intently.

"So what happened?" I jump in before we can continue my obsession with his eyes. His beautiful, dark eyes. And that scar! It only gives him more character. "Let me guess. Some girl's ex-boyfriend hit you? Oh, or was it the boyfriend of a girlfriend you thought was your girlfriend?" I say jumping in my seat. "Oh my gosh! Was she two-timing you?" I say as I slap my hand over my mouth.

"Do you want to hear what happened or would you like me to listen to your imagination make up what happened?" he says in a Daddy-like tone, which is strangely a turn on. I sheepishly tuck my hair behind my ear and smile.

"Go ahead, Scrappy. I'm all ears." He shakes his head and laughs.

"My friend Ben and I spent a few weeks in Greece the summer before we left for college. Ben had an uncle that lives there, so we spent the summer working on his fishing boat." Jack? A fisherman? I *so* need to close my jaw right now.

"Well, he lived next door to a girl named Helen that was about our age and very beautiful." He smiles and looks up at the ceiling. Oh, please. She couldn't have been *that* beautiful.

"So, of course Ben and I did what all eighteen-year-old guys do when there's a pretty girl thrown into the equation." I lean in eagerly.

"You competed for her," I say as the waiter takes our plates.

"Exactly. And being the cocky kid I was back then, I made a move on her, which wasn't my brightest idea." He laughs.

"Oh no. You and Ben fought over her," I say, taking a sip of my drink.

"Actually, Helen punched me when I tried to kiss her," he says plainly, which causes me to spew my water all over the table. Oh crap. It's coming out my nose.

"You got that from Helen?" I say, dabbing my nose with a napkin. He nods.

"So I take it the two of you aren't pen pals?" I joke as I place my linen napkin back in my lap.

"Actually, Ben and Helen are still together."

"Are you kidding me?" He crosses his arms.

"Nope. They're married and have a little boy."

25

"It's funny how things work out," I say with a pun totally intended.

"Yes it is," he says. The waiter bends over to refill our water glasses. Jack rubs his hands together.

"Now it's my turn," he says.

"Take your best shot, Rocky," I say, tossing my head and leaning back in my chair.

"Tell me three things about yourself that nobody knows," he says.

"Three things." I scoot around in my chair.

"Yep."

"About me?" I ask.

"Yep," he repeats. I bite my thumb.

"That nobody knows?"

"Emma, you heard the question."

"I know. It's just that my mom and best friend know just about everything about me." He looks at me sternly. Gosh, why is that so sexy? "Fine. I'm thinking," I say as I look off into space. While I'm thinking, Jack calls over the waiter and orders two coffees.

"I'm scared of the dark," I announce before the waiter leaves the table. He and Jack exchange curious looks. Oops.

"Hey, I'm not ashamed," I say to the waiter. He shakes his head and disappears into the kitchen.

"So do you sleep with a night light then?" he jokes.

"Please," I say, looking out the window.

"Emma?" he asks, laughing. "Do you?" I sigh and wave my hand casually in the air.

"Fine! If you must know, I sleep with my bathroom light on. But that's only because I don't want to trip on something if I get up in the middle of the night." He leans his head back and laughs. It's a good thing I didn't tell him I check under my bed as well.

"I also want to be a CIA agent. I think it all started when I got hooked on 'Alias.' Sidney Bristow is so ..." I start, but the look on Jack's face makes me stop.

"What?" he asks as he shrugs his shoulders innocently.

"You're mocking me," I say as I point my finger at him.

"No, I'm not," he says. He raises his hands innocently. "I think you'd be a great agent."

"You do?" I ask skeptically. He nods with a straight face.

"Yeah. I think a lot of CIA agents are afraid of the dark."

"Shut up," I yell as I throw my napkin at him. A few people turn their heads toward our table. Gosh, this place is stuffy. Don't get me wrong, the food is fabulous—and the company. Well, the company goes without saying, but other than Jack and me, the place is a little hoity-toity for my taste.

"One more, Agent Mosley." I glare at him.

"I'm thinking." I tap my fingers on the linen table-cloth. Gosh, what do I tell him? I gaze out the window for a few moments while Jack sips his black coffee.

"I hate my job," I say, looking him in the eye.

"So do most people," he points out.

"I know, but I've never told anybody that."

"Not even your mom or best friend?" he asks with a smile.

"They know I don't love it, but they have no idea how bad it really is. You see, I was recently up for this promotion at work and, well, I didn't get it."

"I'm sorry," he says, lightly touching my hand. Be still my beating heart!

"Thank you, but the funny thing is that I wasn't even that upset about it. I mean, initially I was, of course. Rejection never feels good, but I was almost relieved because I took it as a sign that I'm not stuck where I am." I add some creamer to my coffee. "It's not that I'm ungrateful for my job and what I get to do every day, but I want more. I want to be passionate about what I do. I want to have a voice and write about things that actually matter."

"You know what I think?" he says after pausing to take in my words. He leans forward.

"What's that?" I say.

"Well for starters, I think what you do isn't who you are. You're a writer by profession, which by the way I had pegged after talking to you for five minutes." I smile. "But you are so much more than that. You're passionate and unique. And there's no doubt in my mind that your personality exudes from what you write. So what I think is that you need to just keep being you and your story will come." I think I'm going to cry. He has no idea how badly I needed to hear that. I pause as I attempt to articulate some sort of response to his flattery.

"But if it doesn't, you can always join the CIA," he adds.

"You can't be trusted," I laugh.

"So seriously, Emma, how big are your feet?"

"Why?" I ask skeptically.

"Just getting to know you," he says through a laugh.

"If you must know, they're a size ten," I confidently reply.

"And why the $500 shoes?" Jack says, leaning over the table inquisitively. If I were dating this guy, I don't think I'd ever get bored of staring at him. I wave my hand casually in the air.

"I was just fooling around, though I bet this benefit will be full of Manolo Blahnik-wearing types. Much like the CEO I'm sure."

"So what type is this CEO guy?" he asks. I wonder where Jack is from. Or what he does for a living. Or if he prefers dogs over cats. Hopefully dogs because I hate cats. Gosh, I want to know everything about him.

"Well," I say, snapping out of my thoughts and back to lunch at Atlantis. "He's probably some trust-fund baby, who looks at life as something to be conquered." With this, I can't help but think of my ex's quest to climb Mount Everest. "And I'm sure he's dating some Paris Hilton type." I don't know what my problem is. I don't even know the guy, or want to for that matter. I guess it's just the fact that the world already has a surplus of cocky, rich boys like Jonathan Carmichael. Or maybe it's the fact that I dated that category before.

"You just have everyone figured out, don't you, Lois Lane?" If only he knew why.

"I know what you're thinking," I say, taking another swig of coffee. Yuck, it's cold.

"You do?" he asks curiously.

"You think I'm too opinionated."

"Well, for someone I just met, you seem to know an awful lot about me," he says facetiously.

"I know you can take a punch," I say with a laugh.

"So you never told me whose benefit you're going to," he says.

"Jonathan Carmichael," I say with a roll of my eyes. "It's to raise money for cancer research. And get this: the tickets were five-hundred bucks, which is quite ridiculous considering the fact that he could just nix the party and spend money on the kids." My gosh. I have got to stop taking my issues out on this Carmichael guy. What is my problem? "But there I go again making opinions about a guy I don't know. He probably just has bad PR people," I add. Jack stares at me strangely. Oh my gosh. I must have food in my teeth, or what if I have a booger hanging out of my nose? He clears his throat and glances down at his watch.

"Oh my gosh, Emma. I didn't realize how late it was. I have an interview across town in twenty minutes." What? There's no way we've been here for two hours. Forget the booger, I'm so gonna get fired. Twice over. Jack throws a few bills on the table.

"I guess I better get back to work too," I say as I follow his lead and head for the door. What's the sudden rush? And why hasn't he asked for my phone number? Oh my gosh, I do have a booger. But he doesn't seem like the kind of guy to get freaked out by boogers. I mean, the guy just witnessed water coming out my nose. I don't understand.

"Well, thank you for lunch, Jack. And for rescuing me," I say trying to hide my utter disappointment.

"You're welcome," he says distractedly as he stops on the street corner. "Can I get you a cab?"

"No. I'm only a few blocks away," I say, stuffing my hands into my plaid coat. Then I do the unthinkable and give Jack my pre-kiss look. Normally I shy away from that look. I mean, kissing is great and all, but on a first date? It's like opening your candy before the movie starts. By the end of the previews, you're empty-handed and disappointed. But it's not like I want him to kiss me. I just want him to want to kiss me.

"And I'm that way," he says as he points in the other direction. Oh my gosh. He just totally looked the other way. Why is he acting funny all of a sudden?

"Well," I say, stalling for more time. Jack reaches out his hand, and as much as I want to slap him as hard as I can, I refrain and do the same.

"I'm glad to have met you, Emma," he says. He squeezes my hand quickly, then lets go. My arm falls limp at my side.

Jack looks at me to respond, but there are no words. I'm too shocked to speak. I don't get it. I have no idea what's going on. Jack and I had an incredible time today. I mean, out of nowhere, like in a fairytale, I meet this guy who, literally, rescues me. Then we spend the next two hours engrossed in conversation at one of the most romantic restaurants in Boston. But now we're shaking hands? I realize I've been out of the game for a while, but somewhere, somehow, I know I missed a step. I had to miss a step. It's like Jack is suddenly a different person.

"See ya, Jack," I manage to get out and walk in the other direction.

I take off through the park without as much as a second glance at him. I'm so mad that it almost saddens me. The park looks so beautiful this time of year. The trees are coated white from the snow, and the frog pond has been transformed into an ice skating rink. An ear-to-ear smile should be spreading across my face as I observe the children playing in the snow, but no. That last two minutes with Jack had to happen. I mean, everything was going great until he looked down at his watch. I don't even think my girl Jane Austen could articulate my feelings at this moment. Well, she could definitely tell you they aren't feelings of felicity. If life were playing music, you wouldn't hear Louis Armstrong's "What a Wonderful World." You'd hear "Things That Make You Go Hmm."

"Emma!" Gwen says, nudging my side.

"Huh? What?" I guess my daydream is over.

"What is up with you?" Gwen asks as everyone packs up to go. The meeting with Natasha is over.

"What do you mean?" I ask innocently. I scoot my way from behind the conference table and make a beeline for the door.

"You didn't listen to a word Natasha said," Gwen says

as she tails me to the door. "And you were late. That's not like you at all."

"I know," I say sheepishly.

"Emma, can I have a word with you?" Natasha cuts in. Shoot a monkey, I was so close.

As I follow her to her office, I can't help but stare at the back of her body. She really is a perfect hourglass.

When we get to her office she shuts the door, turns to face me, and folds her arms across her chest.

"Look, Emma. I know you're Miss Congeniality around here and everything, but that stuff doesn't fly with me. If you don't have the decency to show up on time to mandatory meetings, we're going to have a problem."

"I'm sorry. You lost me at the Miss Congeniality part," I say solemnly. She doesn't crack a smile.

"Just don't let it happen again, okay?"

"Okay," I say slowly.

"And I want that article before you leave. Chop-chop." She snaps her fingers. What am I, a dog? I bite my bottom lip to keep from saying anything else. On the bright side, at least I still have my job.

I return to my desk and begin working furiously for the remainder of the afternoon, but I can't get Jack out of my mind.

Why didn't he ask for my number? And why does this feel strangely familiar? Out of nowhere, I'm feeling some of the same feelings I felt six years ago. Man, I thought these emotions were gone, but I guess they were just dormant. And I was doing so good. I didn't think about him once when I was with Jack. Not once, but out of nowhere his memory is hitting me like a freight train.

Caleb Callaghan. Chills run down my spine at the very thought of him. It was so long ago, but when I really stop and think about him, it's as if it were yesterday. He was the wealthy Carmichael-type I dated in college.

Caleb's "Orlando Bloom" face made him Harvard's most eligible bachelor. He was one of those frat boys who only dated pretty, petite, country club girls. Everyone saw him as the son of one of England's top architects who sat on the Harvard Alumni Board. That is, everyone but me. We had a few classes together, and he always tried to trump me with his photographic memory and natural intelligence.

Aside from the fact that I despise anyone disagreeing with me, I thought he was cocky. And let me tell you, I wasn't shy about telling him that. I don't know why, but for some reason, in between taking out the Chancellor's daughter or dating some beautiful sorority girl, Caleb would ask me out. I, of course, rejected him without flinching, which felt quite liberating. This went on for over a year, but one day he stopped talking to me. And for some crazy reason, I missed him. I missed him throwing things at me in the library. And I missed yelling at him in class. But being the tough girl I thought I was, I didn't let it show. I just put more of a guard up and convinced myself I'd be just fine without him.

Then one day I was contently reading *Pride and Prejudice* under my favorite oak tree on campus. I kept willing Caleb to walk by as I sipped my latte, and the crazy thing is he did. Except he wasn't alone. Some Swedish beauty was riding on the handlebars of his bike. They were laughing, sharing in a secret joke. He even had the audacity to wave at me. Gosh, I felt ill. I wanted to come out of my skin. That's when I knew: he did a number on me, and I didn't even realize it. Two days later, he was my boyfriend.

Every day was an adventure with him. Apart from our attraction for each other, the two of us had nothing in common. From religion to politics, we disagreed on just about everything. But maybe that was the spark that held us together. I don't know. I didn't think, I just felt. But faster than it started, it crashed. It's like Kelly

Clarkson sings, "Beautiful Disaster." Yep, that was Caleb. He was my Beautiful Disaster.

Apparently his family had an agenda for him that didn't include me. I still can't tell you why they hated me so much, but it didn't really matter to me because I was crazy in love. Unfortunately, Caleb loved his dad and his pride much more than he loved me. Two days after I met Mr. Callaghan, he gave Caleb an ultimatum. He could choose his father's multimillion-dollar architectural firm and a fat inheritance or he could choose a life with me. I didn't stand a chance. Caleb took the road to wealth, and the rest is history.

I haven't thought about him in a long time, but occasionally, when I do run across someone from the male species, he comes back to haunt me. It's been six years, but every time I even think about moving on, the scar is reopened and every issue, every insecurity rushes to the surface.

But I thought Jack was different. Seriously, for the first time in six years, I didn't think about Caleb. I wasn't scared, and call me crazy but Jack seemed interested in me. I thought we connected. Gosh, how could I be so stupid? Why did I open my heart to the idea of a stranger? Why do I ever open my heart to the idea of love? It only leads to heartache. Shame on me. I should know better.

7

The February wind cuts my face like glass as I walk home from work. 'Tis the season for moisturizer. And frozen snotcicles.

The bad thing about living in the South End is the lack of transportation. It's one of the most historic parts of the city, but the "T" won't get you very far. The winter is miserable, but I still love walking along the cobblestones, admiring the rows and rows of brownstones. I can't think of a more perfect place to live. Not only is it the most charming neighborhood in Boston, but even the people are friendlier here.

After what seems like a Lewis and Clark expedition, I make it to Appleton Street and sprint up the front steps. (Does that count as exercise?)

"Hey," Mandy calls from the den.

She's curled up in one of our two oversized chairs, digging into a carton of Ben and Jerry's ice cream. We had Chandler/Joey syndrome and spent a fortune on those chairs.

"Hey, hoochie. How was your day?" I pant, peeling off my coat, hat, gloves, and scarf. I make my way to the coffeemaker and make a fresh pot.

"Good," Mandy says, sitting up in excitement. "I got a sneak peek at the Ritz. Emma, it's breathtaking. And you wouldn't believe how much money this is costing Carmichael Advertising! I wish I were going."

"Really?" I ask, half amused.

"Really, and I interviewed the CEO this afternoon," she says, ignoring my skepticism. "We had the greatest conversation. He's nicer than I thought he'd be. A bit standoffish but with good reason. Everybody was eyeing him like he's a celebrity or something. Poor guy."

"Oh yeah, poor little millionaire," I snort.

"Well that millionaire happens to be your type." I pause as I pour myself a cup of coffee. I still can't get Jack out of my mind, which is quite frustrating because I'm usually able to do that.

"You have to date to have a type," I say as I plunk down onto the other chair.

"That's not true. You like them tall, dark, and handsome. And he looks great in a suit."

"Mandy, don't tell me you've bought into that pompous act of his!" I say as I spill a little coffee on my shirt. I've got to simmer down about this guy. I've never even met him. Maybe it has a little to do with Caleb. Not to mention my foul mood due to the disappearing act that went down a few hours ago. I still can't believe that happened.

"Are you okay?" she asks suspiciously.

"Speaking of tall, dark, and handsome, I need to talk to you." I sigh and stare into my cup. I promised myself that I'd never mention Jack to anyone, that I'd go on living as if he'd never existed, but I have to tell Mandy about him. It's bothering me too much. I set down my favorite Harvard mug and give her my serious face.

"What is it?" Mandy exclaims as she drops her Chubby Hubby.

I grab her carton of ice cream and recap my day down to the very last detail.

"I mean, out of nowhere he just had to go," I finish.

"One minute I'm thinking I could totally date this guy." I close my eyes, trying to retain the image of him smiling at me over lunch. "But then two minutes later I'm left feeling like I did when ..." I trail off.

"I know," Mandy says, reaching over and squeezing my hand.

"So why do you think he scrammed like that?" I set down the ice cream in despair. "He didn't ask for my card or anything."

"Maybe an important meeting came up. You did say he seemed like he did something pretty important." I nod my head, though I'm not convinced. "Or maybe he got scared. Men get really scared about this stuff," Mandy adds lamely.

"As if I don't?" I say as tears fill my eyes. Gosh, I feel so stupid. Even when talking to my best friend, who knows me better than anyone, I feel so pathetic that I'd let a guy I hardly know get to me.

"Emma, I know there has to be an explanation for his quick departure. And I know you'll see him again." She smiles and places her hand on my knee. "You'll be coming out of Starbucks and you'll bump into him or something romantic like that."

"Gosh, I don't know." The mere thought makes me pick up my friends Ben and Jerry and take another bite. I set down my spoon helplessly.

"But I'm sick of talking about it. I'm fine." Mandy looks at me as if she's unconvinced. "Really, I am. I mean, the date wasn't that great. And he had this scar above his eyebrow that kinda bugged me." I am such a liar.

"You know what you need?" she asks, jumping up from her chair.

"Please, no more food," I moan as I curl my knees into my chest. Not only did I just inhale a pint of ice cream, but I ate an entire bag of peanut butter M & M's at work. Not to mention the big lunch I had at Atlantis. I need to have my jaw wired shut.

"Nope, you need a date with Bridget Jones," she says with a squeal.

"Sounds perfect," I say as I grab a nearby blanket and get lost in one of my favorite movies.

I once read that if you go to bed thinking about something, there's a 95 percent chance you'll dream about it.

Well, whoever wrote that probably also said that cutting carbs will help you lose weight, because I went to bed thinking about Mark Darcy a la *Bridget Jones's Diary*, but dreamt about Jack instead. I'm sitting at Starbucks reading a book when he comes prancing in sporting Manolo Blahniks and the Calvin Klein dress I tried on. He sits down next to me and asks me to help him with his zipper. Then somehow we end up at my grandmother's house baking a pumpkin pie. Just as I'm taking it out of the oven, I sit straight up in the bed. What did I forget to do today? My mind goes through a mental list of To-Do. I got milk. I mailed the rent. I took Mandy's dress to the cleaners. I ... oh my gosh! I forgot to get shoes today!

I force my dry eyes open and glance at the clock. It's 2 AM. A sudden panic rushes over me as I jump out of bed. I can't believe I forgot to get shoes when the benefit is tonight!

As I retrieve my dress from the hall closet, it occurs to me that Mandy may have something I can borrow. I know this can probably wait until tomorrow, but she's a heavy sleeper and I'm wide awake. I tiptoe toward her room and slowly open the door. After rummaging through her closet for a few minutes, I realize that I don't hear her breathing. In a state somewhere between fright and worry, I run to her bed, throw back her covers, and see that she's not there.

"She's been kidnapped!" I yelp. I have sudden flashbacks of the Lindberg kidnapping. I bet they crept in through the fire escape. What am I going to tell her mother? And why didn't they come after me? She probably sacrificed her life saying, "Take me instead."

In the midst of my thoughts, I see a dark shadow move outside on her fire escape. Okay, Emma, don't panic. Think Enya. You're breezy.

Who am I kidding? I dash to the kitchen and grab a butcher knife. As I run back to Mandy's room, I fling open the door and see her climbing through the window.

"What are you doing?" we ask each other at the same time.

"Have you gone mad?" she shouts as she glances at the butcher knife clutched tightly in my hand.

"I thought you were kidnapped," I gasp. "I was coming to save you." Now that I've said it out loud, I realize how ridiculous it sounds.

"Thank you, Nancy Drew. But I meant what were you doing in my room at 2 AM? And with a butcher knife!"

"What were you doing on the fire escape?" I snap back.

"I was getting some air." She turns calmly and closes the window.

"Air? There's a blizzard outside. Oh my gosh! Have you been smoking? Mandy, you know better. Weren't you the one who told me that—"

"I wasn't smoking, all right? I just have a lot on my mind," she says, brushing flecks of snow off her arms.

"Like what?" I press.

"Hey, Psycho. You want to put the knife down?"

"Oh." I realize it's still poised above my head. I place

it on her night stand. "So who were you talking to on the fire escape?" I ask, hoping she'll say our Mark Consuelos-looking neighbor.

"Look, Emma," she starts.

"Oh man, this can't be good." I plop down on her bed. The last "Look Emma" I got from her was when I borrowed her Louis Vuitton purse and spilled coffee in it.

Mandy studies my face for a minute. "I didn't want to tell you this earlier, but I saw Caleb today."

"Caleb who?" I ask.

"*Caleb*," she says slowly.

"Wait a second. Caleb-Caleb? My Caleb?"

"It was just after the Carmichael interview." She sits down next to me.

"Is it hot in here?" I ask, jumping up and unlatching the window. Her eyes follow me, concerned.

"Some of the crew and I went to Grill 83 for lunch, and I bumped into him, literally," she says as she plays with the corner of her down comforter.

"I think I'm having a hot flash," I say. I begin pacing the room. I stop and turn to face her. "Why didn't you tell me earlier?"

"Because you had such an emotional day."

"Did you talk to him?" I ask, beginning to gnaw on my thumbnail.

"Briefly." She grabs a pillow and hugs it to her chest.

"And?" I blurt. She sighs.

"Emma, it's late. Do we have to do this now?" she asks with a fake yawn. She gets up and walks over to her dresser.

"Do you remember this picture?" she asks. She picks a frame up off the dresser and stares at it. "What was our cruise director's name again?" I walk over to the dresser and take the picture from her.

"Stop dodging the question. What happened?" I say in her face.

"Fine. He's been here for a few days," she says, plunking herself on her bed. I pause in my pacing and force a laugh. "He said he wanted to call you."

"But he hasn't." I continue pacing her room while I contemplate if I'm upset or relieved about this fact.

"Well, I told him you wouldn't want to hear from him anyway, seeing how things were left."

"Thank you," I say.

"But he kept asking questions," she says, looking up at me. I join her on the bed.

"Like what?" I ask. She turns to face me.

"Well just, you know. Questions about you," she says as she resumes her fixation with her down comforter. Why do I get the feeling she's hiding something from me?

"What did you tell him?" I ask as I put my hand on top of hers. She looks up at me.

"I said that everything was wonderful and that you've never been happier."

"Thanks," I say softly. My girl always gets my back.

"He also asked if you were seeing anyone," she says as she picks at her cuticles.

"What did you tell him?"

"The truth. That guys fall all over you, but you've yet to date anyone worth your while."

"Right." I walk over to the window. "Ew! That ugly, white cat is on your balcony again." Mandy gets up and joins me at the window.

"There's more," she says as she puts her hand on my shoulder. I knew it. Mandy always fidgets when she's nervous.

"Don't tell me he's married," I joke.

"No." Is it wrong that I want him to serve punch at my wedding?

"Well then, what is it?" She takes a deep breath and pauses. "Mandy, come on. Like you said, it's been six years. I can handle it."

"He's getting married." The breath has just been knocked out of me.

"What?" I gasp, though I heard every word she just said.

"Her family's from here, and she wants to get married at Trinity Church." I feel like somebody just punched me in the stomach. "Oh Em," she says, putting her arm around me.

"So let me get this straight," I say as I wiggle from her embrace. "He broke up with me because I'm from the States and didn't fit into his little British world, and now he's marrying someone from here!" I begin pacing her room again, this time faster and with more intensity. Oh my gosh. It's hot in here.

"That was a long time ago. Things change. People change. Besides, you know there's a lot more to your breakup than that."

"You mean maybe he finally got the guts to stand up to his father?" I say. I pull off my sweatshirt before I overheat.

"No, I mean that he's not good enough for you!" she shouts. "Emma, if he chose money over you then why are we having this conversation?" Tears begin welling up in my eyes and I look at the ground.

"He did, didn't he?" Mandy walks over and puts both hands on my shoulders.

"I know you didn't get much closure. It all happened so fast, but Emma, you have to let it go." I continue looking at my unpolished toes and watch as a tear falls to my foot.

"I can't," I say, shaking my head in defeat.

"Then why don't you talk him?" she says. I look up at her as she walks over to her dresser drawer. She opens the top drawer and pulls out a tiny piece of paper. "Here you go," she says, placing it in my hand. "He's staying at the Ritz."

"The Ritz, huh?" I glance down at the number.

"Get your closure and move on. It's been long enough." I continue to stare at the piece of paper as if it were a Magic 8 Ball.

"How did he look?" I can't help but wonder. It's been a while, but I'll never forget his adorable face.

"You mean, has he gained massive amounts of weight and gone bald in the last six years?" she laughs. Has it really been six years? Am I completely psycho to still hold onto to anger after six years?

"Well, it would make things a lot easier," I say sheepishly, though I can't imagine ever being turned off by him. I take a seat on the edge of her bed.

"He looks the same." She joins me. "Well, except for the suit." I look at her in surprise.

"He was wearing a suit?" Never in my life did I see him in a suit. Or with his shirt tucked in, for that matter.

"So, what are you going to do?" Mandy asks after a moment. I sigh.

"Go back to bed." I stand to my feet. "I can't think about this right now." Translation: Leave me alone.

"I understand." She always does. I turn to exit her room. "But tell me this." I stop at the door and turn to face her. "Why were you in my room at 2 AM?"

"Well, the thing is..." I shift my weight from one foot to the other. "It's that ... with all the excitement at Saks," I say as I burst into tears, "I never found shoes. I came to borrow yours." I cup my face in my hands and continue sobbing.

"I figured this would happen," she says. She kneels down and pulls a box out from under her bed. I walk over to her and open it. Oh my goodness. There, hidden beneath tissue paper, is a beautiful pair of size ten Steve Maddens. They're clear sandals, with two straps covered in little rhinestones. They're also about three inches tall. Tears stream down my face as I look at them. Mandy is such a wonderful friend.

"When did you do this?" I ask in disbelief.

"Yesterday." She smiles.

"Yesterday? Then why did you send me looking?"

"Call it intuition," she says with a wink.

"You're the best!" I drop the shoes and give her a hug. "Thank you. I love you, Panda Bear."

"You're welcome, Little Emma." She hands me the shoe box and nudges me toward the door. "Now get out so I can get some beauty sleep. I have to do the morning show tomorrow."

9

Well, I can't sleep. I have too much on my mind. I thought I was over Caleb. Sure, I think of him on the rare occasion when I watch the BBC Channel or read Harry Potter, but I hardly ever daydream about him anymore. Or think about what might have been. I even put all my Caleb scrapbooks in storage.

At 5 AM I toss the covers back in defeat. I need some air. As I bundle up, I head for the Public Garden. I used to storm this park whenever Caleb and I fought, which was just about every day. Things were so simple back then. We'd fight and make up like it was nothing. How did things get so complicated?

And why am I still bothered after six years? I'm supposed to hate him, not be grieving that he's getting married. I don't want to feel insecure about this, but how can I not? Caleb didn't want to be with me because his family had another life picked for him, yet he's back in the same situation with someone else. And he proposed to her. It's taken me a long time to find confidence again, and just as I have, stupid Caleb comes back and reopens the can of insecurity. That is just like him to come and mess things up when I finally have it together.

Minus the dramatic breakup, he was a great boyfriend. No one could make me laugh like he did, and I've never met anyone so unselfish. He used to spend his summers in places like Africa and India helping other people. He wanted to save the world, one country at a time. And I believe he could. But his character was never the problem.

He was such a guy's guy and a lot more sociable than me. He never wanted to stay in and eat pizza, and he hated watching movies and reading books. He used to say, "Why read a book about someone else's life when there's a story out there to live?" He was so passionate that I never really got to be the dreamer that I am. It's like the roles were reversed, but somehow we had a great thing going. That is, until I met his family. That's when our relationship began its downward spiral. On site, they were warm and friendly, but they hated me. And they were pretty good actors because it wasn't until I overheard them talking about me that I actually picked up on it.

After a long day of touring London, we returned to Caleb's house. I was exhausted so I went up to my room to lie down. Well, not really because I never take naps, but I wanted to recap my day to Mandy. After spending an hour on the phone, I went downstairs to find Caleb and stumbled onto a conversation that I should have never heard.

"But Caleb, she's an American," I heard his mother say from the den. I peeked around the corner and saw her standing by Caleb's father at the fireplace. Caleb sat on the sofa facing them.

"So?" he said defiantly.

"Look, son," his father interjected. "I know a Daddy's Girl when I see one. Do you honestly think she's going to leave her family for you?" Daddy's Girl! I wanted to punch Mr. Callaghan in the face for saying that, but I knew Caleb would defend me. Or so I thought.

"I'm afraid your father's right, sweetie. You can't possibly ask her to do that. And even if she did, she might resent you for it." Caleb let out a huge sigh.

"I know you think you care about her," his father started.

"Care about her? Dad, I want to marry her." I clasped my hands over my mouth to keep from screaming. I didn't care what Caleb's parents thought. He wanted to marry me!

"That's why I brought her here," he added.

"You will do no such thing!" his dad interjected.

"Why not? Because she's not who you picked?" Caleb retorted.

"You threw away any chance of who I picked," his dad said.

"Who? Elizabeth?" At the time, I had no idea who Elizabeth was, but I didn't care. I was still in shock to hear Caleb say that he wanted to marry me. I was floating on a cloud.

"Okay everyone. Time out," his mom said. She was always the peacemaker. It wouldn't surprise me if she secretly wanted us together, but she's was just like Caleb: too scared to stand up to her husband.

"Look, son," Mr. Callahan said firmly. "I know you have a good time with her. She's a charming girl, really. But you have no future with her. She's in a different class entirely. Do what you have to do and move on." As much as I wanted to come out of my skin when I heard this, I knew Caleb would defend me. I knew he loved me. I knew that any minute he would jump off the couch and get in his Dad's face. I waited for Caleb's reply.

"What are you saying?" he finally asked, choking on his words. I could hear his father walk toward him. I had no idea what was about to happen, so naturally, my heart was pounding in my chest.

"I'm saying cut this girl loose or I'll have to cut you loose." Tears streamed down my face, but I stayed to hear more. I was so naïve at the time that I stood on the steps waiting for Caleb to tell his dad to shove it, but he never did.

"But why?" he asked. At this point everything in me felt weak and ill. I saw a side to Caleb that freaked me out. I saw a passive stranger sitting before two people afraid to speak up for himself. I saw a person I didn't even recognize.

"Because she'll hold you back," he said.

"But..." Caleb started. I peered my head around the corner because at this point I didn't care if I got caught eavesdropping. Caleb was still sitting on the couch, but now his parents had closed in on him. His mother had her arm around his shoulder and his father was looming in front of him.

"No buts son." I collapsed on the stairwell and waited patiently for Caleb to defend me. To tell his dad that no amount of wealth or prestige was worth sacrificing what we had, but he never did. And a huge part of me knew he wouldn't.

"I'll need to think about this," Caleb finally said.

With this, I turned up the stairs and cried myself to sleep. I couldn't think much less speak to him after that. I was blindsided. I didn't know what to do. Whoever coined the phrase, "It's better to have loved and lost than to have never loved at all" is a liar. I wish I'd never met Caleb. The good times didn't come close to outweighing my hurt in the end. I was heartbroken.

We broke up the next morning, right there, in the very room I heard him say he wanted to marry me.

"Whatcha doing all by yourself?" he asked, unaware that I was about to erupt like Mt. Vesuvius.

"Waiting for you," I said softly. Thinking nothing of it, he grabbed my arm and snuggled up next to me on the couch. I'll never forget the thoughts that raced through my head at that moment. I was so mad at him for cowering in front of his dad. I was so angry that he pursued me knowing full well that his dad would object. I was so mad that he was a different person once he got to London. But at the same time, I still loved him. I loved him so much that it gutted me to say what I was about to say to him, but I had to.

"Do you know how much I love you?" he asked, tracing my hand with his finger. My face grew hot with anger.

"You must really think I'm stupid," I said, pulling my hand away.

"What are you talking about?" I stood up and walked to the fireplace.

"Just do it," I said, turning to face him.

"Do what?" he asked, standing up. "What are you talking about?"

"I heard you!" I shouted as I choked on my words. I think his parents were upstairs, but I didn't care. I wanted them to hear us.

"What are you talking about? You heard what?" He grabbed my shoulders.

"I heard your dad tell you we have no future." I said, walking over to the other side of the room.

"You heard that?" he asked, raising his eyebrows.

"Yeah, but I missed the part where you stood up for me." My eyes filled with tears as I collapsed on the sofa.

"Emma," he said as he approached.

"Don't touch me!" I shouted, turning my back to him.

"Please talk to me," he said, touching my shoulders.

"Why would you do this to me? Why would you bring me here when you knew full well how your parents were going to react?"

"I didn't know. But my dad needs me. You're close to your family. What would you do if your dad needed you?"

"Oh come off it, Caleb. Your dad doesn't need you. He wants to control you. My dad would never try to control my life. Your dad asked you to pick between me and your trust fund. I'm not stupid!" I was shouting at this point. Caleb shook his head.

"That's not it."

"You know what, Caleb? I really don't care anymore." I jumped to my feet. "I've heard all I need to hear." With this I brushed past him, but he jumped up and blocked me from leaving the room.

"Move," I said as I fell into his arms and sobbed hysterically.

"No."

"Move!" I yelled again as I pushed him back.

"Not until you understand," he said stubbornly.

"Understand what exactly? That I wasted two years of my life on a coward?"

"If you want to look at it like that. But I'm just trying to do the right thing."

"You mean do what your dad wants," I said, looking into his eyes.

"He's my family," he said helplessly. I turned and walked back to the center of the den.

"News flash Caleb," I said, crossing my arms and turning to him. "You're not the only one who's getting pressed by your family. My parents are barely speaking to me because of you."

"Why didn't you tell me?" he asked as he walked toward me and placed his hands on my shoulders.

"Because I wasn't going to dump you over it," I yelled as I moved away and plopped myself onto the sofa.

"Look Emma." He joined me. "You don't know what it's like," he said in a hushed voice. I looked at him blankly.

"My family isn't like yours. I can't just ..." he started.

"You can't just what? Make your own decisions?" Caleb's face turned red and he looked at the ground.

"Why did you bring me here?" I asked with a lump in my throat. He looked up at me with his sad, green eyes.

"If you knew your dad was going to give you an ultimatum, why did you even put me through this?" I asked. At this point, my heart was pounding in my chest. I was so scared at what he was about to say.

"I thought my dad would see you the way I do. I thought he would fall in love with you the way I did the moment I saw you." A part of me wanted to get lost in his words. I wanted to plead with him to pick me. I even thought about sacrificing my last year at Harvard and the life I had there in order to stay by his side, but I couldn't. Not after seeing what a coward he was.

"Let me ask you something," I said as I turned my body toward him and looked into his teary eyes. Gosh, that was hard. "Do you really love me?"

"Yes," he said as he pressed his forehead up to mine.

"And would you do anything for me?"

"You know I would," he whispered.

"Then don't follow me," I said as I got up and walked toward the door. My bags were packed and I had already arranged for a driver to take me to the airport.

"You're leaving?" I looked at him with tears streaming down my face and saw that he was crying too. Until then, I'd never seen him cry. I'd never seen a lot of things.

"Yes, and I don't ever want to see you again. Don't call me. Don't try to see me. Don't come near me." It killed me to say this to him, but I couldn't let him linger. I wasn't strong enough to say no again, and I knew things had to end. We were a dead end. I realized that after his conversation with his parents.

"I know you're angry, but you—"

"I'm not angry," I interjected. Caleb looked at me confused. "I just, I just, I don't know you," I said as I cupped my face in my hands and started sobbing like a baby.

"Emma, Emma," Caleb kept saying over and over as he hugged me, but I couldn't speak. I could only cry.

"Please just let me go," I said, finally looking up. He looked at me for a long moment, then silently picked up my bags and helped me into the car. Part of me wanted him to get in the car with me so that we could run away together. But he never did. As the car drove off, I watched him get smaller and smaller. Gosh, I felt as if my insides were being torn apart. After staring into the distance until he was out of sight, I slumped down in the back seat and cried my heart out, vowing never again to give my heart away so freely. And I never have.

Keeping to his word, Caleb never tried to contact me when he got back. Part of me was angry that he didn't try, but another part of me was relieved. You see, on the way home from London it struck me that I would have given up everything for Caleb. All he had to do was say those four words: "Will you marry me?" I would have left everything behind and followed after him.

I didn't see Caleb until graduation a few weeks later. I didn't want to go, but I had to. I knew he was moving back to London, and I'd probably never see him again. I know I told him I never wanted to look at him again, but I had to see his face one last time. Something bigger than me was burning to. I knew he'd be with his family, and they were the last people I wanted to see, so I sat in the back wearing Jackie O. shades and a black dress. Mandy begged me to take her, but I had to go by myself. Sometimes your friends and family can't fix things. Though it would've been nice to have her holding my hand, I had to face him alone.

When the ceremony ended, I turned to leave and saw him standing with his family about thirty feet away under our beautiful oak tree. For a moment, we stared at each other, and in that moment it felt as if we were the only two people on earth. He started to approach me, but I shook my head in protest. After a brief moment, I turned and walked away. I couldn't bear to talk to him. Part of me was afraid he'd say he was over me. But the other part of me was afraid that I'd surrender my heart, my dreams, and my future to follow him. I'd like to think Caleb knew that, but that's just too optimistic. The bottom line is that I wasn't enough.

I glance down at my watch. 6:30 AM. Normally a walk and a cup of coffee cheer me up, but not today. I don't think anything could unbreak my heart. Maybe Mandy's right. Maybe I should call him and get closure. But what if I fall for him all over again? What if his fiancée is with him? I mean, what could he possibly have to say to me after all these years? And do I even want to hear it?

10

I absolutely, positively, dreadfully despise getting dolled up. Don't get me wrong, I love the after part, but all the preparation is exhausting. And I'm usually in such a rush that I'm sweating like a pig by the time I apply makeup, which really just defeats the whole purpose of showering.

As I step back and glance in my tilted mirror (which makes me look ten pounds thinner), I admire my backless dress. And what better occasion to wear red lipstick?

Giddily, I fasten my grandmother's yellow diamond necklace, grab my wrap, and lock up. Okay, so I'm excited. Yes, Carmichael Advertising isn't the equivalent of Enron, but I'm still going to a $500 dinner at the Ritz. I'm moving up in the world!

"You look beautiful," I say the moment I see Zoë. Miss Size Zero looks perfect in her little black dress.

As we pull up to the Ritz, I can't help but lose my breath. It feels as if we're arriving at the Academy Awards or something. Limos galore, and there are so many good-looking people clad in the likes of Armani and Versace. I feel like Daisy Buchanan living in West Egg at one of Gatsby's summer parties. It's like a dream.

"This little soiree probably cost a million dollars!" I say as we enter the ballroom. "Why didn't the generous

Mr. Carmichael just donate all this to cancer research?" Zoë cuts me off.

"Emma, you need to chill out and enjoy this. I saw your eyes. I know you're loving it. Now, I'm going to get us some drinks. Can I trust you to keep your opinionated mouth to yourself?" Maybe she's right, but of course I don't say that. Maybe because I'm speechless.

As Zoë sets off for the bar, I wander around the ball-room like a kid in a candy shop.

A friend of mine had her wedding reception at the Ritz a few years back, but it was nothing like this. And rumor has it that she had to mortgage her house just to pay for the event. All the same, it was lovely.

As I make my way to the window overlooking the Public Garden, I lean back in order to take in my surroundings. There must be at least three hundred people swirling around the grand ballroom. The tables are set with the finest of china, while bouquets of red and white roses sit in the center. Caterers are making their way through the room with trays full of hors d'oeuvres and champagne. I grab a crab cake and continue scanning the room. Most people seem to be in their 40s and 50s, with the exception of a tall, dark, and handsome figure whose back is only observable. I get up from the window and take a few steps closer to James Bond. As I squint my eyes, I see the figure turn around to greet a group of people. No way, I think as my mouth opens like a Venus flytrap. I pinch myself to see if I'm dreaming, but the pain that shoots up my arm tells me I'm very much awake. Oh my gosh, I think as I move in closer. It can't be. Oh, but it is. It's Jack! Oh my gosh. Engrossed in conversation with two older gentlemen, I see the face of the man I had lunch with only yesterday. What's he doing here?

Suddenly he looks up. As the jazz band, clad in white tuxedos, continues playing "The Way You Look Tonight," I watch Jack excuse himself and make his way toward me. My heart is pounding so hard. I think it may bust through my flat chest. That can't be normal.

Oh gosh, what do I say to him? Should I be mad at him for not wanting my number? Or maybe he knew I'd be here and wanted to surprise me. My head is flooded with so many thoughts. Okay, Emma. Think hard. Say something articulate.

"You butthead," I say as I playfully hit him in the stomach. Ouch! He really does have abs of steel.

"Excuse me?" he grimaces.

"Why didn't you tell me you'd be here?" I say.

"Did you really just call me a butthead?" he laughs. Yeah. What was that?

"What are you doing here?" I wonder if he's here because of me. I bet tickets were a fortune. How sweet is that! Oh my gosh. All this time I've been so afraid to let my heart go. I was afraid of being let down again. I was afraid of rejection, but I'm not anymore. I let my mind go wild about this stranger. This perfect stranger. He didn't ask for my number because he wanted to surprise me here.

"Emma, there's something I should tell you," he says. "Do you mind if we go somewhere quiet?" he asks seriously.

"Um, okay," I say as I follow him to a quiet corner all the while wondering what he's going to say. Maybe he's going to tell me why he left so abruptly the other day. Or that the moment our eyes locked on the dance floor, he knew in his heart that he'd never be the same. Okay, that would be a little cheesy, but it would still be great to hear.

"So?" I ask with a toothy grin.

"Emma," he says the smile falling from his face. "When I asked you to lunch yesterday, I never thought I'd see you..." he starts, but before he can finish Zoë walks up.

"What are you doing in the corner?" she asks as she

hands me a drink. "It took me forever to find you." I'm so glad she's here. Now she can meet her future brother-in-law.

"Zoë, this is—" I start.

"Jonathan," she interrupts. "It's nice to see you again," she says as she kisses his cheek. Jonathan?

"No, Zoë," I chime in to save her from further embarrassment. "This is—" I start.

"Zoë, what a surprise," Jack says warmly. "Look at you. You look great." Wait a second. I swear she called him Jonathan, I think as I fidget with my ear.

"Thank you," she says looking back and forth between the two of us. "Wait a second. Do you two know each other?" Finally, a little clarity.

"Zoë, he's the guy I was telling you about yesterday. You know, the shoes. Saks. My big feet."

"Oh!" she says giving me a knowing glance. "You're the guy my sister met."

"You're Emma's sister?" he says coolly.

"Yep," she says as she puts her arm around me. "Gosh, it's a small world," he says heartily. I wonder if he'll notice if I text Zoë and ask her if they love each other.

"So how do you two know each other?" I say a bit too perkily. If the two of them dated, I'm stabbing myself with an ice pick.

"I met Zoë at a party in New York. What was it, two years ago?"

"I think so," she chimes in. "Emma, Jonathan throws the greatest parties." Jonathan. She called him Jonathan again. Is he too nice to correct her or did I miss something? "He's the one who threw that Labor Day party I tried to get you to come to New York for." I give her a blank stare. My brain hurts. "You know, the one where we all wore white. Gosh, it felt like we were a Utopian society or something." I feel like I'm being Punk'd. I open my mouth to speak, but Jack beats me to it.

"Did you really like that?" he asks earnestly, turning to face her. Um, hello? Did they forget I was here? "I thought it was kinda cheesy, but my client's PR people really wanted to do it." His client's PR people? Who is he, Donald Trump?

"If anything's over the top, I'd say it's tonight. You really outdid yourself." Hold the phone.

"This is *your* party?" I jump in.

"You didn't know that?" Zoë asks, glancing quickly at Jack. Suddenly, it all makes sense.

"You mean, you're..." I start.

"Emma, I had no idea I'd—" he begins in a low voice.

"But you told me your name was Jack!" I say a little louder than intended. I step back a bit, and Jack steps forward.

"Emma, maybe I should hold your drink," Zoë says nervously. She takes my glass from my hand. Oh my gosh. This is not happening. I'm dreaming. Wake up, Emma. Wake up. Oh my gosh, I'm not waking up. This is real.

"Why didn't you tell me you were Jonathan Carmichael?" I say in almost a whisper. Zoë puts her hand on my back as if to tell me she's still standing here. Jack spreads his hands out innocently.

"I didn't think it mattered until—"

"So you make it a habit of picking up women and trying to make them feel stupid?" I say, looking down at my feet. This very gesture only reminds me of how I met Jack. My heart has sunk 20,000 leagues. I look up and see a jaw-dropped Zoë holding two drinks.

"Does anybody care to tell me what's going on?" she forces through a laugh. I swallow hard as I glance at Jack from the corner of my eye. He runs his fingers through his wavy hair.

"Well sister dear," I say, giving Jack an eat-crap-and-die look, "let me fill you in." She looks at me nervously.

"It turns out that not only is *Jonathan* Carmichael a rich, Gatsby, fun-loving, advertising tycoon, but he also likes to pick up women using an alias. Isn't that right, *Jack*?" Zoë still looks confused and very much like she wants to head back to the bar, but stays in case we resort to killing each other.

"Emma, you don't understand," he starts.

"Just Jack, huh?" I look at Zoë. "Did you even know he went by Jack?" She shrugs her shoulders and gives me an I-don't-have-a-clue look.

"I didn't lie to you," he says earnestly. He takes a step closer. "I didn't even think I'd see you again."

"Oh come off it, Jonathan," I say rudely. This day couldn't get any worse.

"Listen to me, Emma," he says in a low voice. "Jonathan Carmichael is my professional name, but my close friends have always called me Jack." I look up at him, skeptical. "When I met you, I had no idea I'd—" he begins.

"There you are," says a voice behind Jack. Okay, I've definitely been Punk'd. Natasha sidles up next to Jack. "Why are you hiding in the corner with your back to all your guests?" She looks at our small gathering and smoothes her hair.

"Emma," she says coolly, though I can tell she's appalled we're at the same event. "What are you doing here?"

Okay. So not only is Natasha standing right in front of me, but she's also wearing my dress, the Calvin Klein I tried on just yesterday, though I doubt hers is a size six.

"Natasha," I manage to get out. "You look beautiful. What is that, Calvin Klein?"

"Straight off the runway. And look at you. You look so … cute." She flashes a cool smile. What am I, five?

"Natasha," Zoë says in her peppy workout voice, "you're Emma's boss, right? I've heard so much about you." I grab my drink from Zoë and begin to chug.

"You're Emma's boss?" Jack says, glancing at me. I remove the cup from my face.

Why does he care if she's my boss? Oh crap! Jack knows Natasha. He's totally gonna get me fired. Gosh, I hate him. Why would he do this to me? Why would he set out to make an idiot of me? But can I blame him? I tore him up. And to his face. Why am I so critical of people I hardly know? Why do I let complete strangers take me to lunch without showing me some sort of ID? And why is my jaw wide open?

"Sweetie, Emma's the writer I was telling you about," Natasha says, placing her hand lightly on his arm. Wait a second. Did she just call him "sweetie"?

"Jonathan," Zoë prods politely, "aren't you going to introduce us?"

"Of course," he says as he snaps out of it. "Where are my manners?" Yeah. Where are they? Not that I can talk. I've acted pretty rash tonight, even for me. "Natasha," he says as he places his hand on the small of her back. "This is Zoë. She's Emma's sister. We met in New York a couple years ago. And Zoë, this is my girlfriend, Natasha." Did he just say girlfriend? Oh, I think he did, though I should have known. I bet they even planned the whole thing just so I'd get fired. Why can't I just be at home eating Ben & Jerry's and watching TGIF like all normal 26-year-olds?

"It's nice to meet you," Zoë says, reaching out to shake hands with Natasha.

"And how do you know Emma?" Natasha bats her long eyelashes, which look awfully fake. I hope they fall in the punch bowl and Jack swallows them.

"I just met her yesterday at Saks," Jack says lightly, avoiding my gaze. That's it? I opened my heart to the idea of a complete stranger, and I'm just the girl he met yesterday at Saks. Why did I even entertain the notion of him?

"You mean when you were supposed to be buying a purse for Carolyn?" she asks with a laugh. They sound like an old married couple.

"Who do you think helped me?" he asks as he smiles back at her.

"Well, I'm going to mingle," she says, obviously sick of making small talk with one of her underlings. "Save me a seat," she tells Jack as she kisses him softly on the cheek. Oh, I feel like vomiting.

"Well, if you would excuse me too," Zoë says awkwardly. "I see someone I know." She walks away before I have time to respond. Why is she leaving me alone with him?

"Emma," he says as he turns his full attention to me. "I had no idea you worked for Natasha."

"So you and Natasha, huh?" I interject. I take another sip of my drink.

"Yeah," he says, trying to read my expression. I can tell he's uncomfortable, which doesn't seem like something he's accustomed to. Good. I'm not accustomed to throwing myself at strangers, so we're even.

"Well, isn't that just precious!" I say sweetly, clasping my hands together on my glass. "I mean, what a power couple! And how considerate that she lets you take other girls to lunch?"

"I know you're upset." He takes a step toward me. "And you have every right to be, but I promise I didn't—"

"You don't know a thing about me, Richie Rich." I take a step back. Oh crap, that's the wall. "So please don't presume that you do."

"Emma, please just calm down and let me explain. I think you're overreacting." I open my mouth as if he just insulted my mother. Man, if there's one thing I hate more than being shushed, it's being told to calm down.

"Don't tell me to calm down," I say rather loudly. A few people at a nearby table turn their heads. I lower my voice. "And don't tell me I'm overreacting," I say with a point. "If anything, I'm underreacting." Is that even a word? "You had no right letting me go on about you when you were, well ... you." He looks at me with his usual brow raised, which is so distracting because it is such a cute gesture, especially with the scar. I shake my head in frustration. "You know what I mean. And I'm already on thin ice at work, yet you made me sit with you through a two hour lunch." I cross my arms in defense.

"I didn't kidnap you," he says, a faint smile creeping onto his face. He does have a point, but how dare he laugh at me?

"Yes, I know that," I say, gesturing with my hands. My drink sloshes over the rim of the glass. I jump back before it hits my dress. "Crap!" I mutter as I shake my hand dry. I jump back into my attack. "Then you act all interested in my life. What are you, The Bachelor?"

"Are you finished?" he asks patiently. He signals a waiter to bring some napkins.

"No!" I say. "Did you wake up thinking, gee, in between my million-dollar enterprise and my bombshell girlfriend, I think I need another hobby? Oh, I know! How about I lead someone on? There's a sucker over there. The one with the shoes stuck on her big feet." A waiter walks up and hands me a napkin. I wipe my arm and hand him my glass. I take a minute to catch my breath.

"Emma, will you just listen to me for a minute?" he asks. I sigh in annoyance. I can't believe he's mocking me. "Look, I'm not going tell Natasha you lied to her. And as for tricking you. Emma, I didn't even know you worked for her. I'm just as surprised as you are. And you're right. I shouldn't have taken you to lunch. I'm sorry if I mislead you. I never thought I would see you again." A lump grows hard in my throat. So he regrets the date? My eyes fill with tears and I look at the ground.

"But I told you I was coming," I start. I cut myself off as I remember his speedy exit. "Oh, that's why you bolted. But why didn't you just tell me you were—"

"Richie Rich?" he interrupts. "Because it was too late. You had already formed your opinion of me. And you don't seem easily persuaded." His eyes twinkle. He has a point there. "It's kinda funny though."

"What's funny?" I snap.

"The way that people think they know you and set false pretenses for you." I cross my arms.

"Cry me a river."

"Can I finish?" he asks earnestly.

"Sure." I huff like a bratty little princess. I know I'm freaking out over a big misunderstanding, but this represents much more than that. This is me taking a chance and once again being humiliated.

"Everybody around town brownnoses me because they know I have a lot of pull in Boston. You're the first person I've met who actually has an opinion of me, and I like that. I can't say how off base you are, but at least you aren't afraid to speak your mind." I'm afraid it's my curse. I toss my head.

"So I'm supposed to feel sorry for you because people kiss your butt?"

"I'm not asking for your sympathy," he says calmly. "I'm just trying to explain to you why I didn't tell you who I was, but I don't think I need to explain myself any further. You obviously don't want to hear it." He backs away in defeat.

"Wait a second," I say as I step closer to him. "You don't get off that easily! What if I liked you? What then, huh?" Why did I just let an already cocky guy know that he got to me? I'm seriously going to consider having my jaw wired shut. I hear it's a fairly inexpensive procedure.

Jack touches my elbow. "Emma, if I led you on in any

way, then I'm really sorry." He steps closer and looks at me intensely.

"Don't do me any favors, Jack Carmichael," I choke. "I would never like a guy like you." I turn and storm off.

Okay Emma, don't cry. Don't cry! You don't even know him. You liked the dream of him. Look on the bright side. Your heart isn't dead. At least you know there's someone out there you're capable of being attracted to, even if it's just for a day. My eyes start burning with tears, but I bite my lip. Forget him. He's not worth it. Besides, I don't even like the name Jonathan.

11

As I storm my way back to the table, I spot Zoë talking on her cell phone. I can only imagine who she's talking to, which is really quite pathetic. She just saw Michael an hour ago. So maybe I'm in a bit of a bad mood, but that's absolutely ridiculous.

She hangs up the phone and turns to me.

"Oh Em, I'm so sorry," she says, patting my bare back. Her hands are freezing. "I should've known. You described him to me." I shiver and try to change the subject.

"Your hands are freezing." Zoë looks at me intently.

"And he's dating Natasha. I mean, what are the chances?" She leans back in her chair, incredulous. I breathe deeply through my nose.

"Are you trying to get me all worked up again? Because if you are then don't bother. I'm over it."

"I'm sorry," she says defensively. "But I was just trying to talk to you about what happened. Some people actually express their feelings instead of trying to play them off."

"What are you trying to say, Zoë?" I lean in to the table. You've got to be kidding me! Is she really giving me a lecture on feelings right now?

"Nothing." She flicks her hand casually in the air. "I just think you're upset about all this and rather than talk about it, you're acting like you don't care." I look down and examine my cuticles.

"I don't care," I lie.

"Right. So somewhere on your walk back to the table, you just got over the guy. Either that or you're gonna sulk around all night." She's so right. I lean back and sigh.

"Can we change the subject, please?" I say, giving her an earnest look. Zoë looks right past it.

"And you're being really selfish. Michael spent $500 on tickets, and the least you can do is enjoy them." Okay, I'm officially mad. How can I let that go?

"Are you kidding me, Zoë?" She gives me a blank stare. "Are you really trying to bring Michael into this? You always do this. Gosh, you're so obsessed with him!" I watch Zoë's face go red.

"I'm not obsessed with him. You're just jealous!" I lean back and laugh.

"Jealous! Of what?" I'd rather die alone than have a relationship like hers, but that's another story. Besides, this is about me and how stupid I am to have let my heart go.

"Forget it," she says as the waiter brings out our lobster. I'm so not in the mood for all this drama. I lean over and grab her arm.

"Look, I'm really sorry." I stare at my plate. "I just don't want to talk about it, okay?"

"I know." She shrugs her shoulders as if everything is okay. But everything isn't fine and dandy. At least not with me. True, I hardly know Jack, but for some reason I feel this jab in the pit of my stomach. Gosh, I'm such an idiot. To actually think that I could know someone after spending three hours with them. That's just unheard of, though you don't see Julia Roberts running into this crap.

"Wanna get some air?" I offer in hopes that she'll decline. I need to be alone, even if it's for five minutes.

"I'm okay," she says. I leave my lobster and head for the exit.

As I strut through the lobby, I can't help but mutter Destiny's Child under my breath.

"'I'm a survivor. I'm not gonna give up. I'm not gonna stop. I'm gonna work harder.'" Gosh, Beyonce is brilliant.

"Emma." Did someone just call my name? Probably not. I keep walking.

"Emma," I hear again. Wait a second, I know that voice. Oh, dear heavens! It can't be. I stop dead in my tracks. Unable to turn around, I shut my eyes and will him to go away. What is he doing here?

"Hey," I hear as footsteps approach. Oh gosh. He's like five feet away. Opening my eyes, I turn around and face him. Big mistake. One look at those beautiful, green eyes sends a rush of déjà vu through my entire body.

"Caleb," I say rather shakily. I can't look at him anymore so I opt for the floor instead.

"Emma, you look beautiful," he says as he leans in for a hug. Are you kidding me? He wants a hug?

"Caleb, um, this really isn't a good time," I say as I dodge his embrace. "I'm in a hurry. I have to go."

"Wait a second!"

"I can't. I'm late," I say as I drop my purse. I stand still for a moment watching the contents go rolling everywhere. Could this day be any worse? Oh, crap. It can.

"Here you go," Caleb says with a smile as he hands me my rose-scented tampon.

I've day-dreamed of future run-ins with Caleb, and I've come up with some really good ones. My favorite is the one where we end up sitting next to each other on the same airplane. I have a beautiful tan, have lost about twenty pounds, and look absolutely classic in my strapless sundress. We're stuck together for five hours eating bad airplane food, while he professes his undying love for me. Of course I tell him he's too late. I'm engaged to Prince William.

"Thanks," I mutter, shoving it back in my purse. Unsure of my next move, I stand there absolutely dumbfounded.

"What are you doing here?" he asks with a huge smile. He looks so different, yet just the same.

"I really have to go," I say. I turn around and walk back toward the ballroom.

I hear him call after me, but I don't turn around. I duck into the crowded ballroom so he can't follow me. He's on crack if he thinks I'm going to stay and shoot the breeze with him. I can't decide if my heart hurts out of unresolved anger or out of pure emotional exhaustion. Either way, I don't care. This night has been a total nightmare. All I want to do is go home.

As I find my seat, I see that the presentation is about to begin. I start to tell Zoë about Caleb but am rudely interrupted by Jonathan Carmichael. As if it couldn't get any worse, I now have to hear him give some fake speech about how wonderful Carmichael Advertising is. While he presents a big check and talks about his great passion for finding a cure for cancer, I sit nervously and tap my feet. After two very long minutes, I can't stand it anymore.

"Zoë," I whisper.

"Huh," she says. She's listening attentively to Jack, which makes me wonder if she's buying into his pompous act.

"I'm feeling sick all of a sudden. It may have been all that rich food," I lie. I hardly touched my plate. "Would you be upset if I slipped out?"

"No, but don't lie to me. I know you're upset so I'm coming with you." She reaches for her purse.

"That's really sweet, and I love you for being so understanding. But you stay and enjoy everything. Michael would want you to."

"Are you sure?" she asks doubtfully.

"Absolutely," I say as I get to my feet. She leans toward me.

"Are you going to be okay?"

"I'll be fine. I'll call you tomorrow," I add as I kiss her on the forehead. "Love you, sis," I whisper.

"Love you too," she adds as I walk off. I take one last look at the front and see Jack staring at me. He's so cocky. I bet he thinks I'm leaving because of him. What a jerk, I think as I stick my tongue out at him.

12

As I flip on the den lights, I see Mandy passed out in her chair. A bag of Chex Mix has spilled onto the floor and *Gone with the Wind* is playing on the TV. I slip into my PJs and make us some hot chocolate.

"Mandy," I say, shaking her a bit.

"Hey," she says groggily, sitting up. "How was it?"

I try to calmly hand her a cup of hot cocoa but suddenly burst into tears. As I explain the Jack saga to her, I can't help but get all worked up again. Mandy bangs her cocoa down on the coffee table.

"What a scumbag! If I'd known that you and Jonathan, or Jack, or whatever-his-name-is had just had lunch, I'd have killed the guy. And I'm so sorry for saying he's your type. He's *so* not your type. He and that little waif deserve each other." She picks up her cup and takes an angry slurp. Call me childish, but I can't think of anything better than a friend taking my side, no questions asked.

"It gets worse." I swallow hard as I manage to get the rest out. "I saw Caleb."

"No!" she says, spraying hot chocolate all over herself.

"Yep. And he looks really good." She nods her head in agreement while mopping hot chocolate off her shirt. "But I couldn't talk to him. I tried to look him in the eyes, but my heart burned in my chest so of course I looked at the ground. And he knows I do that when I'm uncomfortable."

"Emma, I'm sure he understands why you were so uncomfortable."

"Yeah, well, it gets even worse." I set down my mug.

"I don't think it can," she laughs.

"Trust me, it can. I told him I had to go and so I ran off. But well, he called after me, and it startled me so I jumped and dropped my purse." I begin crying hard.

"Well, he knows you're clumsy." She looks at me sympathetically.

"That's not it. My ... my ... my tampon was in there," I say in full sob.

Mandy pats me on the back. She knows I have the worst luck of anybody on the planet. I am always the statistical outlier. I'm the one who gets strip-searched at the airport. I'm the one who gets pulled over for speeding when people are flying past me. And I'm the one who, after six years, has a run-in with my ex-boyfriend involving a tampon. This goes well beyond having a slice of humble pie!

"Where was your sister during all of this?" Mandy asks after I finish hyperventilating. She tends to get annoyed with Zoë and her boyfriends too. "I can't believe she made you sit through the entire night just because Michael paid for the tickets. That's pocket change to him. Besides, if he were any boyfriend, he'd have gotten off work to be with her. That's just shady if you ask me." I wipe my eyes and take a deep breath.

"She didn't make me stay. I didn't want to leave her alone. You know how she is."

"Yeah," she says softly.

"Oh Mandy, it's all so terrible. And I didn't even eat anything." This disturbing fact makes me cry all over again. Who doesn't eat a free meal?

"Okay, Emma. The last thing you need to do is re-hash the entire evening over and over again. You'll only drive yourself crazy." She jumps out of her chair and heads for the freezer. She returns with two pints of ice cream. I laugh for the first time all evening.

"I can't believe you bought more Ben & Jerry's." Mandy gives me a triumphant look.

"Of course I did. Now what do you say we watch the second *Bridget Jones' Diary* and forget the night ever happened?" I stare mournfully into my empty mug. "After all, no matter what you do, Bridget always does something worse."

"This is true."

"Good." She plops a carton in my lap.

"But I'm not that hungry," I add.

"Too bad. I'm not eating this crap by myself."

"It's never stopped you before."

"Very funny. Now grab a spoon and dig in because we're eating both pints." Aw, girlfriends are the best!

13

After what seems like a catnap, I awaken to Mandy
rubbing my face with a feather. I swear she'll never grow
up.

"What is this, a sleepover?" I groan. There's tooth-
paste all over my face.

"Good morning," she chirps. I don't know about her,
but I'm definitely sluggish the day after eating two pints
of Ben & Jerry's.

"I hate you," I moan, glancing at the clock. It's 6:30.

"Wake up, Sleeping Beauty." She pulls open my blinds,
sending a stream of sunlight right on my face.

"Are you on something?" I yell, yanking my comforter
over my head.

"Get dressed. We're going to New York."

"What?" I sit straight up. Wow, she wasn't kidding. I
look at Mandy and she's all dressed and ready to go. She
looks cute too. She's wearing red pants and a red-and-
white-striped shirt. She even has on a cute red hat to
match. It's very Cameron Diaz.

"You heard me. We're going to your favorite museum
and we're going shopping." She goes over to my closet
and starts searching for a decent outfit.

"Oh," she adds, tossing a pair of pants on the bed,
"and I'm taking you to Serendipity for some frozen hot

chocolate. You barely touched your Ben & Jerry's last night."

"What are you talking about? I scarfed down more than you did."

"Get dressed, Emma." She pulls the covers off me. "I want to get there by lunch time." I rub my eyes.

"You're serious?"

"Hurry up."

Twenty minutes later, I emerge from my bedroom clad in dark sand blasted blue jeans and a butter-colored sweater. I throw on a beret and striped scarf as we head for the door. We're going to New York City, baby. Yeah!

"Coffee?" I ask as we walk to our car. And I meant to say "our" car. It's kind of silly to have a car in Boston, but it's a nice treat to be able to pick up and go somewhere for the day. It's no BMW, but it's taken us all over New England.

Mandy parks illegally while I run into Starbucks.

"Hi," I say as I walk up to the counter. I've worked in customer service before, and if there's one thing I can't stand, besides men using an alias to pick up women, it's a rude customer. "How are you today?" I ask cheerfully.

"Ugh," I hear a woman call from behind me.

"Hurry up," someone else groans. Oh my gosh, Starbucks' customers are so rude.

"Can I please have two small cappuccinos with a shot of vanilla?"

"Two tall vanilla cappuccinos," the girl calls over her shoulder.

As I wait in line for our drinks, I can't help but feel like a dope. Don't get me wrong; I am a Starbucks junkie. And there's nothing like a fresh latte on a crisp day, but come on. Is it absolutely necessary to yell my order out loud? And I feel like they're correcting my grammar or something. If the "customer is always right" then why on God's green earth does the Starbucks lingo make me feel the size of an ant? It's like one big inside joke in here. And the menu! It's so large and overwhelming that I'm afraid to try anything new, which is almost a tragedy. There's probably some perfect drink out there just waiting to be sipped, but I'm too afraid to take a chance. Oh no. That sounds too much like my love life.

"That's what's wrong with this city," I say as I hop in the car. "Everybody's in such a hurry to be somewhere, they can't even sit down and enjoy a cup of coffee."

"We're in a hurry to get somewhere," Mandy points out as she turns onto Highway 93.

"Whatever," I say. I hate when people correct my wrongness.

14

After what seems like forever, we finally arrive in the city. Mandy's favorite uncle lives in Manhattan, so the good thing is we'll have no trouble finding a parking spot. I wish we were staying with him because he and his wife have an amazing apartment on Park Avenue. He lives in the very building where John Jr. and Caroline Kennedy were raised. Of course this does us no good now, but it's what sealed the deal on the apartment. As their realtor put it best, "If it's nice enough for Jackie, it's money well spent."

After parking the car, we decide on brunch at Tavern on the Green. Sure, this is going to cost us a small fortune, but I can always donate blood if I run out of money, right?

Tavern on the Green is one of Manhattan's finest establishments, restaurant to the rich and famous. And what better tourist trap than to have common folks dish out their life savings for one silly meal? The idea is to make us feel like *we're* the rich and famous. I hate to admit it, but I totally buy into the marketing ploy. When it snows, it almost feels like you're dining inside a snow globe. The floor-to-ceiling windows display a perfect view of Central Park. At night, the trees glimmer fairy lights, making you feel as if you're in a movie. With over fourteen rooms to choose from, you can never get tired of this place.

After stuffing our faces with French toast, eggs benedict, and what feels like a pound of bacon, we're ready to hit the town. There's no better place to walk off a gluttonous meal than New York City, though I wish I hadn't eaten so much. I hate trying on clothes after I've just pigged out.

We spend the first few hours getting lost in my favorite museums, then hit the stores, where we manage to accumulate quite a few packages. I buy a Burberry hat from Barneys and Mandy buys cream jersey knit pants from BCBG that make her butt look amazing. I don't know how she pulls it off. She's 5'9", eats like a horse, and still wears the same size as me. But the thing that's so unfair is that she's fat in all the right places. And she hasn't exercised a day in her life, not that I'm one to talk. I've spent more money on my gym membership than I care to admit, but at least I've thought about it. Shouldn't that earn me a few courtesy pounds off?

"Want to get lost in Central Park?" Mandy asks as she loosens her belt. We haven't stopped eating since we got here. I even bought chocolates at The Met. That, and a book on Da Vinci that I didn't need. I read *The Da Vinci Code*, enough said.

"You read my mind," I say, unbuttoning the top button of my jeans.

Central Park is fifty-eight miles of heaven. I've been to New York a million times, and I've yet to see even half of it. I did, however, spot Catherine Zeta-Jones jogging its perimeter. I've tried to jog it myself in hopes of spotting more stars, but I find it more effective to buy a cup of coffee, sit on a park bench, and just wait for them to come running by.

We spend the rest of the day strolling through the park and playing "Who Would You Rather?"

"Okay, Em, who would you rather choose: Brad Pitt or Matthew McConaughey?"

"You can't ask me that," I snap. "It's like having to choose between carbs and chocolate. It's just not possible."

"Just answer the question," Mandy says matter-of-factly. Gosh, she sounds like a schoolteacher.

"Well, Brad is one gorgeous dude. I mean, did you see *Troy*?"

"Oh, I saw every angle of Achilles," she laughs.

"But that Texas twang of Matthew McConaughey's is pretty darn cute. I'd love to have him whisper sweet nothings in my ear. And those dimples! Okay, I'm sold. Matthew McConaughey for sure."

"Good answer," Mandy says. We plop down on a bench.

"Okay, my turn... I got it," I say, barely able to contain myself. "Dylan McKay or Brandon Walsh?"

"You can't do that to me!" Mandy says, setting down her bags. "You know I'm president of both their fan clubs!"

"Sorry, sweetie. You know the rules." I tap my foot impatiently.

After a minute's thought Mandy comes to a decision. "Well, Brandon has that intellectual, ambitious thing going on. And you know how I love that."

"Me too," I say as I think of Jack.

"But Dylan is a bad boy with a green Porsche. I'd definitely pick Dylan."

"You'd pick Dylan!" I exclaim, shocked. "But he's so skinny. And a surf bum."

"But he's hot. I only wish that he'd ended up with Brenda," she says mournfully.

"I know! I was so mad that he ended up with Kelly. What about poor Brandon? What was Aaron Spelling thinking?" I still have issues with this.

"It can't be as bad as the way *Dawson's Creek* ended. I mean, Pacey! Why didn't Joey pick Dawson? He's so much cooler and I mean, the show was called *Dawson's Creek* for Pete's sake!"

"Do you think Tom Cruise ever watched the show?" I interject.

"Don't even get me started," Mandy says, rolling her eyes. We pick up our bags and make our way out of the park.

After browsing through Bloomingdale's, we head to Serendipity for peanut butter frozen hot chocolate.

"Promise not to freak out," Mandy says between licks of whipped cream.

"I hate when people start sentences like that." I set down my spoon. "I mean, you could have stolen my boyfriend or something."

"I booked us a room at the Plaza," she says excitedly.

"You did what!" I exclaim.

"Well, when I woke up this morning, I went on Priceline.com and bid on a room, and you wouldn't believe the deal we got. It'd be silly not to take it." She takes a gleeful bite of dessert.

"But I don't have any clothes or anything."

"Yeah you do. I threw together a few of your things when you were in the shower." So that's why she was so insistent I take a shower.

"You rock," I say as I get up to hug her. Mandy is my spontaneity. Somehow, over the years, I've become anal and serious. I used to stay awake watching *The Nanny* reruns. Now I stay up watching *Dateline.*

Luckily, the walk from Serendipity to the hotel is only a few blocks. As we stroll up the famous red-carpeted stairs, I daydream I'm a movie star. This is the very place where Catherine Zeta-Jones wed Michael Douglas in a one-million-dollar ceremony.

And look at that! There's the fountain where Barbara Streisand says her tearful goodbye to Robert Redford in *The Way We Were.* "Your girl is lovely, Hubble," she says as she strokes his cheek sadly. I tear at the very thought of it. Why couldn't they make it work? Why?

I feel like a kid on Christmas morning, except now I'm grownup, checking into the Plaza, and spending Saturday night in New York City with my best friend in the whole world.

As Mandy checks us into our room, I listen to my messages.

"Three messages," I say to myself as I wait at the white, mirrored elevators. "Don't I feel special?" The first one clicks on.

"Hey, Em. It's Zoë. Listen, I talked to Michael last night about some stuff. Basically, he's been so busy and I haven't seen him in a while, whatever. Anyway, we've both decided to turn our cell phones off for the day and spend it with each other. I hope you're feeling better. Call me if you need me. Mine is really on vibrate. Love you." This puts a smile on my face. She sounds good, though I'm still not convinced about Michael. There's something about him that's very unsettling, but I can't seem to put my finger on it.

The next message is from my mom. "Hi, sweetie. How are you? Zoë told me everything that happened. Why didn't you tell me about Jack? And as far as that sconehead Caleb, don't give him another thought. You're much better without him. I love you, dear." I think I'll save that one. Who could the last one be from?

"Hey, Em. Can you believe I remembered your number after all these years?" I cringe at the very sound of Caleb's voice. Why is he calling me? I should just delete it. Right now. Okay, I'm doing it. Oh, who am I kidding? "Listen. I hate that you felt like you had to run from me last night. I know it's awkward, but I need to talk to you. Please phone back when you can. I have to see you. I ..." Okay. That's enough. I hit delete.

"All checked in," Mandy says as she meets me at the elevator. I give her a half smile. "What's wrong? You look like you just got a bad haircut or something?"

"I'm good," I say rather shakily. Or at least I will be.

15

I love walking in the front door after having been away for a few days. It's one of those simple pleasures that gets a dork like me excited. It's good to be back in Boston, though I hate that I have to face the real world tomorrow. Before dozing off, I make one last call to Zoë.

"How was your weekend?" I ask.

"Oh, it was wonderful. Michael took me to Top of the Hub for dinner and moonlight dancing." I guess now's not the time to tell her I think Michael's hiding something.

Top of the Hub is a very upscale restaurant on the top floor of Boston's Prudential building. It's very romantic. The lighting is dim, and you get a panoramic view of the entire city.

"I bet that was nice," I say, forcing some enthusiasm into my voice. I'm sorry. Top of the Hub is great and all, but I still don't think he treats her like he should.

"It was magical," she says in her head-over-heels tone. I may be a dreamer, but Zoë is a hopeless romantic. And she always seems to fall for those John Mayer-types. Yuck! But I guess if we liked the same type it would be a problem. "But how was your weekend?" she asks.

"Refreshing." Zoë pauses for a moment on the other end.

"Emma, there's something I need to tell you."

"Oh great." Holding the phone to my ear, I sprawl out on my bed. The last time she started a sentence with "there's something I need to tell you" she told me she was moving to New York.

"Michael told me something last night, and it's pretty shocking. But I'm only going tell you if you want to know." Oh good, maybe he confessed his heart to her.

"He's not secretly dating your boss, is he? Oh wait, that's me." At least I haven't lost my sense of humor.

"Emma, I'm serious."

"Okay. Okay. I'm all ears." I wiggle around, trying to get comfortable. Gosh, I was only trying to break the ice. I hear her take a deep breath as if she were in the midst of a yoga session.

"Well, it turns out that Michael knows Jonathan rather well."

"Jonathan who?" I ask absentmindedly.

"Carmichael!"

"Oh," I say a little taken back. "So they're old acquaintances. Jack knows everybody. What's the big deal?"

"It's not that simple." It never is with me, now is it?

"It couldn't be any worse than him dating my Scrooge of a boss. So just come out with it."

"Okay. Well, I never told you this but before Michael went to medical school he was going to start his own business."

"Michael, a businessman? I don't see it."

"Well, believe it because he was going to do it with Jonathan."

"What? That's weird."

"I know," she says.

"So what's the big deal?"

"They were best friends, then had some big fight, and now they haven't spoken in years." I sit up, unable to relax. My mind is buzzing.

"Then why would he buy tickets to a benefit Jack was hosting?"

"Because he was going to try and patch things up. Apparently, he's been trying to for years. But then they saw each other on the street a few weeks ago and Jonathan blatantly ignored him, so Michael asked to work that night. He's sick of trying to apologize. And it's such a shame because they were really close." Wow. Do I know how to pick them or what?

"Come to think of it, Jack did mention something about parting ways with an old friend, but that's all he'd say. I figured it was a love triangle or something like that. Did Michael tell you what happened?"

"Yes, but if I tell you, it'll definitely make you think less of Jonathan."

"Zoë, I don't think that's possible." I flop back on my pillows.

"Well, let me start from the beginning. Michael and Jonathan met at Berkley. They'd been friends since high school and had always planned on moving to New York to start their own business. But when they got there, Jonathan started changing. It was very subtle, but Michael said it was like he became another person. He got all cocky and greedy. Oh, and he started using women like they were ATM machines."

"Why doesn't that shock me?" I start to chew my thumbnail.

"Well, Michael was dating this girl Kate pretty seriously at the time. And one night when Jonathan didn't show up for poker night, he found them together."

"No!" I gasp.

"Yeah. So they had this huge blowout, and Jonathan started telling their friends all this stuff about Michael, which I only thought girls did. But that's beside the point." I stand up and start pacing the room.

"And they believed him?"

"Well yeah. He's got that politician thing going on and a whole lot of power because apparently his father is some hot shot lawyer." Well that figures.

"So what happened to Michael?"

"He moved to Boston, studied for the MCAT, and got into medical school. He hasn't spoken to Jonathan or any of their other friends for like eight years." I close my eyes.

"I feel sick."

"I know," Zoë says softly. "I liked him too." I fall back on my bed.

"Why do I always fall for that type of guy? I should know better."

"Emma, stop blaming yourself. He presents himself like a Kennedy."

"Who donates money to cancer research and helps girls get shoes off their big feet?" I add. I roll off my bed and resume pacing. "Gosh, I'm so naïve. When will I learn?" I'm on the verge of tears at this point. "And poor Michael." I sit down on the bed again. I never thought I'd say that, but poor, sweet Michael. I suddenly have a newfound love for that guy. Maybe that's why he acts so guarded. He's been burned. If anyone can understand that, it's me.

"I know, but Michael's happy now. He always wanted to be a doctor. It was Jonathan who told him not to do it." I let out a huge sigh. I mean, you think you know someone and then bam! "Look Emma, I debated telling you this, but I figured it would help you see why he's with someone like Natasha."

"I'm so glad you did because now I see how perfect they are for each other." At least I can see that now. When a guy doesn't like me, no matter how confident I may be, it's inevitable that I second-guess myself. And I hate that. I hate that someone like Jack Carmichael has power over my emotions. Shame on me for allowing him.

"Are you going to be okay? Should I come over?" she asks.

"I'll be fine. I'm pretty exhausted," I say, yawning into the phone.

"I'll call you tomorrow."

"Bye," I mutter and hang up.

Suddenly, I'm overcome with emotion. Why does this always happen to me? I'm so tempted to turn on Celine Dion and feel sorry for myself. Why do girls do that, anyway? As if being sad isn't enough. We have to throw sad music and a candlelit bedroom into the mix? But instead of crying in my pillow, which I'm notorious for doing, I stomp around the apartment. I want to talk to Mandy, but she's had a hard day.

When we got back from New York, there were three messages from her boss on the machine. He wants to meet with her first thing tomorrow. After running through twenty different reasons as to why he'd need to meet with her, we came up with nothing. And I know she's on pins and needles about it. She thinks she's going to be fired for making out with the new intern.

"I thought you went to bed," she finally calls from her bedroom. I don't respond. I just walk into her room and sit on the edge of the bed.

"Are you okay?" she asks, shutting *Pride and Prejudice*. I smile as I look down at her book. I conned her into reading all of Jane Austen's classics. I told her Katie Couric said these books have been beneficial to her career. What a dope! I didn't expect she'd believe me.

I relay everything Zoë told me, while she wears a look I'd imagine very similar to the one Minnie Driver wore when Matt Damon announced he was single on *Oprah*. (And I thought I had problems.) After listening, Mandy leans against the wall.

"I don't know what to say."

"You could throw me a when-God-closes-a-door-He-opens a-window speech," I offer half seriously. "Or how about telling me there are other fish in the sea?" I put my face in my hands. Mandy clears her throat.

"You know what, Emma. I'm glad this happened."

"Huh?" I ask, looking up.

"Don't get me wrong, the guy is scum, but look at what you learned from it."

"That there's only one kind of man in the world?" I joke, though I half mean it. Does that make me a feminist? And if so, do I have to shave my head and start listening to Ani DiFranco music?

"No, that you're capable of liking someone again, even if it was only for a day." She lays her hand on mine. "Emma, you've shut every man out since Caleb. I'm sorry this had to hurt, but look at how open-minded you were with Jack."

"Yeah and look where it got me." I scoot away.

"I am looking at where it got you. And you're here. You're alive and breathing and doing just fine."

"You know what," I say with a sudden surge of empowerment. "You're right."

"I know I'm right," she smirks. "And you even get closure on this one. Plus, it explains why he and Natasha are so perfect for each other."

"Right again." Why don't I buy into my own words? My mind is quick to understand that Jack sucks at life, but my heart has trouble keeping up. It just won't follow. Is that normal?

"Sweetie, you're going to be just fine. There's some amazing guy out there who doesn't even have a clue as to how lucky he's going to be when he finds you."

"Hopefully yours is a rich doctor," I joke as I get up to leave.

"Wouldn't that be nice?" she smiles. I turn at the doorway to face her.

"Thank you, Mandy. Not just for the encouragement,

but for being my rock this weekend. I hate that I've been such a drama queen, but you've been there for me with ice cream and Bridget Jones in hand. I love you for that, you know."

"I think I owed you a few," she says with a smile. Mandy's had a couple of bad breakups herself. And I think we both gained five pounds when her dog died.

"And I'll be thinking about you tomorrow, meeting with your boss. I'm sure it's nothing." She sighs.

"I hope so," she says.

16

Oh my gosh! The power must have gone out last night. I stare at my clock flashing twelve. I jump out of bed and run to look at the clock on the oven. Eight fifteen! Oh my gosh! I'm going to be so late. Crap! Okay, no time to think and definitely no time for a shower. I pull my dirty hair back in a clip. Hey, at least my outfit is cute. I borrowed Mandy's power suit, and it looks great with my yellow tank top.

Two minutes later, I dart out the door and hail a taxi. This turns out to be a good idea because Gwen rolls into work complaining about public transportation.

"The T is broken again," she says, collapsing into her swivel chair. "I waited for thirty minutes and when I finally hopped on, it stalled for another fifteen minutes. And the worst part is, I didn't even have *The Metro* to read." *The Metro* is the newspaper that the transportation system puts together for commuters to read on their way to work. I realize the editors aren't Pulitzer Prize winners or anything, but can you believe they misspelled a headline?

As we head to the conference room, I tell her all about Jack, leaving out my true feelings, of course.

"Oh my gosh!" she whispers. "Natasha would flip if she knew her boyfriend took you to lunch." I hadn't thought about that. We enter the boardroom and sit down.

I look down at my watch and see that I have three minutes to spare. In the midst of my morning crisis, I didn't even have time to go to the bathroom.

"Will you save my seat?" I ask, getting to my feet.

As I head to the restroom, I see that Helga, the bathroom Nazi, has yet again blocked the door while cleaning. I step over her mop bucket, but immediately Helga blocks my path.

"I'm sorry Miss, but this bathroom is closed for cleaning," she says firmly. Oh my gosh. Last week, I distinctly asked her not to do this, seeing as how everybody drinks coffee in the morning.

"I know," I say through clenched teeth, "but it's really an emergency. Please," I say, crossing my legs.

"Come back in fifteen minutes," she says and ushers me out the door. I can't believe she won't let me in after I told her it was an emergency.

"You know, I could have a kidney problem." Helga continues mopping without so much as looking up. "Seriously, I don't understand why I can't go to the bathroom while you mop. You're not anywhere near the stalls." Helga closes the bathroom door on my face. Oh my gosh! That's so rude. I mean, what's she doing in there that's so secretive, anyway? Espionage?

In attempt to avoid a fistfight, I pop my head in the men's room.

"Hello?" I call out. Okay, the coast is clear. I quickly slip into a stall. As I flush the toilet, I hear the door open.

"Someone's in here," I say without thinking. Why didn't I just stand on the toilet seat like any normal person would have done?

"You do realize this is the men's room?" a male voice calls out. Well, there's no denying it now.

"Um, yes." How much I wish I went down the pipes as well. "Look I'm really sorry, but the girl's bathroom is closed, and I had to use the bathroom really bad," I say as I attempt to walk out with my hand over my eyes. "You see, my alarm didn't go off this morning, and I drank the largest cup of coffee ever. And well, you know us girls. We have to go like every five minutes. And ..." I stop. Why am I telling this poor guy all of this? "Ouch," I say as I bump into him.

"Emma?" I take my hand off my eyes and to my horror see Jack Carmichael. How? What? Why?

"What are you doing in here?" I ask. I look at the ground in horror.

"I was about to ask you the same question, but it seems you already told me." I glance up at him. Okay. That cute grin has got to go.

"Why didn't you tell me you were in here? You always do that." I point a finger at his face.

"I always do what?" he asks, folding his arms.

"Keep things from me."

"What was I supposed to do? Announce my presence in the men's room?" He has a point there.

"Yes," I say very matter-of-factly, walking to the sink. "Helga is cleaning the girl's bathroom, and if you had any intuition whatsoever, you'd know that girls come in here." I dry my hands on a paper towel and throw it in the trash.

"Right," he says, his eyes twinkling. He so deserves a swirly.

"And besides, when you have to go, you have to go." I'm so digging my own hole right now. Am I really having a conversation with Jack Carmichael in the men's bathroom? "So what are you doing here, anyway?" I turn to face him again. Okay. I guess I am having a conversation with him in the bathroom. He clears his throat.

"The same as you, Miss Mosley," he says with a straight face. He glances over at the urinals.

"Not here," I say, pointing to the toilets. "Here. At the

office." Why am I using my arms to talk? And why does he look so amused?

"I have a meeting with the magazine. Now if you wouldn't mind..." Jack has a meeting with the magazine?

"You have—" I start.

"Hey lady," Helga says as she pops her head in the restroom. "I'm finished cleaning."

"I should call immigration on you," I say storming past her. Helga follows me out and starts screaming what I assume to be Polish obscenities, but I just hold my head high without looking back. What else can I do?

17

As I make my way back to the conference room, I take a moment to gather my thoughts. Okay, surely I can find the silver lining here. So what if I ran into Jack in the men's bathroom? It could have been worse. I could have walked in on him actually *going to* the bathroom. Now that would have stunk. And I still have my health, though a dozen Dunkin Donuts are calling my name right now.

I slip into my seat just as Jack walks in after me. Oh man, was he walking behind me the entire time? What if he saw me picking my wedgie? This day couldn't be any worse, and it's only 9 AM!

"I hope everyone had a nice weekend," Natasha says in her little pink suit. She looks like Barbie. "I'd like to welcome Jonathan Carmichael from Carmichael Advertising." She looks over and smiles at him.

Please woman, do you have to flaunt yourself to the entire staff room? She reminds me of Heather Locklear's character on *Melrose Place*. I think she ended up dying or faking her death or something, not that I'm saying I want Natasha to die or anything. Well, maybe just gain fifty pounds and be banished to the Middle East.

"He's going to be using *Bean Town Scene* to promote his new clients."

"He's gonna what?" I mutter under my breath.

"Jonathan," she says as she calls him to the front to take over.

"Thank you, Natasha," he says, giving her a look that makes me nauseous. "Good morning, everyone." The lights dim for his power point presentation. "As most of you may already know, I have acquired a few local clients who target the same demographics as your magazine. In front of you are the names of two of them who will be using your magazine for their campaign launch. If you would please look on with me." He turns to face the lit screen. Oh great, I have to put on my Lisa Loeb glasses. I feel like such a geek.

"My first client is up-and-coming fashion designer Chloe Zimmerman. She made quite an impression at Fashion Week last fall, and she has a very promising career ahead of her. She's making her way in New York City but will be opening a boutique here in Boston this spring. We're going to be doing a five-page spread in *BTS* as well as other regional magazines in order to advertise her new collection. I have all the numbers and information you'll need in your booklet, so there's no need to read them aloud."

"He probably can't read," I whisper to Gwen. She laughs. Aw, I'm witty.

"Do you have a question, Emma?" Natasha asks sweetly. "Your Mom," I want to shout so badly. But I don't.

"Uh, no," I say and sink lower in my seat. Jack clears his throat and continues.

"My second client is Edward Kelly." What! Since when does our magazine endorse politicians? "For those of you who don't watch the news, Mr. Kelly is running for mayor of Boston. He has his own team running the campaign; however, he hired me to help boost his popularity." I know my jaw is on the floor. Jack looks at me, then continues. "We're in no way endorsing Kelly over the other candidates. We're just informing the public about him as a person. As you know, Boston is a very diverse town, and Mr. Kelly is hoping to gain favor amongst the hard-to-reach residents. Since there are over fifty colleges in the Boston area, we're going to be targeting college students, as well as young professionals. We'll be featuring Edward Kelly in your magazine next month. Any questions?"

"Yes," I yell rather loudly, raising my hand as the lights come on. I don't know why I still raise my hand. It's not like I'm in the sixth grade anymore.

"Emma," Jack says, not at all surprised I'd be the first one to open my mouth. Oh man, I'm still wearing my librarian glasses. I slide them self-consciously off my face.

"What if a portion of our readers dislike Mr. Kelly? We could lose them and circulation would go down."

"That's true, Emma," Natasha says, straightening herself in her chair, "but all our readers favor Edward Kelly." Why is she acting nice to me? She usually eats me for supper during meetings.

"No they don't," I blurt. I look over and see Jack raise a brow. Why is he always amused by me? I'm trying to be serious here. Gosh, my cheeks are burning. If there's one thing I hate most, it's when people don't take me seriously.

"They don't?" Natasha says, throwing me a challenging look. I shake my head.

"I don't think so. I mean, I can't stand the guy, and I fit the magazine's demographics."

"Well, you don't represent every person in Boston," she says crisply, tapping her fingers hard on the table.

"True. But if we didn't survey our readers, how do we know what we're up against?" I'm really not trying to be difficult here.

"You didn't survey your readers?" Jack asks, turning to look at Natasha. How great would it be to witness a lover's quarrel from the power couple? I'm talking a full out, *Days of Our Lives* meets *Dynasty* kind of fight. And we've got front row tickets.

"Well," she says, rising to her feet. My goodness, the woman has got to be at least six feet tall. "We didn't find it necessary to poll the readers because this is Boston. It's made up of left-winged Democrats. Kelly's a liberal. Plus, he's from Wellesley, so he's politically similar in beliefs to most of the people around here."

"That's not true," I retort without thinking. Oh great, all eyes on Miss Short Bus.

"No?" Jack asks, obviously amused with my Tourette Syndrome.

"No," I say confidently. "I'm from Boston, and I'm not a left-winged liberal. And like you said, there are a lot of college students. They're from all over the world. They're not all from Wellesley or even New England. A lot of them come from the Bible Belt South and overseas. So I don't think it's fair to generalize our readers. Boston's a melting pot with diverse cultures." I think that was a quote from an article I wrote a few months ago, but I'm allowed to plagiarize myself, right?

"She's right," Jack says as he looks at Natasha.

"I could take a survey," a little voice squeaks from the back of the room. Oh shut up, Justin. He's our numbers guy. I don't mean to sound like a snob, but he's your typical MIT geek. He even has a pocket protector. Yes, a pocket protector! I haven't seen one of those since Screech donned one on *Saved by the Bell.*

"That won't be necessary," Jack says, placing his hands on the table. He looks at me, and I can see his eyes are dancing with amusement. "Emma's going to work with Edward Kelly."

"What!" I gasp.

"What?" Natasha asks calmly, though you can see the veins bulging on her neck. Now don't get me wrong. I'd love to trump Natasha any day of the week, but if I have to work on Edward Kelly's promotion, I'll die.

"Jonathan," Natasha says in a low voice. "Emma's our entertainment writer. We need her to keep with that because there's a lot going on this season. Besides, she's not even fond of Edward Kelly. Let's have one of the other editors do it." Jack, obviously thrilled with his latest idea, paces the front with excitement.

"But if we use Emma, we'll save time surveying readers." I scowl and cross my arms.

"How do you figure that?" I ask. For once, I agree with Natasha. Jack turns to look at me.

"Well, if you dislike Kelly, then I'm sure there are others who feel the same way you do."

"So?" I ask, waiting for the light to go off.

"So you can represent those people. Tap into the heads of the readers who oppose him."

"You want me to lie!" I retort as if we're the only two people in the room.

"No," he says calmly. "I want you to spend time with him. To find the good in him and use that to win reader approval." I glance around the room. Everyone is waiting for my answer.

"What about my entertainment article?" As much as I hate my column, I'm not liking this very much either.

"Natasha?" he asks, glancing at her silently seething in the corner. High society girls only throw tantrums in private. Or in her case, when I'm around.

"You're the client," she says, flashing an empty smile. "It's your call."

"Great," he says. "Thank you everyone." He shuts his laptop. Natasha steps to the front.

"Gwen, you can write Emma's column for the time being," she says. "Now, that's going to be all for now. We have a lot of work to do so everybody get to it." We collect our things to go.

"Emma, can I see you a minute?" she asks as I make my way to the door. Why am I always in trouble? I'm not in the third grade.

"I just need to work out some details with Emma," she says sweetly over my shoulder to Jack, as she ushers me outside.

"What's up?" I ask in an attempt at civility.

"Look," she says in a hushed tone, "I completely disagree with Jonathan, but he's the boss so my hands are tied."

"But I don't even want—" I start.

"Just remember this is a weekly thing. If I find your articles aren't up to par then I'm yanking you. Got it?" She's standing just an inch too close to my face. I'm tempted to take a step back, but that would be admitting defeat.

"I'll do my best," I say defensively. Natasha smirks.

"Just make sure your best is good enough." At this point, I almost want to get fired. I'm fuming. I mean, did she and Jack conspire on how to best ruin my life? Well they are wasting their time because it's not going to work. I was here way before Long Legs and Jack the Ripper.

I storm back to the conference room to find Jack packing up his presentation materials.

"What is your problem?" I ask hotly.

"I'm sorry?" he asks, not looking up from his materials. I clench my fists at my side.

"Oh, don't act so nonchalant. You know you did that to me on purpose."

"Did what to you?" he asks distractedly while fumbling through some papers. Who is this guy? What happened to the man I had lunch with a few days ago? The man who spent the summer in Greece and got punched by a girl? Does he even exist? Was all that a lie?

"Should I check the back of your head for the number 666 or something?" Jack glances up and smiles, and I find once again I'm having an argument with myself. "What did I ever do to you? I was fine before I met you, but now everything seems to bite." I guess there really is a thin line between love and hate. Three days ago I had our wedding china picked out; now I want to serve his head on a platter.

"Do you want to know what your problem is?" Jack says, sliding his laptop into its case.

"*My* problem?"

"Yes, your problem. You take everything so personally and create drama." He places his last folder in his briefcase and turns to face me. I stand there open mouthed.

"Wait a second. Because I take my life seriously, I'm a drama queen?" Jack shakes his head.

"I didn't say that. You just put words in my mouth." In hopes that he'll read my cues, I let out a large sigh. Okay. That didn't work so I do it again. What's the deal? I inhale sharply to sigh yet again but am rudely interrupted by Jack's laughter.

"Are you done now?" he asks, smiling. Why doesn't he care that I'm mad? I want him to know that I hate him. I let out another sigh, just for good measure.

"I have asthma, okay." I flip my hair over my shoulder and cross my arms. Jack lays a hand on my shoulder.

"Emma, this is business, not personal. No one is out to get you. You're the best person for Kelly's campaign. It's as simple as that."

"Is it that simple, Jack?" I say softly. I glance into his face, though I wish I hadn't. Those eyes. And that scar. His look only reminds me of who I thought he was.

"Yes," he says. "Aren't you the one who told me that you wanted to write about things that matter?" I shrug his hand off my shoulder and look down at the floor. "Well, here's your chance." He's absolutely right. Besides the internship I had at *Boston Magazine* back in college, I've never had the chance to write a story that really matters. Sure my entertainment column is fun, but I want to do more than make people laugh. Maybe writing about Edward Kelly can help me do that. As much as I loathe Kelly, Jack is right.

"You're asking me to write about someone I detest," I say uncertainly, tucking my hair behind my ear. Jack sits on the edge of the conference table.

"You of all people should know that's journalism. You have to see both sides of a story." As much as I hate to admit it, he's right. I once had a professor who made me give a speech on an issue I completely opposed. The point was to put my personal issues aside and be unbiased. He told me that my strong opinions would get me in trouble one day, and I hate to say it but the wise, old professor was correct. Of course, I'd never admit this to Jack. All I can think about is what he did to poor Michael, and how stupid he made me feel. Gosh, I hate him. I hate him for being such a disappointment. I hate him for humiliating me. I hate him for teasing me into thinking there was life after Caleb. But most of all I hate him because despite all that's happened, I don't hate him as much as I should.

"I guess I was sick the day we covered that in school. But thank you for that point to ponder, Professor Carmichael," I snap. "So what do you want me to do?" I cross my arms impatiently. Jack stands up and snaps back into his professional mode.

"Well, for starters, you can lighten up. We're going to be working together for the next few weeks, so you're going to have to let go of whatever grudge you have toward me and be professional." If he means knock down my tough girl wall, then he's on crack. Had I built it the day we met, I wouldn't even be in this mess.

"I can do that," I say in a state of defeat.

"Great," he says, reaching into his briefcase. "Now I've scheduled lunch for you, Mr. Kelly, and myself at noon today, so we'll discuss everything then. In the meantime, I'd suggest you brush up on his campaign. This might help." He hands me a press kit put together by Edward Kelly's advisors.

"And where do I meet you?" I ask, taking the papers from his hand. My fingers brush his, sending chills up my spine.

"The Oak Room, but I'll be here until then so I can give you a ride," Jack says casually.

"No thanks. I'd rather walk," I say as I whip my head around and strut off haughtily. Okay, that was a little dramatic, but at least he's getting the message.

18

I look down at may watch and see that it's time for lunch with the Menendez brothers. Time really flies when you're not looking forward to something.

"Bye Gwen," I holler as I bundle up in my winter gear. And yes, I do mean gear. I've got the gloves, hat, scarf—even the hand warmers.

"You're going out in this?" she exclaims, eyeing my Eskimo ensemble. "Are you crazy?" Maybe she's right, though I suspect prideful would be a better word. After all, there is a blizzard outside, which means I'll never get a cab, and Jack has offered to give me a ride. But rather than accept his gallant offer, I opt to trek almost a mile in high heels and falling snow. Yep, I'm definitely prideful.

"I'll be fine," I call back to her.

I push with all my might against the wind to open the door to the office building. Maybe this wasn't such a bright idea. The snow pelts my face like paint balls. Normally I'd use my walking time to do something worthwhile, like envision my wedding or rehearse my Pulitzer Prize-winning speech, but the only thing I can think of at the moment is the movie *Alive*.

I cut across the historic Trinity Church grounds and make my way into The Fairmont Plaza's Oak Room just as Jack pulls up in a shiny, black Range Rover. Before he can spot me, I dash inside. As I make my way through the lobby, my cell rings. I flip it open and see a number I don't recognize. I hate unknown numbers, but my curiosity always gets the better of me.

"Hello?" I say warily into the phone.

"Emma, it's me."

"Mandy? Where are you calling from?" I say, removing my hat so I can hear better.

"A pay phone. Listen, you're never going to believe this. Are you sitting down?"

"Yes," I lie. That's just a cliché anyway.

"I got my own show!" she squeals.

"What!?" I pause in my attempt to unravel the scarf from around my neck.

"Wait. Before you get too excited I have to tell you the bad news."

"There couldn't possibly be bad news." Well actually, there could be. The cameras do add ten pounds, but now isn't the time to bring that up.

"I'm moving to New York," she says and pauses as if waiting on the jury to reach a verdict. What? Did she just say what I think she said? That she's moving? Surely my ears have deceived me. I collapse onto a couch in the hallway.

"Emma?" Now is one of those moments in life where my response truly matters. On one hand, I'm going to be miserable without her, but come on. This is her dream. How can I tell her I'm devastated that she's leaving when that will only hold back her happiness?

"That's not bad news," I say, forcing some pep into my voice. There's a painful lump developing in my throat. "You're moving to New York City, baby." Now I know how daddies feel when their little girls get married.

"Do you really mean that?" she says doubtfully. Should I continue to lie? Because I'm really starting to feel bad.

"Because I couldn't be happy unless you were happy too," Mandy says. Gosh, we sound like a married couple. I swallow hard.

"Of course I'm happy. No, I'm ecstatic!"

"You don't sound it," she says.

"That's because I'm shocked, and I just walked through a blizzard." I finish yanking off my scarf and shove it into a ball with my hat and gloves.

"Dare I ask?" she laughs.

"So when do you leave?"

"Well, I'm actually at the airport right now. I'll be gone all week. Gosh, there's so much to do. Find a fabulous apartment, work out all the details with the producers, lose ten pounds, etc." Find a new apartment? Oh my gosh! I'm losing my roommate too!

"Do you need any help? I could take off a few days at work." Which is so another lie. Between Jack and his bulimic girlfriend, I doubt I'll even get a Christmas vacation.

"You're sweet to offer, but I'm fine. Oh, crap. We're boarding." Is this really happening? "I'll call you ASAP," she says as she hangs up the phone.

It's funny how much life can change in less than a week. Mandy is moving to New York City to become famous. Caleb is getting married. I'm working for Satan and his little helper. Yet I'm the same old, boring person who has yet to accomplish anything on my dream list. I have yet to go to Africa, learn another language, publish a book, get married, or move to New York City. Nothing ever changes in my life. I'm stagnant. Gosh, I could die and no one would even notice. Would anyone even be at my funeral?

"You okay?" Jack asks as I sit down at the table without saying hello. I wonder how long I've been here.

"Uh huh," I say, staring despondently out the window. My eyes are burning. Okay Emma, don't cry. Quick, think of something funny. Think about the time you got lockjaw in the middle of a make-out session with Ben Cummings in the ninth grade. Not working. What else? How about the time Zoë ate the ex-lax® cookies you baked for Dad when he took away the car? Oh great. I can feel the tears forming. You'd think you had control over a small little tear duct. It's not even the size of an ant.

"Kelly's running a few minutes late," Jack says somewhere in the distance. "He's caught up in a meeting with his advisers. He said to go ahead and order."

"Fine." I hear Jack, but I can't comprehend what he's saying. Don't cry, Emma. Not in front of Jack. Oh, but I can't help it.

Do you ever have the feeling that you're so utterly alone? You could be standing in a crowded room, surrounded by friends and family but still feel this deep hollowness in your heart. That's my exact state at this moment. Man, here they come. They're rolling down my face.

"Emma?" Jack says. He reaches across the table and touches my hand. I jump and slip my hand down to my lap.

"You okay?" he asks.

"Yep," I say all too cheerily, trying to dab away the tears with my napkin. "I just have something in my eye." That excuse is almost as lame as "you're not fat, just big-boned."

"Do you want to talk about it?" he asks, furrowing his brow. Since when did he start caring about my feelings?

"There's nothing to talk about." I take a cleansing breath and open my menu. "Well actually, there is. Is your company paying for lunch?"

"Mine," he says, raising a brow of curiosity. As much as I despise Jack Carmichael, he looks so yummy when he does that. It's amazing how one gesture can momentarily make me forget how much I dislike him. As I glance at him, I can't help but realize how hard I could have fallen for this guy. After a moment of thinking, I snap out of it, reminding myself how much he disappointed me.

"Well in that case," I say pertly as I look down at my menu, "I think I'll have the lobster." A few awkward moments of silence later, Edward Kelly joins us.

"Sorry I'm late," he says, walking up to the table. "My advisers are pretty long-winded, and do you believe this weather?" He flashes me a Colgate smile. Wow, Mr. Kelly is a hottie. Not in a Brad Pitt sort of way, more like an Ed Harris, but still.

Jack rises to shake his hand, then turns to me.

"Edward, this is Emma Mosley from *Bean Town Scene.* She'll be the writer working on your campaign."

"Miss Mosley," he says, shaking my hand. "I'm delighted to meet you. I've heard only good things," he says with a smile, glancing at Jack. I give Jack a somehow-I-find-that-hard-to-believe look, and he smiles as if he read my stare.

"Please, call me Emma," I say. "And the pleasure is all mine." I still can't get over how cute he is.

After playing twenty questions with Mr. Kelly, I've learned that he's a Democrat from the rich town of Wellesley. His parents are blue bloods that sent him off to prep school at the age of six. He went to Harvard, and then on to Georgetown for law school. He practiced for a few years but found his true passion in public service. Though I hate his politics, he seems like a good man. And if I didn't know better, I'd like him. But I know better.

"Tell me about your family," I say between bites of my $60 lobster. This is due justice, since Jack was the one who ruined my lobster the other night. I mean, it's only fair that I order something equally as fine. Just thinking about the way he treated me that night makes me want to order dessert. I hope his company goes under and he's forced to live in a box.

"I'm glad you asked," Kelly says, smiling warmly. "My wife, Kathleen, is a social worker. We met when I clerked at her father's law firm about twenty-three years ago. She was bringing her father lunch, and then we got to talking and after a few weeks, she was bringing me lunch. We have twin boys, James and John, both at Yale, and a daughter Lauren, who's still in high school."

"You must be a proud father," Jack says as I take notes. Of course it sounds nice on paper, but is he really this good to be true? I mean, I do watch Lifetime.

"I am," he says, adjusting his tie. "Family has and will always come first," he adds.

"Can I quote you on that?" I ask, looking up.

"I wish you would." He smiles. Family First. I like that. I return his smile. But I still dislike his politics.

"Are you religious?" I ask. A million dollars says he's Catholic.

"I'm an active member of St. Paul's Catholic Church. My great-great grandfather helped start the church when he came over from Ireland. He was a priest." Irish and Catholic, huh? I bet he drinks like a fish.

"Right," I say as I close my note pad and put it away. "Well, I think that about covers it."

"Great," he says, setting his napkin on the table and getting to his feet. "Thank you for your time, Emma."

"The pleasure was all mine," I say, trying to swallow a mouth full of bread. Carbs, carbs, carbs.

"Now if you would excuse me, I have a press conference in half an hour. Jonathan, you'll call me if anything comes up?"

"Will do," he says, standing up. "Let me walk you out." Edward places his hand on Jack's shoulder.

"Now Jonathan. You wouldn't want to leave this beautiful young woman all by herself, would you?" Gosh, he's good, but then again he's paid to flatter people, kiss babies, lower taxes, and all that other stuff.

"Now that would be tragic," Jack says teasingly. That was so rude. I hope he gets food poisoning.

"Have a wonderful afternoon," Mr. Kelly says as he grabs his jacket and exits. Oh great. It's just me and butthead now. What on earth do we have to say to each other?

"So why'd you tell me your name was Jack if everyone else calls you Jonathan?" I ask without thinking. Jack sits back down in his chair.

"Because that's what I go by professionally," he says plainly. "But my good friends call me Jack." So what, we're good friends now? Remind me to call him Jonathan.

"So what did you think of Mr. Kelly?" he says.

"I've only known him for an hour," I say, crossing my arms.

"You formed an opinion about me after only an hour." He smiles.

"And I won't be making that mistake again," I say with a grimace.

"Mistake?" he asks, amused.

"Oh, nothing. Never mind." I stuff my mouth with another piece of bread. My gosh. That makes three.

"No way," he laughs. "You don't get off that easily."

"Huh?" I ask with my mouth full. I so need another roll.

"How did you make a mistake?" Gosh, he's persistent.

"Oh. That." Dude, where is the bread basket? "Well," I say as I shrug my shoulder and look up at the ceiling. "You appealed to me the first time we met."

"But," he starts, leaning in. I turn my head to look at him.

"You're digging your own hole here. You know that, right?"

"Right behind you," he says with a smile. A smile, I might add, that almost makes me swoon. Almost, but I have self-control.

"And look who you turned out to be? That guy." I flick my hand in the air.

"What guy?" he asks curiously.

"Why do you care what I think?" I ask. Tired of this conversation, I grab my coat to leave. Oops, I think I was supposed to check it.

"Because you seem to get defensive whenever I'm around," Jack says, rising to his feet with me. I open my mouth to speak, but he continues. "And I know you're not really like that because I've seen you with other people, and you're usually very sweet." So now he's watching me? He thinks for a minute and smiles. "Well, except to Helga. She definitely hates you." He thinks I'm sweet? That is so ... so—who cares what it is? He has a girlfriend. And he embarrassed me. I make my way through the lobby but stop at the door. Jack follows close behind.

"Look," I say as I turn to face him. "I know you think we're all buddy-buddy and all, but really, Jonathan, we just work together." Why don't I believe this? "And for the record, I think you underestimate me." He gives me a this-should-be-interesting-look and allows me to continue. "You don't know a thing about me, but I know all about you."

"Who told you about my drug problem?" he jokes.

"For someone as perceptive as you claim to be, you seem to forget that I'm a reporter."

"I haven't forgotten that, Lois Lane. I just hope you haven't dug up my old yearbooks. Now that would be tragic." He really doesn't take me seriously, does he? Well if he only knew what I knew about his true character.

"You know, Jack, sarcasm is a sign of insecurity," I snap back.

"So is a critical spirit," he says calmly. We're like oil and water.

"I am not critical," I say as I exit the hotel. Well, actually I am, but only to him. And maybe to Zoë, but only because I want what's best for her. Besides, who is Jack to label me? Gosh, I don't think I've ever been this bothered by another human being in my entire life. And I was quite the firecracker during my adolescent years.

"Wait," he says, gently grabbing my arm. The hair on the back of my neck begins to tingle. "Do you need a ride back to the office, or are you going to snow plow your way back?" I almost forgot about the snow. I glance at the street. Oh my Dairy Queen! It looks like a snow globe after it's been shaken up.

"You really think I'm a joke, don't you?" I retort hotly.

"No," he says, shaking his head. "I think you're a dreamer and very passionate." Okay. That caught me off guard. I expected a joke.

"What are you talking about? I'm realistic." I'm so lying. I'm the most unrealistic girl in the world. Jack takes me by the shoulders.

"Emma, I had no idea you worked for Natasha," he says softly. "I didn't think I'd see you again." I shrug him away.

"You have no idea what I'm talking about, do you?" I'm so tempted to tell him that I know about Michael. I'm so tempted to tell him that before him, I hadn't so much as looked at another guy in six years. Maybe I am critical. And maybe I'm guarded, but it's only because I'm so scared of this guy. I'm so scared because I really don't hate him like I should.

"I guess not. But if you don't tell me then I—" he starts, but I interrupt him.

"You know what, Jack? It doesn't matter. You're right. I've already formed an opinion about you."

"And?"

"And seeing as that I'd rather pay ten bucks for a cab then to be stuck in a confined space with you," I say as I wait for the doorman to hail me a taxi, "you can make an educated guess."

"Wait a second," he says as he steps closer. Oh great, what's he going to say now? That he was never attracted to me because I'm too psycho? Well, I know that already and I'm over it. Kind of.

"What?" I snap.

"Do you have a card or something with your cell phone on it?"

"Why?" I take a step back.

"Well, I'm no rocket scientist, but I'm thinking that maybe I'll need to contact you sometime. You know, since we're going to be working together."

"Oh yeah. That," I say. I fumble through my purse, finally digging out my business card. He's probably going to write it on the bathroom wall at some sketchy gas station.

"And here's where I can be reached," he says in a businesslike tone. He hands me a card to the Ritz.

"You're staying at a hotel?" I ask surprised.

"Is something wrong with that?" he asks. Why is it that the one guy I truly dislike is the one guy who can read my mind? And it's not a normal mind either.

"I just figured you'd be staying with Natasha. She is your girlfriend, and most guys ... well, you know." He crosses his arms and stares at me curiously. "You know, most guys aren't ... I mean, most couples stay together. In the same room. Or place." Quick, Emma. Retreat. "Not that I care or anything. I mean, it's your life. Stay where you want to stay. The Ritz is an excellent choice." I need a clincher here. "You know what? I should've guessed you were staying at the Ritz. That's where the benefit was, wasn't it?" Three words: Flintstone back pedal.

"Are you finished?" he laughs, obviously amused by my gibberish.

"Yep," I say as I look down at the ground. Oh, how I wish I were the pavement right now.

"And here I thought Yankees were short and to the point."

"Well, I'm not your average Yankee," I say, tossing my hair and looking straight into his dark eyes.

"I'll give you that," he says. He gives me a look so cute it could easily kill me. Houston, we have a problem.

19

My eyes are burning. I've been staring at this stupid computer since lunch. I think my backside has molded into the shape of my chair.

I blink uncontrollably as I turn off the computer and gather my stuff. I've been researching Edward Kelly all afternoon, and I must admit that he does sound good on paper. I'm not saying that I'd vote for him or anything, but he seems like a very nice man. He's definitely a family man, and not bad looking either. If he were mayor, I'd definitely watch local news more.

Right on schedule, I enter my favorite coffee shop and order a large, extra-whipped mocha. My English class is tonight and this is my Monday night ritual. A cup of coffee, Jane Austen, and some good jazz music. It's great to be alive. And I'm so excited about class tonight because we're discussing *Emma*. I've already read it like four times, but it's yet to bore me. I was, after all, named after Emma Woodhouse, so you could say it was predestined I would adore this story. I love how Emma plays matchmaker to everybody else, yet the entire time, she's falling in love with her best friend. I cry every time I read Mr. Knightley professing his love for his darling friend under the large oak tree, which only makes me wonder where my Mr. Knightley is. Knowing my luck, he probably got hit by a falling tree.

Okay, enough of that. What has gotten into me?

I take off my coat and flip to the chapter where Emma realizes that she loves Mr. Knightley. I squirm in my seat at the very anticipation of his proposal, yet am rudely interrupted by a familiar voice.

"Tall skinny cappuccino," I hear her say. You have got to be kidding me. I look up and see Natasha, and oh dear goodness, there's Jack. Crap. I bury my face in my book. I'm so that idiot who puts a newspaper in front of her face to appear inconspicuous. I pull the book down to my nose in order to catch a glimpse of them, and just as I do so, Jack looks up and ruins my Sidney Bristow moment. He ruins everything.

"Who are we spying on?" he asks, sidling up. He glances around, then sits down in the chair across from me.

"Did I say you could sit there?" I ask, shutting my book. "I mean, you automatically assume I'm by myself. I could have someone with me, you know."

"I'm sorry," he says standing up. "Did I just sit on your imaginary friend?" I almost want to laugh, but I'd rather die than give Jack the satisfaction of knowing that he made me laugh. He sits back down and leans toward me. "So what are you reading?" I hold up the book, and he lets out a roar.

"Are you mocking me?" I ask between sips of my mocha. My goodness it's hot. "Ouch," I say, spitting it back into the cup.

"You okay?" he asks, handing me a napkin.

"I'm fine," I say, panting. I just burnt my taste buds. Man, now food will be tasteless for a week.

"So has Emma realized she's in love with that Knightley chap yet?" Jack asks, leaning back and placing his hands behind his head.

"How do you know about Mr. Knightley?" I ask. Jack never ceases to amaze me.

"I was an English major."

"*You* were an English major," I say with a smile. Not that I care. I can't stand this guy. Why do I keep forgetting that? I wipe the smile off my face.

"Yep."

"Well, did you like the book?" I lean forward, curious. Jack thinks for a moment.

"Not really."

"What, not enough war and masculinity?"

"Actually, it was the lead character I didn't like. She's kind of annoying."

"Excuse me," I say as if he just insulted my mother. "How can you not like Emma? She is only one of the most heroic female characters in British literature."

"And she's also nosy, emotionally immature, and stubborn."

"She's nosy in a good way," I retort. Jack laughs.

"There's no good way to be nosy."

"Yeah there is. Prying into people's lives in order to make them happy is honorable."

"Or it can mean you have intimacy issues of your own." Somehow I think we got off *Emma*. Oh my gosh. I hate him. As if he knows a thing about me or my plethora of issues.

"What are you talking about? Have you even read the book?" I stand up in fury as my chair goes screeching across the floor. "Emma is a caring and innocent person. She plays matchmaker because she cares more about other people's happiness than her own." I'm, of course, shouting this and people are looking at me.

"You act like I'm offending you or something," he says softly, insinuating that perhaps I'm talking too loudly. I sit back down and cross my arms. "All I said was that I didn't like the book. Why do you take things so personally?"

What is the matter with me? I'm about to commit

murder because Jack doesn't like my favorite book. It's not like I wrote it. But still. Everything he's saying about Emma holds true to me. I'm a matchmaker. I pry into people's lives. I'm emotionally immature. Oh my gosh, my eyes are starting to tear. I wipe them quickly.

"Because you make me take things personally. Ever since I met you, you've seemed to go out of your way to make things difficult for me." I dramatically start collecting my things. He tries to talk, but I cut him off. "As always, Jack, it was a pleasure." And just like that, I exit the shop. I even walk past Natasha, who's still waiting on her tall skinny cappuccino.

Tall skinny cappuccino, huh? Like I should be surprised. I mean, who wants a regular, extra whipped mocha when there's a tall skinny cappuccino waiting at the bar?

20

After what seems like a nap, I'm waking up to "Matty in the Morning" blaring on my clock radio. Days like yesterday make it close to impossible to sleep. I mean, who is Jack Carmichael to challenge me? And will somebody please tell me what about me is so unlikable? Why does Jack go out of his way to belittle me?

After a quick shower, I throw on my tan suede pants to conceal the bag of dark chocolates I inhaled when I got home last night. I'm not sure where all my fat has gone, but I don't care as long as it stays gone.

Thirty minutes later, I walk to my desk and find a sunflower sitting on my chair. What is this? I examine the flower. I look around and find only a card.

"Truce?" it says.

I roll my eyes and slump into my chair. Jack is such a ladies' man. Does he really think some cheap CVS-bought flower is going to make up for all the attacks he's made on my character? And I'm not stupid. He probably had some poor assistant go fetch it. But on the other hand, it was pretty endearing. Especially since I told him the day we met that sunflowers make me happy.

After a couple hours of writing, Natasha pops her little head in my cube.

"Where's Gwen?" she asks.

"At a press conference."

"Nice flower," she says as she looks down at my sun-flower.

"Thank you," I say with a huge smile. Not an "I love you" but definitely an attempt to be civil.

"And how sweet of Jack to spare one for you and Helga," she adds.

"You mean, he—" I start.

"Yeah. Isn't he cute? And so sweet!" He gave me and the cleaning lady leftover flowers?

"Yeah, he's a real keeper," I say as I reach for my ringing phone.

"You will never guess who I just met!" It's Mandy. She sounds terrific.

"Who?" I ask, pitching the sunflower in the trash.

"Kelly Ripa."

"What!" I exclaim.

"She was having lunch with her producer, and my producer is friends with him. Long story. Anyway, she's such a sweetheart and way cuter in person. If that's possible. Okay, enough about me. I called to see how things are with you."

I want to give her a complete rundown of everything that's happened with Jack, the article, the *Emma* debate, and the flower, but for the first time in the history of our friendship, I hold back.

"Oh, nothing new. Tell me more about you."

As she talks about fancy lunches in SoHo and apart-ment shopping on the Upper East Side, I fight back my tears. I know I haven't experienced a great tragedy like losing a loved one or battling cancer, but sometimes I feel like I missed the dream train. Like my whole life has been a huge waiting room.

"Listen, I have to get back to this stupid article," I say as tears stream down my face. I don't want Mandy to know I'm upset. This is her time to shine.

"You okay?" she asks.

"Yeah, I'm fine," I lie. "I'm just exhausted."

"I know the feeling. I've been running on caffeine all day. I'll call you again soon."

"Bye," I say as I hang up the phone.

Not wanting to break down, yet again, I put my elbows on the desk, rest my head in my hands and take a few deep breaths. In times like this, when there is no food in sight, yoga is the answer. I push my chair under the desk and lift myself into a backbend. This always relaxes me, though it feels a little awkward in suede pants. I close my eyes and just think. Man, I'm exhausted. I'm so tired of writing about things I'm not passionate about. I should've just married Caleb. We'd probably have kids by now, or I would be writing for some classy British magazine. And Jack. Boy did he throw me for a loop. I wish I'd never tried on those stupid shoes. All that boy did was remind me why I never put myself out there.

After most of the blood rushes to my head, I open my eyes and see an upside-down Jack standing at my feet. Oh my gosh! How long has he been there? Maybe if I shut my eyes, he won't be able to see me.

"That doesn't work, you know," he says.

"Can I help you with something?" I ask as I scramble to my feet and adjust my shirt. Oh my gosh. My stomach was totally showing. I hope he didn't see my nonexistent six-pack.

"How's the article coming?" he asks, stepping into my cube.

"It's fine, thanks," I say, trying to catch my breath.

"Well, I just wanted to stop by on my way out to see if you need any help on my part?" I look at him blankly. "Press releases, contacts, or anything like that." Now that he mentions it, that would be nice, but it would be asking Jack for help. And I'd rather die than let him help me.

"No thanks." I sit down in my chair and begin typing.

"Suit yourself," he says and just stands there.

"Is that all?" I ask, glancing at him over my shoulder. He leans casually against my desk.

"I think so. Unless you want to grab some lunch. I have an afternoon meeting with some investors, and I could use a sandwich."

"I'd rather beat my head in with a hammer," I mutter under my breath.

"What?" he asks, leaning in. Oh crap. Did I just say that out loud?

"I said why do you want to have lunch with me?" I swivel my chair around to face him.

"Because I'm hungry, and because it's lunch time." He must think I'm a real loser. I mean, how does he know I don't already have lunch plans?

"Thanks, but I can't," I say, avoiding eye contact.

"Why's that?" he asks with a challenging look. Does the guy ever give up?

"Because I'm not hungry," I say as my stomach growls abnormally loud. That's just great. Even my stomach is against me.

"Right," he says, but before I can speak my phone rings.

"Excuse me," I say as I reach for it.

"This is Emma."

"Emma, it's Edward Kelly."

"Hello, Mr. Kelly," I say, glancing up at Jack.

"Please. Call me Edward."

"Okay, Edward. What's up? I was just sitting here with Ja...Jonathan." I feel so weird calling him that.

"Wonderful. Put me on speaker, will you?" I reach over Jack, who has now found residence on the corner of my desk.

"Edward," Jack says, leaning closer to the phone. As he does, his arm brushes my bare skin. A feeling of excitement rushes through my body.

"Hey, hey. What's it looking like today?" Edward says.

"Everything's right on track," Jack says.

"Great. Listen, Emma. I know this is last minute and I'm sure a pretty little thing like you has quite the social life, but my wife and I were wondering if you'd like to join us for dinner tonight. I'd love for you to meet Kathleen, and it may even help with the article."

"I'd love to," I say, beaming with excitement. Just because I won't vote for him doesn't mean I can't like him, right?

"Is seven o'clock okay?"

"Seven sounds great," I say as I pull out my day planner.

"Great. Well, Jonathan has all the details. I'll see you two tonight."

"You two?" I ask, glancing up at Jack in surprise.

"You didn't think I'd make you go alone," Jack says softly in my ear. I look up at him to see a little boy grin plastered to his face.

"Emma? Did I lose you?" Kelly asks.

"No, I'm here," I say weakly into the phone.

"Okay. Well, I'll see you tonight then." He hangs up before either of us have a chance to respond. Unbelievable, I think as I click the phone off.

"Why didn't you tell me ... ?" I start, but wheel around and see that Jack is gone. Right. Whatever. Back to work.

21

When five o'clock rolls around, I'm forced to call Jack because he's nowhere in sight. I hate calling guys, even when it's work related. I dial the first six digits and then hang up.

Okay Emma, relax. This is Jack. Don't be stupid. You hate the guy. Who cares what he thinks? I take a deep breath and dial his number again. My heart pounds in my chest as I wait for him to pick up.

"Hello," he says after the longest three rings of my life. I think I'm gonna barf.

"Um ... hey, uh, Jack. It's Emma. Emma Mosley." What was that? How many Emma's does he know?

"Hey, Emma Mosley," he says with a laugh.

"Did I get you at a bad time?"

"As good as any," he says warmly. "Sorry I haven't called. The meeting ran late, and I had to run some errands." I hear children laughing in the background.

"Where are you?" I ask suspiciously.

"Oh, just out and about," he responds vaguely.

"Do I hear kids?" I press. He sighs.

"I'm at the hospital."

"Are you okay?" I ask quickly. I may have wanted Jack to get sick, but I only meant with something curable, like a bad rash on his butt.

"Yeah, I'm fine. I'm just visiting someone."

"Who?" Boy, I really do sound like Lois Lane.

"A few of my buddies."

"Your what?" I ask.

"Can you say hi to my friend Emma?" I hear him say in the distance.

"Hi Emma," I hear in unison. Oh my gosh! He's at the children's hospital.

"Oh," I say completely dumbfounded. I'm suddenly taken back to the conversation we had a few days ago. The one where I assumed he'd never even seen a hospital before.

"Do you visit there often?" I ask. Open mouth. Insert foot.

"Whenever I'm in Boston," he says. "Which has been a lot lately."

"Oh," I say again. I'm a terrible, terrible person. I want to cry. "Look Jack, I'm really sorry I accused you of—"

"Don't," he interrupts.

"I want to," I say sternly. "I was completely out of line when I accused you of being heartless. I ... I ..."

"Don't sweat it." Awkward silence.

"Okay. Well, I totally forgot why I called." Seriously, my mind is a complete blank. It's like dialing someone's number and then forgetting who it was you dialed. I hate it when that happens.

"Emma?" he says after a moment of silence.

"Huh? What?" I say as I snap out of it. "I lost my train of thought." Why do I always do that with him?

"You were probably calling about dinner." Oh yeah. "Sorry I ran off before I got to tell you why I scheduled it. I had an urgent phone call." Maybe he scheduled it just to be with me. Hey, just because I don't like the dude doesn't mean I don't want him to fall all over me.

"Let me guess. You thought it'd be good for me to see him with his wife because she's his backbone."

"Very good," he says proudly.

"And you're tagging along so I don't have to be alone with them."

"You know me too well," he laughs. I think not, but I'd really like to. No, I wouldn't. Oh my gosh. I can't even control my thoughts anymore.

"So my question is," I say slowly, "why don't you think I can get a date of my own?"

"Oh, there's no question about that," he says confidently. "I just want your date to be me." He's totally trying to play me again. Well not this time.

"Why don't you just bring your girlfriend?" I ask defensively.

"Because she's not writing the story." So that's why he's coming. To baby-sit. Well, I'm perfectly capable of having an adult conversation with well-to-do people.

"So where should I meet you?" I ask in defeat.

"I can pick you up," he offers. Are you joking? I'd rather make out with Lyle Lovett.

"That's okay," I say quickly.

"Okay, Miss Independent. The reservation is at Clio at 7 PM."

"I'll see you there," I say and hang up. Do you want to know a secret? I have this gut-wrenching feeling that there's so much more to Jack than I know, but I'm so frustrated because I can't know it. And I'm even more frustrated because I find myself wanting to know him. What's wrong with me?

I turn my attention back to my article, but the phone rings almost immediately.

"This is Emma."

"Stop being so stubborn and let me pick you up," he says.

"Why?"

"Because that's what guys do. You know, you didn't strike me as a feminist when we first met, but I'm beginning to think otherwise." And you didn't strike me as a two-timer, I want to say, but I refrain.

"Begin to think all you want but that just shows how little you know me," I say airily.

"That's just it, Emma. You won't let me know you."

"That's because the last time I checked, you had a girlfriend."

"So I'm not allowed to be your friend or drive you to dinner?" he asks. "You had no objections to lunch the other day."

"That's before I knew you were dating Miss Perfection."

"Emma," he says softly. I hate when he says my name like that. It makes me want to melt. And I don't know why because I hardly know him. But never in my life have I ever wanted to know another person so badly. Oh my gosh. When did I start feeling this way?

"I'll see you there," I say quietly.

"Wait," he cuts in, but I hang up. What does he want from me? I'm trying so hard to be professional, to keep my guard up, but he's making it so difficult. Why can't he just be the selfish man I assumed he was? The guy who writes a check for cancer-stricken children. The jerk who dates supermodels like Tall Skinny Cappuccino.

I start typing again, but I can't concentrate. Does Jack really go to the hospital once a week? I should check the visitor's log. I stand up to stretch. Gosh, these pants are tight. I unbutton the top button and head home.

22

"You look beautiful," Edward says as he and Jack stand to greet me. I do look pretty good, if I must say so myself. I'm wearing an off-the-shoulder sweater and my favorite black satin pants. I even rolled my hair in school-girl ringlets. Eat your heart out, Jack Carmichael.

"Thank you," I say, sitting down.

"Emma, this is my wife, Kathleen," Edward says. "Honey, this is Emma Mosley."

"It's a pleasure to meet you," I say, reaching across the table to take her thin little hand. What a well-put-together woman. Clad in a mint green suit, this woman is the essence of tact. And that hair! Not one fly-away. I'm impressed.

"Hey, Emma," Jack says as I look everywhere but in front of me. He would have to look good, wouldn't he? I try to avoid his gaze as long as possible, which isn't for very long. I love how his wavy, Hugh Grant hair falls in front of his dark eyes. And you can tell it annoys him. I smile as I watch him gently push it away from his face. Oh, man. He had to show me his scar.

"Hey, Jack," I say politely, placing my napkin in my lap. My mom would be so proud that I remembered to do that.

We make small talk until our appetizers arrive. As the plate is passed around, I attempt to decline whatever it is that's in front of me. What is that? Bird poop?

"You have to try the escargot," Edward insists.

"No really. I'm good." Why couldn't we have gone somewhere simple like Taco Bell?

"Come on," Jack says with a nudge. "Live a little. I dare you." Never one to turn down a dare, I cram a huge spoonful into my mouth. Almost instantly, I spit it out into my napkin. Both Edward and Kathleen stop talking and look at me curiously.

"I'm so sorry," I say between gulps of water. "But I think this is rotten or something. It tastes like ..."

"Fish eggs," Jack suggests, trying not to laugh.

"Here, eat this," Kathleen says kindly and hands me a cracker. Edward and Jack laugh hysterically as I cram it into my mouth.

"I'm glad we're all mature adults here," I joke, though inside I'm furious at Jack for making me look stupid. I finish off my glass of water.

"So, Emma," Kathleen says as she leans forward, "are you seeing anyone special?" I so badly want to lie, but I know better.

"No," I say as I reach for Jack's water.

"Well, it just so happens that I have two handsome boys, both unattached," she says with a smile. This is definitely not the way I intended to start the evening. What happened to discussing politics?

"You'll have to forgive my wife," Edward interrupts, placing a hand on Kathleen's. "She's always on the lookout for the children."

"Oh Edward," she says, smiling at him, "you know I'm only half serious."

For the next two hours, Jack and I laugh hysterically as we listen to stories about the Kellys and their three children.

"Well, we better get going," Edward says, rising to his feet. "I have an early meeting tomorrow. Can I give either of you a ride home?" He helps Kathleen into her fur coat.

"I'm okay," I say as I finish off my coffee. "But thank you so much for dinner. I had a wonderful time."

"Thank you for your company," Jack says as he gets to his feet. "I'll be in touch." He shakes Edward's hand and kisses Kathleen on the cheek. I stand and do the inverse.

"Take care," Kathleen calls back as they exit the restaurant.

"I want that," I say, looking toward where the Kellys exited.

"What?" asks Jack, sitting down again.

"A marriage like that. Someone I still like after twenty years."

"So you want to get married then?" he asks.

"Of course I do," I say, appalled that he would think otherwise. "What about you?"

"Yeah. Someday." I'm sorry, but I don't see him married to Natasha.

"Ever been close?" I ask without thinking.

"Yeah," he says quietly. "You?"

"Yeah."

"Want to talk about it?" he asks.

"Nope? You?"

"Another day," he says as he sips his black coffee.

"So I think Zoë's getting pretty close," I add, making it completely obvious that I want to change the subject.

"Really?"

"Yeah. I set her up with some doctor I met ..." I start, but trail off.

"Let me guess. That you weren't interested in," he says, smiling. How does he do that? I open my mouth to tell him the story and then it hits me. Oh my gosh, Michael! I totally forgot about him. Now would be a great time to tell him that I know what happened, but I can't help but wonder if it really did happen. It doesn't make any sense. Jack would never do something like that. I just know he wouldn't.

"You know what? It's getting late," he says as he gets to his feet. Why don't I want this dinner to end? I hate Jack. Or at least I'm supposed to. All of a sudden a bad book review and an accusation from a guy I didn't trust to begin with don't seem to hold up anymore. But the fact that he has a girlfriend does: a girlfriend that may be breathtakingly beautiful, but an absolute snob.

"Can I give you a lift home?" he asks as we exit The Elliott Hotel. Why am I wanting to say yes?

"No thanks," I say, hailing a taxi. Where could this go anyway? He has a girlfriend. And regardless of the validity of Michael's accusations, I can't fall for my future brother-in-law's enemy. Can you imagine Christmas?

"You know, I don't think you hate me as much as you think you do," he says, as if reading my thoughts.

"Excuse me?" I ask as I turn to face him.

"Emma, you are one of the most stubborn people I've ever met. And more than you dislike me, you fear letting down your tough-girl wall." I swear the man reads my journal. I look at him blankly.

"And I think you were smoking some crack in the bathroom?" I say, rounding the block to a busier street corner. He laughs loudly and follows after me. Good, now we can change the subject. A few moments pass and we're still standing next to each other in awkward silence. "So what?" I ask out of nowhere as a taxi pulls up. I hate awkward silence, though it doesn't seem to bother him all that much.

"So, it wouldn't hurt to let your guard down and be nice to me," he says as he opens the taxi door for me. His arm is practically around me. Oh, I have to pee.

"I can't," I say, looking in the other direction. At what, I couldn't tell you. Gosh, this is straight out of a movie.

"Try," he says softly. I feel goose bumps forming all over my body. He's less than six inches from me, staring at me with those intense, dark eyes of his. My body has gone numb, though the only thing I can think about is how much I regret eating garlic for dinner. Medically, I can only hold my breath for so long, you know? After falling in a trance for a few more moments, I snap out of it.

"Listen Romeo, why don't you save your lines for some other Juliet because I'm not falling for them again?"

"Again?" he asks.

"Drop the act Carmichael," I say as I shut the door and the car drives off. Oh great, I just vocally admitted my feelings not only to myself, but to him.

Why did I have to say that? I think as I climb into bed. For the past hour, I've been going over and over tonight's dinner. Oh man, I think as I switch off my lamp. Jack knows I have feelings for him. Worse, I know I have feelings for him. I mean, I started feeling "the thing" in my stomach a couple days ago, but I thought it was just a hunger pain so I ate a cookie. I didn't realize it was "the thing."

Oh man. This would happen to me. Life would be so much easier if I was just normal, but I'm not. I first realized it when the movie *ET* came out. Every girl on the block was in love with Elliot. They had his posters and were in his fan club. It was like Beetle Mania all over again. But of course I had a crush on ET.

I pull the covers over my head, but it's no use. I can't sleep. My mind is thinking about Jack. How is it that he's able to read through my wall? No one has been able to do that, not even Caleb. And how on God's green earth is he able to make me go weak at the knees? I thought that was just a metaphor. But it's not. I've turned into "that girl." I am trying so hard to mask my feelings for him with abruptness, but deep down my heart leaps at the very thought of him. And people are starting to see through that. Maybe if I were meaner to him, if I avoided him more, then maybe he will go away. It's worth a shot.

In attempts to fall asleep, I brainstorm different ways in which I can avoid Jack tomorrow. I could act like I lost my voice. Then he wouldn't try to talk to me. Or I could tell him that it's against my religion to talk to men. I could even cover my head like they do in the Middle East. Maybe I'm overreacting. I probably won't even see him. But just in case I do, I'm going to wear my red satin shirt. Oh, and a beret.

23

Not that I care, but it's noon and I still haven't seen Jack. And I know he's here because I saw his car parked on the street, not that I was looking. That would be psycho.

A few moments later, he emerges from the elevator and begins walking toward my office. Great, what do I do? Without thinking I pick up my phone and pretend to be engrossed in some important conversation.

"If I didn't know better, I'd say you were trying to avoid talking to me," he says, crossing his arms and smiling at me.

"Please," I say as I sheepishly hang up the phone. "If I were avoiding you, then that would mean you intimidate me, which you don't." Gosh, he looks good. He's wearing all black, like he stepped out of a Brooks Brothers catalog. But I don't care because today I choose to hate him.

"True," he says and then pauses. Um, awkward silence. What do I do? I look around the room, then at the floor. Gosh, I'm looking everywhere I can but into his eyes. I just don't think I can handle it.

"So, um," I start. I cross my legs and kick my foot nervously.

"So, um, there's a press conference for Kelly at three today. I know it's last minute, but can you make it?"

"Isn't it my job to make it?" I say defensively.

"Do you know where my office is?" he asks with a half smile.

"Why would I know where your office is?" I cross my arms.

"I'm sorry. I thought you knew everything," he says as he reaches across me for a sticky note.

"Do I detect an attempt of sarcasm?" I say without looking up. He's too close for me to look up.

"Here's the address, Yoda. I'm sure you'll find it." He scribbles down the address. Naturally, it's in Beacon Hill, the ritziest area of town. "I'll see you there," he says as he sticks it on my forehead and walks away. As soon as he leaves, Gwen peers her head into my cube.

"What's going on with you two?" she says, sitting on my desk. I peel the note off my forehead.

"Come again?" I ask, a little taken back.

"Emma, please! I can feel the attraction from my cube."

"Have you been drinking?" I ask. I can feel my face turning red. Gwen throws her hands up.

"I only call it like I see it." Like she sees it? Apart from our staff meeting the other day, when has she even been in the same room as Jack and me?

"Well, then you should see that there's absolutely nothing going on with Jonathan Carmichael and me." Oh my gosh, my fear has been confirmed. Ever since I saw the movie *The Truman Show*, I've been a little concerned that my entire life is being filmed on camera. And if that were true, I'd just die. Just this morning, I crashed to the floor when putting my pants on.

"Fine," she says, crossing her arms and leaning back. "Then I won't tell you what I overheard this morning."

"What did you overhear this morning?" Jack chimes in.

Gwen and I both turn sharply to see Jack standing behind us. Oh crap. How long has he been standing there? Gwen and I stare at Jack.

"There's an interesting article about Kelly's opponent on page four," he says as he drops a copy of today's *Boston Globe* between Gwen and me. I look up at him blankly and then at Gwen who seems to wear the same expression. "I thought you'd want to take a look at it." I'm still at a loss for words. He turns to leave, but before I can say anything, he wheels around to face us. "Oh, and next time you decide to gossip, look behind you," he says with a laugh and walks off gallantly. Hot dog, he has the backside of a baseball player. I bury my face in my hands.

"Oh my gosh, Gwen."

"I wonder how long he was standing there," she says as she moves back into my cube.

"So tell me what you heard," I say as I look behind me.

"Well, this morning I was in the elevator with Jonathan and Natasha, and he seemed very annoyed with her." She moves in closer. "I think they just had a fight or something."

"So they fight? What's the big deal?" I ask as I reach for my mouse. Gosh, I haven't checked my e-mail all day.

"Well, if you would let me finish," she says.

"Sorry. Go on." I give her my full attention.

"Then about an hour ago, I followed him to the coffee room and overheard his phone call," Gwen whispers as if revealing who shot JFK.

"No you didn't!" I gasp.

"I most certainly did, and it's a good thing I did because he called his office, and apparently there was some mess up with the flowers."

"What do you mean?" I ask, leaning in.

"Emma, he only meant to send one sunflower, and it

was meant for you." For me? But why? "I think he ordered another dozen roses for some sick client of his or something, but KaBloom messed it all up." I lean back in my chair.

"But that doesn't mean anything. He just knows I love sunflowers. Besides, he was already getting Natasha a dozen." I scratch my head in contemplation.

"Then how did one flower make its way to your desk?" She crosses her arms in satisfaction.

"There has to be some logical explanation for that." I tap my fingers nervously on the desk.

"Well then tell me this. Does Natasha look like a sunflower kind of girl?" Come to think of it, she doesn't.

"Gwen, Jack and I had another argument last night so he was probably utilizing the company's budget to keep his employee happy. That's all it was."

"So it's Jack now?" she asks. "You are in such denial." She hops off my desk.

"Denial? Gwen, please. The guy was doing what he does best. You should have seen his arrogance last night. You should have seen him all—"

"Whatever," she interjects and turns to leave.

"Gwen," I say but she's already gone.

I resume my typing, but can't concentrate. I can't stop thinking about what Gwen said. Were the flowers really meant for me? But why would Jack send me flowers? And why is he being nice to me when he knows I hate him? Though I can't for the life of me remember why I hate him. I mean, the guy did lead me on. Kind of. But what if he really meant what he said? That he never thought he would see me again. And what if, in the back of my mind, I thought the same thing? Maybe that's why I let my guard down. And what if he's not really a jerk? What if he's just dating the wrong person? We've all done it. I know I have.

And what about Michael? Sure I've had my reservations about the guy, but is he really capable of making up such an elaborate story about Jack? And why would he? What could he possibly gain from that? Man, I can't decide what's worse: A shady Jack or a dishonest Michael. If Jack's a liar, that means I'm working and secretly enjoying a sleezeball. But if Michael is lying, that means Zoë's in trouble. Oh, man. My brain hurts.

But what if Michael is the backstabber, and Zoë and I have been duped? You know what, I'm sick of this. I'm going to ask Michael right now and get this all out in the open. The worst that can happen is that he'll kill any interest I have in Jack, which is a good thing seeing as he's dating my boss. I throw on my coat and head for the hospital.

Half an hour later, I'm standing before an 80-year-old receptionist who acts as if she's guarding the cure to cancer.

"Young lady, I told you. He's at lunch in the staff room." She resumes her typing.

"Great. Is it back this way?" I ask as I point to my left.

"Yes, but you can't go back there." She glares at me over her bifocals.

"Why not?" I ask as sweetly as possible. This old hag is a real patience pusher.

"Because you're not a doctor."

"So let me get this straight." I lean over the counter and look her in the eye. "I have to put myself through med school just to have lunch with my friend?"

"Don't sass me," she says, wagging a crooked finger. Okay. Where's the camera? Surely people aren't really this dumb.

"Ma'am, I'd never intentionally sass you. It's just that this is urgent." I clasp my hands together for effect.

"I'm sorry, but security is more important."

"Do I look like a terrorist?" I ask. What is it with people and their stinkin' power trips? It's so annoying.

"Miss, I'm afraid I'm going to have to ask you to leave," she says as she gets up from her chair.

"What?" Am I really getting kicked out of the hospital? The overhead intercom beeps.

"The charts for patient #456 are needed in Room 17." The woman sends me a withering look.

"I want you to be gone when I return." I smile innocently.

"Yes ma'am." Sucker, I think as I watch her disappear down the corridor.

I wait around the corner for a few minutes and when the coast is clear, I slip past the desk and search for the staff room. I peek my head in, but no one's there. I look around the wing. No sign of Michael. Where is he? Finally, I see what looks like a young medical student walk by.

"Excuse me," I say, stopping him. "Do you know where Dr. Lancaster is?" I've always liked a man in scrubs. What a hottie.

"Are you his girlfriend?" he asks warily.

"Gosh, no," I say with a fake laugh. Then I realize I could get in trouble for sneaking back here, so I tell a little white lie. "I'm his sister. Why do you ask?"

"Because I'm on the lookout for his girlfriend." He looks around.

"Why's that?" I ask casually, leaning in.

"Because he's indisposed at the moment, if you know what I mean." He smiles and nudges me with his elbow. What does that mean? Before I can even formulate a question, the guy walks away. This is precisely why I never dated a doctor. They're too busy for their own good.

"Indisposed?" I ask myself as I slump into a nearby chair. Is that medical lingo for him being in the bathroom?

Before I have time to contemplate, I see Zoë's friend Samantha emerge from a dark room. As I open my mouth to call out her name, I see Michael following her out. What is going on here? I jump up and crouch behind a large plant. They stand for a minute, talking in low voices, then Michael glances around and pulls Samantha in for a finale kiss. My jaw hits the floor. As much as I want to turn my head, I stare at them in a state of shock. As the two continue their make-out session, I get up and walk away as fast as I can.

I exit the hospital trying my best not to hyperventilate. What was that and why did I have to be the one to see it? Did I really just stumble across Michael and Samantha making out? Maybe I'm reading into things. Maybe he was giving her an exam or something. Yeah right. He's totally cheating on Zoë. Worse, he's cheating on Zoë with a friend of hers. Worse than that, I have to be the one to tell her.

I look down at my watch and see that it's 2:30. I have to be at that stupid press conference in thirty minutes. What am I going to do? This is all my fault. I'm the one who set her up with that scumbag. What is it with men? Do they receive special instructions on how to break a girl's heart? Poor Zoë. She's going to be devastated.

By the time I reach Jack's office I want to kick myself. Why didn't I jump up and say something? I could've let them have it. I could've even snapped a picture with my camera phone, yet I hid behind some stupid plant like a coward.

I climb the stairs to Jack's office and step into the nicest lobby I've ever seen. It almost feels like a log cabin. The walls are made of wood, and there's a plethora of bay windows giving a panoramic view of the cobble-stoned streets of Beacon Hill. I make my way into the press room and spot Gwen.

"What are you doing here?" I ask, taking the seat next to her.

"Natasha still wants me coming to these things," she says, rolling her eyes. Right. Or maybe she sent Gwen because she still doesn't trust me. "By the way, I hear her and Jonathan are on the rocks."

"You are relentless," I say jokingly. She pats my arm.

"I'm just looking out for my girl."

"Do me a favor and keep your day job," I whisper as the press conference begins.

As Jack gets up to speak, I go into daydream mode. Maybe I should confront Michael first? I could bring my tape recorder like they do in the movies. Or maybe I should just go straight to Zoë. You know what? It doesn't matter because either way she's going to be devastated. I can't win.

About thirty minutes into the press conference, I hear my cell phone go off. Shoot a monkey. I thought I put that thing on vibrate. Jack stops talking and like the domino effect, heads begin turning to my row. As "I Can't Get No Satisfaction" goes off repeatedly, I panic and kick my purse in Gwen's direction. She's way more cool and collected than I am.

"Excuse me," Gwen says as she digs in my purse and turns my phone off. Jack continues, but I see him hiding his smile.

"Call your sister," she whispers as she zips my purse.

"You hate me, don't you?" I ask as I pretend to listen to Jack.

"You have no idea," she says. She starts taking notes, but I see her smile.

After another hour of gibberish, the press conference comes to an end. Finally. After declining Gwen's offer to share a cab, I make a beeline for Edward Kelly.

"Emma," he says as I approach him. "How are you, dear?" He kisses my cheek.

"I'm wonderful. I just wanted to say hello and thank you again for last night."

"Aren't you sweet! Kathleen and I had a wonderful time," he says. He and Kathleen are the modern day

Jack and Jackie Kennedy. I'll have to mention that in my article. Edward leans toward me. "I'd watch out if I were you. I think my wife wants to adopt you. By the way, how's the article coming?"

"Oh, it's great. You're a very easy man to write for."

"Well good. You call me if you have any questions," he says. He shakes my hand. "It's great to see you again, Emma."

"You too, Edward," I call after him.

"I can't get no ... satisfaction," I hear Jack sing in my ear. Chills run up my spine as I take in his hot whisper. What is wrong with me? I turn to face him.

"Gwen wanted me to apologize for the cell phone incident," I say with a straight face. "She's so embarrassed." I look around the room in order to avoid his gaze. I'm sure my cheeks are as pink as Barbie's wardrobe. Why am I lying? This guy has seen me do yoga, and he's removed shoes from my big feet. Why should I be embarrassed that my cell phone went off in a meeting?

"You're a terrible liar," he says with a half grin. I look up into his slate eyes and immediately regret doing so. My gosh, the man is beautiful. He could stop traffic. For a moment, I'm unable to speak. Literally, I'm unable to formulate words because I'm lost in his gaze.

"I'm sorry," I admit as I come to. "All I've done today is lie, so you Jack, are the first person who gets the real story." I play nervously with my Burberry scarf. "Yes, that was my cell phone that went off. And yes, I like to download cheesy rings at odd hours of the night. And while we're on the subject, I happen to love Britney Spears' music thank you very much." He looks at me with a smirk. Sometimes I wonder where my words come from. Seriously, isn't my brain supposed to filter stupid comments like that?

"While we're confessing," he says as he nudges me with his arm, "I stayed up late downloading Jessica

Simpson songs on my phone." I send out a loud laugh. Gosh, he's cute. And funny. One would think Jack's a serious, intense person, but he has such a light-hearted humor. It's almost like comic relief. I give him a toothy grin. Man, it is impossible to hate him. He's too irresistible.

"Listen," he says more formally, "I have some papers for you, but I left them at the hotel. Would you mind coming to get them?" I look at him with my brows crossed. "I'm really pressed for time today, and it would really help me out a lot."

"What sort of papers?" I ask, as though I'm afraid he's going to kidnap me or something. But would that be such a terrible thing?

"A few news clippings, and there's also a bunch of stuff for Natasha." The very utterance of her name makes me sick to my stomach. Everything in me wants to say no to this guy. I mean, why can't Miss High-and-Mighty trot her little stilettos over here and get them herself?

"Is this how you get women to come up to your hotel room?" I joke in an attempt to buy more time. I even cross my arms for effect. Crap. What do I do?

"I do what I can," he says teasingly. I open my mouth to say not on his life will I go anywhere with him, but he beats me to it. "I'll meet you in the lobby in five minutes so don't even think about taking a cab."

24

Okay, what am I doing? I'm sitting here in the car with Jack. How on God's green earth did he con me into going to his hotel room? And why did I buy into it? He probably has some black book full of girlfriends all over the globe. Though I must admit, he really knows how to make a girl feel special. Stop it Emma, bad!

We take the elevator up to the top floor, where naturally, he's staying because it's the best floor in the hotel. And do you believe there's a couch in the elevator? It takes everything I have not to pull a Julia Roberts a la *Pretty Woman* by throwing my leg up and saying, "Well color me happy, there's a sofa in here for two." But I don't.

"So this is home," I say as I attempt to break the ice. Oh my gosh, his bathroom is bigger than my apartment!

"Yeah, well, I've been too busy to look for an apartment. Besides, I'm not sure how much time I'll be spending here." He offers me a drink as I take a seat.

"You don't like us Bostonians," I say playfully. "I can't say that I blame you. We're not exactly known for our kindness."

"It's not that." Jack sits down across from me. "I just miss New York."

"Well, what about your family? Don't you miss them?"

"Very much. That's partly why I opened an office in San Francisco. It gives me an excuse to see them." He takes a sip of his drink and looks at me interestedly. "What about you? Have you ever thought about moving?" I squirm a little in my seat.

"Well, I almost moved to New York when I graduated, but I backed out at the last minute." I tuck my hair behind my ear.

"Why's that?"

"Because my family's here," I lie. So much for telling the truth today. Jack cocks an eyebrow.

"Good one. Now try telling me the real reason." The man can see straight through me. I sigh heavily and look at my hands.

"Because New York is a dream, and I don't want to ruin it by actually living there."

"How would that ruin it?" Jack asks with an amused look on his face.

"It'd become a reality that I'd stop appreciating." Now that I'm saying it out loud, it sounds a bit ridiculous. Jack sets down his drink on the glass coffee table.

"Do you want to know what your problem is?" he says, leaning toward me.

"My problem? I don't have a problem," I say, crossing my arms, though secretly I'm thinking: Which one? He looks at me as if waiting for my answer. I roll my eyes. "Okay, Dr. Phil. What's my problem?"

"Your expectations are too high."

"Excuse me?" I ask, dropping my hands.

"You expect too much out of people. It's a sweet thought and all, but I bet you're always disappointed." That's so true.

"That is so untrue," I say defensively. I get up and walk to the window.

"Tell me something..." he starts, following me. I turn around to face him.

"So how about those papers?" He opens his mouth to continue, then closes it and smiles.

"I'll go get them," he says with a laugh.

Okay. So I know I'm not supposed to care what other people think about me, but how can I not be bothered by what he's saying? He's known me for what, a week, and already he's criticizing me? I mean, look at his life. Look at his nut case of a girlfriend. The worst thing is that I do care what he says. His opinion matters a lot to me. No it doesn't. I won't allow it to. I'm rubber, and he's glue. I need to be rubber. I have to be rubber!

"So maybe I do expect a lot from people," I say, following him into his bedroom. "But it's a lot better than expecting the worst of people. That's just sad." Here it goes. Mt. Emma's volcano of emotions has just erupted. Jack looks up from a stack of folders on his desk. Gosh, he's neat as a pin.

"No, Emma, it's reality. People mess up. We're human."

"Sounds like an excuse to screw up if you ask me," I huff.

"What's this really about?" he asks gently. He steps closer to me.

"Excuse me?" I step back and hit the wall.

"What's really eating you?" How does he know?

"You've known me for a week, and what? You think you can read me?"

"All you have to do is say you don't want to talk about it," he says, returning to his desk. I walk over to his desk.

"Why do guys cheat?" I ask, slumping into his chair. Ouch, I think I just sat on a stapler.

"Huh?" he asks, a little caught off guard.

"Is the fact that we're human grounds for cheating?" I place the stapler on his desk.

"Well, I can't speak for every man," he says with a

wry smile. I look straight into his eyes.

"Then speak for yourself."

"Not all guys cheat, Emma," he says quietly, pulling over a chair and sitting next to me.

"You mean to tell me that you've never cheated on a girl?" I say through a laugh.

"No," he says with full confidence.

"Then why did you, um, never mind." I look away in frustration.

"Why did I what?" He leans in. Now would be the perfect time to ask him why he took me to lunch knowing full well that he had no intention of following through. But of course, I wuss out.

"So I caught Zoë's boyfriend with another woman today," I blurt, pulling my knees into my chest.

"Oh," he says leaning back in his chair.

"It was just before the press conference." Why am I confiding in Jack? And why is he so easy to talk to?

"Well that explains your foul mood," he says, nudging me with his elbow. I give him a half smile as if to thank him for putting up with me. I know I'm not a cup of tea.

"And the girl is a friend of hers. Her only friend, in fact." I swallow my tears. "I don't know what to do." I run my fingers through my hair, and call me crazy but I feel Jack staring at me. Probably because it's so greasy.

"Tell her," he says as if that were some easy solution.

"Are you always so practical?" I say, throwing down my hands.

"It's not a simple situation, but the solution is very easy." I raise my brows. "Wouldn't you want to know if she found someone cheating on you?"

"But it's my fault."

"Why? Because you set them up?"

"Well, yeah." I tap my fingers nervously on the arm of the chair.

"You didn't know this would happen. And more importantly, stop bearing the burdens of other people. It's no wonder you're exhausted."

"But it's gonna devastate her." Jack shakes his head. "She'll survive."

"Maybe." We sit there in silence for a moment, and in that moment, I almost feel like he's looking into my soul. But that's crazy.

"Are those the papers?" I ask, snapping out of it. I've got to get out of here. I can almost hear Jenny saying, "Run, Forest, run." Jack glances at the papers in his hand.

"Yes. Thank you so much, Emma." He stands up and I follow him to the door. "This really helps me out. I have about ten more meetings today."

"Don't mention it," I say while Jack helps me into my coat. So much for being mean to Jack. Okay. From here on out, I promise to only see Jack at the office. I mean, this is ridiculous. We can't be friends. It's not right.

"Let me walk you out," he says as he closes the door behind us and we walk to the elevator. Why my heart is beating faster than a jack rabbit, I don't know. Just standing next to him makes me excited. As I inhale his signature scent of fresh laundry combined with a hint of cologne, a feeling of nostalgia runs through me. It takes me back to the day we met. It already seems like ages ago. Things were so easy back then. I was walking on Cloud Nine. Now everything is so complicated. I feel stuck. Here I am falling for a man who's dating somebody else. Somebody so beneath him. And if he really saw me, if he's really been looking into my soul all this time, then why hasn't he tried to win me? Why hasn't he done what he has to do to get to me? Why doesn't he get weak at the knees at the nearness of me? As I glance at him I can't help but wonder what's going on in his head. Am I just somebody who amuses him or is this real? Because it feels so real to me.

"So, how long have you been matchmaking your friends, Miss Woodhouse?" he asks, smiling. I pause in attempts to conceal my surprise. I thought Jack was lying when he said he read *Emma*.

"Doesn't that just make me nosy?" I say with a smirk.

"I think it makes you sweet." He turns and presses the down button on the elevator.

"But I thought you said ..." I start.

"Well, if you hadn't darted out in the middle of our debate, you'd have seen that I was just messing with you. I didn't know you'd get so worked up." I shrug my shoulders in defeat.

"That's what I do." I lean against the wall.

"Yeah, I've noticed that," he says as we both laugh.

"So you didn't hate the book?" I ask a little too eagerly. Jack shakes his head.

"No, Emma. I didn't hate the book."

"You never cease to amaze me, Jack Carmichael."

He opens his mouth to say something, but the elevator opens and he's interrupted. For a second I think I'm dreaming. I even pinch myself. Nope. This is definitely real. I swear, my life should be titled "What Not to Do."

"Emma," Caleb says, stepping out. Okay, there are like a million people in this metropolis. And only five rooms on this private floor. Why do I keep running into the same people? After a brief moment of awkward silence, Jack jumps in.

"Hi. I'm Jonathan Carmichael," he says, extending his hand out to Caleb. Ten points for Jack.

"Caleb Callaghan," he says. He takes Jack's hand and shakes it warily. Jack gives me a little nudge, but I'm still mute. Caleb and I are just staring at each other, while Jack holds the elevator with his foot. He nudges me a little harder, and I'm still unable to speak. Jack clears his throat.

"So, how do you two know each other?" he asks cheerfully.

"Um," he says as he looks at me intensely, "I guess you could say we go way back." Suddenly I find my voice. "Yeah, it's a really funny story," I blurt. "You see, Caleb was my college boyfriend. I was ready to move to London to marry him, but he dumped me because he didn't have the guts to stand up to his father. I guess waking up with money was more important than waking up next to me." I shrug my shoulders and look at Caleb with a smirk. Jack's smile vanishes.

"Emma," Caleb says, reaching out for my arm. I yank it quickly and look away as tears form in my eyes. I can't let Caleb see me cry. Oh, I need an angel.

Jack looks at my face and without hesitation grabs my hand and pulls me into the elevator. Unable to speak, I back into the corner and face the wall as the doors shut. I can't believe that just happened. I can't believe I just said that to Caleb. After all these years, I'm still so angry with him.

We reach the ground floor and step into the lobby. I'm not sure where I'm going, but I just walk numbly next to Jack. I don't know what's worse, the fact that I just saw Caleb and mouthed off to him or the fact that Jack just saw me do that.

"Do you want to talk about it?" he asks as we exit the Ritz.

"You pretty much heard everything," I mumble. I look away as my eyes start to water again, which seems to be a regular occurrence for me lately. My poor tear ducts are so confused. I take a few deep breaths and try to think of something funny.

"Listen," Jack says as we stop under the outside heater. "What do you say we blow off the next couple of hours and go somewhere?"

"But what about the papers?" I ask, looking down at my feet. "And your meetings? You have so much to do."

"Forget about that." He raises my chin. "I could use a

break. What do you say?" he asks as his car pulls up. I know I shouldn't add another piece of drama to my life, but how can I say no to this man? He's standing there in his long black coat, and I can see his cold breath as he talks. This is a picture-perfect moment. I feel like Lady Guinevere, and he's my Sir Lancelot. Except that instead of a horse, he has a Range Rover, but you get the idea.

"All right," I say as I take his hand and crawl into his car. Crap! I think I was supposed to enter butt first.

"I've never seen an entrance quite like that," he says as he gets in and shuts the door.

"You automatically assume that I'm a lady," I say lightly. Of course, he just laughs, which makes me feel good. Very few things feel as good as the joy of making somebody laugh. He flips on the radio and we pull off. I have no idea where we're going, but I don't really care.

"Do you want to talk about it?" he asks again. Say no, Emma. Say no. You can't form a friendship with this guy.

"Why not," I say. For the next fifteen minutes I give Jack a summary of my relationship with Caleb. I tell him about the trip to London, the breakup, and bumping into him at the lobster benefit. I even mention the tampon incident, though I wish I hadn't because he laughed for a good five minutes.

"So that's why you left early," he says.

"Well, that and ..." I cut myself off, though I'm afraid he knows I'm talking about him. "I guess when it rains, it pours. You know the other day when we met Edward for lunch?"

"Yeah."

"Well, I had just gotten off the phone with my best friend and roommate who was all of a sudden moving to New York." I inhale sharply.

"How'd you take it?" He glances over at me. Okay. We've hit a fork in our relationship here. I can either be the strong, I-don't-need-anyone Emma or I can show him my heart.

"I'm happy for her, but of course there's room for me to be sad."

"Well naturally. She's your best friend."

"Exactly," I say. And my spooning buddy, I think but dare not say.

"So are you still in love with him?" he asks casually, keeping his eyes on the road. This catches me by surprise because it's not like Jack to push my boundaries.

"I thought it was my job to ask all the blunt questions."

"You're changing the subject," he says seriously. I sigh.

"The thing about Caleb is, well, we were pretty much doomed from the start. I was young and very unaware of the way the world works."

"What do you mean?" he asks.

"I was too naïve to see that money always trumps love," I say bitterly.

"That's not true for everybody," he says, turning toward me. My goodness. The boy has given me goose bumps and butterflies at the same time. That's definitely journal worthy.

"If it's not true for everybody then I wasn't enough for Caleb, which I find a little harder to stomach."

"How can you think that?" he asks as he puts his hand on mine. "Caleb's an idiot if that's why he broke up with you. And call me crazy, but I think you know that, Emma." I quickly pull my hand away and he places it back on the wheel.

"So you and Natasha, huh?" I ask as if I'm just now receiving the memo. I know Gwen is trying to investigate this, but at the rate she's going I'll be ninety by the time I actually hear something concrete.

"Me and Natasha," he repeats.

"Is that all you're gonna give me?" I ask.

"Pretty much," he says shortly.

"Since when did you become so passive?" I demand.

"Since when did you get so inquisitive?" he throws back. He looks at me and grins.

"Come on, Jack. You know I've always been inquisitive." And that's just to his face. If he only knew the amount of time I've spent Googling his name. Oh, and I bought the *People* where he was featured after all.

"Well, there's not really that much to tell," he says casually.

"Okay. I'll just ask you questions then. How long have you been together?" He exhales with a laugh and tightens his grip on the steering wheel.

"About a year." Gulp.

"That's all?" I say, looking out the window. My heart just sunk down to my toes. I hadn't realized it had been that long. Relationship speaking, a year at this age is like three years when you're younger. I bet he's gonna propose soon. Oh man. What if we're on the way to Tiffany's to pick out her ring? He probably needs my help. That's why he was so insistent on me leaving with him. He's going to ask me to try it on. How cruel is that! I hate him.

"Yeah," he says, breaking into my runaway thoughts. "A lot of it has been long distance, so it hasn't really been that long. Look, I know you aren't too keen on her," he interjects.

"Isn't that the understatement of the year?" I mumble. He smiles.

"Look, I would love to be open with you the way you were to me with Caleb, but given the fact that Natasha's your boss, I probably shouldn't talk to you about our relationship troubles."

"Troubles?" I press curiously.

"Did you not hear what I just said?" he says with a laugh.

"I'm a sink when it comes to words I don't want to comprehend," I say sweetly.

"I love your metaphors, Emma. Your outlook on things is so ..."

"Weird?" He shakes his head.

"No, that's not it. You have this unique way of getting people." I'm suddenly feeling something I've never felt before. It's a feeling of being sad and scared and jittery all at the same time. "You're smart. A lot smarter than most people give you credit for." Well, I didn't see that one coming. He thinks I'm smart? Wow. Maybe I should tell him he's too good for Natasha. That he needs to be with me. Would that make me a home wrecker if I said that? Because my friends are always telling me I need to put myself out there more.

"Can I be honest with you about something?" I blurt without thinking. Oh man. There's no turning back now.

"Since when did you need my permission?" he says. Okay, here I go.

"Say hypothetically someone else comes along. Then what?" Maybe I'll just dance around the issue a bit.

"What do you mean?" he asks. He would say that, wouldn't he?

"I mean, how would you handle that? As a guy, I mean. If a girl came along that you thought might ... Oh, never mind. Me and my stupid hypotheticals." I turn away again and look out the window. This conversation is so not going the way I thought it would. I'm so inarticulate. Jack glances over at me.

"Emma, I know what you're trying to say."

"You do?" My face is so red right now. It's getting hot in this car.

"Yeah, and I'm sorry." He's sorry? Okay, I'm sweating. I try to press the window button.

"Can you unlock the windows? It's hot in here." He unlocks the windows and I roll mine down. He pauses a moment.

"I'm sorry that I can't talk about this. Natasha and I are working through some things, but I can't make emotional decisions about you just like that when—"

"I'm not asking you to," I say defensively.

"Well then I'm telling you. I hate that this bothers you, but I can't just—"

"Wait a second. Bothers me?" Oh, no he didn't.

"I know it's not easy working so closely with me, especially when I'm with—"

"Jack," I interrupt sharply, whipping my head around to look at him, "I get it." I get that I'm not good enough for you, I so badly want to say, but he can't know that. He can't ever know that. I can't believe I opened my big mouth. What was I thinking?

"Emma," he starts.

"Can you just take me back to work?" I ask coldly. I lean back and fold my arms across my chest. He knows me well enough to know that I'm full of it, but I don't care. I'm sick of being everybody's second choice.

"Why?" he asks sincerely. Quick question. Why are men so dumb? Take Jack for instance. He went to Columbia and owns his own enterprise, yet he is so oblivious to why I no longer want to ride in the car with him.

"Because I want you to take me back, okay?" I look out the window. I can't bear to look at him because I'm too embarrassed. Gosh, why did I have to say anything? I could kick myself.

"Emma, please don't get upset. I'm trying so hard to do the honorable thing here. I know you've had a rough day, and..."

"Just drive, Jack."

"But—"

"Please," I say as I choke on my words. "Just drive."

A few minutes later, he attempts to make small talk but gets the hint when I turn up the radio. It's 5 PM by the time we return, but I still insist he drop me off at the office.

"Okay," he says as we pull up. I turn to get out, but he grabs my arm.

"What do you want from me, Jack?" I ask hotly.

"Please don't be upset. I hate that I've hurt you. Emma, I wish I could offer you more, but I can't right now. I've got to work through some things." My mind understands what he's saying. It really does, but my heart won't listen to it.

"Then I guess we have nothing else to say to each other," I say and slam the door shut. And for the third time today, my heart falls to my toes.

25

"There you are," Natasha says as soon as I step off the elevator. Naturally she's the first person I'd see after playing hooky all day.

"Oh, hi-ya Natasha, I've just been ..." I start.

"Jonathan told me," she interrupts. I give her a quick glance over. That red suit totally clashes with her auburn hair. Not that I'm one to talk. I mix blue and black all the time, but still. It's her.

"Good. Then I should get back to work," I say brushing past her.

"Can I see you in my office first?" she asks. Where have I heard those exact words before? Oh right. From my high school principal. "It'll only take a second," she adds.

"Uh, sure," I say slowly.

"So, how's the article coming?" she asks as we walk into her office. What's with the small talk? Did Tall Skinny Cappuccino suddenly grow a heart?

"It's great." Though I've only written about half of it, that's for me to know and her not to find out. "Great," she says perkily. "Then I'll expect to have it by the end of the day." Bummer.

"Okay," I say as I turn to leave.

"Listen Emma," she says, closing the door behind her. "I'm not sure what your take on my Jonathan is, but I don't like it." If she's going to give me some lecture on why I have to be nice to Jack, then I'm going to barf.

"There's no problem between Jonathan and me anymore."

"Problem?" she says as she laughs sarcastically. "I wouldn't really call it a problem, Emma."

"Huh?" What is she talking about?

"Oh, stop acting so innocent. It's obvious that you have some sort of crush on him. It's cute and all, really, but let me save you the embarrassment."

"Crush?" I say at a loss for words. I'm still waiting for her to say she's kidding.

"Look, Emma." She leans over her desk and looks me in the eye. "Jonathan's far too nice to say anything, so he's obviously going to play it off. But between us girls, let me just give it to you point blank. You need to back off." I can feel my blood pressure rising. I wonder if I'm about to have an aneurysm.

"Natasha," I say as calmly as possible, "I wouldn't date Jonathan if he were the last man on earth. And you may be my boss, but since this is personal and I assume off the record, let me just give it to you point blank. If there's a problem with your love life then you need to deal with it outside of the workplace. And because this conversation is both unprofessional and inappropriate, I'm ending it right now." With this, I walk out of her office. Every bit of me wants to slam the door shut, but I don't. I act as cool as a cucumber. That is, until she's out of sight.

Oh my gosh, I think as I stomp furiously to my cube. I can't believe that evil woman had the audacity to confront me like that. And what has Jack been telling her? I may have formed some very small, minute feelings for him, but he's initiated everything. He probably called her as soon as I got out of the car to tell her about the stupid entertainment writer who has a crush on him. I'm probably the topic of conversation as they eat caviar and sip champagne by the fire.

Well you know what? If that arrogant jerk thinks he can wine and dine me into thinking he's wonderful, then he's got another thing coming. I'm deeper than that. Sure the guy is gorgeous, but I see past the surface. At least I thought I did. I thought we both did. Shame on me for thinking he saw my soul. I so want to kick myself for even thinking I was attracted to him. He's been playing me from day one. I was right about him. Gosh, I hate him. I'm never talking to the dude again.

I sit down at my desk and type away furiously. Call me crazy, but I'm actually looking forward to staying here late. As long as I'm at work, I can hide behind my computer. Unfortunately, you can only spell check your document so many times.

26

After inhaling an entire package of Velveeta Shells back at my apartment, I go into deeper thought. What happened today? I hated Jack this morning. I caught Michael with another woman. I left the press conference with Jack. I bumped into Caleb and pulled a Jerry Springer act on him. The next thing I know, I'm in the car with Jack, wanting to crawl out of my skin because the very nearness of him makes me want to melt. But then out of nowhere, his catty girlfriend corners me like I'm some Jezebel trying to sink my claws into her man. No, wait a second, that's beneath Natasha to see me as a threat. I'm more like the band nerd with a crush on the head cheerleader's boyfriend.

After another hour of thinking, I crawl into bed. Normally, it'd take a miracle to fall asleep at 10 PM, but the rain serves as a tranquilizer. I can hear it clanging on the fire escape. Ignoring the fact that I need to call Zoë, I pull the covers over my head. It's not like Michael won't still be a cheater tomorrow. I'll call her first thing.

Just as I doze off, I'm rudely interrupted by the phone ringing. I glance at my clock. Maybe I didn't just doze off, because it's 1 AM.

"Hello," I say in my how-dare-you-call-me-this-late tone.

"I'm engaged!"

"Who is this?" I ask. I sit up and flick on the lamp.

"Zoë." I still haven't registered a word she's said.

"Zoë. Hi. What did you just say?" I blink against the glaring light.

"I'm engaged!" she gushes. Okay, I registered that.

"To who?"

"To Michael. What's wrong with you? Listen, I'm sorry to call so late. It's just that he took me on this beautiful drive and after he popped the question, we just kind of enjoyed it. Look, I know I don't have to ask, but I still want to. Will you be my maid of honor?" This isn't happening. Why does procrastination work for everybody else but me?

"Is Michael with you?" I ask cautiously. "Can I talk to him?" I realize now isn't the best time to confront him, but it's better than waiting until after they've told everybody.

"You mean your soon-to-be brother-in-law?" she jokes. Somebody please pull the trigger. "He's not here. He's on call. Listen, I haven't even called Mom yet. I wanted you to be the first to know. Get back to bed, Grumpy. I'll call you tomorrow. I love you." She hangs up before I can say anything back.

I slam my phone down on the bedside stand. Over my dead body is she marrying that two-timing, scumbag doctor. I can't sleep knowing there's a chance of a wedding. I jump out of bed and throw on a pair of jeans. This has gone way too far. I call a cab and head to the hospital. I'm going to confront that philandering adulterer and make him tell Zoë what happened.

27

Gosh, there are a lot of people up at 2 AM, I think as I barge into the staff room. This time, I'm fortunate to find Michael.

"Emma," he says as he drops his cookie into a glass of milk. I wish he'd choke on it. "Is everything all right?" He gets to his feet.

"What are you doing?" I shout.

"Having a midnight snack," he says innocently. "You want an Oreo?" I could rip his head off. I lean over the table and into his face.

"Drop the act, Michael. I know."

"You know what?" I look at him blankly. "Oh, about Zoë and me. Sorry. It's been a long day. Forgive my absent mind, will ya, Sis?" I think this may have been what Hillary Clinton felt when she met a certain intern.

"Michael, I saw you," I say with a tearful choke. I cross my arms and look down at my feet.

"You saw me what? Having a cookie? Yeah, don't tell Zoë. She gets upset when I eat this late."

"Oh my gosh! I'm in the Twilight Zone," I say, throwing my hands in disbelief. Michael stands up.

"Have you been drinking?" he asks, putting a hand on my shoulder and peering into my eyes. I shrug away from him.

"Have I been drinking? Are you kidding me?" He takes my arm.

"Don't touch me you two-timing scumbag." I yank my arm so hard it almost pops out of joint. "I saw you yesterday with Samantha."

"You did?" he says cheerfully. "Well, you should've said hello. She was trying to sell me some new cardio drug, and I could have used some rescuing. That woman doesn't know when to quit." I shake my head. It's like talking to a two-year-old.

"So you're really going to stand here and lie to my face." I'm so mad I could vomit.

"Emma, I have no idea what you're talking about," he says light-heartedly. He sits back down and pulls out another cookie. "Here," he says, sliding the bag across the table. "Have one." I sit across from him, attempting to make eye contact.

"Michael, I saw you kiss Samantha!" I slam my hand on the table.

"What are you talking about? I'm engaged to your sister." We lock eyes for a moment. The thought of Michael being in my family makes me sick.

"Not for long, you aren't." The smile falls from his face. He leans across the table.

"What are you trying to do, Emma?" he says in a low voice.

"What am *I* trying to do?" I lean in. "What are *you* trying to do?"

"Look," he says calmly. "I know things have been bad for you lately, but that doesn't give you the right to wreck Zoë's happiness." Oh my gosh. This has to be what hell feels like. I let out a laugh. Is this guy for real?

"You're unbelievable!" I say incredulously. I lean back in my chair.

"Or maybe you've been hanging out with Jack Carmichael too much," he says with a smirk. He finishes off his glass of milk.

"Now you're calling Jack a liar." Michael frowns and shakes his head.

"He always had a way of disillusioning women. I just thought you were smarter than them." Now I'm a "them?" I sit up tall in my chair.

"Jack doesn't even know that I know you."

"You mean to tell me that you think *I'm* the bad guy? You're crazy!"

"I don't have to think anything, Michael. I know. But that's not why I'm here."

"It's not?" he asks.

"That's between you and Jack. I'm here about Zoë."

"What about Zoë?" Michael stands up and looks at me testily. I walk over to him.

"Please, Michael. If there's any decency in you, please tell Zoë what you did." I pause. "I really think it should could from you, not me."

"Well then," he says, slipping into his white coat. "I guess it's your word against mine," he says as he walks past me and out of the room. I chase after him, but jump back when I see Ms. Rent-a-Cop from earlier.

Silly me for thinking Michael would confess. Maybe I should call Jack. I may hate the guy, but at least he can confirm Michael's shady character. No, I can't call Jack. I have to handle this myself. I got Zoë into this mess; it's my responsibility to get her out of it. I tear at the thought of Zoë sitting at home, flipping through *Modern Bride*. I slump out of the hospital. I have to tell Zoë. Now. To-night. It's my obligation as her sister.

I get to Zoë's apartment in record time. Since I have a key, I let myself in the building but knock on her apartment door. I don't want her coming at me with a baseball bat. After all, it is 3 AM.

"Zoë, open up. It's me."

"Emma?" replies Zoë's groggy voice. "What are you doing here?"

"Please just let me in. I have to talk to you about Michael." She opens the door and my eyes immediately fall to her hand. My goodness, her ring is massive, though I have two words for that three-carat beauty: pawn shop.

"Can't it wait until morning?" she asks as she yawns. "I just fell asleep."

"No, it can't wait," I say as I shut the door behind me.

"Well, what is it?" We make our way into her den.

"I know you're a little upset with me because I wasn't more excited about your engagement, but I have a good reason."

"You look awful," she says, slumping next to me on the couch. I look at her intently.

"You know how you thought I was avoiding you yesterday?"

"Yeah," she says warily. Okay, deep breath. I can do this. I have to do this.

"Well, it's because I saw Michael with another woman." There, I said it. That wasn't so bad. She looks at me blankly.

"I went to the hospital this afternoon to ask him about Jack." I pause to take a deep breath. "But when I got there, I saw him coming out of a dark room with another woman." Zoë shrugs her shoulders and yawns.

"It was probably a patient of his. You're so silly." She leans her head back on the couch.

"No, Zoë, it was Samantha." She pops her head up. "And I saw them kiss."

"Oh," she says, getting up and moving toward the window. "I see where this is going."

"You do?" I follow her. "Oh, thank goodness." I lay my hand reassuredly on her arm. "I was so worried. I thought you—"

"You're just jealous," she says coldly, whipping around to face me.

"What?" I pull back my hand in surprise. Jealous? Of what?

"Just because you're unhappy doesn't give you the right to rain on my party." Zoë glares at me. "My gosh, this is just like you."

"How is this like me?"

"You would be the bearer of bad news on the night I get engaged." I take a minute to compose myself.

"First of all, I'm not unhappy. I don't know where you got that idea. And second of all, how can you accuse me of making this up? I'm your sister." I lay my hand on her arm. "I only want what's best for you." She pulls away.

"Please. You've been hanging out with Jonathan Carmichael too much." She crosses her arms and turns toward the window.

"What is that supposed to mean?"

"It means that he's totally brainwashed you against Michael." She looks at me coldly. Why is everybody bringing Jack into this?"

"Zoë," I say, turning her to face me. "Jack doesn't even know you're with Michael. He only knows what I saw today."

"Wait a second! You told him about this?" she shouts.

"Well, yeah." Is that bad? "He was there just after it happened, and I needed someone to talk to." She walks into the den and sits on the edge of the couch.

"Since when did you start being friends with Jonathan?"

"Now you're appalled that we're friends?" I throw my hands up in defeat. "I can't win with you."

"You're right," she says, getting to her feet. "You can't win. Now get out!" She walks to the door and throws it open.

"What?" I shout, rushing over to her. This is so not going the way I thought it would. I knew there would be tears, but being kicked out never even crossed my mind. I thought for sure she'd believe me.

"Get out," she yells through tears.

"Zoë," I say softly, laying my hand on her shoulder. "Why would I want to see you anything but happy?" I ask desperately. She glares back at me.

"I don't know what you're doing, but I've heard enough." Tears stream down her face.

"Zoë, I'm your sister. Why would I come over at 3 AM to break up your engagement?" She looks away. "Think about it. Michael could've easily lied to us about Jack."

"So now you think he lied about Jack?" She looks at me coldly. I've never seen her look so mad. Not even the time I wrecked her new car.

"Zoë," I say calmly, "the man's a liar." I'm trying so hard to put things delicately, but you know what? I just can't. I can't sit here and say nothing when my sister is about to marry a sleaze ball. I'd rather die than let that happen.

Zoë rubs her forehead with her hand, and then looks up at me.

"Emma, this is an exciting night for me, and I'm not about to let your stupid theories ruin it. I want you out of here! Now."

"What?!" I exclaim in utter horror.

"Now. Or I'll call the cops," she says, choking back tears. Can you even call the cops on someone who has a key?

"Fine," I say, walking through the door, but I stop on the other side of it. If I continue, she may never speak to me again. But if I let this go, she will make the biggest mistake of her life. Gosh, this bites.

"Think about it," I say gently. "Why would I lie about this? What could I have to gain? Come on, all those late nights at work. He's had plenty of opportunity." She looks at me intensely.

"He's a doctor!" she screams as she slams the door in my face.

29

I can't believe she chose Michael over me, I think as I hop into bed. She's only known him for a few months, and I'm her sister! We've always stuck together. That is, until I set her up with Dr. McFlingy! What is it about a man that infects a woman's mind so much, anyway? I don't get it. Would somebody please explain it to me? There is no love like the love of a sister. Why is Zoë chucking everything we've been through for a stupid guy? My poor sister is entangled in the lies of this sick individual. And you know what? I've been there. Well, I almost went there with Caleb, but I was lucky. Or was I? I finally doze off at 5 AM, but my alarm awakens me two hours later.

As I throw on my favorite pair of jeans and a blue velour blazer, my phone rings.

"Hoochie!" It's Mandy. As usual, her timing is impeccable.

"How's my favorite talk show host?" I ask as I brush my teeth. Gosh, I'm multitasked.

"I wouldn't say that just yet. Oh my gosh, I miss you!" she says.

"I know. The apartment is so empty without you. You'll never believe the things that've gone down since you left."

"Like what?" she asks inquisitively.

"Where do I begin?" For the next ten minutes I tell her about Zoë and about catching Michael with Samantha.

"And she doesn't believe you!" Mandy gasps. I can't explain how great it feels when somebody takes your side. When I was in fifth grade, I remember getting in a fight with this really popular girl. Like most grade-school fights, loyalties were divided. Most of the girls sided with the other girl, but not Mandy. She sided with me, no questions asked. That's when I knew I'd found my soul mate of a best friend. Why can't Zoë stand by me like that?

"I think she's in denial," I say, trying to give Zoë the benefit of the doubt.

"Sweetie, I know she's your sister and all, but that girl is way passed the stage of denial. You got out of bed at 2 AM to help her. That's above and beyond the call of duty."

"Yeah, well, I guess it wasn't enough. Listen, there's something else I need to tell you." Now I tell her about my run-in with Caleb and my almost getaway with Jack.

"Well, isn't that interesting?" she says suspiciously.

"But wait a second. Here's the best part," I interject. "After Jack dropped me off, guess who was waiting for me at the elevators?"

"Tall Skinny Cappuccino?" she asks.

"Yes! And she totally pulled me aside and told me to back off her man." I wander into the kitchen and start rinsing the dishes.

"You've got to be kidding me?" she says with a laugh.

"Yeah. So my question is, how did she come up with that theory on her own? Jack must've said something to her." The very thought of it is so humiliating. What a fool I've been. Mandy is quiet for a moment.

"Not necessarily," she says slowly.

"What do you mean?" I stop cleaning and lean against the kitchen counter.

"Well, it seems to me that Jack goes out of his way to be around you. And I'm sure she's noticed the way he looks at you." Does he look at me any particular way? Maybe with amusement. "Think about it. The woman he's dating may be beautiful, but she reeks of insecurity. And I have no doubt that she watches Jack like a hawk."

"I hadn't thought of that."

"I know you haven't. You never do. He's probably falling in love with you, but you're too blind to see it."

"Right," I say sarcastically, but my heart flutters at the very notion of it.

"Wait a second. What's this?" she asks.

"What's what?" I ask, standing up straight.

"Em, are you falling for him?"

"What? Me? Falling for him? Ha!" I pick up a mug and continue rinsing.

"Oh my gosh! You are! I can tell."

"Mandy, are you kidding? That's ridiculous. We've only known each other a week." I finish the dishes and dry my hands.

"You still haven't answered my question." I let out a huge sigh, which isn't enough because we sit in silence for a moment. I wander into the living room.

"Okay. So, I could easily fall in love with Jack, but—"

"But what?" Mandy interrupts. I start pulling at a loose string on my blazer.

"But he's with someone else. And even if he weren't, it still wouldn't work. Think about what Thanksgiving dinner would be like. Michael in one room and Jack in the other. That's absurd."

"You think too much," she says. "It's February." Life must be great for laid-back people. We analyzers have it hard. I have at least five panic burps a day.

"I know, but I'm just putting my guard up," I finally say, which feels quite liberating, really. I've had so much going on in my head that I've yet to actually speak my thoughts out loud.

"Emma, I know you've been hurt in the past, but you have to let that go now. Jack was put in your life for a reason. Trust that. He isn't Caleb." I pause to ponder her point. She's absolutely right. If she were going through this, I'd tell her the exact same thing. I'd tell her to close her eyes and fall backwards. But I can't do that. I know it's self-centered to think that my case is different, but it is. I wander into my bedroom and collect my stuff.

"Okay, enough about me. How are you? Have you found an apartment yet?" I ask.

"We're going to visit this topic later, okay?"

"I'll keep you updated."

"Good. And yes, I found a two-bedroom loft in Tribeca." Two bedroom, huh? She's so going to try to convince me to move to New York with her.

"I'm so excited! You've always wanted to live in that neighborhood."

"It's a little pricey, but I'm young and single so I figured, why not?"

"I can't wait to see it!"

"You'll love it," she says excitedly. I lay back on my bed. "Listen sweetie," she continues. "Try not to think about Zoë. She's an adult. It's time she starts acting like one. But I do think you should talk to Caleb. And as far as Jack is concerned ..." she starts.

"Yeah?" I prod.

"Get his side of the story. I have a feeling about this one. He seems different."

"He does, doesn't he?" I mumble.

"I'll call you tomorrow. Love you." Gosh, I'm going to miss her.

I apply red lipstick and head off to work. I faxed Edward Kelly my article before I left the office last night, so I immediately check my messages when I get to work. I'm anxious to know what he thinks.

"Emma, it's Edward Kelly. Your article was magnificent. Really, you flatter me. Thank you, thank you, thank you. I spoke with Jack this morning, and he thinks it's brilliant too. Listen darling, I hate to spring this on you so last minute, but Jack and I are meeting this morning and really think you should be there. Let's say, the Ritz at 11 AM. We can grab a bite to eat and go over a few things. Call me if there are any problems. I'll see you there."

Aw, he likes my article. A writer can never hear that enough. Sometimes it feels like people don't even care, and it's really discouraging after putting your heart and soul into a piece. I want to cry every time I see a copy of *Bean Town Scene* in the trash.

I call Zoë before leaving for the Ritz but get her voice mail. Maybe Mandy's right, I think as I close my phone. If she wants to act like a brat, then that's her choice. But she's still my sister, I can't help but think. And the thought of her pain makes my stomach ache.

30

I look around the lobby and see Mr. Kelly waiting for me, but Jack is MIA. Bummer, I think as I join him. I got all cute for nothing.

"Good morning," I say, taking a seat next to Edward. He looks up from his crossword puzzle. "Nine down is serum," I say with pride. One good thing about not sleeping last night was the opportunity to catch up on this week's crosswords and watch *Fox News*.

"Thank you, dear," he says, folding his paper. "It's been so long since I've had a chance to do a crossword that my mind has escaped me." He pours me a cup of coffee.

"Where's Jonathan?" I ask casually. I hate calling him that.

"He had something come up."

"I hope nothing too serious," I say in hopes of acquiring more information. Edward shakes his head.

"Not too bad, though I'm afraid the poor lad was up all night with a client of his on the West Coast."

"Oh," I say, trying to hide my disappointment. I add cream to my coffee.

"So, do you have any ideas for the next piece?" he asks, leaning back in his chair and giving me his full attention.

"Well, I was thinking we'd talk about your community involvement. Mostly your charity and church work."

"What about my platform?" he asks.

"I think it's a little early to discuss politics, but this'll lead into it. We want people to get to know the man behind the platform first." Edward flashes his movie-star smile.

"Brilliant," he says. "When's the first article going to go to press?" I set down my mug.

"It'll be on newsstands Monday." I take out a notepad and piece of paper from my oversized black bag.

I begin asking him questions regarding his various charities and church work. He gives me detailed information about each one. An hour and three cups of coffee later, we're finished.

"Great," I say, tucking away my notes.

"Well, I better dash. I have a meeting across town," he says. He gets to his feet and reaches out to take my hand. "Thanks again for your time."

"It was my pleasure," I say, slipping on my coat. And I really mean that. I'm growing rather fond of Edward Kelly. He's an extremely trustworthy and nice man. You don't see that every day. And that great face doesn't hurt either.

I step into the cold outside air and realize I left my gloves on the table. As I walk through the lobby, I see Edward Kelly stepping through the side entrance of the hotel. That's weird, I thought he had a meeting across town. I hope everything is all right. Retrieving my gloves from the table, I turn to leave, but my curiosity gets the better of me, so I step behind a plant to watch. Edward hands the bellhop a note. I move behind a luggage cart and observe him walking to the elevators. This is probably nothing, but I can't help but wonder about the note. And why is he going upstairs? He's not staying at this hotel, unless he's going to see Jack. Oh my goodness!

What if something is going on with Jack? I *so* need to get a life, but I decide to wait and see who that note was intended for.

Ten minutes later, I see an attractive blonde walk up to the bellhop. I perk up. He's handing her the note! I watch as the mystery woman heads to the elevators. Hiding behind a cart of luggage, I join her on the elevator. This is so *Alias*. I'm Sidney Bristow, and I can be anybody I want to be. When we reach the fourth floor, I take off in the other direction, but peek around the corner. I so need a life, I think as I wait for the door to open.

"What took you so long?" A familiar voice rings in my ears. Oh my gosh! It's Edward Kelly. Okay, calm down. It could very well be his daughter.

"Sorry," she says softly. Dude, she needs to speak up. I can barely hear her. I lean in closer. "I couldn't get away."

"Well get in here, baby. We don't have much time," he says as he pulls her in and I hear the two giggle. Oh my goodness! I don't think that's his daughter.

Dear heavens! Am I the official "it girl" for busting infidelity? Because I seem to be a magnet for catching people in the act. It serves me right for being so nosy. I slump through the lobby and onto the street. Why did I have to forget my stupid gloves? This would happen to me, wouldn't it? Oh my gosh, what am I going to do? I can't write about a man who's openly cheating on his wife. *Bean Town Scene* can't print my article. It's all a lie.

I spend my walk back to the office in deep contemplation. On one hand, I could pretend my eyes deceived me. The girl could have been his daughter or something. Doesn't Angelina Jolie make out with her brother? And look at her. She's very happy with Brad Pitt. Ew, no! That was so not his daughter.

Okay, so even if I did see what I think was an affair, who am I to inform the public? It's not like I'm Diane

Sawyer or anyone special. I'm Emma Mosley, an entertainment writer for a local magazine. Besides, this is his private life. It has nothing to do with his campaign, or does it? You know what? It so does. I mean, how can I work for a magazine that promotes such a scoundrel? Maybe nobody would ever know, but you know what, I would know. What if it got out? Not only would our magazine lose all credibility, but I'd be known as the idiot reporter who missed it. Or worse, I'd be the evil writer who knowingly lied to the world. I'd be the Johnny Cochran of journalism. Why do I get myself into these situations? Life would've been so much easier if I were an astronaut.

For the first time in my life, I'm writing about something that matters. I have a voice. I'm the spokeswoman for the future mayor of Boston. And Jack chose me to do this. But how can I live with myself if I continue writing about Edward Kelly? Sure this is a step up from pointless entertainment gossip, but it's not worth the sacrifice. Nothing is.

31

I climb the steps of the building and walk straight to Natasha's office. My mind is going a mile a minute. I knock furiously on the door. When I hear nothing, I open it to find Jack sitting in front of her desk. If they were making out on her desk, I'm going to be sick.

"Emma," he says as he gets to his feet. "Come in, we were just talking about you." I bet they were. They're probably still laughing at my "crush" on the quarterback.

"We were reviewing your article," Natasha says, nibbling on a California roll. Ew, Natasha's eating sushi. Gross.

"Edward faxed it to me early this morning." Jack adds. "I would have called you but I've been on the phone with a client all morning."

"It was ... good," Natasha forces through clenched teeth. You know, I really don't like to see the worst in people, but please. Can Natasha be any more fake? I mean, what's up with this facade of hers? It's really unnerving. She hates my article and she hates me. I wish she'd just drop the act.

"No, it was brilliant," Jack says, placing his hand on my back as he leads me into the office. Oh man, this is going to be harder than I thought.

"Thanks," I mumble. I sit down and look at my feet.

"Are you all right?" he asks. "I don't think I've ever seen you this quiet." I clear my throat and glance at Jack.

"I can't do this feature anymore," I say quietly. "I want off the story." There, that wasn't so bad. I look up and see that they're both looking at me like I have a third eye.

"Is this a joke?" Natasha asks coolly, rising to her feet. She looks like she's on stilts.

"Emma," Jack says, crouching down next to me. "What are you talking about?" I hope he doesn't resent me for what I'm about to tell him. I know I'm supposedly mad at him for not telling me how he felt yesterday, but more than that, I respect him for it. Even though I don't respect the girl he's with.

"Edward Kelly's having an affair." I exhale loudly. "I saw him."

"What do you mean you saw him?" Natasha says, tapping the desk impatiently with her long nails.

"Well, I ... I followed him." How pathetic does that sound? "I left my gloves at the restaurant this morning and when I went back to get them, I saw Edward with a woman."

"Was this woman tall and blonde?" Jack asks. Natasha whips her mane around at the very mention of another woman. Yes, Natasha, there are other attractive women in this world, I want to say.

"Yeah," I say. He stands up.

"You scared me," he says with relief. He looks at Natasha and the two exchange smiles. "Emma, that's his political strategist. Gosh, you almost had me going." He walks back to his seat.

"Now if that's all," Natasha says, walking toward the door.

"Stop belittling me!" I say, standing up. Oops! This wasn't supposed to get dramatic. "I'm not a kid. I didn't just *see* him with a woman. I saw him pull her into his hotel room."

"Are you sure?" Jack asks as he approaches me.

"Am I sure? I wouldn't be here if I weren't sure. She went up to his room. I saw her with my own two eyes!" What is with the third degree? They're treating me like I'm five! Natasha walks to her desk and faces me.

"Fine. You saw him with another woman," she says. "So what? Men cheat on their wives all the time." No, she did not just go there!

"Are you joking? Like seriously, where's the camera?" I ask, looking around the room. "Are you actually going to stand here and condone adultery?" She sighs impatiently.

"I'm not condoning adultery, but cut the man some slack. He's under a lot of pressure, and it's his business what he does in his spare time. Not yours and certainly not the publics." I throw my hands up in disbelief.

"How can you say that? I just poured my heart and soul into an article that promotes his family values!" My heart is running a marathon in my chest.

"And I'm sure he loves his wife and kids," she adds with a wave of her hand. Oh my gosh. This is like the dream when someone's chasing after you and you can't run. I mean, what is wrong with people? I lean over her desk.

"Natasha, you can't print my article."

"I'm sorry?" she asks tartly.

"Emma," Jack cuts in. I almost forgot he was here. He places his hands on my elbows. "Are you sure you saw him kissing Jocelyn?" Her name would be Jocelyn, wouldn't it? Gorgeous women don't have ordinary names like Emma.

"Do you need a Polaroid?" I yell, prying from his grip on my arms. "My gosh, why am I the only one worked up here, like it's abnormal to think adultery is wrong?" I know Nathaniel Hawthorne wrote a book about it and don't get me wrong, I've read it twice, but to glorify it! I don't think so! Jack looks at me quietly for a moment.

"We need to take her off the story," he says, turning to Natasha.

"No," Natasha says, shaking her head. "I gave Gwen her column because I thought Emma was capable of handling this." Please. She put me on the story because Jack made her. Why are people so unauthentic?

"She's too involved," he says in a whisper.

"Hello, I'm in the room," I say.

"Sorry," Jack mumbles. He runs his fingers through his dark hair. In the midst of a crisis, he still looks good. What's up with that?

"How about I just rewrite the story?" I offer, glancing from Jack to Natasha.

"No!" they say in unison. I almost want to yell "Jinx!" But I'm too worked up to be funny.

"Why not?" I ask, crossing my arms. Natasha looks at me with cold, calm eyes.

"Emma, you're never going write about this. At least, not as long as you work here." It suddenly got really hot in here. I tug at the neckline of my shirt.

"Natasha," Jack says softly.

"What!" I gasp. "You're going to fire me because I won't lie?" My heart is pounding even harder. Isn't that called atrial flutter or something?

"If you want to look at it that way," she says casually. I pound the desk with my fist.

"Are you kidding me?" Gosh, I hope my dad knows a good cardiologist.

"That's not what she said," Jack intervenes. "Nobody is getting fired here." I turn to look at him.

"Of course you'd side with her. She's your girlfriend." The dreamer in me truly thought he'd take my side. Boy, am I an idiot. And you know what else? I don't care that I'm throwing a tantrum. This is ridiculous, and I want them to know how ridiculous they sound.

"I'm not siding with anybody. I just think that you need to calm down so you can think rationally," he says, laying a hand on my arm. I pull it away and begin pacing the room.

"How can I calm down? And why are you taking this so lightly?" Why am I the only one worked up over this? It's like I'm in the Twilight Zone.

"I'm not taking this lightly," he says. "I'm just trying to figure out what to do."

"What's there to figure out? The guy's a liar! He committed adultery! In public! At The Ritz! What else do you need?" My hands are flying all over the place.

"I know, but I'm trying to think about what this would do to his family," he says.

"Yeah, this can't get out," Natasha agrees. Please. She was probably right behind Jocelyn.

"I'm sorry, but I can't promote someone who cheats on his wife and then lies about it. And I don't think our magazine should either." Natasha rolls her eyes.

"So you want our magazine to drop him, and you want to write about his infidelity? How do we even know you're telling the truth?" she asks.

"Now *I'm* a liar?" I exclaim. Oh girl, don't make me take my nails off!

"Emma," Jack says as he gets close to my face. "You've got to calm down," he whispers so only I can hear him.

"Look, Jack. On the walk over here, all I wanted was to be taken off the story. To let somebody else write it."

"Okay, it's done. We'll have somebody else write it," he says. Gosh, I've never seen him look so intense.

"But it's not that simple anymore," I say, shaking my head. I take a few steps back. "Now that I've listened to you defend him, I realize that that isn't enough. I don't want to work for a magazine that promotes someone like

Edward Kelly. I don't even want to be associated with people who do." I glance at Natasha. Jack puts his hand in his pockets and lets out a sigh. "Someone recently told me that we're human and we make mistakes." I pause in hopes that Jack remembers it was him. "And I know I'm hard on people. Probably too hard, but it takes a sick human being to blatantly cheat on his wife during a crucial point in his career. I don't think telling the truth and being faithful to your family is expecting too much from someone. And besides, how do we know he's not lying about other things?"

"Emma, just sit on it," Jack says firmly.

"What?" I ask, perplexed. "You want me to sit on it? Why?" I swallow back my tears.

"Because it's not our business," Natasha chimes in from behind her desk. I almost forgot she was here. I slump into a nearby chair. Jack pulls up a chair next to me.

"Emma, this will tear his family apart," he says searching my face for understanding.

"Well, he should have thought about that before he rendezvoused with Blondie," I say angrily. I look passed him and out the window.

"You're right, he didn't think." He pauses and swallows hard. "But you can." I remove my eyes from the window and look straight into his. "Emma, this is a huge thing you discovered today. So big that you have to be careful with this information." I roll my eyes in annoyance. "Think about it. Kelly's the likely candidate for mayor. Everybody knows that, so we have to find out more about this before we go public with anything."

"My gosh, why is everybody acting like it's my fault he had an affair!" I jump out of my seat and begin pacing the room again.

"Look," Jack says as he gets to his feet. "I know he messed up. And you're right. He should have thought about his family, but you've got to sit on this until we know more. Can you please trust me to do that?"

"You know, I expected this from Natasha, but I thought you of all people would believe me." I stop in my tracks and look at him with disappointed eyes.

"I do believe you," he says softly.

"You do?" Natasha asks as she moves behind Jack. We both look at her, but he continues.

"I know you feel somewhat responsible because you—" he starts, but I interrupt him.

"This goes way beyond feeling responsible, Jack. This goes against everything I believe in. What's so wrong with telling the truth?" If I weren't so mad, I'd be bawling my eyes out.

"Look, I'll see to it that you're taken off the story. I'll do anything, but you have to let this go." Natasha clears her throat but Jack doesn't turn around.

"Why? Because he has a promising career?" I ask.

"No, because it'll tear his family apart. Do you really want to bear that burden? You can't let this leak."

"You know, that's something he should've thought about before he cheated on his family." With this, I turn around and walk out of the office, slamming the door behind me. The door opens and Jack comes running after me. This is straight up soap opera drama.

"Emma," he says as he grabs my arm. This is the part where I'm supposed to throw a glass of cold water on his face and scream something awful. "Emma, don't be silly." Every time he says my name, I want to cry and melt and skip and jump off a cliff. All at the same time. I turn to look at him.

"Silly, huh?" Oh man, I'm starting to tear. "Because that's what you'd expect from me, isn't it? Silly Emma Mosley. What'd she do this time? Well you know what, you're wrong. And if you knew me at all you would never ask me to sit on this!" I turn and walk to the elevators.

Naturally, it doesn't come so I'm forced to stand in awkward silence as Jack and Natasha follow after me. We've even acquired ourselves a little audience.

"If you get on that elevator, you can kiss your job goodbye," Natasha says curtly. Jack stares at me with a concerned look on his face, but he knows there's no changing my mind. The elevator doors open and I turn to look at Natasha.

"I should've quit a long time ago," I say as I press the first floor. I glance at Jack. He's looking at me like I'm the stupidest girl alive. Maybe I am stupid, but at least I have my self-respect.

32

I've been wandering aimlessly around the city of Boston for almost two hours, and it's just now sinking in that I quit my job. I, Emma Mosley, am jobless. I'm unemployed, though I can't decide if this is a good or a bad thing.

On one hand, I'm excited. I've worked my bum off for three years as a dumpy entertainment writer. I've slowly become a statistic. You know, the high percentage of people who go to work every morning with a frown on their face. Not that it's a bad job or anything. Gosh, it was a dream come true for a girl just out of college, but I'm not that girl anymore. Sure, I'm a little scared of the unknown, but it's thrilling to have the freedom to do anything I want. The sky is the limit, and for the first time in years, I feel boundless.

On the other hand, I'm sad. Apart from my Oscar-worthy *Carrie* reenactment back at the office, I'm disappointed. I'm disappointed in Edward Kelly. I'm disappointed in myself, but most of all I'm disappointed that Jack didn't stand up for me. Call me crazy, but I thought he'd believe me, no questions asked. I was thinking Renée Zellweger and Tom Cruise in *Jerry Maguire.* Maybe my expectations are too high.

And if I really wanted to feel sorry for myself, I'd go into my "Why Me" speech. If you calculate all the things that have happened to me over the last few days, you'd think someone put a curse on me or something. My best friend is moving, and look at the mess I created with Zoë. I've developed feelings for a guy that I'm supposed to hate. I lost my job. Jack hates me, and oh my gosh! I almost forgot about Caleb.

Wow. That's a topic I've put on the back burner. And now, more than ever, I could use the comfort of an old friend. He's always believed in me. I can't help but wonder what he's doing. Maybe I should call him. It's not like this day can get any worse. And if it does, I can always fulfill my secret dream of moving to Africa.

Be still my drumming heart! It's thumping so hard in my chest that you'd think I just exercised or something. I take a few deep inhales as I dial his number.

"Hello?" That accent still makes me go weak in the knees. Just hearing his voice sends me back to the days we used to talk until the wee hours in the morning. Gosh, I miss that.

"Caleb, it's me." I didn't ID myself on purpose. I think it's a sign of insecurity, and I want him to think I'm all confident when really, I'm shaking in my fake Uggs.

"Emma," he says with relief in his tone. "I'm glad you finally gave in."

"You know me." Why did I call him again? I know I said I needed a friend right now, but I'm thinking that was a lie.

"Yeah. You usually come around in the end." That's so true. I try so hard to be stubborn, but after a few days it kills me.

"Do you still want to talk?" I ask. This is worse than those late night phone calls my sorority sisters used to make in college. It's kind of like when you eat an entire box of cookies. Sometimes it feels like you're empowered by some outside force that you just can't explain. What am I doing? I should just flee. Right now. Hang up the phone, Emma.

"Of course I do," he says. "When can you meet me?" he asks. Flintstone back pedal. Scram.

"Actually," I say, "I'm at The Parish Cafe." Considering the fact that The Parish Café is around the corner from his hotel, I might as well strap a sign to my forehead that says "stalker."

"Oh," he says taken aback. "Well, I'm across town. I had a meeting in Newton, so it'll be about thirty minutes. Do you mind waiting?" I'm so pathetic. I act like he's just sitting in his room waiting for me to call.

"Did I say I was already there?" I ask nonchalantly. "What I meant was I can be there. And in about thirty minutes." I'm so full of crap. "Talk about perfect timing," I add. Oh my gosh, I've got to stop talking.

"Err ... right," he says, obviously unconvinced. "Then I'll see you in about half an hour."

"Okay, bye," I say and hang up the phone before anything else can fly out of my mouth. Why did I call him? It only complicates an already complicating day. And he didn't even sound happy to hear from me.

After ordering a cup of coffee, I stare out the window and try my best not to think about Caleb. Thus far, I've managed to block him out of my mind, but now I can't seem to shake him. Suddenly, I feel like the girl I was back in college. I wonder if his eye still twitches when he gets really nervous. Or if he still listens to the *Top Gun* soundtrack when he goes running. I wonder if he even goes running anymore.

Okay, I've got to stop this. I pick up a copy of the *Improper Bostonian* and being flipping through the magazine's pages as I shake my leg nervously.

"Can I get you another cup of coffee?" asks a waitress as I nearly jump out of my seat. For a moment, I had forgotten where I was.

"Sure," I say without thinking. "But can you make it a decaf this time?" I put my hand on my leg to keep it from shaking.

"Of course," she says. I look back down at the magazine only to stare at a picture of Tall Skinny Cappuccino. You have got to be kidding me. She's standing next to some billionaire at a charity ball. Not wanting to think about her any longer, I slam the magazine shut and slide it under my chair.

"I guess it's back to staring out the window," I mutter under my breath.

Ten minutes later, I'm watching Caleb approach the cafe. As he walks, it's almost like he's in slow motion and we are the only two people on earth. On a scale from one to ten, he's at least a twenty. Oh gosh. I can't breathe. I wonder if he can see me. I pull out the magazine and act as if I'm engrossed in it.

"Hi," he says, stopping in front of me. Does he expect me to give him a hug? I nervously look up at him. I mean, he's gotta be standing there for something. And I'm sorry, but I really don't think I can hug him as if we're old buddies because we're really not. That is, if he even wants to hug me.

"Hi," I reply as if I put no thought into his standing over me. He gives me an ear-to-ear smile and takes the seat across from me.

"Read anything good?" he asks as he motions for the waitress to come to the table. As she takes his order, I look down to see that the magazine is upside down. Crap. I shut it for the last time. I swear that thing is cursed.

"So, why did you give in?" he asks as he waits for his coffee.

"Honestly," I say, fiddling with the saltshaker, "I needed a friend right now. I've been living out a nightmare for the past week." He raises his eyebrows. He knows I'm full of it.

"Emmy, what's going on?" Hearing him utter my name sends chills up my spine. He's the only one that's ever called me that. I know it's been six years, but all the feelings I've buried so deep within are flooding back as if time has stood still. Why did I have to call him? I shake my head.

"It'd take hours to explain everything," I say as the waitress approaches with his coffee.

"I'm in no hurry." He looks at me intently as I squirm in my seat.

"First, let me congratulate you," I force myself to say. He looks down at his coffee.

"So you heard." It amazes me how clueless men are to the mind of a female. Take Caleb for example. Does he honestly think he can tell my best friend something and expect her not to tell me? Everybody knows "Don't tell anyone" excludes your best friend, your mother, and your sister. "Listen, that's part of the reason I wanted to talk to you." He sets his cup down. I knew we'd have this conversation if I called him, but why should I care? We're so over, and while hearing your ex is getting married when you're still single never feels good, I thought I'd come to terms with this. Caleb is wrong for me. My head has always known that. But not my heart. It didn't get the memo.

Since the first day I saw him, my heart was literally pulled from my chest and into his direction. I spent months trying to convince both him and myself that I hated him, but really, I was madly in love with that boy the first moment I laid eyes on him. Don't get me wrong, the boy is beautiful, but it was so much more than that. There is no man on earth like Caleb and certainly no man who has ever made me feel the way he did. I never let it show, but I would have followed that boy anywhere. Sitting with him now, staring into his beautiful eyes, takes me back to the person I used to be. Suddenly, I'm no longer the tough, independent woman I have become over the past six years. I am the girl who fell so hard for a guy so completely wrong for her.

But I can't go back to being that girl. He's engaged! And even if he weren't, he didn't love me. At least not as much as I loved him. And he left me. Caleb left me for what—a job at his daddy's firm? My heart begins to pick up momentum as my feelings begin to surface. I am so mad at him! I'm mad because he pursued me knowing full well that he had no intention of following through with me. I'm mad that he left me brokenhearted. But most of all, I'm mad at myself for letting my emotions control me.

Not this time, I think as I take a deep breath.

"You mean you want to try and explain why I wasn't good enough for your family and this girl is?" I say harshly. Suddenly, I no longer care about impressing him. I don't even care if he thinks I should be locked up. I am scarred because of him, and I want him to know that.

"Let me explain," he says as he tries to grab my hand, but I pull it away. I wonder what her ring looks like. I bet it's his grandmother's engagement ring. He showed it to me once. Can you believe he used to keep it in a sock drawer?

"Go ahead," I say as I look him squarely in the eyes. This should be good.

"Okay," he says as he draws a breath. "I met Katlyn about a year ago. She was interning at the British Museum." Oh, great. She's all cultured and classy. "We started seeing each other and before either of us knew it, we were in love. She had every intention of moving back to the States at the end of the summer, and I was prepared to let her go, but then I thought of you." I choke on my cold coffee.

"Huh?" I grab a napkin and wipe my face.

"I can't remember a sadder time in my life than the day you left my doorstep. It killed me." He pauses for a second to take another sip of coffee. I start to tear, but immediately swallow them back. I will not show him I'm sad. I have to hate him. "So when Katlyn said she was leaving, I remembered that feeling I had on graduation day. Under the oak tree. Do you remember?" he asks.

"Of course I remember," I say a little defensively. I realize he's being honest and all, but it doesn't make this any easier to hear.

"Well, I didn't want to be that stupid again. So without much thought, I popped the question right there at the airport. My parents had never even met her." I can't help but get pleasure out of imagining Mr. Callaghan's face.

"I bet they went ballistic," I say, getting a strange satisfaction from this.

"I thought my dad was going to have a stroke." We exchange smiles.

"So how were things left?" I ask.

"Not good. He sent me here to meet with a few clients, but mostly to think about everything."

"So where's Katlyn right now?" I look down at my empty coffee cup. Just saying her name is weird.

"At her parent's house. They live in Chestnut Hill."

"Oh," I say, looking up. Of course. She's planning the wedding.

"But in all honesty, Emmy, I came here to see you."

"You did?" I ask skeptically.

"I had to see you again. I know it's been years, but I can't get married until I know for sure that things are over between us. You still linger with me." I look down at my lap in order to hide my wide eyes. I've never been able to think rationally around Caleb, and after six years, I'm still unable to. I take a moment to articulate some sort of response but am unable to do so.

"Em," he says after a pregnant pause.

"I still linger with you?" I say condescendingly, though I know exactly what he means. "Please. That's almost as lame as, 'You had me at hello.'" He winces. I know I'm being harsh, but I don't trust myself around Caleb. Not that he's a bad guy. He's an incredible person, but the way I feel around him can't be normal.

"Well it's true," he says quietly. Okay, so I feel bad for saying that, but it's only because I've been so hurt by this man. More like gutted.

"So let me get this straight. You had to see my face to see if you were still in love with me." He just nods because he knows better than to interrupt my tantrum. "So when it was convenient for you, you decide to come waltzing back in my life without any regard as to how this might affect me!"

"Well ..." he starts. I lean in.

"Do you have any idea how selfish that is?" I think I may be yelling because people are starting to look at us. Gosh, you'd think I just talked above a whisper in the library or something.

"That wasn't my intention," he says as the waiter refills our cups. I look down at my lap and recompose myself.

"Caleb, you broke my heart." Oh man, I'm starting to choke on my words. Deep breath, Emma. You are in complete control of your emotions.

"I know I did, sweetie," he says as he places his hand on mine.

"Don't call me sweetie," I snap as I yank my hand from the table. "You don't get to call me that anymore." I turn my attention back to the window, where I notice a young couple walking down the street hand-in-hand. I stare at them for a moment before speaking.

"You see those people right there," I say, pointing to the couple.

"Yeah," he says with uncertainty in his voice.

"I wanted that with you," I say without taking my eyes of them. I hear him let out a sigh, as I take a hard swallow.

"I had no idea it would hurt you so badly to see me. Believe me," he says softly. "Hurting you is my last intention." I match my eyes with his.

"Caleb, you waited six years to come back. Six years. And now what? You expect us to just pick up where we left off? Just like that."

"Emmy," he starts, but I interrupt.

"Stop saying my name like that!" We pause as we both gather our thoughts. Not knowing what to say, I grab some artificial sugar off a nearby table.

"So, what does Katlyn have that I don't?" I say as I stir it in my mug. Ew, it's not even dissolving. No wonder I don't use this stuff.

"What?" he asks.

"If you're willing to stand up to your father for her, she must have something over me. What is it?" He shakes his head.

"It's not like that."

"Then what's it like, Caleb? Tell me because I'd really like to know," I say bitterly.

"I broke up with you because I wasn't good for you," he says with intensity.

"Don't insult my intelligence. If you're going to fly across the world to see me, then the least you can do is tell me the truth. Really, what was it? Was it my parent's new money? Was I not pretty enough? Did you meet someone else? Tell me, Caleb. What was it?"

"You're not listening to me." He pauses and I can hear him swallow. "You were out of my league, Emma. I knew that from the day I met you. You were this beautiful, passionate, perfect human being, and I knew staying together wouldn't have been the best thing for you." I look down at my coffee.

"Wasn't that for me to decide?" I say without looking up. He lifts my chin with his fingers.

"Yeah, but I knew you wouldn't decide wisely. Emma,

you and I both know that you would've followed me to London, and I know without a doubt that we would've gotten married. It took everything I had to break up with you, but I had to keep reminding myself that you wouldn't have been happy. And I was right. You're such a great writer because of the experiences you've had. You're so independent and courageous because you haven't been overshadowed by someone like me." We lock eyes for a moment.

"You mean to tell me that you broke up with me because I'm too good for you?"

"That's what I've been saying," he says. I frown.

"So your dad cutting you off had nothing to do with it." He shakes his head.

"It was never about the money." I look at him unconvinced. "I know you overheard my dad say he'd cut me off if I married you, but that's not the reason why I broke it off."

"It's not?" I ask with a laugh.

"No, and to be honest I'm pretty hurt that you'd think so little of me." I lean back in shock. He's absolutely right. I was quick to assume he was a pansy who only cared about money when, really, I've never known him to be remotely selfish. Or greedy for that matter. I mean, the boy used to spend his summers volunteering for the American Red Cross in places like Africa and India.

"But you said your dad needed you," I say with full confidence as I recall our last conversation in his foyer.

"Well, if you had ever let me explain ..." He trails off as I give him an awkward smile. I imagine he's insinuating my immature behavior after we broke up. I blocked his e-mails and phone calls. I even mailed back all his unopened letters.

"You weren't very persistent," I joke.

"Well, after a few months, I realized that you were going to believe what you wanted to, so I stopped trying to contact you. Besides, what was the point?" He shrugs his shoulders as we exchange smiles, something we haven't done in years.

"So why did you end things?" I interject when our smiles fade.

"I had to let you go before I drained you. I was so spontaneous and irrational back then. I was in no position to take care of someone when I could barely take care of myself. And to be honest, Em, I think we loved each other too much." I smile, knowing exactly what he means. "It wasn't healthy," he says as he rests his arm on the table. After a moment's thought, I lean in and take both his hands. Gosh, I always loved his hands. And the crazy thing is, they feel the exact same.

"You're absolutely right," I say. Caleb looks at me with a brow raised. "What?" I ask innocently.

"In all the years I've know you, Emma, I don't think I've ever heard you utter those words," he says, smiling. I throw my sugar wrapper at him. That's such a Jack comment. Oh my gosh, Jack! I've been so wrapped up in Caleb that I'd almost forgotten about him. I wonder what's going through his head at this very moment. My guess is that it has something to do with me, a padded wall, and a straight jacket.

"So, who's Jack?" Caleb asks as if he just heard my thoughts. I open my mouth to respond, but close it to take a deep breath.

"Well, um, I'm not sure how to answer that," I finally get out. I lean back in my chair and cross my arms.

"Are you dating him?" he asks candidly.

"Gosh, no. He's ... uh ... working with the magazine that I used to work for," I mumble.

"Wait a second. The magazine you *used* to work for? Didn't I see you with him yesterday?"

"Yeah, well, I quit my job today. Actually, it was just before I called you."

"Your quitting didn't have anything to do with Jack, did it?"

"I wish it were that simple," I say as I chug the last of my coffee. I hate the last sip. It's always cold.

"What happened?"

"Well, one of Jack's clients is this guy named Edward Kelly," I start.

"The liberal?" he says. I love how smart Caleb is. It was one of the things that drew me to him. The first time I saw him, he was reading *Time*. Being the confrontational girl that I am, I started reading it just so I could argue with him. To this day I'm hooked.

"Yeah," I say. "It's a long story." He smiles, as if to acknowledge that everything is a long story with me. "Anyway, my job was to write features for him every other week. You know, to kind of boost him to our readers. I finished my first piece last night, and most of it discusses his family values." He nods. "Well, this morning after we had brunch, I caught him with another woman." Caleb raises his eyebrows.

"Oh."

"But when I told my boss and Jack, they wanted me to sit on it. Jack said that it'd hurt his family and that he didn't want me to bear that burden. But my boss gave me an ultimatum, and I wasn't going to lie, so I quit."

"I'm so sorry," he says as he takes my hand again. However, this time it has a different affect on me. It's almost like mentioning Jack has brought me back from Memory Lane and into reality.

"It's not your fault," I say as I slip my hand from his.

"Well if it's any consolation, I'm very proud of you. That took guts."

"Thanks," I say, tucking my hair self-consciously behind my ear.

"You know I'll always be here for you." I don't say anything. It's way too bizarre. Here I am, sitting in front of Caleb, staring at a face that I used to stare at for hours, yet all I can do is think about Jack. About a man I've known for less than a week: a man who wants nothing to do with me.

"So, what exactly do you want from me?" I ask quietly.

"I don't want anything from you, Emma. I just came here to say that I still love you." Did he just ...? No. "I've never stopped loving you." Yep, I think he just did. He grabs both of my hands. "And I'm here because I need to know if there's any chance that you'll have me again. I've changed ..." he starts.

"Are you mad?" I ask as I jump to my feet. My heart just skipped about three beats. "You have a fiancée for crying out loud!" Every head turns toward our table. I slither back to my seat.

"I know, and I thought I was here to tell you goodbye, but sitting across from you, looking at your face, it just makes me fall in love with you all over again." Why did I have to call Caleb? Why didn't I just go home and drown my sorrows in carbs like normal people?

"Aren't you the one who just got done telling me we were unhealthy? And now what? We're just going to sail off into the sunset and live happily ever after as if no problems ever existed between us?" Who knew I could be such a realist?

"I don't know what we're going to do. I was hoping we'd figure it out together." He may have changed, but this is just like the old Caleb. He'd say all the right things that I always seemed to believe—perhaps because I wanted to. And here we are, six years later, and I still want to believe him. I want to believe that he loved me so much he had to let me go. That he's still in love with me. That this time will be better. I want to believe him so badly, but more than anything I want to believe him so that I can forget about Jack.

"You know what? I can't do this right now. I don't know what to say or how to feel." I run my fingers through my hair. "I need some air." I stand up abruptly and head for the door. Caleb follows me with my jacket.

"Listen, Emma," he says as he grabs my shoulders and turns me toward him. "I don't know how this is all going to play out. All I know is that when I saw you standing in that red dress, I knew that after all these years I'm still in love with you. I love Katlyn. I really do. But she's not you. No one is. And I can't marry her without knowing that I tried everything in my power to get you back." Before I can respond, he cups my face with both of his hands and kisses me. I start to pull back, but after a moment I give in to what I remember. It feels safe. It feels so good, in fact, that I fall into it and kiss him back. My head tells me to pull away, but my heart is still so connected with this person that I can't seem to muster the strength.

My entire body has gone numb, and I have a feeling it has nothing to do with the crisp air. It's as if my brain is on vacation and my heart has been left in charge. This is not a good thing for someone as emotionally bipolar as myself.

After savoring Caleb's kiss for another moment, I snap out of it and push him away.

"What are you doing?" he asks startled.

"This is a mistake. I shouldn't have called you." I turn to walk away. What am I doing?

"You can't just leave," he says, grabbing my arm.

"I have to," I say in a state of panic. It's ten below outside, but I'm sweating like a St. Bernard. I loosen my scarf in attempts to cool off. I'm getting claustrophobic in my own body.

"You can't kiss me like that and just walk away," Caleb calls after me. I turn to face him.

"We shouldn't have done that." I knew this would

happen. Not that we would wind up lip to lip on Boylston Street, but I knew I'd do something stupid. What was I thinking?

"Done what? Show each other how we feel? Emma, you of all people should know it's okay to do that. Don't push me away because of something that happened six years ago."

"Caleb, you're engaged to another woman," I say helplessly. Why am I always attracted to unavailable men? It's a pattern that's going to ruin me. Oh gosh, I'm going to end up like my Great-aunt Wanda: a fat, old woman with a bunch of cats. And I hate cats.

"It's not like that," he says as he places his hand on my arm.

"Really. What's it like then, huh?" I take a step back. For a moment we stand in silence. I look past him because I can't bear to see his face. I'm too ashamed.

"Because I'm engaged I'm sorry for kissing you. The last thing I want to do is make you feel uncomfortable. But Emmy," he says, stepping closer and placing both hands on my shoulders. "I'm not sorry for being in love with you." My eyes fall to the ground. I try and wiggle from his grip but he's holding me too tight.

"Look," I say, looking up at him. "I have no intention of getting stuck in some love triangle, so if you'd kindly let go of me, I have a job to find." I start walking away, but he calls after me.

"Run all you want, but I'll still love you." My heart feels like it's ripping in two. I stop in my tracks and turn around.

"Please don't say that again. It's not fair to me, and it's certainly not fair to Katlyn. Oh my gosh, Katlyn," I say as I pace off into an epiphany. "I'm just as bad as Edward Kelly. No, I'm worse. I'm the other woman. The home wrecker. I bear the scarlet letter." Caleb smiles amusedly.

"Calm down. It's not like you're some floozy I picked up at a bar. You're the love of my life." The more he talks the more drained and helpless I feel. After a moment's silence, he continues. "I know the last thing you need right now is another ultimatum, but I have to give you one." Oh man, why did I have to call him? I should throw my cell phone in the Charles River because I'm obviously not responsible enough to own one. "Emma, you say the word, and I'll break it off with her." I don't even have to check to see where my jaw is. "We'll pick up where we left off, except this time it'll be better because we're both better people." And I thought I was a dreamer. Never in my wildest daydreams did I envision this.

After all these years, he still loves me. And he didn't leave me for the money after all. If I want him back, now is my chance. He's here, in the flesh, asking me to love him. But either way, someone's going to get hurt. It's kind of scary to know that with one word my entire life can change. I could get married and live happily ever after. But would I be happy?

"Caleb, I can't think about this right now. I have so much on my plate." He walks closer to me and brushes a strand of hair from my eyes.

"Take some time and sort it out. I'll be here for a few more days. You know how to reach me," he says as he turns to leave.

I watch him walk away. If this were a movie, I imagine you'd hear some sad James Blunt song. Like buckets of water pouring from the sky, tears stream down my face. And it's so cold that they freeze to my chin. You don't see that in the movies.

33

What am I going to do? I fall face down into my sofa in despair. I'm unemployed. I'm caught in a love triangle. My sister hates me. My best friend is gone. Jack thinks I'm crazy. I'm an adulteress. And I don't have anything to eat for dinner.

My crying is interrupted by a knock on the front door. One of the downfalls of this apartment is that there's no peephole, probably because it's so old. I wouldn't be surprised if Benjamin Franklin lived in this very building.

"Who is it?" Maybe it's a Girl Scout! I quickly get to my feet. How awesome would that be? I could get a box of Samoas. Or Tagalongs? Or maybe I'll get both! Oh, and I just bought some milk yesterday. I run to my purse and grab my wallet. There is another knock at the door.

"Emma, it's Jack. I have to talk to you." Jack! I stop in my tracks. What's he doing here? How did he find me? Oh my gosh! I look like crap. I wonder if he has cookies.

"Um, she's not here," I say in my best old lady voice. I can hear him sigh on the other side of the door.

"I know your voice. Please just let me in." I can't let him see me like this. I look like a punching bag. My face is all splotchy, and my eyeliner is smudged all over my face. Waterproof, yes. Cry proof, no.

"Uh, just a second," I say, giving myself a quick glance in the mirror. Bummer. I look terrible. But who cares? He fired me. Kind of. I throw open the door.

"Can I come in?" he asks, glancing at my ensemble. I'm wearing a wife-beater tank top and my favorite Superman pajama pants. He gives me a half smile, but all I can think is thank heavens I removed my doggy slippers. I step aside as he lets himself in.

"You look awful," he adds. My heart flutters at the very sight of Jack. He looks just as cute as I left him, but wait a second. I'm mad at him. I'm mad at him for saying I look awful. I'm mad at him for not believing in me. But most of all, I'm mad at him for being so wonderful. So wonderful, in fact, that he seemed to make me forget about a guy I've held onto for six years.

"Gee, thanks," I mutter, shutting the door behind him. Okay, Emma. This is crucial. Whatever you do, you can't let him know you care about him.

He takes off his coat and I see that he's still wearing his suit. I swear the man never stops working. As he examines a framed picture of my family, I grab a tissue and try scrubbing the mascara out from under my eyes. Crap. I clench the tissue in my hand. He just caught my glance in the mirror.

"Don't think my being upset has anything to do with you or your skinny little girlfriend," I say, glancing at him nonchalantly. We stand in the entryway for a few awkward seconds. Gosh, he looks good. Being near the guy makes my head spin.

"Are you okay?" he finally asks.

"What's it to you?" I retort, looking him squarely in the eye. He looks hurt, which in turn makes my heart drop to my toes, but I have to be mean. I have to push this guy as far away from me as possible.

"A lot," he says. He steps past me and walks into the den. I follow after him and curl up in my white chair. I'd give anything to be curled up next to him, but I try not to think about that. Why is it that I just had a kind of marriage proposal from a man I've dreamt about for the past six years, and all I can think about is Jack?

"So how'd you know where to find me?" I ask, pulling my knees into my chest. Jack throws his red scarf on the couch and sits on the edge of the coffee table.

"Gwen told me," he says, turning to face me. She's so dead. I mean, a warning would have been nice.

"Well then why are you here?" I ask curiously. Is it ridiculously idealistic of me to think he's here to tell me that he believes in me? That he told Natasha he couldn't be with her anymore because the moment he saw me at Saks he was captivated?

"Because I wanted to talk to you about Edward Kelly," he says firmly. I pause to take a breath as my heart begins pounding in my chest. I swear I'm going to need open heart surgery after today.

"Jack, if you're here to make sure that I don't reveal what a sleaze ball your client is, then I'm afraid you're wasting your time." I jump to my feet. He sighs. Why is he sighing? He's not the one who pretty much got fired for telling the truth and having the integrity to actually do something about it.

"It's not your place to tell people," he says as he rises to my level.

"So you think I'm a liar." I look down at the floor in order to hide my teary eyes. I watch my foot as a tear falls onto its surface.

"Emma, that's crazy. I didn't even come close to saying that." I can feel him staring at me, but I can't bear to look at him. I'll start crying, and he'll want to know why. Maybe I'm crazy, I think as I move to the other side of the room. After all, I did fall for a man who's dating my boss. And I pretty much wigged out on the man I thought I've loved for six years because of a guy I've known for a week.

"You didn't have to," I say, slumping onto the other sofa and crossing my legs. I begin to kick my foot furiously.

"Look," he says as he takes the seat next to me. "I believe you." I look down at my fingernails. "Look at me," he says as he waits for my gaze to continue. I look up at him. "I believe you." He places his hand on my knee to keep me from fidgeting.

"But," I say softly.

"But if you tell this story Edward's people will eat you alive." I roll my eyes in annoyance.

"You mean your people!" I shout. I pull my knees into my chest and look straight ahead. "I can't believe what I'm hearing."

"Look, I know you're not some heartless reporter looking for a story to further your career. I know your heart's in the right place, but—"

"But you don't trust me," I interject as I turn to face him.

"It's not that." He places his hand on my shoulder. "It's just that I'm worried about you. I ..." But before he can finish, my phone rings. He pauses as the machine picks up. I lean back into the couch.

"Emma, it's Caleb. I know you're there." I jump up to the machine in the hall to turn it off but can't find the button. I knew I should have read the manual. "You're probably staring at the machine in your favorite pair of pajama pants." He laughs. "Anyway, I just wanted to apologize about today. I shouldn't have kissed you. I know it only made you more confused. Em, you know I love you and ..." I yank the cord out of the wall. After a moment's hesitation, I return to the couch, where I feel Jack's intense stare. Not knowing what else to do, I grab a blanket and put it over my head.

"Is there any chance you didn't hear that?" I mumble.

"Emma, what are you doing?" he asks, pulling the

blanket off my head and placing it in my lap. I look at him sheepishly. "I thought you were over him," he says quietly. I remain silent. "And I thought you said he was engaged," he adds.

"What are you, my dad?" I ask sarcastically.

"No, but I'm your friend, and someone who ..." he starts.

"My friend?" I say as I put my hand to my chest in exasperation. "My friend," I repeat. "Forgive me, Jack, but you didn't seem like my friend at the office earlier today. Come to think of it, when have you ever been my friend?" My mind wanders back to the hurt I felt the day I found out he was dating Natasha. Then to the rejection I felt today, when I left the office all alone. I start to tear as I think about all the disappointment I've seemed to suppress over the past week, but stop myself. If I cry then he'll know I care about him. And oh, how much I do. I want to tell him how much his support means to me. I want to tell him that he's wasting his time with Natasha. I want to tell him that I can't stop thinking about him, even when I'm with Caleb. I want to tell him everything, but I can't. I have to protect myself this time. I get up and move to the window. Jack follows me.

"Whether you believe it or not, Emma, I care about you. That's why I'm here. And right now, I'm scared for you." My eyes widen, but I keep my gaze on the bustling Arlington Street. "I don't think you realize how much responsibility you're taking on." I turn to face him and end up like three inches from his face. Oh crap, I'm cornered.

"It's the right thing to do," I say softly. I look down at the ground. He has beautiful hands. I've never noticed that before.

"I know," he says sincerely. "But you have to give it some time. I've already phoned Edward's people, and I'm waiting to hear back from Jocelyn. Please, please be patient. Natasha and I are working on it." Tall Skinny Cappuccino? Are you kidding me? She's probably at the office doing cartwheels because I'm not there.

"Please. Natasha doesn't even think what he's done is wrong." I take a seat on the windowsill.

"I know," he says shortly. I pause to give him time to elaborate, but he doesn't. Not that this surprises me. He's too honorable to talk about anybody.

"So did she send you here?" I ask with wide eyes.

"What?" he asks with hurt in his voice. I swallow hard because I see that I've offended him. "No." He loosens his tie.

"Then why are you here?" I ask, closing my eyes. I suddenly feel very tired. Jack crouches down next to me.

"I'm here because I care what happens to you. And now I'm worried about you and Caleb." I look away because truth be told, I'm worried, too, but for a different reason. Not that it's any of his business, but Jack ruined any notion I had of ever getting back together with Caleb. He has set the bar so high that I don't think I'll ever care about another guy again.

"Maybe you should be more worried about your relationship with a girl who thinks adultery is excusable," I say coldly. I know that was harsh, but I'm sorry. The truth hurts. Jack gets to his feet.

"Just call Natasha," he says as he hands me his cell phone. "She'll give you your job back. I've already talked to her. The three of us can work on this together." So that's why he's here! They want to keep an eye on me. Man, he almost had me fooled.

"Maybe I don't want my job back!" I exclaim as I get to my feet. Silly me for thinking he could read my heart. "I know you're mad but—" he starts.

"Mad? You think I'm mad?" I put my hand on my hips and take a deep breath. "Jack," I say through gritted teeth, "I wouldn't work for that woman if it meant never writing again. She treats me like crap, and if you weren't so blinded by her long, skinny legs and big ... teeth, you'd see the way she treats people." I walk over to the chair and put the blanket over my head again.

"Or maybe you're blind," he says quietly.

"Huh?" I ask, pulling it to one side and looking up at him.

"I don't think you have a clue as to how talented you are. You're smart." He pauses and removes the blanket from my head. I can feel the static electricity sitting in my hair. "You're really smart. You can read people." He laughs. "And you have this incredible way of making people laugh. Everybody loves you." Everybody except you, I think as I get to my feet.

"Your PR attempts are touching, really, but I'm not falling for them. I can't be bought with your charm."

"So just like that you're going to put up a wall and act all tough again?" If only he knew why.

"Don't act like you know me," I say coldly. He's right. I am putting up a wall, but only because I'm scared. I don't think I can handle any more disappointment from him. I'd rather him think I'm mean than to have to feel as foolish as I have today.

"I know you better than you think I do," he says. "My gosh, Emma. Don't you let *anybody* get close to you?" he asks. A lump forms in my throat and my eyes fill with tears. He's right. I don't let anyone get close to me, but it's only because of situations like this. I want to let him in. I really do, but what does he expect? He has a girlfriend for crying out loud! Gosh, I'm sick of this. Over the past few days, I've managed not only to kiss someone engaged to be married, but I've also fallen for a man with a girlfriend. Forgive me for putting up a wall.

"Why are you here?" I ask as I cross my arms and lean against the wall.

"To tell you that you're in over your head. If there is a story to be told, you need to be very careful. Edward Kelly has a lot of pull around this city, and I don't think his advisers would think twice about dragging your name through the mud. Please just think about it. Think about letting somebody else tell it."

"And you and your girlfriend are defending him," I say. "Isn't that classy? But then again, you are part of his team."

"You're talking like he's some sort of criminal. Yeah, what he did was dead wrong, but Emma, he's still a human being. You can't just run a tabloid on his life. You haven't even talked to him. You have no idea what goes on behind closed doors. Maybe Kathleen already knows about it, and they're working through things. Do you really want to embarrass his family when you know so little about what's going on?" I take a few steps closer to him.

"Jack, the guy's openly cheating on his wife. And I'm both horrified and disappointed that you're going to stand here and defend him. I thought you had better morals than that, but once again I stand corrected." I turn to walk back in the den, but he grabs my hand and pulls me back into the hall.

"You're not the only person who has morals, Emma." He's still holding my hand. "Just because I didn't quit my job over this doesn't mean I'm any less offended than you are." I look at his grip on my hand and he lets go.

"What about Natasha?" I ask matter-of-factly. "I mean, she obviously couldn't give a rip about Kelly's morality. Do you really expect me to keep working for her when she clearly has no respect for my opinion?"

"I can't speak for her," he says as he drapes his scarf around his neck, "but I think you can do more good from the inside than you can unemployed. I also think you should find solid proof before you start attacking his character. For all you know, it could've been a one-time thing that his wife already knows about." He takes a few steps closer. "Have you even asked him?"

"Don't patronize me," I say, tossing him his coat. "I'm not out to get the guy. Gosh, why are you trying to make me feel guilty for taking a stand?"

"That's not what I'm doing," he says as he throws his hands up in annoyance.

"You act like there's something wrong with me for standing up for what I believe in. I don't care if she's your girlfriend, Jack. She's wrong. I can't believe you don't see that!" I make my way to the door, but he doesn't move. He just looks at me. I turn and fiddle with the lock.

"And I know Caleb has his flaws," I say as I turn to face him, "but at least he believes in me." It's kind of ironic. I was miserable with Caleb because I lacked the independent, strong spirit I now have. I couldn't be that person with him. But with Jack, I am that person. So my question is, why does Caleb believe in me and Jack doesn't?

"Or maybe Caleb doesn't challenge you and it feels easy," he adds tersely. I'm so mad I could throw up.

"You don't even know him!" I yell.

"No, but I know you," he says calmly. "And I saw your face when we ran into him at the hotel. Emma, he's not good for you." Jack steps closer.

"Try not to let the door hit you on your way out," I say, throwing open the front door so hard it hits the wall. Jack walks to it, but pauses right at my face. My breathing slows down as I look deep in his eyes.

"Emma," he says with a sigh. "I'm really sorry about today. I'm sorry you don't think I'm on your side. I'm sorry about a lot of things." He pauses and looks at me. "I don't understand your thinking at all. I really don't, but I guess you have to do what you have to do." He tucks a loose strand of hair behind my ear, which gives me chills. How is it that with one touch, I can go from livid to weak at the knees?

"Just like you're going to do what you have to do," I say as I choke on my words. His dark eyes are so intense that my heart wants to leap from my chest. I look at the scar above his brow. What I wouldn't give to trace my finger across it.

"I think you and I are more alike than you think."

"We are not the same," I say with a fake laugh.

"I didn't say we were the same. I said we're alike." He pauses. "We're just working from opposite ends." I watch him put on his coat and can't help but want to get in it with him. "Please be careful with Caleb. You may not think I know you, but I do know that you deserve so much more than he can give you." And just like that, he turns down the staircase.

I slam the door shut and lean my forehead against the wall. I just want to hide. I want to fall in a dark hole and hide. Actually, there is a place I can hide: my place I can always go when things are out of control. I quickly throw some things in a bag and lock up the apartment. Without calling, without telling anyone, and without even changing, I hop in my car and head home.

34

"Emma, come in, sweetheart," Mom says as she closes the door behind me. She takes one look into my distraught eyes and immediately pulls me in for one of her medicinal "Mom" hugs: the ones that charge hope and comfort back into a broken heart. Some things in life simply have no explanation.

I step into the den and inhale the familiar scent of home. My mom is an interior designer, so it's nothing short of perfection. I take off my coat as my mom clicks off the television. We sit on the sofa and she looks at me, waiting for me to talk when I'm ready.

"I quit at life," I say finally, falling into her arms. She just cradles me and strokes my hair. I may have disaster written on my forehead, but being home reminds me to count my blessings.

"This can't possibly be just about Zoë," she says quietly. I sit up and wipe my eyes.

"Oh, that's just the beginning," I sob. "Mom, this has been the worst few days of my life. Zoë thinks I'm a liar. Mandy's moving to New York. Caleb's engaged, and I kissed him today, by the way." She raises her eyebrows. "I quit my job. And the one person whose opinion matters more than anything to me doubts my judgment. And he doesn't even want me. Mom, what's wrong with me?"

I begin crying again. Mom pats my arm.

"I know things seem bad for you right now, but darling, you get so wrapped up in things. How could they not come crashing down on you?"

"So it's my fault all this is happening?"

"I wouldn't call it your fault. You just get so interested in people and their problems. You take on their burdens." I nod. That's exactly what Jack said.

"You want to fix things, and I think that's wonderful. It shows what a sensitive, compassionate person you are, but Emma, it's not your job to fix people."

"My acts of chivalry do tend to backfire."

"Have you eaten anything?" she asks. Come to think of it, I can't remember the last time I ate. That's amazing.

"I'm not hungry," I say mournfully.

"How about a glass of milk and a warm brownie? You don't have to be hungry for chocolate, you know."

"Mom," I say as she takes my hand and helps me up. "I love you."

"I love you, too, little Emma," she says, giving me another hug. "And I'm very proud of you."

As we head to the kitchen, I realize that I'm proud of me too. My mom is absolutely right. I'm lucky I've come this far without having my projects backfire on me. And you know what? Jack is right too. My expectations of people are way too high. How could I not get let down? I walk into our French country kitchen and inhale the smell of Mom's cooking.

"Here you go, darling," she says, handing me a glass of milk and a warm brownie. She sits next to me at the bar. "Let's start with Zoë."

This is one of the many reasons why I love my mom so much. Like a kid, she's gossiping with me over brownies and milk.

"Have you talked to her?" I ask.

"Yes. And sweetie, she doesn't think you're a liar. She just needs to figure things out on her own."

"I take it the engagement's still on," I say bitterly.

"As far as I know. She leaves tomorrow morning for that fitness conference in San Francisco. I think being away will do her some good. Emma, you did the right thing in telling her."

"Well, I'm the reason they're together," I say as I cram another brownie in my mouth. Chocolate and peanut butter. They're the greatest pair since Humphrey Bogart and Lauren Bacall. "If I weren't such a matchmaker, I wouldn't have pawned Michael off on her."

"That was beyond your reasoning. Michael has the charm of a Kennedy. We all bought into it. There's nothing you can do for her until she figures things out on her own. Now tell me about Caleb," she says. She puts another brownie on my plate.

Over the next two hours, the brownies in the pan diminish as I fill her in on everything that's happened with Jack and Caleb since the ball. Gosh, has it been that long since I talked with my mother? That never happens.

"Can you back it up?" she asks after I tell her about the kiss. I hate when she asks me that. I swear, I kissed over a dozen guys my freshman year in college, and I had to stop telling her because she'd always ask me if I had the guts to back the kiss up with a relationship. If my answer was no, she'd tell me to move on.

"I don't know how I feel. I thought I was over him, but seeing him again makes me wonder."

"You know I trust your judgment, but just remember that while you both may have changed, you still have the same obstacles. They don't just disappear with time."

"I know," I say.

"And you have to ask yourself if you want to marry this man. You can't jump into a relationship with him simply because Jack is unavailable." Is that what I was doing? "What about Jack?" she asks.

"I used to think my soul mate got struck by lightning, but it turns out that he's dating my boss." My mom laughs.

"Well, if he wasn't with Natasha, where do you think you two would be?"

"But he is." I get to my feet, though I know what she means. I would've been scared to my wit's end if I hadn't known him as my friend first.

"I'll clean up," she says, picking up my plate. "You get yourself a good night's sleep."

"Thanks," I say, giving her a quick hug. "And I'm sorry I waited so long to tell you about Jack."

"It's okay, honey. I know you always come to me when you're ready." She's right. I don't think I've ever kept a thing from her, I think as I turn to leave. I'm such a mama's girl.

"Remember," she calls after me. "Weeping may come at night, but joy comes in the morning." I pause and give her a huge smile. My mom has said that to me since I was a little girl.

"I love you," I call as I climb the stairs to my bedroom.

35

I wake up at 7 AM to my dog Max licking my face.

"Gross, Max," I say, pushing him away. I know they say a dog's mouth is cleaner than a human's, but with all do respect, we don't lick our backsides.

"Time to shake the stink off," my dad calls from my doorway. The downfall to being home is that there's no way to sleep past 7 AM. "I brought you some fresh coffee," he says. He hands me a warm cup.

"Thanks," I say, squinting my eyes.

"Your mom made pancakes, so get your bum out of bed and come eat breakfast," he calls over his shoulder. Max trails off after him. My parents are nuts. Who gets up at 5 AM and works out when they don't have to?

I join my parents at the table for breakfast. I know they've already eaten a bowl of Raisin Bran, but that's what you get for waking up so early. You're ready for your second breakfast by 8 AM. It's kind of a contradiction to working out if you ask me. I figure the later you sleep, the less likely you are to eat breakfast. And if you skip breakfast, you certainly don't have to work out. It's so simple.

"So, what's next?" my dad asks between bites of pancakes. I shake my head.

"I don't know," I say, drowning my pancakes in syrup.

"Emma, we're worried about you," my mom says. She shuts the refrigerator door and joins us at the table.

"Why?" I ask innocently. I exchange looks with my dad. He knows I hate it when people tell me they're worried about me because I inherited his pride. He used to say it made him feel like a burden to have people concerned about him.

"Maybe Jack's right about Edward Kelly," she says. "He's a very powerful man."

"So he should get away with adultery?" I say as I set my coffee mug down.

"She's right," my dad says as he looks at my mom. "You can't expect her to do nothing. We've taught her better than that." This is why I love my dad so much. He's always pushed me. That's why I'm so passionate. And I hadn't realized it until now, but my mom reminds me a lot of Jack. Very steady and extremely practical.

"I didn't say he should get away with infidelity. I just want her to be careful," Mom says. She stands up and starts collecting dishes.

"I will."

"So, what's the plan?" my dad asks again.

"Well, I can't hide here anymore," I say, throwing my napkin on my plate. "And I'm certainly not going to let Natasha or Edward Kelly intimidate me. Kelly's a liar, and I'm going to prove it. But first, I have to get Natasha to pull my article."

"How are you going to do that?" Dad asks. I sigh.

"I have absolutely no idea." He smiles knowing full well that I'll figure something out. And the reason he knows is because I'm his daughter.

36

After three hours of contemplation, I still haven't a clue as to what I'm going to say to Natasha. I double-park my car in front of the office. I'm sure I'll get a ticket, but what's new? I have an entire glove compartment of proof that there's no avoiding a ticket in the city of Boston.

As I hop into the elevator, I glance at my pale appearance. I wish I hadn't. I'm wearing faded Levis and my dad's Red Sox sweatshirt—not exactly professional. I get off the elevator and march straight through Natasha's open doorway.

"I hope you're not here to beg for your job dressed like that," she says, casually hanging up the phone. Tall Skinny Cappuccino is wearing a white mini-skirt and sheer black shirt with, get this, her bra showing. I realize they dress like that in Hollywood and all, but this is Boston for crying out loud. And February for that matter.

"Does Jack know you talk to people like this?" I ask, shutting the door behind me. Wow, being unemployed has really given me the confidence to say pretty much whatever I want.

Natasha ignores the comment as she leans back in her chair and crosses her legs on her desk. I wish she'd fall out the window and bounce twice. Is that mean? "I take it you're here to pick up your stuff," she says. Come to think of it, I totally forgot about my stuff. I lean over Natasha's desk.

"No. I'm here to ask you not to run my article in Monday's edition."

"Sure, I'll get right on that," she says sarcastically.

"I'm not kidding, Natasha. You can't print that."

"With all due respect, I can print whatever I want. That's what makes me your boss. Or should I say, *made* me your boss?" She laughs. Ignoring her, I continue.

"Natasha, you didn't even want me on the story to begin with. Surely you can find someone else to write it. Someone better." Natasha puts her feet down and stands up.

"You're right about that," she says, pouring herself a glass of water. I bite my tongue and wait for her to continue. "That's why I pulled it." I drop my arms in surprise.

"You did?" I ask, raising my eyebrows. Don't tell me she suddenly grew a heart. She waves her hand casually in the air.

"Jonathan wants to wait. You do remember my boyfriend, Jonathan?" she asks with a smirk.

"Why does he want to wait?" I ask cautiously.

"Because he wants to talk to Kelly before he reacts."

"Oh," I say, obviously taken back.

"That doesn't mean he believes you," she says quickly. "And as far as I'm concerned, you're just trying to further your career." She takes a sip of water.

"And where did I hint that I cared where you're concerned?" I blurt. If there's one thing I've learned this week, it's that there's nothing wrong with sticking up for myself. I'm not a doormat, and it's about time I stop acting like one.

"Whatever," she huffs.

"Well, if we're done here, I'm going to get my stuff." I turn to leave.

"Emma," she says, walking around the desk, "I'm not sure what's running through that crazy head of yours, but if you even think about writing this, you'll be sorry."

"Is that a threat?" I ask, stepping closer to her, "or a challenge?" I can't help but smile as I say this. My daddy would be proud.

"Good luck getting a job in this town," she calls as I open the door. "You're not getting a reference from me."

"I thought references were supposed to be credible," I say proudly, shutting the door. A mature person would simply leave it at that, but I can't help it. I peep my head back in her office. "By the way, isn't there a dress code here?" Before she can react, I smile and shut the door.

I arrive at my desk and see that my stuff has already been packed up. I thought Natasha was bluffing when she said someone else would be hired, but I guess this time she was telling the truth. Gwen must have done it. I leave her a thank you note and walk to the elevator. It opens and Jack steps off.

"Oh," I peep, hidden behind my plant.

"Hi," he says, holding the door open for me. Gosh, he looks good. He's wearing gray pants and a red cashmere sweater. He has to workout. I mean, that body can't be all genetics.

"I'll ride down with you," he says as the doors shut. If you think watching an R-rated movie with your grand-parents is awkward, try riding an elevator with a guy who makes you melt *while* a big plant rubs your nose. As soon as the doors shut, I sneeze.

"God bless you," he says. I sneeze again. And again. "Maybe you should move that plant away from your face," he says, laughing. He reaches over and takes it out of the box. Oh great, he's kidnapped my plant. Now he has to walk me to my car, which has probably been towed by now. So he'll probably offer me a ride, which I obviously can't accept. Bummer.

"Thanks," I muster.

"You're the last person I thought I'd see here," he says. I tap my foot impatiently. We stand in silence.

"Is it just me, or is this the longest elevator ride ever?" Jack looks at me, and I make the mistake of looking at him. Why does he have to be so wonderful?

"Emma," he starts, moving closer, but I interrupt.

"Don't," I say as I look up at the numbers. "Five more floors to go. Come on!" He looks at me hard.

"This is ridiculous," he says. He pulls the emergency stop button and the elevator screeches to a halt in between floors three and two.

"What are you doing?" I shriek. "Oh my gosh, claustrophobia!" I close my eyes and start breathing a Pilates breath of fire. Jack removes the box from my hands and places it on the floor.

"We're staying right here until you talk to me," he says.

"Why don't we talk outside? Where there's plenty of oxygen," I say between shallow breaths. I'm starting to see stars. Jack grabs my arm.

"Emma, you're okay. There's plenty of air in here. You're standing next to a plant," he points out. True.

"*Okay*?" I say as I turn to look at him. "*Okay*? Jack, I am not *okay*. I'm not *okay* at all. And I haven't been *okay* since I met you."

"Okay," he says hesitantly.

"Do you have any idea how bad this week has been for me?" Here I go. You'd be amazed at the things you say when trapped in a small, confined space with someone. "Apart from losing my job, Zoë hates me. That's right! My sister hates me because I caught her fiancé cheating on her."

"Zoë got engaged?" he interjects.

"Yeah, and do you want to guess who her fiancé is?"

"You never told me."

"That's because it's Michael Lancaster, your old buddy from Berkeley."

"Oh." He drops his arm, which has been gripping mine.

"And he told me all about you, Jack. He told me you trashed him around school and that you stole his girl-friend, Kate. And the sad thing is I believed him."

"You did?" he says quietly.

"Well, at first I did. Yeah. I had no reason not to." Jack shakes his head.

"So that's why you were so mean to me."

"But that's only the beginning." Jack raises his eye-brows.

"There's more?"

"Oh, there's more. You only heard part of it. Caleb's still in love with me. And I kissed him, which you already know. Are you hearing me? I kissed a guy that's engaged, which makes me just like Edward Kelly. And I hate myself for that. But more than anything, more than I want to say yes to Caleb's proposal to pick up where we left off, I want to hate you." Jack stands quietly, looking at me. "I want to hate you so badly, Jack, but I don't. I don't even dislike you. I dislike myself for not disliking you." Jack smiles but doesn't interrupt. "And your opinion matters so much to me. It shouldn't, but it does. So the fact that you think I should sit on Edward Kelly's scandal made me think. And I did. I drove to Nantucket, ate a pan of brownies with my mom, slept in my childhood bed, and thought about every-thing. And you know what I came up with?"

"Was that a rhetorical question?" he asks.

"Jack, I can't sit on this. Your opinion may matter to me, but you know what? My opinion matters to me too. And not only do I feel right about this, but I also feel like it's my responsibility. I know you think my expectations are too high, and you may be right. My mom seems to agree with you, but Edward Kelly let a lot of people down, not just me. And who knows? America is forgiving. Maybe they'll see past what he did. But they have a right to know what they're voting for."

"My opinion matters to you?" he says as if this were the only thing I just said.

"Yes," I say quietly. "And I'm so sorry I believed Michael and was so horrible to you."

"That does explain a lot," he says with a smile.

"For the record, I knew he was wrong almost as quickly as Zoë told me. And FYI, you're wrong about me." Jack takes a step toward me.

"How am I wrong about you?" I take a deep breath.

"I know you think I'm a silly little girl who—" I start.

"I don't think that," he interrupts.

"You don't?" I ask skeptically.

"You couldn't be more off." Okay. He's definitely got my attention. "Emma, I think you're the strongest, most passionate human being I've ever known." I look down at my feet. "Why won't you look at me?" he asks, raising my chin with his hand.

"Because," I say quietly.

"Because why?" he says softly. He steps closer.

"Because you're not mine to look at." I reach past him and press the elevator button and the doors suddenly open.

"Emma," he calls, picking up my box and following me outside.

"I think I've said enough," I say, making my way to my ticketed car. I take the box from him and throw it into the passenger's seat. "Fifty bucks!" I exclaim, ripping the ticket off the windshield.

"Talk to me, Emma," Jack says, following me to my door. This is complete torture. He's standing at my car looking unbelievably cute, and all I want to do is ride off with him.

"Why are you saying this stuff to me when you're with Natasha, anyway? And why are you even with her?" He opens his mouth to speak, but I interrupt him. "Let me guess. She warms up. Or there are things I don't know about her," I say, opening the car door. "Well you know what, Jack? I warm up too! And there are things you don't know about me. Things you will never know, because you're with her." I pause and look into his eyes. "Now please leave me alone," I say softly. I shut the door and drive away.

37

"You have no messages," my machine says. That figures. I hurl my keys across the room.

Did I really just confess everything to Jack? I sink into my down comforter. It's not like I was on death row or anything. We were in an elevator, and it wasn't even stuck. Have I completely lost it? I guess I really don't have anything left to lose at this point. Well, maybe my pride, but I lost that the day I got a pair of Manola Blahniks stuck on my big feet. Was that only a week ago? Can you fall for a guy in just a week's time?

Gosh, I have so much to do, but I can't think about it right now. My brain is on emotional overload. I need a break. I have to get out of here.

An hour later, I step off the T clad in baby blue pants and a tan sweater. The night air is thin and cold. There's a special showing of *Casablanca* at The Coolidge Corner Theater that sounds intriguing. I cross the street and head into the old building. Naturally, it's filled with gag-me couples, but that's okay because I'm confident.

Before finding a seat, I make my way to the concession stand and buy a box of Whoppers, a cheese pretzel, and a large Diet Coke. The Diet Coke is essential because, you know, every calorie counts.

I make my way up the red-carpeted stairs and into the crowded theater. I smile as I overhear one guy telling his girlfriend that next weekend she has to go to the *Rambo* marathon. I try to sit in the back, but seeing as everyone wants to make out, I'm pushed to the front of the theater. Bummer. As I make my way down to the reject seats, I swear I hear my name.

"Emma," I hear again. I slowly turn my head and see Gwen with her husband, Matthew.

"Hey," I say, relieved at the sight of some familiar faces. I know I'm supposed to be confident and all, but who am I kidding? A movie, alone, and at night? That's like three strikes. I open my mouth to speak, but someone beats me to it.

"Are you here by yourself?" I hear Natasha laugh. You have got to be kidding me. Please allow me to misquote Jane Austen here. It's a truth universally acknowledged that if you go to the movies alone, you will run into someone you know. I look over and see a very quiet Jack. Okay Emma, say yes. You're at the movies by yourself, but you're proud of it. Be confident. Just say yes.

"No," I say smoothly. See, I can't help it. My brain and mouth just don't work together.

"Good, because that would be totally pathetic," she says, leaning back into her chair. Bite me, Natasha. In fact, bite my pretzel. You could use the calories.

"Is this a double date?" I whisper to Gwen, trying my best to sound chipper, though my feelings are definitely hurt. What is Gwen hanging around with Natasha for?

"No, we actually ran into them at dinner," Gwen says. I can tell she's uncomfortable.

"Oh," I say, slurping my drink.

"Do you and your friend want to meet us for dessert after the movie?" Gwen asks, loud enough for Natasha and Jack to hear. What friend? Oh man, why did I have to lie?

"Perhaps," I say vaguely as I look around the theater. "Speaking of, I think he got lost." I purposely stress the "he" in attempts to make Jack jealous, but he doesn't even look at me. "It was good to see you," I say as I trail off.

Okay, I want to cry. What am I going to do? Why do I always get myself in stupid situations? Why can't I just be normal? You know what? I'm leaving. I can't do this. I can't go inside and face those people alone. I can't do it. I just can't. In a state of defeat, I turn to leave but stop just before exiting the building. Yes I can. I can do this. I will do this. I reascend the staircase. And I don't even have to go in there alone. I've watched enough movies to know exactly what to do.

I stand outside the theater, searching for someone flying solo. My gosh, doesn't anyone come to the movies alone? Oh, there's one. I spot a short, bald man in a plaid suit. No time to be picky, though he kind of looks like George from *Seinfeld*.

"Excuse me," I say, grabbing his arm.

"Yes," he says.

"Are you here alone?" I ask, trying not to sound like the desperate loser I fear that I am.

"No," says a woman who marches up behind him. "Now would you kindly take your hands off my husband?" I have hit rock bottom. Even Plaid Suit Guy has someone to sit with. I hope this isn't a glimpse of my future. Emma Mosley, party of one. I will forever check the single box. I will always be Emma Mosley and Guest on wedding invitations. I'm going to die alone. And who will I be buried next to? My old dog Skippy? Or maybe I should have my ashes thrown into the Atlantic. No one will notice anyway. They will all be Resting in Peace with their significant others and my ashes will be at the bottom of the Atlantic.

I snap out of my epiphany when I see a Chinese guy

walking alone. I check around and see no sign of a wife or even a girlfriend. He's wearing thick glasses and a Disney World T-shirt, but I'm in no position to be choosey, so here goes nothing. How can I ask him to sit with me without sounding too desperate?

"Excuse me," I say as I stop him.

"Yes," he says in a thick accent.

"I'll give you my Whoppers if you'll sit with me." I hold out my Whoppers. He looks at me confusedly and after a moment's pause, he grabs my Whoppers.

"No English. Thanks much," he gestures and walks off. I don't believe it. He just stole my Whoppers. And how can he sit through *Casablanca* if he doesn't understand English? I should've just stayed home. I could be eating a pint of Ben and Jerry's, watching Jay Leno, but no: I'm across town begging lonely men to sit with me. And the worst part is, they've all rejected me. Tail between my legs, I turn to leave again but hear a voice call after me.

"Excuse me, Miss," says a cute Irish accent. The dreamer in me hopes to turn around and find Colin Farrell staring at me.

"Yes," I say with wide eyes. Okay, Emma. Blink.

"Did you just offer your Whoppers as bounty to sit with you?" he asks. Wow. Move over Colin Ferrell. This guy looks to be about six feet tall and has a five o'clock shadow that's very sexy. His hair is a little unkempt, but he has that I-don't-care look. He's wearing a pair of jeans and an untucked black shirt.

"Yeah," I say sheepishly. "But I'm not a loser, I promise. I'm just in a bit of a bind." Irish man grins.

"I'll tell you what. How about you explain it to me over my box of Whoppers," he says, holding out his arm. I take it, and he escorts me into the theater.

"I'm Lance," he says.

"Emma," I say as we find seats that just happen to be

two rows directly in front of Jack and Natasha. We're just out of earshot, but in his direct view, which is perfect. I can't help but wonder what's going on in Jack's head right now because this guy is really hot, and well, he's with me.

"So what's the story?" he asks as he pops a Whopper in his mouth.

"I just ran into my ex-boss, and I told her I wasn't here alone."

"Why did you lie about it?" he asks. I take a sip of Diet Coke and think for a minute.

"I'm not sure. It just kind of came out. I used to have this thing for her boyfriend, and I guess I didn't want him to think I was alone on a Friday night."

"Which one is he?" Lance asks.

"He's next to the girl in the red shirt." Lance turns slyly to look at him.

"Cute but not my type." I laugh.

"I thought only girls could say stuff like that."

"In your country," he says, handing me a Whopper. "So, what's a beautiful girl like you doing alone on a Friday night?"

"I don't do the dating thing very well," I say flatly.

"Psycho?" he jokes.

"Picky," I say as I hit him in the arm. He looks at me curiously.

"Do you still have a thing for this bloke?" he asks. I sigh.

"I don't know."

"Well, just in case you do, let's make him squirm a little." Lance leans back in his seat and puts his arm around me. Perfect timing too. The curtains part and one of the greatest movies of all time begins.

"By the way, what's a guy like you doing watching *Casablanca* on a Friday night?" I whisper.

"I have three sisters," he says. Wow, this guy is a dream come true. But no matter how appealing Lance's rogueness may be, the only thing I can think about is whether Jack is looking at us or not. Just in case he is, I snuggle a bit closer to Lance, where I remain for the entire movie.

38

"Whatever you do, don't tell any of these people we just met," I whisper to Lance as the lights come on.

"Got it," he grins. We make our way to the lobby.

"Emma," I hear Gwen call after us. She's standing with Matthew and Jack. Natasha is MIA. Thank God for small miracles. "Did you enjoy the movie?"

"How could she?" Jack mutters. "She was talking the whole time." What was that? I've never heard Jack say anything less than polite.

"That's because I've seen it a million times," I say, exchanging confused looks with Gwen.

"Then why'd you pay ten bucks to see it again?" he challenges. I shoot him a look, but he glances away.

"Um, Lance," I say, grabbing his arm. "This is Gwen, her husband, Matthew, and Jack." Lance extends his hand to all three of them.

"Where are you from, man?" Matthew asks.

"Dublin."

"What brings you to Bean Town?" I ask, forgetting that I'm supposed to know him already. "I mean, tell them what brings you here."

"I'm just visiting an old mate."

"How do you two know each other?" Jack cuts in. Think, Emma. Think.

"We used to go out," Lance remarks casually, putting his arm around my shoulder. What? He did not just say that. Gwen knows I haven't had a boyfriend in the last three years.

"In college," I add.

"You really have a thing for foreign guys," Jack says testily. Is it just me or is he mad?

Natasha walks up and breaks into our conversation. My gosh, she's wearing the tightest pair of jeans I've ever seen. I bet she has to pee every five minutes.

"Sorry," she breathes coolly. "That was the new entertainment editor. Can you believe he's managed to weasel his way into a VIP party at Sonsie tonight? It's his first day on the job and already he's making a splash." Everybody just stands there and stares at her. "I mean, never has the magazine had such a wonderful writer. Emma, thank you so much for quitting." Okay, there's a stark difference between being the bigger person and being a doormat. I take a deep breath.

"Can I ask you something, Natasha?" I ask as I stand a little taller.

"Of course you can," she says with a sweet smile, leaning her head on Jack's arm.

"Did they forget to teach you manners in finishing school?" She throws me an evil stare and I match my eyes with hers.

"How about we step outside?" Jack suggests in attempts to break things up. He takes Natasha by the arm.

"Excuse me?" she asks, pulling away from his grip.

"It's really a nice night," he continues. We both shoot him a look.

"Seriously, were you absent that day?" She lets out a fake laugh.

"What are you jealous or something?" she asks innocently. She reaches for Jack's hand, but he doesn't take it.

"Why? Because you're skinny and successful?" I cross my arms.

"Well, whatever it is, get over it. I'm accomplished because I've worked my tail off to get here. Maybe if you worked a little harder ... " she starts. I look out of the corner of my eye and see Jack shifting uncomfortably. At least he isn't acting like a jealous boyfriend anymore.

"Let's go," Jack says as he tries to pull Natasha away from the group.

"I'm not finished," she says, yanking her arm away from him.

"Natasha, cut it out," Jack says through clenched teeth. Natasha ignores him and takes a step toward me.

"You know what your problem is, Emma? You're just average. Your writing is mediocre. You're only kind of pretty. And well, you're never going to be anything special."

"Come on, Emma," Lance says, tugging gently at my arm.

"I mean, look at you," she continues. She looks me up and down in disgust. "You're unemployed, single, and you dress like you're still in college. You're a sad act Emma Mosley. You're nothing." I look over at Jack. Natasha's words have sliced right through me, but all I can think about is Jack. He can't be the person I think he is if he knowingly chooses to be with a girl like Natasha.

"Let's go," Jack says shortly as he guides Natasha away from the group. As they walk away, he turns to catch my eye, but I quickly look away.

"Emma," Gwen says as soon as they're out of earshot. "I had no idea she was that awful." I take a deep breath.

"Yeah, well, that's the Natasha I've always had the pleasure of knowing."

"She's evil," Matthew adds.

"I hope you didn't listen to any of the things she said," Gwen says, giving me a hug. "Because you know she's full of crap. She's a sketchy judge of character."

"And insane," Matthew adds.

"I know," I lie. "Listen, I'm going to pass on dessert. I'm exhausted. And I'm sorry if I ruined your evening with all my drama."

"Don't even apologize. We'll do lunch next week," Gwen says, squeezing my hand. "We have so much to talk about." I smile.

"Sounds wonderful."

After saying our goodbyes, Lance and I step into the cold night.

"I thought for sure a cat fight was about to break out," he says with a laugh.

"I'm sorry," I say, shaking my head. "I promise I didn't grow up in a trailer park."

"Don't apologize to me. That lady is crazy. It's no wonder you quit working for her." He pauses. "Listen, do you want to pop into the pub for a small bite?"

"Sure," I say as we turn toward the Coolidge Corner Clubhouse. Forget this small bite stuff. I want a fat piece of pie.

39

"You mean to tell me that Jack's still talking to you after the way you've been treating him?" Lance asks as he takes another bite of my peanut butter pie. I've been telling him about Jack for the past half hour. When I told him about the shoe incident, he nearly choked on his chicken tender. The truth is, he's really fun to be with. We've been talking as if we were old friends.

"I know," I say, fighting him for the Oreo crust.

"Do you want to know what I think?" he asks. He lays down his fork and leans back.

"Of course," I say with a smile.

"I think Jack's in love with you." I drop my fork in surprise.

"What are you talking about?" I manage to get out. "You saw his leggy little girlfriend." Lance shakes his head.

"Yeah, but I also saw the way he looked at you. Besides, that girl has nothing on you."

"Did he look at me in a special way?" I ask casually.

"He looked at you the way a little boy looks at a fire truck."

"You have to say that because you're my friend," I say in attempts to play off his compliment.

"Actually, I wouldn't say that because I'm your friend. Giving someone false hope is the worst thing a person can do. But I feel confident about what I'm saying. Trust me on this one. I'm a guy." The words "trust" and "guy" should never be used in the same sentence, but I'll let it slide because he saved my butt earlier.

"So, what's your story Lance?" I ask, leaning my elbows on the sticky table. Ew, gross.

"I already told you. I'm visiting a mate from school."

"You're holding out on me," I tease.

"And what makes you think you know me so well?" he asks, tossing his head defiantly. "I could be a serial killer for all you know."

"Dodge my questions all you want, but it'll only make me more interested. Come on," I say, pinching his cleft chin. I love a good "booty chin."

"I'm visiting an old friend from St. Andrew's," he starts, but I completely interrupt him.

"In Scotland? Oh my gosh! That's where Prince William and Harry went to school!" I practically scream. "Do you know them? Oh my gosh. I knew William would find his way to me. I can already picture our wedding at St. Paul's Cathedral. You think Diana's train was long, just you wait! Oh, I always wanted to be a princess."

"Do I need to be here for this?" Lance jokes.

"Sorry. Please continue." I put my hand over my mouth. "I'm taking some time off to travel because—" he stops to take a swig of his drink.

"Because why?" I ask anxiously. He clears his throat.

"Well, about three months ago, I was supposed to get married." I nod my head to give him some nonverbal feedback, which is killing me because I'm still thinking about Wills. "But a week before the wedding, I called it off. And a lot of people are pretty upset with me, so I took off for a while."

"Why'd you cancel your wedding?"

"It just didn't feel right," he says, staring into his glass. Men just don't know how to elaborate, do they? I reach over and pat his hand.

"Sweetie, you're gonna have to give me a little more than that." Lance shrugs.

"That's the thing. I can't give you more. It was just one of those things where I just knew she wasn't right for me, though very few of my friends see it that way."

"If they're your friends, why wouldn't they stand by you?" I ask. Thank heavens I never have to worry about that. Mandy and I made a pact to drive the getaway car should either of us get cold feet on our wedding day.

"It's more complex than that. We all grew up together, so they're her friends too." I open my mouth to tell him how very Ross and Rachel this is, but I don't. Now is not a good time for TV metaphors. "They don't get why I broke it off." I lean back in my chair and fold my arms.

"Then it's good you took off. You need some time to clear your head. They'll come around if they're your true friends." Oh my gosh, a light bulb just went off in my head. Mandy! This guy is perfect for her. I lean forward again. "So, have you been to New York yet?"

"I was actually heading there next," he says, looking up. "Why do you ask?"

"Well, my best friend lives there. Kind of. She's in the process of moving. Anyway, I'd love for you to meet her. She's really cool." Oh my gosh, the more I think about it, the more it makes sense. They'd be perfect together. And how great that I got to meet him first? It's almost like test driving a car. I should get the Nobel Peace Prize for my act of humanitarianism.

"Is she anything like you?" he asks, smiling as he sips the last of his drink. I don't know if yes or no would be a good answer here.

"Yeah, a little lower maintenance," I say, grabbing the check from his hand. "But just as cute."

40

I know it's stupid to let a complete stranger walk me home, but I had to let Lance escort me back to the apartment so I could show him Mandy's picture. And it's a good thing I did because he wouldn't shut up about how beautiful she is.

I know I said I was going to try and stop butting into people's lives, but this is my best friend we're talking about. And Lance needs friends in his life. I'm really doing him a favor. I mean, I can't just sit back and let him return to Ireland. We need guys like him in America. This is my duty as a United States citizen. Plus, I have to end my matchmaking schemes with a bang. I can't possibly let Zoë and Michael be the last couple I ever set up. I promise after this one I'll stop.

After an hour of telling Lance everything he needs to know about Mandy, we exchange numbers and make plans to meet before he leaves for New York the next day. I hope Mandy doesn't have plans.

I sprint to the phone to call her. I had intended on just telling her about Lance, which she was thrilled to hear, but we end up talking for two hours. I know that seems like a long time, but I'm having best friend withdrawal. I'm used to flopping myself on her bed and gossiping over Ben & Jerry's. Don't get me wrong, I love to eat, but it's no fun to eat alone. I miss her. No, I miss her terribly.

I get myself ready for bed and force myself to fall asleep. I even set my alarm because tomorrow is such a big day. I have to have the story ready for Monday's paper. Talk about a deadline. In hopes of a romantic dream, I try to think about Jack, but as usual I have a dreamless sleep.

At 8 AM I practically jump out of bed. My body can't relax when I know I have to wake up for something. After spending a few minutes of deciding where to begin, I start to research some of Kelly's speeches. Thank goodness I have a ton of information on him already.

I reread my notes from our first interview. This is almost laughable. I asked Kelly how his marriage has stood the test of time, and he had the nerve to say, "Why buy a hamburger when you can have a steak at home?" On sight I thought that was the sweetest thing I'd ever heard. Now I just want to vomit.

As I continue to write, I'm careful not to throw in my fancy journalistic training. There's nothing worse than reading a newspaper with some journalist using tricky vocabulary in attempts to shove her biased opinions down readers' throats. I don't want to write like that. I keep reminding myself that as I write this, I'm abandoning my profession. I'm writing this story as a Bostonian, as a layman.

After scarfing down a bowl of Ramen Noodles, I dial Jocelyn's number. My hands are really shaky. As much as I need to talk to her, I so badly want to get her machine. But after the third ring, she answers. Talk about facing the music.

"This is Jocelyn," she says.

"Hi, Jocelyn. This is Emma Mosley. I'm sorry to bother you on a Saturday, but I was wondering if we could talk."

"Emma," she says quietly. "I heard you might be calling." She heard I might be calling? From who?

"Then I guess I don't have to beat around the bush."

"Listen, I'm a little tied up at the moment, but I'll be free in an hour or so. Can we meet up then?" she asks. I pause in complete shock that she's willing to talk me.

"Uh, yeah," I say slowly. "Where do you want to meet?"

"It's probably better if I come to you. Give me your address, and I'll be there at four o'clock."

"Great. I live in the South End. It's 3 Appleton Street. Apartment 303."

"Got it," she says. "Listen, Emma. Please don't tell anyone I'm coming over. I'll explain later."

"Of course," I say. "I'll see you at four." I hang up the phone with a feeling of hope. It's a little odd that she's coming to talk to me in secret, but I try not to think about it.

I jump in the shower and throw on my favorite pair of jeans. I even tidy the place up a bit, making sure to flip the chair cushions onto their clean sides. At 4 PM Jocelyn is still not here, so I phone Lance.

"Hello, gorgeous," he says. Okay, he's a keeper.

"We still on for dinner tonight?" I ask.

"Certainly," he says, just as the doorbell rings. Crap.

"Lance, I have to go. I'll see you tonight." I hang up and go to the door.

"Hi," I say as I open the door.

"Hi," Jocelyn manages between short breaths. Wow. She's young. Maybe even younger than me.

"Don't worry, the stairs get everybody," I say as I take her coat. Gosh, she's pretty. Like beautiful.

"It's me too. I haven't worked out in weeks." When I get a closer look at her, I see that she can't be a day over twenty-four.

"Can I get you anything?" I ask as I show her into the den. "Coffee? Soda? Girl Scout cookie?" I stole a few boxes from my parent's house.

"Thin Mints?" she asks with a smile.

"No. I'm afraid I ate that box." And I'm not exaggerating. I popped them like potato chips on my ride back yesterday. She laughs nervously.

"Better you than me," she says as she takes a seat on the couch.

"Can I ask you something, Jocelyn?" She nods. "Who told you I might be contacting you?"

"Jonathan."

"Really?" I say as cool as I can, but I'm perplexed. Why would he do that? Jocelyn fiddles with her necklace, then puts her hands in her lap and looks up at me.

"Let me just cut to the chase, Emma. I know what you saw in the hotel," she says directly. "And I'm aware that you're writing a story on Edward Kelly." Oh man, this is the part where she reaches into her purse and shoots me.

"And you still wanted to meet?" I ask incredulously.

"Listen Emma," she says as she scoots forward in her seat. "I got fired today."

"What!" I exclaim. I sit straight up.

"It seems Natasha called Edward this morning, and he's livid. He thinks I'm the one who told you about us. He even accused me of taking money from you," she adds. Her eyes are full of tears.

"But that's ridiculous! You didn't tell me anything. I saw you with my own two eyes." I hope Natasha's leaking this to Kelly has nothing to do with what happened last night. I mean, if she was going to call him, why didn't she yesterday? Surely, she wouldn't do something just to spite me. And even if she would, Jack would stop her. But then why did he warn Jocelyn that I would be contacting her? Gosh, my brain hurts.

"I know," she says as she pulls out a handkerchief. I know this is a sad moment and all, but I can't help but cringe at the sight of a hanky. How these things ever took off is beyond me. They're dirty tissues contaminated with snot and eye boogers. And the grossest thing of all is that you just stick them back in your purse until your next snotty episode.

"I'm really sorry if I cost you your job," I say gently. Jocelyn shakes her head.

"Oh no, Emma. You couldn't have possibly known I'd get fired. Besides, he needed an excuse to get rid of me." She pauses to regain composure.

"Actually, it was Jonathan who suggested I talk to you," she says as she wipes her eyes.

"What?" My heart just skipped a beat. Now he wants her to talk to me?

"He felt really bad that Natasha called Edward without his knowing and wanted to apologize." I can't believe Natasha did that, though I smile at the fact that perhaps Jack has finally seen her true colors.

"Of course, I had no idea any of this had leaked until he called this morning. You can imagine my state when he dropped the bomb. I barely know him and there I was crying on his shoulder." I guess now's not that time to tell her he's seen a lot worse. My mind flashes back to the day we met in Saks. Then to the day he saw me in Superman pajama pants. Yep, he's definitely seen worse.

"He said you could probably help." Now he wants me to help? I thought he was adamantly against what I was doing. I wonder if he's changed his mind. Or maybe he just wants the two of us to sink together. But how could I possibly think he would want me to fail? No matter how mad he's made me, the truth is Jack's never wronged me. The only thing he's ever really done is not want to be with me. I swallow hard and feel a lump in my throat. Oh gosh, I don't think I hate him at all.

"Emma," Jocelyn says. Oh gosh, I wonder how long I've been looking into space. I can't do this now. I can't think about Jack.

"So did you love Edward?" I ask, shifting my body as to show her she has my full attention. She gives me an I-can't-believe-you-just-asked-me-that look. She pauses.

"Look, I want to help you. I really do, but I don't want to be the Monica Lewinski in all of this."

"Jocelyn," I say, leaning forward. "You can tell me whatever you want. Anything you say will be kept off the record unless you specify otherwise."

"Thank you," she says as she reaches for my hand. I can't explain the thrill I get when I can connect with people. I love that she trusts me. "I don't know where to begin."

"Start from the beginning," I say. She takes a deep breath.

"Okay. Well, I started working for Edward about a year ago. I know I don't have to tell you what a charmer he is," she says with a smile. "He flirts with everybody, and it feels good." She's right about that. "We spent a lot of time together, but when we first met, I had no intention of starting anything with him. I was in a relationship, and he's married." I nod in agreement. "But at the end of the summer, my boyfriend broke up with me. I was really hurt, and Edward was there for me. We started spending more and more time together, and well, one thing led to another. We started having an affair in December." She gets up and walks to the window.

"At first, it was a lot of fun. He made me feel so beautiful, but after a month or so, it stopped being fun." I walk over to her and sit on the windowsill. "I got attached," she says through choked words. "I started asking him where it was going, and he told me that he loved me." I look away to avoid her seeing the expression on my face. "Of course I loved him, too, but he said that he couldn't leave his wife because of the circumstances."

"And you believed him!" I can't help but blurt. I have never been one to kick someone while they're down, but because of this affair a family has been hurt.

"I guess I believed what I wanted to believe," she says as she wipes her eyes. I can understand that. "You see, I grew up in about ten different foster homes, and I've never had a person tell me they love me. I've been in some terrible relationships." She pauses. "And as awful as the circumstance was, it felt good to be wanted. At least at first," she adds. As crazy as this may sound, I can feel my heart softening toward this person. I am so blessed to have the support I have. It hasn't even occurred to me how lucky I am. I disagree in every way with what Jocelyn did, but my gosh. She is a product of her past.

"Emma," she says as she turns to me. "I held on to the fact that he loved me. After a few weeks, his words became empty, but I chose to believe otherwise." She places her head against the window and closes her eyes. "How dumb am I?" I may not have done anything as severe as this, but I understand clinging to a person and believing what you want to believe. I also understand being blind to that fact until all is said and done. It's the worse feeling in the world.

"Jocelyn," I say as I stand to my feet. "I'm so sorry. Really, I can't think of anything else to say except that I'm sorry." I watch as tears stream down her face. "No one should feel unloved, especially someone as beautiful and as sweet as you." She turns toward me.

"I'm not sweet. Look at what I've done. It's awful!"

"I'm not gonna sugar coat things and tell you that what you did is okay. But I will say this." I take her shoulders. "You aren't the one who's married. You aren't the one who sat me down and told me to my face how very much you love your spouse when all the while you were cheating on them." She looks down at her toes. I see more tears trickle to her feet.

"But the entire thing was consensual. I'm just as

responsible as he is."

"I know you are," I say. "But that's not what this is about. This is about Edward Kelly. He lied. Plain and simple. And not only that, he asked me to print his lies."

"I'm such a fool," she says as she slumps onto the windowsill. "It wasn't even worth it."

"It's pretty scary how easy it is to do something stupid, huh?" I place my hand on her back in attempts to console her.

"But his poor family," she says through choked words.

"Unfortunately, there's nothing you can do about that. You can't undo what's been done. It happened. Now it's over." I pause. "But I know what you can do." She looks up at me with hope shining through her red eyes. My gosh, this girl has no clue how beautiful she really is. Not to condone her behavior, but she probably got into this mess because no one has ever told her that. When I first called Jocelyn, it didn't even occur to me how I would react. I guess I thought I would hear her story and that would be that. But in all honesty, I'm really moved. What she did was wrong, but I still can't help but feel sorry for her. I mean, this could have just as easily been me.

"What can I do?" she asks.

"You can ask yourself what you can do to make this right."

"Actually, that's why I'm here." I look at her with my brows raised. "I didn't just come here to tell you my sob story." Oh crap. Do I want to hear her out?

"Then why are you here?" I ask skeptically. Jocelyn sniffs and dabs her eyes.

"Well, the thing is ... I'm not the only girl on Kelly's campaign that he was messing around with." Oh my gosh! This is straight up Rickie Lake.

"You're not?" I say as cool as a cat, but inside I'm totally freaking out. What a scumbag! I wonder if Jack knows about this too. Probably, otherwise he would have never suggested she contact me.

"No. I know for a fact there have been quite a few women before me, but I didn't want to tell you because it makes me look even more pathetic. I mean, here I am having an affair with a married man who can't even be faithful to his mistress." How did this sweet, beautiful girl get stuck in such a crap situation with such a loser?

"How many other girls do you know for sure that he's been with?" I ask.

"Three that are on his campaign." Oh my gosh! This is huge! Three other women, and they're all working on his campaign.

"Um, Jocelyn." I pause in attempts to articulate some sort of a question. "Do you know if his wife is suspicious about his behavior?"

"She's made some comments that have made me think she's fishing for something, but she's never said anything overt. She's a real controlling woman." Actually, I got the exact opposite impression of her. I guess I lack that discerning spirit. "It wouldn't surprise me if she knew, but she'd never leave him. People are already saying they think he'll eventually become a serious candidate for president of the United States."

"Is that right?" I say with my brow raised. Something is definitely not right here. It all seems a little too JFK.

"I really want to help, Emma. I mean, he already thinks it's me who leaked this anyway, what do I have to lose?" She stands to her feet. "But I want to read anything before you send it."

"You can trust me," I say as I grab her coat.

"I know," she says with a smile. "Here's my e-mail address and all of my numbers." She hands me a scratch piece of paper so I can give her mine.

"Jocelyn, thank you so much for your help. And I promise I'll do my best to keep you out of this."

"Thank you," she says as she gives me a hug. I open

the door to let her out, but she stops.

"Jonathan was right about you," she says.

"How so?" I ask, taken back.

"He said that you have a big heart." I'm surprised he didn't say I have a big mouth. "Emma, before I came here I was feeling pretty hopeless. I was pretty ashamed and wanted to run away." I know the feeling. "Jonathan said that you always do the right thing, and for the first time in my life that's what I want to do." I smile at her. "I know I can't undo what I've done, but I can do my best to help you."

"I admire your courage," I say through choked words.

"Bye, Emma."

"Bye," I say, locking the door behind me. I slide to the floor and pull my knees into my chest. It still amazes me that someone so sweet can do something so wrong and not even realize it until she gets caught. And to know that she's one of three other women? Did they do it for the same reasons? And I wonder what Jack is thinking? I so badly want to talk to him. I want to ask him why he sent Jocelyn to me. Is he still representing Kelly? Does he now see what I always saw in Natasha? I have so many questions for him, but one thing is for certain. Jack was right. I'm in way over my head.

41

"I'm sorry, but Mr. Kelly is unavailable," his secretary says with annoyance in his voice. Is there such a thing as a male secretary?

"Well then perhaps you can tell me a good time I could reach him?" I swear the man is avoiding me. After calling his cell and his home twice, I thought I'd give his office a final try.

"Want a piece of advice," he whispers.

"Uh ... sure," I say reluctantly.

"Don't call here anymore," he says with a laugh and hangs up the phone. Oh my gosh! That is so inappropriate. I should call the Better Business Bureau or something, but I have bigger fish to fry today.

I make myself a cup of coffee and trail off into thought. I should have known Kelly would dodge my calls. Am I completely naïve in that I thought he would want to talk to me? I mean, who wouldn't want a chance to defend themselves? Why is it that I feel more like Linda Tripp than Barbara Walters? It's not like I'm making up some story to sell to *The National Enquirer*. I'm writing a personal piece that hopefully someone will print.

I get back to my laptop and add details from my unidentified source. Initially, I set out to call Kelly out on all his crap. Shortly after Jocelyn left, I made a mental plan to call around and get as much dirt on the man as possible. I wanted to put a billboard in Times Square announcing what a scoundrel Edward Kelly is. After all, that's what he deserves. But somewhere between a cold shower and my second pot of coffee, I've had a change of heart. I don't want to lash out against the man; I want people to see his true character. It's hard to imagine that less than a week ago, I looked at Edward and Kathleen Kelly with starry eyes. I thought they were happy.

Three hours later, I lift my hands in victory. I want to shout from the rooftops. But before I click print, I have to call Jack. Not that I want to, but I have to try and get a statement from him. After all, it is his client. I dial Jack's number as I shake my leg nervously.

"Jonathan Carmichael's phone," says a voice that is definitely not Jack.

"Uh, hi. Is Jack there?" I thought this was his cell phone.

"He's unavailable. Can I take a message?" Wait a second. I know that voice.

"Natasha?" I ask.

"Emma? Why are you calling him?" I so want to punch her in the face.

"It's about a client," I say matter-of-factly. What is she doing with Jack's phone? And what on God's green earth is she doing with Jack? Don't tell me they're still together. Okay, Emma. Calm down. You don't know the facts. I let out a deep sigh as I try my best not to assume anything negatively about Jack. After all, look what he did with Jocelyn.

"Whatever," she huffs. "He's in the shower." He's in the shower! Okay, Emma. Don't lose it.

"Well, I'll hold then," I say stubbornly. I so feel like crying. And vomiting. It's the strangest feeling.

"It'll be awhile. I'll tell him you called, and if he wants to call you back, then he will." This is what I'm talking about. There's no need to be nasty.

"Please have him call me," I say with urgency. "It's very—" I start. Click. She just hung up.

Okay, Emma. You have every right to be mad right now. You have every right to cry and scream in your pillow, but you're stronger than that. No more tears, no more emotional eating, no more racing heart for Jack Carmichael.

Twenty minutes later, I throw on my North Face and head to Cheers, where Lance and I are meeting for dinner. As I cut through the park, it suddenly occurs to me that Valentine's Day is tomorrow. How could that have slipped my mind? I bet this is what birthdays feel like when you pass the age of forty. You stop getting excited about your birthday because you realize that every candle on your cake represents a step closer to senior citizenship.

As I continue to walk, my mind wanders back to last year's Valentine's Day. Mandy was dating two guys at once so she was busy keeping them apart all day. I, on the other hand, sat at home, ate a box of chocolates, and watched a special on the mating rituals of tribal animals on The Discovery Channel. I'm afraid tomorrow will be no different. I could call Caleb. Oh my gosh, Caleb. Why do I keep forgetting about him? If he were really the love of my life, don't you think I would've thought about him at least once today? I don't know what's worse: that I'm not in love with Caleb anymore or that I have to tell him that I don't love him anymore.

I arrive at Cheers just as Lance walks up. He is such a hottie. Don't get me wrong, I'm not rethinking my matchmaking game, but if he and Mandy do get married, their children will be lovely. Absolutely lovely.

"Hey," I say as I give him a hug.

"Do you look beautiful or what?" he says. Quick question: If he and Mandy start dating, can he still call me beautiful?

We walk down the flight of stairs into the famous Cheers bar. I was a little disappointed the first time I came here. The outside looks just the way the TV show portrays it, but the inside is completely different. It's not spacious like the fictitious set. There's no Sam, Woody, or Diane, and most definitely everybody does *not* know your name. Reality bites.

Lance and I laugh and tell stories over hamburgers and fries.

"Well, speak of the devil," I say as I reach for my ringing cell phone. It's Mandy.

"Hey hoochie mama."

"Did you finish the story?" she asks.

"Yep," I say. I really want to tell her about Jocelyn, but I can't. Not in front of Lance. Being a grownup stinks sometimes. "Listen, I'm actually sitting at Cheers with Lance right now. I want you to talk to him." I hand him the phone and smile at the fact that she's probably salivating over his accent.

I listen to them chat a few minutes, and let me tell you, romance is in the air. I can smell it from here.

"Great. I look forward to meeting you too," he says after a few more minutes. "Here's Emma."

"Emma!" she screams. "Is he as cute as he sounds?"

"What do you think?" I say as I look at him. We exchange smiles. She doesn't know this, but he can hear her. He's definitely as hot as his accent, though no one, not even Caleb and Lance put together, is as good looking as Jack Carmichael. And I'm not being biased. He's beautiful in every single way. I so have to let him go, don't I?

"You're so good to me," she gushes. I laugh.

"I'll call you later, okay?" I hang up before she can further embarrass herself. I take a sip of Diet Coke and smile at Lance.

"You know what I just realized?" I say.

"What's that?"

"That you've yet to tell me what you do for a living."

"That's because you haven't asked," he says as he shoves another fry in his mouth. Did I mention that I need to curl in fetal position? So much for my pact to not emotionally eat over Jack. I unbutton my jeans in attempts to breathe. "I owned a pub with a buddy of mine, but when I took off, I sold him my half."

"Oh," I say a little surprised. Don't get me wrong, Lance doesn't look like a vagabond or anything, but I had no idea he was an entrepreneur.

"You really wanted to get out of there, huh?"

"I was pretty desperate. I was thinking about opening a restaurant here in the States, but I'm still looking for a place to live. I really liked San Francisco, but I want to check out New York." Aw, San Francisco. Jack. Stop it, Emma. Bad!

"San Francisco's beautiful, but there's no place on earth like New York City," I say, pushing my plate away. "By the way, how are you getting there?"

"I rented a car."

"Oh, good," I say, "because I printed out directions before I left." I hand him my Mapquest printout. "Thank you," he says as he throws down thirty bucks for our meal.

"No, thank you," I say as we walk outside. I button my pants when we reach the street. I hope he didn't notice.

"Do you want a ride home?" he asks.

"No, that's okay. I'd like to walk." There's actually somewhere I need to go. I have to talk to Caleb. Oh gosh, I'm dreading this.

"Okay," he says, pulling me in for a bear hug. And I have to tell you that it feels so good to be hugged by a man. I don't think I could ever be with a man who didn't give great, big, bear hugs. After saying our goodbyes, I turn in the opposite direction. I can do this. I can talk to Caleb. I am The Little Engine that could.

42

As I walk into the Ritz-Carlton, I think of all the awful experiences I've had at this stupid hotel this week. It's a shame that I'll never look at this magnificent hotel the same again.

I step off the elevator and walk toward Caleb's room. What am I going to say to him? Okay, Emma. Deep breath. I knock softly on his door. My heart is beating wildly in my chest. Part of me doesn't want him to be there.

"Emma," he says as he opens the door. Oh man, he's wearing the Harvard sweatshirt I gave him. This is going to be harder than I thought.

"Can I come in?" I ask.

"Of course." He smiles and steps aside. It's kind of strange going from an Irish accent to an English one. My brain is so confused.

"Thanks." I step into his room. Not that it matters, but Jack's room is much bigger. Don't get me wrong, this room is nice and all, but it's not the penthouse. Oh my gosh, that's it! Jack is the penthouse. And no matter how great Caleb is or how much I used to love him, he's not the penthouse. And maybe I'll never get the chance to have the penthouse, but at the same time, there's no way I can go back to wanting anything less. Now that

that's settled, my question is how I am going to say this without using my dumb penthouse metaphor.

"I'm a bit surprised to see you here," he says, interrupting my epiphany. He stoops to collect the newspapers from the couch. Caleb was never one to be tidy. He used to say that it's a waste of time to clean up when instead you could be out somewhere making a mess. I used to love his life philosophies, but now they seem silly. We really have changed, Caleb and me.

"I was walking home, and my body just kind of steered its way here," I say, sitting down. Jack's sofa was more comfortable too. Okay, I've got to stop with that.

"Have you thought about what I said?" he asks as he joins me on the couch. So much for breaking the ice.

"Yeah. I've thought about it," I say, but immediately feel guilty because that's a rationalization. Don't get me wrong, I've definitely spent a lot of time reflecting on my love life, but to be honest I've hardly thought about Caleb and my love life. It's all been about Jack. But how can that be? I must have some serious issues because not only is the guy unavailable, but I've only known him a week. And here sweet Caleb is ready to try again, and I'm about to shoot him down. It's almost better to get dumped than to have to tell someone you care about that you don't want them in your life anymore. Or in my case, you don't want them in your life again.

"Well," he says, placing his hand on top of mine.

"Caleb," I begin. I take a deep breath and look up at him. "You know I'll always care for you."

"But you're not in love with me anymore," he says, leaning back. He slides his hand away and crosses his arms.

"I do love you," I insist. I reach for his hand again. "I love you very much, but not in that way." I pause and look down at my lap. "We're different people now."

"So?" he says.

"So, I think you know that." He pauses. "It's not as simple as it used to be. We can't just pick up where we left off. The same problems still exist, and we hardly even know each other anymore." He rests his elbows on his knees and looks at the floor. Oh my gosh, do I have to do all the talking? "Caleb, I'm so glad you came to see me. All these years I thought you broke up with me because I wasn't enough for you, and to hear you tell me that it wasn't because of that." I place my hand on his back. "You've mended my heart."

"I'm glad someone's happy," he mutters. I wouldn't say happy, more like content, but I won't get into that now.

"You will be too. I promise you will be. And I'm so proud of you. Look at the way you've stood up to your father."

"I haven't done anything yet." He shrugs hopelessly.

"But you will," I say, taking his hand. "I know you will. Caleb, what is it that you want more than anything in this world?" He sighs.

"I thought it was you," he says. Okay, I totally set myself up for that one. "But being here has made me realize that it's over. It's been too long, and you're right. We're different people now."

"And if we'd stayed together, you and I both know that it wouldn't have worked. You were right to break up with me," I say. "You are so honorable for doing that. My life is better because of you." He looks into my eyes and tucks a strand of hair behind my ear.

"I will always love you," he whispers. A lump rises in my throat.

"You have no clue what you mean to me," I say as I hug his neck and sob. I hadn't planned on crying, but now that I've started, I can't stop. I cry and cry while Caleb strokes my hair.

"Can I tell you a secret?" he asks.

"Of course." I pull back and wipe my eyes with my shirt.

"I want to start my own architectural firm. I'm sick of being in my dad's shadow. I'd rather build gas stations than keep doing things his way."

"Someone wise once told me to live like there's no tomorrow." I take his hand in mine. "So take your own advice, and do it. I know you can."

"Emma, I have to confess that one of the reasons I came back for you is because I know how much you believe in me, and I guess I needed to hear it."

"I know," I say, looking down at my lap. "I came to see you the other day for the same reason." I look up to see him smiling. "It would be so easy to ride off with you in the sunset and venture into the unknown."

"But we can't," he says slowly. I lean back into the sofa and shut my eyes.

"If only life were a movie." I rest my head on his shoulder. Caleb lets out a soft laugh and the two of us sit for a moment. Just being here next to him makes me feel far away from all the chaos going on outside this room. For the first time in weeks I feel peace, and you know what? I even feel hope.

"I broke up with Katlyn." So much for peace.

"What?" I ask sitting straight up and turning toward him.

"I care about her, I really do, but part of the reason I proposed was to spite my father." He lets out a sigh. Is it wrong that part of me wishes I had eloped with him to spite his father? "I think I need to be on my own for a while."

"Good decision," I say as I get to my feet.

"I'm flying home tomorrow to talk to my dad, so I guess this is goodbye."

"Not goodbye," I say as I wrap my arms around his waist. "This is see you later." We hug for a few moments but eventually, I step back and look deeply in his eyes. "No regrets?" I ask.

"No regrets," he says, smiling at me. I take his hand and we walk to the elevator. Man, this is harder than I thought. Part of me doesn't want to let go of his hand because this could be the last moment we ever have alone together.

"One day some amazing woman is going to come along, and you're going to sweep her off her feet, just like you did me." I shake my head. "Gosh, she has no idea how lucky she is."

"I love you, Emma," he says as the elevator doors open.

"I love you too," I say quietly. I step onto the elevator and end what I thought was the most important chapter of my life.

When I push open the doors to the hotel, I can almost hear Celine Dion singing, "A New Day Has Come." I walk home feeling at peace because I suddenly realize that I'm going to be okay. Sure I'm out of a job, but at least I'm writing about something I believe in. So Caleb and I are never going to be together. At least I was lucky enough to have an opportunity to be with him for two of the most amazing years of my life. So Zoë hates me. Oh well, at least she knows the truth about Michael. But there's one thing I can't be optimistic about and that's Jack. All he did was open up a door I kept locked for so long.

Do you know how rare it is to meet someone and just know? Before I even spoke to him, I knew my life would be different because of him. Better because of him. I'll be the first to admit that things have been rocky between us, but that's only because he takes my breath away. Do you know how frustrating it is to have finally found your soul mate only to learn that he belongs to someone else?

I climb the stairs to my apartment and check my messages. Jack never called, but that's okay. It's his loss. I e-mail my story to Jocelyn and with a feeling of hope and excitement close my eyes and drift off into a wonderful night's sleep.

43

I jump out of my bed at 11 AM. Mandy!

"Oh my gosh!" I exclaim. What if Lance is really a serial killer? Mandy could be lying dead in an alley, and it's all my fault. What am I going to tell her parents? I sprint to the nearest phone and dial her number. It takes me three tries because my shaky fingers keep pressing the wrong buttons.

"Hello?" she answers in her tired voice.

"Oh my gosh! Are you okay? I thought you were dead!" She laughs.

"Calm down, Emma. I'm fine."

"What are you doing asleep?" I say suspiciously. Never mind the fact that I just woke up myself.

"What time is it?" she asks, yawning.

"Eleven," I say.

"I stayed out late last night. Can I call you later?" I ignore her.

"You stayed out late? With Lance?"

"Who's Lance?" she asks.

"What?" I shriek.

"I'm kidding. Maybe you should eat a bran muffin or something. You're being really uptight."

"I'm sorry. It's just that I set my best friend up with this wonderful guy and I'm—" I start.

"He's great," she interrupts.

"He's great?" I ask. "Is that all you're going to tell me? Mandy, what is my Golden Rule in matchmaking?" I ask condescendingly.

"I know, I know, you're the boss. You get to know all the details. But Emma," she says with a whisper. "I can't talk right now."

"Why can't you talk right now? Do you have flem caught in your throat or something?" Then suddenly, there goes the light bulb. "Oh!" I exclaim. "You mean, he's there?" Oh my gosh! This is huge. This is beyond huge.

"Nothing happened," she whispers. "It was really late, and I felt bad making him pay for a hotel room when I have an extra bedroom."

"Do you like him?" I ask.

"Yes, now stop making me blush. Look, I think he's waking up. I'll call you later."

"Okay," I say a little disappointed. I so wanted the dirt.

"Emma," she says before I hang up, "there were sparks." I hang up the phone in a state of joy.

Things are still looking up. I can't remember the last time I had two consecutive wonderful days. I kind of have that feeling you get on the last day of school when you pack up your books and clean out your locker. I've cleaned out my locker with Caleb, my job, even Mandy, though I can't help but wonder why I'm having all this closure. Maybe it's time I pick up and move somewhere. Or maybe I'm about to die.

I pour myself a cup of coffee, trying not to think about the fact that I might die today. After savoring what could be my last sip of caffeine, I nervously make my way to the phone. I've been giving it a lot of thought and decided to pitch my story to *The Boston Globe*. An old professor of mine is an editor there. I cross my fingers and dial what used to be his old work number. I can't believe I kept his class syllabus.

"Ian Embry," he says sharply. I hope he remembers me. Better yet, I hope he likes me. The class certainly hated me, but surely *he* loved my questions. After all, he did tell me to contact him if I ever needed a reference. I clear my throat.

"Hi, Professor Embry. This is Emma Mosley. I was a student in your class a few years ago. I was the one—"

"Miss Mosley," he says in a more relaxed tone. "Of course I remember you. Are you still as inquisitive as you were in graduate school?" he jokes.

"Yes, sir. I'm afraid I am," I say reluctantly. I knew he'd remember me. You know how some people are able to get through life by blending? Well, that's definitely not me. I'm not a blender.

"Good. I always liked that about you." I pause.

"I bet you're wondering why I'm calling you on a Sunday morning," I say.

"The thought did cross my mind."

"Well, it's kind of a long story. Okay. Let's see. Where do I begin?"

"How about from the beginning," he suggests.

"Okay." I take a deep breath and explain the Edward Kelly situation with as little detail as possible. I tell him about what I saw. I tell him about quitting my job. I even tell him I have an unidentified source that can give me credibility. After five minutes of explanation, I stop talking and take another deep breath. I'm beginning to think that talking is a form of exercise. You know, all that jaw movement. But I guess then that would mean that eating is also a form of exercise, which contradicts my theory.

"I see," he says calmly. "Are you pitching your story to me or do you have another agenda?"

"Uh ... well, actually, I've already written the story. I know it's a lot to ask, but I'd really like to send it to you."

"Miss Mosley," he says after what seems like the world's longest pause. "You have to see the predicament I'm in. I don't doubt your writing ability because I know it's superb, but if I print a story that contains any false information, I could get in big trouble."

"I'm aware of that, sir. But I give you my word that there's no false information in the story. And it's not the kind of story that you'd think it is. It's more of an essay than a tabloid tale," I say.

"Interesting," he says. "Like an opinion piece?" he asks.

"Yes, but factual. I took quotes from Edward Kelly's speeches and interviews. Then I used facts from his actual life to contradict what he said."

"Are you aware that most people in this city are avid supporters of Edward Kelly? He has a great reputation, you know. And he's getting national attention as a rising star."

"Yes, sir. I'm fully aware of that. This is why I wrote an opinion piece instead of an article." He sighs. "Professor, not only did he blatantly lie to my face but he also lied to the rest of this city. My city," I add with emphasis.

"I'll tell you what," he says with a laugh. "How about you e-mail me your story? I'm assuming it's ready for press?"

"Of course."

"Well send it to me. I'll look it over and if it's appropriate, I'll pitch it to the senior editor."

"Thank you," I gasp.

"I'm not promising anything, but it's worth considering," he says.

I give him my information, send him the story, and attempt to wait. I attempt anything and everything I can to take my mind off Professor Embry's decision. I put in a yoga tape but shut it off after three minutes. I try vacuuming the rugs, but then freak out when I realize I may not hear the phone ring. I finally opt for pacing around the apartment. It's amazing how slowly time goes by when you're anxiously awaiting news. I wonder if OJ felt this way when he was awaiting the verdict. After what seems like an eternity, the phone rings.

"Hello," I gasp.

"Emma," Professor Embry says.

"Yes," I say nervously. This is one of those situations where your heart is beating so fast and with just one sentence, your whole life can change.

"Your piece was really good," he starts. Oh man! I can feel it. He's letting me down gently. What am I going to do? I put all my eggs in this basket. I really and truly have no back up plan. Man, this bites!

"But ..." I say trying to beat him to the punch line.

"There's no but. It was really good, and we're running it in tomorrow's paper." I think my heart just stopped.

"I'm sorry, but did you just say that you were running my story?"

"Yes, and in tomorrow's paper so we have to get on it." Oh my gosh. My entire body feels numb, but in a good way. Be still my beating heart, I want to jump out of my skin!

"There's no chance you'll ID your unidentified source, is there?" he asks. "It would definitely strengthen your story." This is one of those defining moments where everything I believe in is riding on the line. If I tell him yes, it would help my credibility immensely. But as tempting as it is, I know better. My credibility to myself is much more important than any story I'll ever tell. I may be passionate about writing, but at the end of the day I have to live with myself.

"No, sir. I can't do that."

"Even if it means not running your story?" he asks. Sometimes it bites to take the high road. I shut my eyes and let out a huge sigh.

"I'm sorry, but I can't betray her trust. I've given her my word."

"Good answer," he says. I pop my eyelids open.

"You mean that was a test?"

"Yes, and you passed with flying colors. Always stick to your guns, Miss Mosley. That's what makes you a great writer." I'm flattered, and for once, nice guys don't finish last. "Now listen. If things turn out the way we think they might, it could get pretty ugly for you." Why does everybody keep saying that?

"Am I going to get shot or something?"

"No," he says with a laugh. "But Kelly's people will sure want you to." My mother would be so happy to hear that.

"So what do you mean ugly?" I ask, hoping he was kidding about the last part.

"You're going to have a lot of people talking about you, both good and bad. Reporters are going to call you and even follow you around for a few weeks. In a nut shell, you're going to create a media circus."

"So basically I'm like *Celebrities Uncensored*, without Sunset Strip."

"Something like that," he says, chuckling.

"Professor, can I ask you something?"

"Of course," he says.

"If you were me, what would you do?"

"I'd write the story."

"Really?" I ask with a smile plastered to my face.

"Absolutely. You may get a lot of attention that you're not used to, but very few journalists are given the opportunity to cover a story like this. And your piece is very well written. I didn't have to edit a thing."

"I owe that to your teachings, Yoda." He laughs. I

always loved Professor Embry for his lightheartedness. Most of my professors walked around as if they needed laxatives, but not Professor Embry. He always taught us to think freely, which was so refreshing because Harvard was very intimidating.

"I'll be in touch, but look for it tomorrow."

"Thank you so very much," I say.

"No, Miss Mosley. Thank you." We hang up and I just sit there for a second.

Is this really happening? Is my story really going to be in *The Boston Globe* tomorrow? Words don't even begin to describe my state. I'm ecstatic. I stand on the top of my sofa and scream at the top of my lungs. Gosh, that felt good.

44

I go into the kitchen and fix myself a bowl of spaghetti. As I reach for the marinara sauce, I drop it down my favorite white T-shirt.

"Crap," I yell as I reach for a dish rag, but before I have time to clean up my mess, I hear my cell phone ring. Thinking it may be Jocelyn, I rush over to it.

Oh my gosh! It's Jack. Can he see me? I jump behind the couch in case he can. Screen his call, my head is telling me. But my heart longs to talk to him—to hear his voice. I take a deep breath and answer the phone.

"Hi," I say softly.

"Hey," he says softly. For a moment, we sit in awkward silence. Why is he calling me now? What could he possibly want? He has to know I've already written the story.

"Hi, Jack. Hi," I say again. Shut up, Emma!

"You sound a little weird. Are you all right?" I plop down on the floor.

"Yeah, I'm fine. I'm just a little surprised to hear from you now. But at least you called me back."

"You called me?" he asks with surprise.

"Yeah, yesterday. I left a message with Na—" I stop to let out a sigh. "I should have known."

"I'm sorry," he says, understanding the unstated. "I left my cell phone at the office yesterday and didn't pick it up until this afternoon." I pick at my half-polished toes. "I hope you know I would have called you back," he says sincerely.

"I know," I say softly, though really I want to scream in frustration and get some answers from him. I want to know what his flaw is. And I want to know why he is calling me out of the blue. Why can't he just leave me alone?

"Listen, I know things are a bit awkward between us, but I really need to see you." Did he just say "us"? Are we an "us"? Because the last time I checked, he was dating the Anti-Christ.

"Okay," I say. I hear someone buzz my apartment.

"Can you hang on a second? Someone's at my door."

"Actually, it's me," he says.

"What!" I jump to my feet.

"Do you want to let me in or should I stay out here and freeze?" he says in a laughing tone. Oh my gosh, I can't let him see me like this. Why does he always have to come over? What happened to the telephone? And e-mail? I love e-mail.

"Uh, sure," I say as I buzz him up. I open the front door so he can let himself in, then make a mad dash to the bathroom. Forget the marinara sauce on the floor: my appearance takes precedent. Once again, I have less than a minute to make myself look halfway presentable. I grab my Levis out of the hamper and sniff them. They smell okay. I throw them on. The very thought of Jack catching me in my boxers sends chills up my spine. I dart to my bedroom and throw on my favorite red tank top.

"Emma?" I hear him call as he shuts the door. My gosh! Did he sprint up the stairs or something?

"I'll be right out," I say, glancing at myself in the mirror.

"Hey," I say casually, coming out of the bathroom. As usual, Jack looks great. He's wearing blue jeans and a T-shirt that's just tight enough to show off his pecs.

"You look nice," he says as I approach him.

"Are you on crack?" I respond without thinking. He smiles. "I mean, thank you."

"How are you?" he asks as he follows me into the den.

"I'm okay." I sit down on the sofa and curl my knees into my chest, but he remains standing. "I finished my story."

"I know," he says. Okay, he's obviously not going to sit down. I get to my feet and walk toward him.

"You know?"

"Well, I figured you'd write it pretty soon." He stares at me intently, which causes me to look at the floor. Why is he acting weird? He never acts weird. I'm the weird one.

"Oh," I say, shifting my feet uncomfortably. "So, that's why you're here. I should have guessed. I mean, why else would you be here?" To see me is the correct answer, but isn't that the joke of the century. I continue to look at the ground.

Do you want to know something funny? If I could have any wish in the world, I wouldn't wish to fly. I wouldn't wish for a higher metabolism. I wouldn't even wish for world peace. (How wrong is that?) I'd wish that this man standing only a few feet away would tell me that he's amazed by me. I wish he'd scoop me up in his arms and tell me that he's lucky to know me. You have no idea how frustrating this is. And I thought the rabbit never getting to the Trix was bad. My whole life I've daydreamed about this man. How will we meet? What will he look like? How long do I have to wait for him? And here he is, standing three feet from me.

Never has a man's presence made it hard for me to breathe. Never have I been able to relate to Celine Dion and Michael Bolton. Never have I felt weak at the knees by a simple brush of someone's arm. Never have I needed someone's approval. As I stand here and look into Jack's dark eyes, I can't help but be sad. It's a cruel thing to think that you have met your match, only to discover that he doesn't want to be with you.

"I came here to say something that needs to be said in person." He steps closer to me, and my heart starts pounding. Maybe he does want to be with me, I can't help but wish. "I'm proud of you," he says placing his hands on my bare shoulders. Chills run up my spine.

"For what?"

"For being you." I raise my eyebrows. "For always acting on what you believe in, no matter what the cost. You have courage, Emma, and I admire that." He brushes the hair out of my eyes. I back away.

"That's what you came over to tell me?" I slump into the sofa in defeat. He's supposed to tell me I'm his soul mate, not give me a pep talk. What is he, my soccer coach?

"Partly." He sits on the edge of the coffee table. I perk up in hopes of what the other part may be. Okay, he's like two feet away from me. My heart is literally leaping from my chest because his gaze is so intense. "I gave you a challenge when I assigned you Edward Kelly's campaign, and not only did you give him the benefit of the doubt, but you put your prejudices aside and embraced him. And when things got bad, you stood up for yourself." I shrug.

"Anybody would've done that," I say, looking down at his feet. He's wearing Wallabees. I love Wallabees!

"No, anybody wouldn't have done that." He lifts my chin with his hand. "You're rare. You lost your job for something you believed in. That's what makes you special. And strong." I would talk, but I'm speechless. "Emma, I didn't come over to talk you out of writing the story. I came over to tell you that I dropped Edward Kelly as my client." I smile, place my hand on his knee and scoot a little closer. Our faces are a mere inch apart, which kinda scares me because I'm so broken out.

"I did a lot of thinking, and I still don't like the fact that your story could hurt his family or you, but you were right. He lied. And I can't represent a liar." He looks down at the ground.

"I'm sorry I stirred all this up. I didn't mean to hurt anyone." I am so tempted to run my finger across his scar, something I've wanted to do since meeting him. "Especially you." We stare at each other a moment and this time, I don't shy away from his gaze.

"You're not the one who hurt people. He is." I want to tell him so badly that his opinion matters to me more than anybody's. I want to tell him that the moment I laid eyes on him, I knew I'd never have that feeling again.

"So why are you really here?" I ask with a laugh. I lean back into the couch and plop my feet next to him on the table. "You don't owe me anything. I'm not mad at you. I'm not even disappointed, if you can believe that." He gives me a half smile. Is it stupid that I'm still waiting for him to say that he loves me?

"Actually," he says, playing with a loose string on my Levis, "I'm here to say goodbye."

"Goodbye!" I exclaim jumping to my feet. "Where you going?"

"Back to New York," he says, standing. "Things are running smoothly here, and there's a lot going on there." I'm so tempted to throw a pillow at him.

"But ... why ... I mean, when are you leaving?" I manage to get out.

"You're my last stop," he says, placing his hands in his pockets.

"But you can't just leave!" I begin pacing the room.

"There's no need for me to stay." No reason to stay?

What about me?

"What about Natasha?" I ask after a moment's thought. "Do you really want a long-distance relationship? They never last." Hum, not a bad idea. Maybe he should go. Jack watches me for a minute.

"We broke up," he says finally. I stop in my tracks, while he walks over to me in the kitchen.

"I wish I could say I'm sorry."

"No you don't," he says with a laugh.

"You're right. I don't," I say hitting his arm. We look at each other until our smiles fade. "So what happened?" He gives me an I-can't-believe-you-just-asked-me-that look. "Please," I say with a smile. "Like I wasn't gonna ask." He laughs as I plop myself on the bar.

"It's been a long thing coming, but every time I wanted to end things, something would come up so we'd move on. Plus, the whole thing was long distance so we really hadn't spent more than three days together until I came to Boston a few weeks ago." Well, shoot. Why didn't he tell me all that from day one? It's just like him to keep his cool, even about a recent ex. But wait a minute. He wasn't supposed to say that. He was supposed to say that he broke up with her for me. He's available. I'm available. What's standing in our way? Why doesn't he ask me how I feel about him? Okay, maybe he just needs a little encouragement. After all, I've spent more time hating him than being nice to him.

"Well, just so you know, I always saw you with someone else." I look down at the ground in embarrassment. Okay, if that's not a hint, I don't know what is.

"I better get going," he says, reaching for his coat. Wait a second. He was supposed to ask me who I saw him with. This is so not going according to plan.

"Uh, okay," I say as I hop down and follow him to the door. He's practically running. This isn't happening. He can't really be leaving. I'm so shocked that my mouth can't even muster the strength to explode all the emotions of my heart.

"Goodbye, Emma," he says as he takes my hand. He kisses it gently and walks out the door.

"Jack," I shout after him, and he turns his head around.

"Are you kidding me? Can you really just pick up and leave after everything that's happened here?" We stare at each other for a moment.

"No, but I have to," he says and walks down the steps. I shut the door and slide to the floor. A wave of emotion rushes over me. It was never about Natasha. He never wanted me. I cup my face in my hands and sob like a baby.

45

I splash cold water on my face and call my mom.

"Well then he's not worth your tears, honey," Mom says gently when I tell her about Jack.

"I know," I mumble. The truth is, he is worth my tears. He's everything I've ever dreamed of in a man, and then some. But how could he just leave like that? If it was so easy for him to just pick up and move, why did he bother telling me? I feel so helpless. Here I am ready to take a risk, and the guy doesn't even want me. Maybe people are right. Maybe there isn't such a thing as love at first sight. I'm so naïve.

"Do you really know that?" she asks. I sigh and wipe my eyes for the hundredth time.

"I know that I need to get my head out of the clouds and start living in the real world. Mom, I barely know the guy, and here I am, acting like he was ..." I trail off. "You know." I can almost hear her smiling through the phone.

"Sweetie, that's okay. You're a dreamer." I wander into the kitchen and start taking out my aggression on the dishes. Mandy would die if she saw the state of the apartment.

"I wish I'd never met him," I say, digging the coffee grounds out of a mug.

"Don't say that. He may have hurt you, but at least he gave you something to dream about." That's true. I've spent countless hours daydreaming about Jack. Want to know something crazy? That day in Saks, when he freed my over-sized feet from prison, I thought he was the one. And I have never used that phrase lightly. Ever since Caleb, I've laughed at the concept of The One. I couldn't understand the idea of waiting for someone your whole life. What does that mean? That life begins with a guy? But the day I met Jack, the day his slate eyes matched mine, I knew exactly what people were talking about. Or so I thought I did. I throw the mug into the sink. Boy, do I have good instincts or what?

"So, are you going to read the paper tomorrow?" I ask in attempts to change the subject.

"You bet I am. I've alerted the town. Daddy and I are so proud of you." I smile and set the mug on the counter.

"Thanks."

"You call me if you want to talk, okay darling? I don't care what time it is."

"Okay." I love my mom more than life itself, but nothing she can say will cheer me up. I have an emptiness in my heart that feels all too familiar.

"Love you," she says. I hang up the phone and scrape cemented Velveeta Shells out of a bowl. When did I turn into such a slob?

Okay, I can do this. I can let this go. I'll be fine. I take a few deep breaths in attempts to relax but am interrupted by a knock at the door. I jump a mile out of my seat. Maybe it's Jack. Oh my gosh! What if he turned his car around? A smile forms as I imagine his Range Rover busting a U-turn on the freeway as he accelerates back to Boston. Back to me! So much for forgetting him. Okay, if this isn't him, I'm going to let him go for good. I shut my eyes and hope with all my might that it's him because you know what? I don't want to let him go.

"Zoë!" I say when I open the door. She hesitates.

"Can I come in?" she asks. I give her what I imagine to be a confused look because she looks at me blankly. "Please?"

"Of course." She has a key to my apartment, so I'm surprised she didn't just let herself in. "How are you?" I ask as we walk into the den. I guess this means no U-turn on the freeway.

"I'm great," she says, then stops and turns to face me. "Actually, no I'm not great. Emma, please forgive my stupidity. I'm so sorry about what I said to you. You were right about everything. You were right about Michael, and you were most definitely right about me. I had my suspicions and you completely confirmed them, but I was too scared to do anything." Would I totally ruin the moment if I told her she had me at hello?

"Why don't you sit down," I say. She looks so keyed up.

"Look, I know that I need to be by myself for a while. I knew that even before Michael, but I've just been so scared. And I'm so sorry I was mean to you. I'm deeply sorry, sis. I guess I've always just envied you."

"Me?" I ask, eyeing her perfect little figure. "Why?"

"Because you're so together." Glancing down at my still-stained T-shirt, I laugh.

"I think you have me confused with someone else." She laughs back.

"Don't get me wrong, you definitely have your share of silliness," she says. "But you always land on your feet. You've always gone after what you want, and you're so content with yourself no matter how bad things get." She takes my hand. "I admire that." My eyes fill with tears. "I want to be like that."

"Come here, you," I say, pulling her into a big hug. We cry a little, and then shake it off with a laugh. "Tell me about the conference in San Francisco."

"Oh, Emma, it was amazing. I really got to have some 'me' time. I even ditched the last day of the conference to go to Alcatraz."

"You must be sick," I joke as I put my hand up to her head.

"I am," she says as she gets to her feet. "I'm sick of not going after what I want. But that's all about to change." I look at her and shake my head in disbelief.

"What's gotten into you? I like it."

"So do I." She sits down and takes my hand. "I did something impulsive this weekend."

"I'm scared to ask." Knowing her, she got engaged again.

"I gave my landlord notice, and I'm moving to San Francisco."

"What?" I sputter.

"Because I love it there. I met this girl at the conference who's going to open a new gym. It's in this really swanky part of town. We hung out the whole time, and well, she asked me to work for her. She said she'll handle the business end of everything if I'll run the place. I can teach, personal train, whatever. It's all up to me." I shake my head in disbelief.

"I don't know what to say." She shrugs quickly and smiles.

"Say what you think," she says.

"I'm thrilled!" I squeal. Zoë's grin widens.

"I was hoping you'd say that."

"Have you told Mom?" I ask.

"Yeah, I called her last night." I pound my fist on the armrest.

"I'm going to kill her for not telling me. We just talked for over an hour." Zoë pats my arm.

"I told her not to say anything because I wanted to tell you myself."

"When are you leaving?" I ask. Oh my gosh, the word "leaving" shoots sadness through my heart. Now Zoë's leaving too. This is so surreal. Saying goodbye is a sad thing, but leaving is more bearable than being the one who gets left. I'm always the one who gets left.

"In a few days," she says. "I found an apartment in this really cool part of town. Emma, I'm so excited!"

"Well, you should be," I say, managing a half smile. First Mandy, then Jack, now Zoë.

"Mom told me about work," Zoë says with a sympathetic look. "She also told me about your story and about Caleb." She shakes her head. "My gosh, how have you handled all this on your own?" I let out a heavy sigh and fall back in my chair.

"I wouldn't say I've handled it. More like made it through the day." I don't tell her the amount of chocolate I've consumed this week, though I'm afraid my swollen backside might give me away.

"Do you want to talk about anything?" she asks quietly.

"Not really," I say, poking at the hole in my shirt. I pause and look her in the eye. "But I do want to talk about you and Michael. I'm so sorry that I set you up with that creep." She shakes her head.

"Oh my gosh, Emma. It's not your fault," she gasps.

"It is partly," I say guiltily. "And did you know that Michael lied to you about Jack?"

"Yeah," she says. "But wait a second. How do you know?"

"I just knew." She eyes me warily for a minute.

"Promise not to be mad if I tell you something?" she asks. Why does that phrase always scare me?

"What did you do?" I ask suspiciously. She clears her throat and leans forward.

"When I was in San Francisco, I called Jack."

"What?" I ask, straightening up in my chair. "Why?"

"I wanted to ask him about Michael. I promise it had nothing to do with you. I just needed to hear what a scumbag he was in order to have closure. I'm not like you, Emma. I can't read people." I let out a bitter laugh.

"And you think I can?" I shake my head. "I mean, I actually thought Jack was the one, and I couldn't have been more off base. How's that for reading people?"

"You thought Jack was ..." She brings both hands to her mouth in a gasp. "Oh my gosh! You're in love with him!"

"What?" I say nonchalantly, though the thought has definitely crossed my mind. She looks at me like a wide-eyed school girl. "I think that California air has made you loopy," I say as I playfully hit her arm.

"Emma, what happened? The last time I talked to you, you hated him. You've got to fill me in." As much as I would love to share with Zoë, I just don't think I can bring myself to rehash everything that's happened since she left town. I let out a large sigh.

"Let's just say that a lot's happened over the past few days, but it doesn't matter." I chomp down on my lip to keep the tears from welling up in my eyes. Zoë reaches for my hand.

"What's this?" she asks, rubbing my hand.

"He doesn't want me," I say. Tears roll down my hot cheeks.

"How do you know that? Did you tell him how you feel?" I take a deep breath to stabilize my emotions.

"No, but I gave him plenty of opportunities to tell me how he felt." Zoë shakes my hand in exasperation.

"What are you, June Cleaver? Things don't work like that anymore. If you care about someone, you tell them right then and there. Shoot, sometimes you even grab them by the neck and make out with them furiously!" We both laugh. The idea has definitely crossed my mind. I think of the day Jack and I were stuck in the elevator.

"Emma? Earth to Emma?" Zoë shakes me and I come to.

"Huh? What!"

"What are you thinking about?"

"Uh, nothing. So why did you think I'd be mad at you for talking to Jack?" I ask in attempts to change the subject.

"Because we talked about you," Zoë says mysteriously.

"What? When did you talk?"

"A few days ago. He told me you were pretty upset about Michael, and he was really concerned about you."

"He was?"

"Yeah. And he said that you had all this stuff going on and that you ran into Caleb."

"What does he care?"

"A lot, actually. He said he thought you and Caleb were getting back together. Is that true? Because I called Mom and she didn't even know." I stand up, incredulous.

"What? No. Caleb and I ended things. But why would he think ... oh crap!" Now I remember that Jack heard Caleb's message on my machine. "I wonder if that's why he left."

"Jack left?" she asks.

"Yeah, like an hour before you got here. He told me he broke up with Natasha and silly me, I thought he was coming to confess his undying love, not to tell me he was leaving!" I begin pacing the room and chewing off my nails. Zoë stands and grabs my shoulders.

"Look, I know I'm in no position to dish out relationship advice. And I have no idea what's gone down the past few days, but Emma, the guy's crazy about you. And look at you. I've never seen you so unglued. Jack *so* did a number on you!" I shrug her off and continue my pacing.

"Sister dear, I think you're suffering from a little jet lag."

"No I'm not." She gets up and grabs me by the shoulders. "Emma, that boy is crazy about you. I heard it in his voice, and look at you! I see it in your eyes. You and Jack fell in love." I spin on my heel to face her.

"Then why didn't he stay?"

"Because you never asked him to." Zoë moves closer and puts her arm around me. "Sis, I love you dearly, but sweetie, you weren't exactly nice to him. You've hated him, what ten out of the twelve days you've known him?" She tosses my hair behind my shoulders. "Can you blame the guy for leaving? He's not a mind reader, you know. And he probably thinks you wanted to get back together with Caleb so he did the honorable thing and left. Emma, he doesn't know how you feel. *You* probably don't know how you feel." My eyes start to water.

"Yes I do," I say, slumping back in my chair. "For the first time in my life, I know how I feel. Zoë, I always pitied you for your hopeless romantic stupidity. I thought you were nuts to be head over heels for a man you hardly knew, but I understand now."

"So go get him," she says, sitting next to me. I stare blankly out the window.

"It's too late. He's gone."

"Since when did you become a quitter?" she asks.

"I'm not quitting. I'm just being realistic." For the first time in my life. "Listen, can we not talk about this anymore?"

"Sure," she says, popping up. "How about dinner? It is Valentine's Day, and seeing as that we are both dateless."

"Only if you promise not to order a salad." She laughs.

"It's a deal," she says.

46

I change my clothes in an attempt to make myself look somewhat presentable. People ought to start calling before they just come over. I throw on black tuxedo pants and a red sweater.

After a few minutes of brainstorming, we decide on Finale. It's a cute little café located next to the Park Plaza Hotel. Actually, I wouldn't really call it a café. It's more like a romantic hideaway that serves as a hot spot for couples, theater goers, and well, silly girls with a chocolate fetish. Mandy and I come here all the time because it's only two minutes from the apartment and oh, so delicious.

After scanning the menu for a moment, I con Zoë into the Chocolate Indulgence. It's this huge plate consisting of small, fancy, chocolate desserts. It's kind of like a box of Godiva chocolates. You don't really know what's what so you bite into everything.

Zoë and I spend the next hour sipping lattes and laughing over endless chocolate. I can't tell you what a treat it is to be sitting here, sharing her excitement. She's glowing with happiness. She tells me stories from her trip to San Francisco, but the highlight of the evening is hearing about what she did with Michael's ring.

"You didn't," I gasp.

"I did. I gave it to a homeless woman on the street."
She bursts out laughing.

"Did you tell Michael?"

"Better. I took a picture of her wearing it, and I texted it to him." She shows me the picture she stored in her cell phone.

"Oh my gosh! I'd give anything to see his face when he opens it," I say. We finish our last bites of chocolate and stroll out under a darkened sky.

I give Zoë a big hug. "Call me if you need help packing, okay?"

"Thanks sis. And thanks for everything."

I walk back to 3 Appleton Street, realizing that in the 26 years I've known Zoë, this is the best time we've ever had together. I'm getting to see the woman that she really is, not the person she pretends to be in a relationship. And you know what? She's never looked more beautiful. Today has been the best Valentine's Day I've ever had, and it's not because of a man. It's because I got to spend it with my sister.

I hop into bed and switch off the lights. I lie awake thinking, ticking off my blessings. I used to think that was just a metaphor, but I'm really counting tonight. Things were rough for a while, but look how fast they came together. My story is going to be read by thousands of people tomorrow. Caleb and I have resolved everything. Gosh, if he hadn't come here, I'd probably have died angry and romantically insecure. Mandy is leaving, but at least she's happy. She may have even found herself a boyfriend. Well actually, I found him, but that's beside the point. Zoë is moving to the other side of the country, but I've never seen her so confident. And for the first time in years, we're really talking to one another. I have a wonderful family, incredible friends, and although I haven't a clue as to where I'm going to be a month from now, the sky is the limit. It's blessings like these that make me realize that with or without Jack, or any other man for that matter, I'm going to be just fine.

47

"I can't believe I'm doing this!" I say as I breathe heavily into a brown paper bag.

"Relax. You're going to be fine," Mandy assures me with a pat on the back.

"Easy for you to say. You do this for a living."

"Look, I gotta go, but I'll see you out there." Mandy slaps me on the bum and struts off onto the set.

I stare at my reflection and pinch myself hard. I'm sitting in a bathrobe in a New York City studio, getting my hair and makeup done.

It's been a long two weeks. After my article hit newsstands, my life as I knew it changed dramatically. It was just as my wise professor predicted, times one hundred. The media swarmed my phone lines—and I'm not just talking local Boston media. I had national networks like *MSNBC* calling me. When I wrote the story, I promised myself that I wouldn't seek out more publicity than was necessary, so with all the strength I had in me, I refused to take any calls. Not answering the phone may seem like an easy gesture, but I assure you that it isn't. I mean, Diane Sawyer left a message on my machine. *The* Diane Sawyer!

After turning my phone off, I was stalked, literally. The only difference between the media and a stalker is a camera. But to be completely honest, the media attention wasn't the hardest to stomach. In the midst of this ridiculous media frenzy was Edward Kelly. Not only did he publicly deny every word I wrote, he even took the liberty of dragging me through the mud. At first I tried to ignore him. That's what all the celebrities do when the tabloids attack them, right? But when Kelly started lying, it was only natural to stand up for myself.

The most hilarious part of the entire mess was when Kelly pulled Natasha into it. Well, it wouldn't be fair to say he pulled her into it. I can almost picture her begging him for a piece of the action. About a week ago, I was helping Zoë pack for San Francisco, and we had the TV on just for background noise. You can imagine my state of shock when I heard Natasha's raspy voice on the ten o'clock news. Apparently Edward Kelly contacted her, and she had no problem telling the city of Boston that I'm an unstable, vindictive phony. Can we say dagger in the back? I don't profess to be super-intelligent, stable, or even likable for that matter, but vindictive and phony? I may think some mean thoughts, but I won't even drive past a lemonade stand without buying a glass. Is that an act of a vindictive person? And fake? Are you kidding me? What you see is what you get. It's almost a downfall.

But even with Natasha's ten-minutes-of-fame attempt, I managed to keep it together, though it got worse. Much worse. Not only were stories about me run every day for over a week, but Natasha managed to weasel some intern into printing awkward pictures of me. And when I say awkward, I mean mortifyingly awkward because this guy followed me around all day snapping candid photos. I mean, I understand America's obsession with candid shots. I've even jumped on that bandwagon a few times. I used to think I liked seeing Jessica Simpson without a full face of makeup or Jennifer Aniston walking her dog, but I've come to the realization that it's a total invasion of privacy. It's one thing to take someone's picture when they're out publicly, but it's another thing entirely to snap them when they're lugging an armful of groceries.

And that's exactly what Natasha had her little gofer do to me. When I opened the magazine, I about died! There, in the center spread of *Bean Town Scene*, was a picture of me picking a wedgie. First of all, everybody picks their wedgies. Who wants underwear riding up all day? Moreover, why would anyone want to see that? I'm almost positive that was how Jude Law felt when he got busted with the nanny. Except this is an innocent, little wedgie. (Actually, the wedgie was big or I wouldn't have picked it, but the gesture was innocent.) But how on God's green earth this picture informs the public about my character is beyond me. All it does is show the world that my big backside doesn't fit in my too-small underwear.

But after that incident, I decided that it wasn't a bad idea to defend myself. This is precisely why Mandy came through for me, as usual, and lined up an interview for Edward Kelly and me. Her one-week-old talk show, *Coffee Talk*, has scheduled fifteen minutes in which the sleazy politician and I are allowed to talk face-to-face.

So here I am, having my face painted so intricately that even Tammy Faye Baker would be appalled. Mandy and I went shopping yesterday, and I'm wearing a stunning black dress with tan, suede boots. I wanted to wear red, but Mandy informed me that the camera really does add ten pounds. I know today's show is a serious, professional occasion, but am I completely shallow for worrying that I may look fat? Surely serious journalists like Ann Curry worry about these things.

"That's it, Emma. We're all done," the makeup artist says as I get up from the chair. My gosh, you could carve your initials in my face. Don't get me wrong, she did a great job. I used to think applying makeup was just another annoying hassle, like shaving your legs, but this girl made it a work of art. I hardly recognize myself, but whoever I am looks pretty good.

"Thanks," I say as I check myself out in the mirror. Is this really my hair? Maybe I fell asleep and they put a wig on my head. I give it a little tug, but it doesn't budge. That's amazing. I take a mental picture of myself because I'm pretty confident that I'll never look this good again. Maybe on my wedding day, but I don't see that happening in the near future.

When I return to my dressing room, I find a black box with a red ribbon sitting on the couch.

"What's this?" I raise my eyebrows as I search for a card. Normally, I'd tear right into the package, but I'm pretty curious as to who it's from. I can't seem to find a card, so I take my chances and open the box, praying it's not a bomb. I *so* need to lay off *Dateline*.

"Oh my gosh!" I gasp and drop the box. Oh my gosh, oh my gosh, oh my gosh!

I pick up the box and open it again.

"No, he didn't," I say as I take out the very pair of black slingbacks that Jack helped me remove from my feet just a month ago. Well, not the very pair because these look to be my size.

My heart flutters as I kick off my tan, suede boots and replace them with the shoes. They're a perfect fit. I walk over to the mirror. After taking a few steps, I feel something in my right shoe. I sit down and remove a folded piece of paper. I unfold the paper and read it aloud.

"For old time's sake. Love, Jack."

My heart starts beating rapidly in my chest. I sit back down to keep my knees from buckling. You know that feeling you get when you have some amazing dream about kissing Matthew McConaughey but wake up snuggling your body pillow instead? Well, take that dream, multiply it times one thousand, and omit the waking up alone part. That is a fraction of the breathless excitement I feel at this moment. My head promised not to allow Jack in after he left that day, but this gesture makes my heart think otherwise. I wonder how he got back here. Oh my gosh. I wonder if he's in the audience.

So many things are running through my head right now. Does he know about Natasha's part in my public humiliation? And what if he saw me picking my wedgie in public? Okay, stop thinking about it, Emma. How dare Jack come back into my life when I finally started to forget him! Well, I wouldn't really say I started to forget him, more like I started to suppress him, but still. That really makes me mad! Who does he think he is? I'm not that easy to win over. He's too late.

I get to my feet and glance in the mirror. These shoes look much better with my dress. Okay, so if Jack didn't care about me, why would he send me expensive shoes with even more expensive sentimental value? And maybe I'm reading into things, but why did he sign the card "Love, Jack"?

"They're ready for you," says a man in a headset holding a clipboard. Wow, doesn't he look important?

I follow him to the set and suddenly it all hits me. I'm about to debate a politician on television. God help me. I feel the chunks beginning to rise.

"Um, excuse me," I say to Mr. VIP Dude. He doesn't hear me because he's busy doing something more important. "Excuse me," I say again, this time tugging on his shirt.

"Yes?" he says rather annoyed. The tugging technique works every time.

"I think I need to throw up," I say.

"Can't you hold it?" he asks impatiently.

"It's not like it's my bladder," I snap.

"Fine. The bathroom's right there," he say, pointing to a nearby door. I take off with my hand over my mouth.

"Hurry," he yells after me. "You're on in five!" What-ever. I grab the door knob. I mean, you can only puke so fast.

I slam the door shut and barf up my breakfast. Quick question. If the stomach is supposed to digest food, why are my Lucky Charms still intact? I run the sink and gargle some water. Okay, Emma, relax. Deep breath.

"You're on in three minutes. Let's go." I would so love to kill Mr. VIP Dude right now. What is this, boot camp? And does he know who my best friend is? I open the door and shakily walk to the set. My knees are bobbling like Elvis' pelvis, but the moment I see Mandy's cute face, I'm put at ease.

"You look green," she says lightly, taking my hand for reassurance. She's wearing a red, cap-sleeved dress. I guess she can wear red because she's so skinny. The stage is set up so Mandy and her co-host are on a love seat, while Edward Kelly and I are diagonally facing them in plush chairs.

"Where'd you get the shoes?" she asks, glancing down at my feet.

"I'm about to go on television and we're talking about my shoes?" I clench my fists to keep my hands from shaking and try and take a peek at the audience. "Shouldn't you be prepping me or giving me a pep talk?" But suddenly I get it. She's trying to keep my mind off Edward Kelly, who just walked onto the set. Is it wrong that I want a piece of stage equipment to come crashing down on his head? I don't want it to kill him or anything, maybe just give him amnesia. Or even better, a Harry Potter scar.

"Are you okay?" Mandy asks. "You're talking a mile a minute."

"You'll never believe this, but Jack left these shoes for me in the dressing room." She opens her mouth in shock.

"Are those the—"

"Yes." I cut her off. "The ones I was wearing the day I met Jack."

"Do they fit?" But before I can answer her, Mr. VIP Dude announces that we're on in one minute. Mandy moves to her sofa and the makeup artist follows her. This gives me time to glance into the audience.

Oh my gosh, it's Jack. He's sitting with Jocelyn. I can't make out what he's wearing, but I imagine he looks good. He'd look good in a Don Johnson blazer. He spots my gaze and gives me a playful nod. How cute is that? I see my parents sitting a few rows in front of Jack and Jocelyn. My mom gives me a thumbs up, while me daddy mouths an "I love you." I'd like to mouth it back to him but for fear that Jack will think I'm saying "I love you" to him, I opt for an ear-to-ear grin instead.

"Thirty seconds," yells Mr. VIP Dude. Oh gosh, oh gosh, oh gosh! Is it too late to back out? Kelly leans over with an icy smile.

"Are you ready to be humiliated?" he says. It's hard to imagine that just three weeks ago I was eating lobster with the man. I still can't believe I bought into his lies.

"Honey, if I'm going down, we're going down together," I say with confidence, looking him right in the eye.

"We're on in ten, nine ..."

Suddenly, I'm no longer concerned about how fat I may look. I'm worried that people won't connect with me. The whole reason I agreed to this was so that people could hear what I have to say. I want them to understand why I did what I did. My worse fear is that people will think I'm a phony. That Edward Kelly will come out smelling like roses. For the first time in my professional life, I'm doing something that really makes a difference, and to be honest, I'm scared to death.

"Five, four ..." I wonder if I have time to throw up again. Not knowing what else to do, I look up at Jack, who gives me a reassuring smile. We lock eyes for a moment, until I'm blinded with a million bright lights.

"Good morning. I'm Mandy Blake," she says confidently into the camera.

"And I'm JD Atler," says her cute co-host. JD Atler was a surprise. Initially, Mandy thought she was going to be working with another woman, but at the last minute, the producers decided flirtation took precedence over yappy, gossiping women. Can anyone say *The View*?

"And this is *Coffee Talk*," they say together. Mandy hates that part. She told me the other day that she feels like a cheese ball saying that in unison.

"I'd like to extend a warm welcome to Edward Kelly, Democratic candidate for Boston's mayoral election," JD says.

"And Emma Mosley, the brilliant writer who blew the lid on his wandering eye," Mandy adds. She looks at me and winks.

"Thank you for having me," Kelly says warmly. Oh, are we supposed to start talking now? Okay, I can do this. I will not look at the red light on the television. "And let me just tell you what an honor it is to be here," Kelly continues. "I'm hoping that after today's interview we can put this mess behind us, and I can concentrate one hundred percent on the citizens of Boston." Half the audience starts applauding. What a lie! He's just wasting time. It's like when basketball players dribble and pass the last twenty seconds of the game. I hate that.

"Thank you for that wonderful introduction," Mandy jumps in. "Now let's get down to business. Mr. Kelly," she says all professional.

"Please, call me Edward," he says as he takes a sip of his coffee and winks at her. The man is flirting with her on national television. What a creep!

"Edward," she says trying to hide her annoyance. "Am I to understand that you deny all allegations that Miss

Mosley has made against you?" Okay, it's been two minutes, and I still haven't said anything. I guess the only way to get me to shut up is to put me on television.

"That's correct," he says. Mandy looks at me to say something, but I just sit there like a deer caught in headlights. "Miss Mosley is an angry employee who was fired for making false claims that I'm having an affair with my former political strategist." He laughs. "Which is absolutely ridiculous. I have been happily married for over twenty years." Okay, I can either sit here like an imbecile or I can do something. I look to Mandy, and she gives me a speak-now-or-else look. Oh, dear. Here I go.

"Mind if I say something?" I ask with a half smile.

"Of course not," Kelly says heartily. Gosh, I'd love to use him as target practice.

"First of all, Mr. Kelly, I wasn't fired."

"Your former boss would disagree," he says.

"Well, my former boss also took the liberty of printing photographs of me picking a wedgie," I say bluntly, "so I'm not so sure of your source's credibility." The audience laughs. Wow! I wasn't even trying to be funny. "Second of all, I saw you having an affair with my own two eyes."

"Really? You saw me?" he asks raising his eyebrows in amusement. Okay, that came out wrong.

"You're right. I haven't a clue as to what you did behind that closed door on that particular occasion, but I guarantee it wasn't rehearsing a speech," I say. "Look, Mr. Kelly. What you do in your spare time is your business. I couldn't care less. You're a grown man. You're allowed to make your own decisions, but when you invite me to dinner, dote on your wife for me to see, and then ask me to write about your family values, I'm going to make sure that you practice what you preach. So when I found out that this wasn't the case, I stepped down from my position. And I almost let you get away with it."

I pause. "Then I realized that not only did you deceive your family and myself, but you also deceived the city of Boston. And if you can't even keep appearances up during your campaign, something tells me we're going to have our very own Oval Office scandal. And I'm sorry, but I can't let that happen." On a scale from one to ten, how *Jenny Jones* was that? Because that's so not what I was going for.

"Uh," JD says. "Edward. Would you care to respond?"

"Yes, I would. Thank you." He smiles at the camera. What a kiss up. "Miss Mosley is an up-and-coming journalist who'll do anything to further her career. It's rather disappointing that she would use me to do so, but it comes with the job." Mandy shoots me a look. I know she wants to jump in and help me out, but she can't. And truth be known, I'm glad she can't.

"Do you have anything to say to that?" Mandy asks calmly.

"Mr. Kelly," I begin calmly. "Why did your advertising consultant drop you as a client?"

"Excuse me?" he asks. He taps his fingers impatiently on the armrest.

"Why did Carmichael Advertising drop you?" He clears his throat.

"They didn't drop me. I dropped them."

"Really?" I say. "So would you change your response if I told you that I had documentation that would prove otherwise?"

"I'd say your documentation is fabricated," he says. Oh my gosh, the man is sweating like a pig.

"Okay. Would you change your answer if I said that I'd present that evidence and a source on tonight's news?" I hope Jack doesn't kill me. Besides, I'm bluffing. I'd never ask him to come forward like that, though I bet he'd do it.

"Uh," he says. Call me naïve, but I feel sorry for the guy.

"Mr. Kelly," I say in an attempt to rescue him from complete humiliation. "I'm not here to embarrass you. Unlike you and your campaign, I don't play unfair. I'm here today not as a reporter, but as a member of the Boston community who's been lied to. If you want to cheat on your wife, then that's your business. However, it becomes my business when you feed me lies to write to the public." I give him a chance to talk, but he says nothing, so I continue. "When I first found out what you were doing, someone told me not to come forward because it would hurt your family." I look in Jack's direction, and though I can't see him because of the bright lights, I know he's looking at me. "But you know what? I didn't hurt your family. You did. A huge part of your campaign focuses on the importance of family. And like I said before, if you want to cheat on your wife then that's your business. But please don't lie to the public because it's really insulting." I take a sip of my coffee, which really isn't coffee. Bummer.

"Edward," Mandy asks with a huge grin. "Would you care to respond to Miss Mosley?"

"Yes, I would," he says quickly. "Miss Mosley snooped into my personal life. She's ranting on about her good ethics yet has no problem harassing me in public. Look at the media circus created by one woman." You have got to be kidding me.

"I believe I'm the one who's being smeared all over the news," I say as I hold up copies of various magazines in which he has publicly sought me out. I count them out for the audience. "That makes eight," I say. "Eight times Edward Kelly has tried to drag my name through the mud. But this one is my favorite," I say as I reach for *Bean Town Scene*. The camera zooms in on the article I'm holding. "'Emma Mosley is a sloppy journalist,'" I read from the article written by Natasha's intern. I laugh. "With all due respect, I think this is sloppy journalism at its finest." The camera zooms in on the picture of me picking a wedgie. "This, Mr. Kelly, is insulting." I pause with a straight face. "I mean, have you never had a wedgie?" The audience roars in laughter. I'm so going to regret this tomorrow.

"Well, it looks like we're running out of time. Do you have any closing remarks?" JD asks Edward Kelly.

"Miss Mosley is using my good name to further her career." He stops. He has nothing else to say. The man is sweating bullets. He takes a sip of whatever he's drinking and looks around the studio. After ten seconds of silence I can't help but jump in. I'm not devoid of my humanity.

"Ladies and gentlemen, Edward Kelly made a mistake. We all make mistakes, so I don't think anybody should hold that against him." I pause and look at him. "It would be much easier if he'd just admit it, but like Bill Clinton, he wants to talk around the issue." I press my hands together in earnest. "We could go on about this all day long, but let me try and make a point. Yes, I pick my wedgies," I say as I hold up the infamous picture. "And if you want another confession, sometimes I pick my nose." Did I just say that I picked my nose on television? That's it. I'm packing my bags and moving to Europe as soon as I get off the set. "But the bottom line is that I admit that I do these disgusting things. I wouldn't go around telling millions of people that I oppose nose picking." Okay, bad metaphor. Must move on. "Mr. Kelly, you have a chance to be the mayor of a wonderful city. What you do in your private life is your business. All I ask is that you don't lie about what you do behind closed doors. You'd be surprised at how forgiving America is." I stop to take a sip of my mystery drink. Ew, I think it's Tab.

"Well, I think that's about all we have time for," JD says.

"Mr. Kelly, Miss Mosley," Mandy says as she looks at us. "Thank you for coming out today. It's been a real pleasure." She looks back into the camera. "We'll be right back with headlines." I assume that means we're about to go to commercial. Thank goodness.

As soon as the lights dim, Mandy runs over and gives me a hug.

"You were brilliant," she says, squeezing my hand.

"Did I really tell America that I pick my nose?"

"You did," she says. "But everybody does."

"Mandy, we need you at the desk," Mr. VIP Dude says.

"Thank you, Mandy. Thank you not only for this, but for being my very best friend," I say as I hug her tightly.

"You're welcome," she says as she kisses my forehead and sprints to the other set. I turn to say something to Edward Kelly, but he's nowhere in sight. I begin walking to my dressing room.

"Emma," my parents yell in unison. How did they get back here so fast?

"You were fantastic," my mom gushes, giving me a hug.

"You sure had the guy sweating," my dad adds. He puts his arm around my shoulder. Now that I'm off the set I feel so at ease.

"I kinda feel sorry for him," I say.

"Don't," my dad says, looking me squarely in the eye. "He got off easy."

We head to my dressing room to watch the rest of the show from a TV monitor. Mandy is interviewing Enrique Iglesias. How she does so without fainting is beyond me. I'd love for him to be my hero, baby.

"Are you ready to go?" my mom asks after the last commercial break.

"Actually, I think I'm going to hang around for a few days," I say, standing up to stretch.

"Are you sure?" she asks.

"Yep," I say. "A few extra days in New York might be nice."

"Well, we're going to take off," my dad says.

"Call us when you get a chance," my mom adds, giving me a parting hug.

"Okay." I smile.

"We love you," they say in unison and then shut the door.

48

For a moment I stand at the door and meditate on everything that just happened. After a few moments of deep thought, I hear a knock at the door. Maybe it's Enrique, I think as I jump to my feet. He's come to take me to his Miami mansion. Move over Anna Kournikova.

"I'm coming, Enrique," I say as I fling open the door. Only it's not Enrique Iglesias standing at my door asking to be my hero, baby. It's Jack.

"Enrique, huh?" he asks with a grin.

"Iglesias. We're running away together." All I can say is thank heavens he can't see me blush underneath all this makeup.

"Why? Because you told America that you pick your nose?" he asks. I give him a smirk. "Just don't do it while you're driving. I hear you can puncture your brain." I can't help but laugh at this.

"When did you get to be so funny?" I shift my weight awkwardly from one foot to the other.

"I've always been this funny. Can I come in? That is, before Enrique takes you away," he adds. I step aside. He walks into my dressing room, which is about half the size of my college dorm room. I inhale his cologne and can't help but think of the day we met. We stand there for a few moments in an uncomfortable silence, and this time Jack doesn't ease the awkwardness. My goodness, he's blatantly staring at me. This is so awkward. What do I do?

"Why are you looking at me like that?"

"How am I looking at you?" he asks seriously.

"I don't know," I say uneasily. "Funny." Have you ever stood next to a man you just wanted to grab by the neck and kiss? So much for putting him behind me. I stare down at the floor.

"You were unbelievable today," he says. I look up and to my astonishment see that he's a foot away from me. Okay, there goes that weak-at-the-knees thing again.

"Thank you for the shoes," I say quietly, taking a step backward. "I can't believe you remember."

"Of course I remember." He steps even closer, and I back further away. What is he doing here, anyway?

"Why are you backing away from me?" he asks, furrowing his brow.

"Because I ... I ... I need a breath mint," I manage to get out. Did I just say that I needed a breath mint? And why am I stuttering like Rain Man?

"Have dinner with me tonight," he says, picking up my hand. I wriggle it free.

"I can't," I say, tucking my hair behind my ear.

"Why not?"

"Because," I say and then turn my back to him like a spoiled little brat who didn't get a pony for her birthday. I feel him walking toward me.

"Because why?" he asks, placing his hands on my shoulders. I can feel his warm breath in my ear. All the hairs on the back of my head stand straight up. It takes every bit of strength I have not to kiss him, but since all my strength is being used on not looking at him, there's none left to hold back my tears. I feel my eyes begin to water. This is the closest I've ever been to him. We're an inch from each other. If I were to boggle my head like a turkey, we'd definitely be lip to lip. Oh, I want to kiss him. I want to kiss him so badly. I turn to face him. "Because," I whisper.

"Because why?" He touches my face. I take a deep breath and pull away.

"Because you suck." Such an intense moment and I have to ruin it by talking.

"I suck?" he asks, confused. Clearly that wasn't the answer he was expecting. Nor was I.

"Yeah, Jack. You suck." I walk past him to the other side of the room.

"You know what really bites?" I ask, pacing back and forth.

"No, but I'm sure you're going to tell me."

"Of course I am," I say matter-of-factly. "You never show any emotion. You're so calm about everything, and I'm just the opposite. I'm emotional about everything and calm about nothing."

"What does this have to do with us?" he asks patiently.

"My point is that we're opposites."

"So?" He starts walking toward me again. I resume pacing. You can't kiss a moving target.

"So, it wouldn't work even if we wanted it to. Not that I'm saying *you* want it to." I stop and clap my hands over my mouth. "Oh gosh. I need to shut up."

"Have dinner with me tonight," he says again.

"I don't know what's worse. The fact that you're missing the point or the fact that you're so incredible that I can't even get to the point." I pause as I digest my own words. "I'm not having dinner with you." I turn toward the wall.

"Why not?" he asks, taking my shoulders and turning me gently to face him. I can't think of a single reason as to why I should reject this man. Why am I pushing him away? Here he is, single, asking me to dinner, and I'm too prideful and scared to show him my heart.

"Because you can't just come after me when it suits you. Do you have any idea how it felt to have you not stand up for me? And what about the fact that you left town with some lame excuse that I'm still not sure of? I was in the midst of all sorts of crap, and you just left." I pause to swallow my tears.

"I didn't leave you," he says hoarsely. I shake my head.

"Do you have any idea how I felt when you took off? Do you even have a clue how rejected I felt? And now what? You want me to just forget that ever happened? Forget how insecure and alone I felt." I kick off my Manola Blahniks, pick them up, and place them into his hands.

"These were a gift," he says.

"I don't want them." I'm so full of it. I'd take Manola Blahniks from Osama Bin Laden if he offered me a pair. "Jack, you can't just keep coming in and out of my life when it's convenient for you." I look down at the shoes. "Besides, Manola Blahniks are a bit out of my league. I'm more of a Payless kind of girl."

"Emma," he begins, but I cut him off because I'm scared to death to hear what he's going to say.

"Jack, I don't need a man to be happy. I'm fine on my own," I say matter-of-factly. Gosh, I sound like such a feminist.

"Maybe a man needs you to be happy," he says softly. Was that a hypothetical or does he mean him? You know what? It doesn't matter. It's too late. I'm too hurt, and nothing he can say will get me over that.

"Or maybe we need to accept the fact that we're not going to happen. I mean, look at our history. It's been one obstacle after another. We've spent more time hating each other than ..." Was I about to use the L-word? Do I love him? Oh my gosh, I think I do. So why am I saying this? Why am I pushing him away? I'm scared, that's why. I'm petrified that he'll see the real me and be disgusted. And what if it doesn't work? I can't survive another Caleb. I refuse to feel like that again. The benefits don't outweigh the pain.

"Than what?" he presses. I set myself up for that one.

"Nothing."

"Just say it," he says, taking my hand.

"You doubted me, Jack."

"I never doubted you for a second. You know exactly how I feel, but you're too scared to let me say it." I pull my hand away.

"Why wouldn't I be scared? You ditched me the second things got rough. You broke up with Natasha, came to my house to tell me, got me all excited, and then just left. Why the heck do you think I'd be real with you after that?"

"Look, I'm really sorry I left without an explanation. I—" he starts, but I cut him off again.

"I don't care," I interject, which of course is a lie.

"What is wrong with you?" he asks. "Where's the Emma I know so well?"

"You don't know me, Jack." I put my hands in my face. "Please, I don't want to hear any more."

"You're scared to hear more just like you're scared of needing somebody. You're scared of reality. You're scared of disappointment. And most of all, you're scared of love." I turn my back to him as my eyes start welling with tears. This time, I don't even care. They stream down my face to the point where I can actually taste the salt.

"Just go," I choke.

"Emma, please don't do this." I turn to face him.

"Jack, I need you to leave, okay?"

"No," he says firmly.

"Please," I beg. "If I mean anything to you then you'll just leave. You'll turn around, shut the door behind you, and never look back." Oh gosh. I said the same thing to Caleb six years ago. He looks down at the ground and shakes his head. For a moment we stand there in silence. The tears are still rolling down my face, so I don't look up.

"Okay, Emma. I'll go," he says as he turns to leave, but when he reaches the door he stops. "But not until I tell you this." Oh, man. "Look me in the eyes." I look up into his dark eyes. My gosh, I've never seen them so intense. "I know you, Emma. I've always known you. Somewhere ..." He chokes on his words. "Somewhere behind all that anger and that fear is the passionate, beautiful Emma that I'm just dying to be near." My heart is racing. As much as I want to throw myself in his arms I can't. It's like my arms are weighed down. I take a step back.

"Please go," I say, crossing my arms and looking off to the ceiling. I feel Jack stare at me for a moment then turn toward the door.

"I know you, Emma." He turns back toward me, keeping his distance. "I know you well. And I know what you're doing. I'm sorry I couldn't let you know me when you wanted to. Things were more complicated then, but I'm here now." He pauses. "It's just a shame that you'll never know me because of your stupid pride." And just like that Jack Carmichael walks out of my life again.

49

It's been over a month since my television appearance and things have finally settled down. When I returned to Boston, I received quite a few job offers, including Natasha's old position, which became available not long after she ran the famous wedgie picture. Naturally I declined, but it was nothing personal. I just thought it was about time I move on, and I couldn't be happier. I'm writing my own column for *New York News*. The senior editor called a few days after my interview on *Coffee Talk*. Apparently he's been looking for someone who's not afraid to speak her mind. Would you believe he liked the fact that I pick my nose?

And people are actually reading my column. They even mentioned it on *The O'Reilly Factor* last week. It's surreal to actually have a voice now. I didn't know how much responsibility it would be, but I have made a vow to always use it for good. I still feel a little guilty that my career took off as a result of the Edward Kelly story. I know I'm not the one who lied, but how can I not feel a little responsible for stirring things up?

Speaking of Edward Kelly, he dropped out of the election two days after our interview. I tried to contact him for over a week, but he wanted nothing to do with me. It was later brought to my attention that he left his wife and family and moved to Barbados with one of his son's former classmates. It's really a sad tale, but I'll let somebody else write about it.

Zoë is doing extremely well in San Francisco. Her gym opens next week so I'll be in San Francisco for that. She hired some posh event-planning firm to promote the place. Rumor has it that Don Johnson will be in attendance. I so hope he wears his *Miami Vice* blazer.

Did I mention Caleb is also doing wonderful? As expected, things did not go well with his father, but he's not letting that stop him this time. I'm so proud of him. He finally stood up for himself, and though he's poorer than he'd like to be, things are looking up. I received a post card from him a few days ago. He's living in Paris working for some up-and-coming architect. It's strange how life kind of works itself out. I'll never forget Caleb, but I'm so glad things are the way they are. It's just a matter of time before some French woman moves in on him and he sweeps her off her feet—much like he did with me. And I have no doubt that she'll make him happier than I ever could.

So here I am, an official New Yorker. It's just like old times, living with Mandy; except this time we're living it up in New York City. Jack was right in telling me to move here so I could live my dream. That's exactly what I'm doing. I'm in this magical city, where I wake up with a smile on my face every morning because I'm so excited about each day.

Lance moved to New York as well. He's opening a restaurant next month. Mandy has been helping promote it with her newfound fame. Isn't that crazy? Mandy is famous. Not a national icon just yet, but she's definitely on her way. We hardly go anywhere without someone stopping her for a photo or an autograph. Most people in my position would be jealous, but not me. I'm happy for her. She's in love. Her career is taking off, and we have each other. Plus, we're making way more money:

of course, her salary is in the six-digit range and mine is in the five, but who's counting?

Our new apartment is fabulous, but that's not the best part. Two actors from *All My Children* live in the building! I don't remember their names, but it doesn't matter because they're soap stars. How cool is that?

"Hey," Mandy says as I walk in the door. She's sitting on the couch with Lance. They're watching *The Simpsons.* Am I a Communist for not liking this show because everybody else seems to think it's hilarious?

"Aren't you guys a little old to be watching cartoons?" I joke as I roll my eyes.

"Just because you don't get the jokes doesn't give you the right to bash the show," Lance says, throwing a pillow at me.

"Oh, go back to Dublin." Not only has Lance become our unofficial third roommate, but he's also like a brother to me.

"It's nice to see you too," he says, turning his attention back toward the television.

"I made fresh coffee," Mandy says. She stands up to stretch. See, things haven't changed a bit. I pour myself a cup and take a seat on my newly covered white chair.

"Your column today was brilliant," Mandy says over her shoulder as she pours herself another cup of coffee. I look at her skeptically.

"You mean you weren't put off by it?" Today I wrote about Hollywood and politics and was a bit concerned Mandy might be a little upset that I ridiculed her community. Don't get me wrong, I love pop culture, but some of those stars need to stick to acting. Can anyone say Tom Cruise?

"Not at all," Mandy says, plopping back down on the couch. "My favorite part was when you listed the educational background of all the outspoken celebrities."

"Isn't that ridiculous?" Lance chimes in. "Half the

morons that are leading protests didn't even finish high school." He's been in America for a month and already he's a patriot. I love this guy!

"Don't get her started," Mandy tells him. "So, why are you coming home so late?"

"Oh," I say as I run over to my bag. "I went shopping. What do you think?" I hold up a leather Coach briefcase.

"You finally got it!" she laughs.

"I know!" Ever since I can remember, I've dreamt of walking down Madison Avenue with my briefcase in one hand and my latte in the other. I used to imagine myself walking fast because I had to be somewhere very important. So maybe I've seen *Working Girl* too many times, but it's so inspiring!

"I think I'm going to let you two do whatever it is you do when I'm not here," Lance says, getting to his feet. "I'll see you tonight." He bends down to kiss Mandy, gives me a salute, and leaves. Mandy smiles as the door shuts, then turns to face me.

"Okay, so Lance told me not to say anything to you, but I have to." I raise my eyebrows.

"Oh no. What is it?"

"Do you remember his friend Andy?" she asks. I wrinkle my nose.

"Andy?" I pause. "Ew! The guy that smells like onions?" Mandy rolls her eyes and sighs in frustration.

"For the tenth time, he had Mexican for dinner," she says incredulously.

"Does he always have Mexican for dinner?" I ask. I've met him at least three times and on every occasion he smelled like fajitas.

"Whatever. So, he's catering a Carmichael Advertising event at the Plaza tonight and wants you to come. Lance and I are going." My face drops when I hear the name "Carmichael."

"Oh," I say, staring into my half-empty coffee cup.

I've been in New York for almost a month and thus far have managed to avoid Jack. Initially, I was pretty angry with him. I guess that explains why I threw him out of my dressing room, but after I had my little pity party, I realized that I'm not angry with him. I'm mad at myself. Yes, I was mad at him for leaving me when I was such a mess. And of course I was humiliated that he left Boston without so much as an explanation. That night he showed up at my apartment, I was so crazy for him that I wanted to come out of my skin. I can't think of anything worse than wanting to be with someone so badly that it hurts, and then being deserted by that person. I felt that same feeling with Caleb the day we broke up, and I swore to myself that I would never feel that way again. I pushed Jack away because I was scared. I know that now.

I have a great life here in New York. I am living my dream, and I did it. I made it here on my own. But if everything in my life is so perfect, then why do I feel that a piece of me is still missing? See, this is why I wanted to be left alone. I was fine before Jack showed up—now look at me. I'm sick of hurting. I'm sick of feeling empty. I try to keep myself busy, but it doesn't help. Jack's the last thing I think about before I go to bed and the first thing I think about when I wake up. For the past month, I've anxiously turned every corner in hopes of bumping into him. I even check my cell in hopes that I missed his call, though I know he doesn't have my new number. I have so become one of those girls.

"Emma," Mandy says. "You kind of zoned out for a minute. Are you okay?"

"Yeah," I say. I get up from the chair and take my cup into the kitchen. "I'm fine."

"So are you going to go?" she calls over her shoulder. As if she doesn't already know the answer.

"Of course I'm not going to go," I shout back. I tap my foot nervously. "Why would you ask me that? You know I have Dinner Club tonight. We're having Italian. My favorite!" I add with fake enthusiasm. Okay, my heart is now officially in my toes. I walk back into the living room. Mandy opens her mouth to say something, then shuts it again. She studies me a moment, then stands up.

"Suit yourself," she says and walks out of the room. I follow her into her bedroom.

"Why should I go? It's not like I was invited." I sit on her bed and cross my arms. Mandy opens her closet and begins tossing her scattered shoes inside.

"Just suck it up and go," she says through clenched teeth. I shake my head.

"Way wrong answer," I say. Mandy turns to face me with her hands on her hips.

"Emma, how you've managed to suppress a guy who's madly in love with you is one thing. But what kills me is the fact that you're madly in love with him too. I don't know what you're doing, but frankly you're scaring me." I gulp hard. My throat burns.

"He's not madly in love with me," I interrupt.

"Can I finish?" she snaps.

"Sure." Mandy takes me by the shoulders and looks me square in the face.

"Why are you hiding from him? He's out there." She goes to the window and points outside. "He's out there, waiting for you to swallow your pride, get over yourself, and go get him." I open my mouth to speak, but her look silences me. "I know you. I know your issues, and I know your fears, but you made it. You made it all on your own. You're in New York, writing your own column. Now why is it such a bad thing to bend and fess up to this wonderful man who adores you?" She sits next to me on the bed. I dig my fingernails into the palms of my hands to keep from crying.

"I don't know," I say quietly.

"Well, I know that you're going to lose him if you don't

get some guts." I stare down at my shoes and sigh. Mandy looks at me with exasperation. "Seriously, help me understand your mindset. Are you waiting for Jack to show up at our doorstep with flowers? Because he already did that, except it was a pair of $500 shoes that you threw back in his face."

"I know," I say. Tears begin to well up in my eyes.

"No you don't know, Emma. This is serious."

"I know it is, but it's too late." I fall back on her bed and drape my arm across my face.

"It's not too late," she says, pulling my arm off. "He'll understand. He knows you. And he loves you. Please take a chance with him. You have nothing to be scared of." She's absolutely right.

"Can we not talk about this anymore?" I say as I wipe my eyes.

"Sure." Mandy hands me a tissue. I blow my nose furiously.

"Thank you. Now do you have anything I can wear to dinner tonight?" She sighs and stands up.

"Of course." She leads me into her walk-in closet. Another great thing about Mandy's newfound fame is her wardrobe. The show lets her keep all the clothes, which is really a great deal considering her stylist works on the set of *Live with Regis and Kelly*. I raid her closet and pick out a Kelly green strapless dress. As I hang the frock on the back of my door, I can't help but frown. I may have all these amazing clothes at my disposal, but when it comes down to it, the fact still remains that I don't have Jack Carmichael to look beautiful for.

50

"You look amazing," Mandy says after I've finished getting ready. "Are you sure you don't want to come to the fundraiser tonight?" I flashback to Jack's last fundraiser. Gosh, that seems like years ago.

"I'm sure," I say, grabbing my coat.

"Okay. Well, have a great night," she says.

"You too," I call over my shoulder. I shut the door and walk to the elevator. I wonder how Jack is handling all this. What if we've been on the subway together and I've been too engrossed in a book to notice? Or what if he's already moved on and he's seeing some beautiful blonde bombshell that actually has a brain and some class?

I step outside into the cool night air and wait for the doorman to hail me a taxi. What if Mandy's right? What if I missed out on something spectacular because of my fear? Initially, I was pretty angry. I even allowed myself to suppress, but now I'm beginning to think I was just plain stupid.

I hop in a taxi at the corner and we head toward Central Park. It's so beautiful this time of year. Spring is almost here, yet the air is still crisp. I crack the window and take a whiff of the New York air. Everything feels so fresh. I catch a glimpse of Central Park. The flowers are beginning to bud and leaves are starting to turn green.

Rich children are running around the park with their beautiful Swedish nannies. Gosh, I love this park. I love this time of year. I love this town. And oh my goodness, I love this song! I haven't heard this song in years.

"Excuse me," I ask, leaning forward in my seat.

"Javier," he says, turning to face me. He opens the plastic window separating us.

"Javier," I smile. "Can you please turn this song up?" He smiles and cranks up the music as I lean back in the seat and reminiscence. This was my first breakup song.

No I can't forget tomorrow when I think of all my sorrows/ when I had you there but then I let you go.

For an entire week, I played this song over and over and cried in my pillow, while holding the teddy bear Tommy Westbrook gave me on our one-month anniversary. Oh my nostalgia! I wonder what happened to the bear.

And now it's only fair that I should let you know/ What you should know.

Tears begin to well in my eyes. Surely, surely I am not crying over Tommy Westbrook. I mean, the last I heard the guy was working at a gas station and still living with his parents!

I can't live if living is without you/ I can't live, I can't give anymore.

Tears stream down my face as I sing with Mariah under my breath.

"Miss? Miss, are you okay?" Javier asks, glancing at me in the rearview mirror. I wipe my eyes on my coat sleeve.

I can't live if living is without you/ I can't live, I can't give anymore.

Suddenly, it all makes sense. Mariah makes sense!

"Stop the car!" I shout.

"What?" Javier asks, looking back at me as if I have a third eye.

"Stop the car!" It's as if a volcano has erupted and my dormant thoughts and emotions are now pouring out like lava. Javier pulls over to the side of the street and I practically jump out of the cab. I hand him a bill and make my way across the street and into Central Park.

I can't go another day, another moment, another second denying my feelings for Jack. I love him. Oh my gosh! I do. I love him. I've loved him since the first moment I laid eyes on him. Those dark eyes. His beautiful soul! I can't live without him. He is the only man for me.

I begin pacing back and forth. I have to see Jack. I have to tell him how stupid I was. How stupid I am! He has to know that I think he's the most incredible human being on the planet. That Caleb and all the other guys along the way were worth the pain because they led me to him. There is no other person on this planet for me. That I love him. He'll probably say it's too late, but I have to tell him anyway because you know what? He's worth the risk.

But I can't tell him. I'm too afraid of what he'll say. What if he's over it? Or, oh my gosh! What if he doesn't remember me? We only knew each other a week, and I'm sure he knows more than one Emma. Exhausted by my own emotions, I find a bench just outside the Plaza, remove my shoes, and curl my knees into my chest. I don't know what to do or what to say. How do I tell him I love him after all this time? And why on God's green earth would he want to be with me after the way I treated him? Gosh, I love him. I love him with all my heart. I wish he knew that I pushed him away because I was so scared that I'd lose him. Seems kinda stupid now, but it really made sense at the time. I shut my tired eyes for a moment but am soon awakened by a golden retriever puppy standing in front of me.

"Well, hi there," I say as I bend down and scratch him behind his ears. "Aren't you a cutie?" The puppy jumps in my lap and starts sniffing me. "And friendly!

Okay, puppy. You're sweet, but I'm wearing borrowed designer clothes. Besides, we just met," I joke. Am I really joking with a strange dog? Gosh, I'm lonely. I'm lonely and needy and the only person who loves me is a dog. A cute, adorable puppy, but nonetheless, a dog. I have hit rock bottom.

"Red!" Be still my beating heart. It can't be! I know that voice. I look up and see Jack walking toward me. He's wearing a black Northface over his white tuxedo shirt and untied black tie. And he's holding a leash. Talk about fate. This crap only happens in the movies. I pinch myself to see if I'm dreaming.

"Emma," he says, surprised. He stops in front of me. My heart is about to burst. I wonder if that's normal. "Red, get down," he says, but the puppy remains sitting next to me on the bench.

"Jack!" I jump up shoeless. "Ah, cold!" I sit back on the bench. I think I just got frostbite. "I thought you were hosting an event tonight." I slip into my green pumps and brush the dog hair off my dress.

"I am," he says as he helps me to my feet. "But I had to take Red out before keeping him cooped up all night." He bends down to hook the leash to Red's blue collar. "I just got him." Only a guy like Jack would be walking his puppy an hour before hosting a huge gala.

"Oh," is all I can think to say. So I love Jack. This I know, but now what? Do I tell him right now? Oh gosh. For the first time in my life, I can't say what I want to say.

"Do you want to walk with us?" he asks. He hesitates, looking down at my dress. "That is, if you don't have anywhere else to be."

"This is exactly where I want to be," I say as I grab Red's leash. We walk in silence for a moment.

"So is New York everything you dreamed it'd be?" he asks. So many questions are running through my head right now. Like how does he know I live in New York? How does he feel about me? And how the heck did his dog find me? Oh gosh! I have to tell him I love him. I should just say it right now.

"Uh ..." I start. I catch his gaze but quickly look at my feet. "Trick question?" he asks with amusement in his tone.

"You know what? Stop." I halt in my tracks, which chokes Red. Oops. Jack turns toward me with a confused look on his face. "Sorry Red," I say, squatting down to his level. "But there's something I have to tell your owner right now, before a plane falls out of the sky, lands on my head, and I die keeping this a secret." Jack raises a brow of curiosity. Oh, dear goodness, why am I talking to the dog? Here I go. All eyes on Jack, though Red is so stinking adorable. I stand to my feet

"Are you okay?" he asks, taking the leash from my hand. I take a deep breath and look Jack square in the eyes. Gosh, I've missed that look. I've missed this man more than I realized. My stomach is in knots just being next to him.

"I know it's probably too late to say this, but ..." I start. "You know what? I can't do this," I say as I turn and walk away. "Oh, but I'm gonna." I pivot and walk back toward him. "It's probably too late to tell you this, but ..." I say as I look down at the ground. I can't do it. I can't tell him.

"But?" he asks. He gently lifts my chin and brings my gaze level with his. I swallow.

"I'm sorry I kicked you out of my dressing room. I'm sorry I've pushed you away since the day we met. I'm sorry about so many things, but I was proud and scared. But now I'm just scared. And—" Jack puts his finger on my lips.

"You're not saying what you want to say," he says quietly. Isn't that the understatement of the century? I look down at Red, who's looking at me curiously.

"I know, but I'm scared of how you'll react." He smiles and looks at me intensely.

"What happened to the fearless Emma who always speaks her mind?" he asks.

"She let her guard down and is so vulnerable right now because what she says really matters." Why am I referring to myself as she?

"Finally," he says with a laugh. He takes my trembling hand.

"You're shaking," he says as he tightens his grip.

"That's because I'm scared," I say as tears begin streaming down my face. I try and let go of his hand, but he won't let me. I use my free hand to wipe my tears, but eventually let them stream down my face. For a moment Jack doesn't say a word, he just lets me cry.

"Emma," he says softly, "look at me." I shake my head and let go of his hand. I cup my face in my hands and sob. Jack moves in and pulls me to his chest. Before I know it, I'm crying and snotting on his white shirt.

"I was scared," I finally manage to say. I look up into his big, dark eyes without pulling away from his embrace. "I've been scared every day since. I wanted to talk to you that day in New York. I wanted to tell you everything, but I couldn't." He strokes my hair. "It's like that nightmare where you're running from the bad guy but your feet are made of lead and you can hardly move." He laughs.

"Emma, I'm scared too." I look up in surprise. Jack? Scared?

"What are *you* scared of?" I say with a smile.

"I'm scared that this unique, complex human being that I've waited for my entire life will keep pushing me away. And for no reason." He's talking about me, right?

"Then why did you leave me in Boston?" I wiggle from his embrace and fix my eyes on Red, who is lying patiently on the ground. Jack sighs.

"Because I know you," he says, stepping over Red. "I know how important it is for you to work things out on your own. I know you had so much on your plate that you couldn't even see straight." I cross my arms and look up at him. "Emma," he says, stepping closer and taking me by the elbows. "You and I had just ended things with other people, not to mention the fact that I had to get back to New York to explain to the board why I dropped Kelly. The timing was bad." He runs his fingers through his wavy hair. "Things were too intense, and I didn't want to start anything in the midst of that." That would have been nice to know when I was on the floor crying, but then again he didn't wait six years to tell me why he left.

"Jack," I say, unfolding my arms and shaking my head incredulously. "I think you may really know me." Jack smiles and touches my cheek.

"Of course I know you, Emma." Would it totally kill the moment if I fainted? "But the question is do you know me?" I look at him confusedly. "You have such high expectations of people and I love that about you, but you have to know how imperfect I am."

"How imperfect *you* are? Do you have any idea how flawed *I* am?" I interrupt. Red jerks at the leash, obviously startled by my tone.

"Maybe it's our flaws that make us so perfect together," he says, cupping my face in his strong hands. I close my eyes in case I have to wake from this dream. I feel like Jane Austen's *Emma*, standing before my Mr. Knightley, holding back my tears of happiness. If this were a movie, now would be the part where Van Morrison's "Someone Like You" starts playing while the rest of time stands still.

"So what are you saying?" I ask, taking his hands and wrapping them around my waist.

"I'm saying that if you're done pushing me away I'd like to spend the rest of my life loving you." This is the part where the choir sings "Hallelujah!" I take a deep breath.

"Jack, I've loved you since the day I got my feet stuck in those stupid shoes." I reach up and run my finger along the scar above his eyebrow. "I knew you were different. I knew my life would never be the same because of you."

"Well then, Miss Mosley," he says as he cups my face in his hands. "If you'd stop talking, I'd like to do something I've been wanting to do since the first moment I laid eyes on you."

After leaning into the greatest kiss known to mankind, I'm tempted to pop my foot like they do in the movies. In my wildest dreams, I couldn't have come up with a more perfect moment to kiss Jack. Here we are, standing in this magical park, underneath a blanket of stars, sharing a kiss more spectacular than any I've ever known.

He holds out his hand and I take it. Together, we head off into the horizon with Red trailing a few feet behind us. It isn't Shakespeare or Hollywood or even Jane Austen, but I'm not disappointed because it's so much better than that. All my life, I've feared that my dreams would never live up to reality, and I was right. My dreams don't hold a candle to reality.

KIMBERLY HUFF was born in Memphis, Tennessee. In 1999 she packed up her SUV and moved to Baton Rouge, where she had her first taste of writing at Louisiana State University. "When I first arrived, I was so sad that I wrote in my journal every day for relief."

After two weeks, Kimberly pledged Chi Omega Sorority and spent the next two years going to parties, experiencing Southeastern Conference (SEC) football, and occasionally hitting the books. Always the dreamer, Kimberly transferred to Emerson College in Boston after two years. "You could say that this is where my adventures began."

Kimberly spent the next two years pursuing a bachelor's degree in marketing and public relations while working at the busiest Starbucks in New England. "Working at a coffee shop put so many stories in my head. The people I encountered, the fat grams I consumed—my first novel pays tribute to some of that. To me, Boston is one of the greatest cities on earth. I was always walking around formulating a story in my head."

After graduating, Kimberly spent the summer in a small Texas town and began writing her first novel. "I always said I wanted to write, but I thought it was another one of my random ideas, like acting classes or marathon training. My best friend once said to me, 'Kim, I'm a romantic, but you are a hopeless romantic.' It's extremities like these that inspired me to write the crazy thoughts in my head. My mind is an emotional time bomb! You could say that it just went off one day. Seriously, one night I opened my laptop and a story just poured out. I couldn't stop writing!"

After her book's completion, Kimberly moved back to Memphis and received a master's degree in social work. She is currently a medical social worker in Memphis and lives with her dog Boston.

Easy Order Form
CHECK YOUR LEADING BOOKSTORE
OR ORDER HERE

Item	Quantity	Price

Please include $1 shipping for each order.
Colorado residents add 7% sales tax.

___ My check or money order for $___ is enclosed.
___ Please charge my credit card.

N a m e _____

Organization _____

A d d r e s s _____

City/State/Zip _____

P h o n e _____ E - m a i l _____

___ MasterCard ___ Visa ___ Discover

Card #_____

Exp. Date_____ Signature_____

Please make your check payable and return to:

Mapletree Publishing Company
6233 Harvard Lane
Highlands Ranch, CO 80130

Call your credit card order to: 800-537-0414
Fax: 303-791-9028
Secure online ordering:
www.mapletreepublishing.com